Praise for

Stay Sweet

"*Stay Sweet* will inspire ambition—and ice-cream cravings."
—*Seventeen*

★ "A delectable mixture of ice cream and romance. . . . While evoking the warmth of rural life and employee comradeship, Vivian writes an empowering novel for young women with big dreams."—*Publisher's Weekly*, starred review

"A rare, enjoyable portrait of a woman-run business. . . . Amelia possesses the qualities she needs to achieve her goals but, like many girls, lacks confidence in using them; watching her evolve is empowering."—*Kirkus Reviews*

"A delightful choice. With a strong message about female empowerment and hard work, this YA book will be a great read for spring break or summer vacation. . . . For fans of Jenny Han looking for a light but touching summer read about first love, feminism, and ice cream."—*School Library Journal*

"A satisfying examination of a girl, used to being in the background, who comes into her own. Summer reading at its finest." —*Booklist*

STAY SWEET

siobhan vivian

SIMON & SCHUSTER BFYR

NEW YORK   LONDON   TORONTO   SYDNEY   NEW DELHI

SIMON & SCHUSTER BFYR

An imprint of Simon & Schuster Children's Publishing Division
1230 Avenue of the Americas, New York, New York 10020

SIMON & SCHUSTER BFYR is a trademark of Simon & Schuster, Inc.
For information about special discounts for bulk purchases, please contact Simon & Schuster Special Sales at 1-866-506-1949 or business@simonandschuster.com.
The Simon & Schuster Speakers Bureau can bring authors to your live event. For more information or to book an event, contact the Simon & Schuster Speakers Bureau at 1-866-248-3049 or visit our website at www.simonspeakers.com.
Also available in a SIMON & SCHUSTER BFYR hardcover edition
Book design by Lucy Ruth Cummins
The text for this book was set in Adobe Caslon Pro.
Manufactured in the United States of America
First SIMON & SCHUSTER BFYR paperback edition April 2019
2 4 6 8 10 9 7 5 3 1

The Library of Congress has cataloged the hardcover edition as follows:
Names: Vivian, Siobhan, author.
Title: Stay sweet / Siobhan Vivian.
Description: First edition. | New York : Simon & Schuster Books for Young Readers, [2018]. | Summary: Seventeen-year-old Amelia has looked forward to her last summer before college working at the Meade Creamery, but when the owner of the local landmark passes away her nephew has big changes in mind.
Identifiers: LCCN 2017048141 (print) | LCCN 2017059682 (eBook) | ISBN 9781481452328 (hardback) | ISBN 9781481452335 (pbk.) ISBN 9781481452342 (eBook) |
Subjects: | CYAC: Ice cream parlors—Fiction. | Summer employment—Fiction. | Entrepreneurship—Fiction. | Best friends—Fiction. | Friendship—Fiction. | Dating (Social customs)—Fiction. | Death—Fiction.
Classification: LCC PZ7.V835 (ebook) | LCC PZ7.V835 St 2018 (print) | DDC [Fic]—dc23
LC record available at https://lccn.loc.gov/2017048141

For Marie

Acknowledgments

Thank you to my editor, Zareen Jaffery, for an abundance of encouragement, patience, and editorial genius.

Extra sprinkles for the all-star team at Simon & Schuster, including but not limited to Justin Chanda, Anne Zafian, Chrissy Noh, KeriLee Horan, Lisa Moraleda, Aubrey Churchward, Lucy Ruth Cummins, Anna Jarzab, Sarah Woodruff, and Alexa Pastor. #houseproud.

Emily van Beek at Folio Literary, thank you for making it possible to live my dream these last eight years.

Pittsburgh is home to two renowned ice cream artisans, and both were gracious enough to share their wisdom with me. Thanks to Chad Townsend and Melissa Horst of Millie's Homemade and Katie Heldstab and Christa Puskarich of Leona's Ice Cream.

I'm grateful to those who helped untangle this book at varying stages. At the very top of that list is my best friend, Jenny Han. Thanks also to Adele Griffin, Morgan Matson, Brenna Heaps, Nina la Cour, Jill Dembowski, Lynn Weingarten, Emmy Weidener, Molly Pascal, and Mary Auxier.

Thanks as well to Jackie Decker, Kelsey O'Rourke, Irene Vivian, Ashley Androkovitch at Fallingwater, and #1 Lady Boss Lisa Krowinski of Sapling Press.

I'd like to call out a few women who have, knowingly or not, mentored me and helped to shape my career—Tsia Carson, Christie Dreyfuss, Nancy Kanter, and Sara Shandler Banks.

And lastly, to my love, Nick Caruso, for supporting me every step of the way—I'll stop the world and melt with you.

May 3, 1945

Nineteen girls came to the lake tonight and each one brought her very own spoon. Up from the sixteen girls last week, and the eleven who showed up the week before. A month ago, there were only four of us.

I climbed off my bicycle and, for a moment, stood back by the trees and watched them. Most of the girls I knew well, some less so, and a few weren't even from Sand Lake. Not that it mattered. They had spread their blankets out edge to edge on the sand to make a huge patchwork quilt, kicked their shoes and sandals off in one big pile. They passed around Life and the latest Seventeen, fussed with each other's hair, chitchatted while the last of the sun disappeared and they waited for me to show.

I could feel my heart pounding underneath my blouse.

I might have tried to slink away if Tiggy hadn't spotted me and rushed over, grinning ear to ear. For her, more girls meant less time she'd have to crank the ice cream maker. Tiggy complains her arm hurts after about a minute of churning, though she sure does recover once the ice cream is ready. But I saw more girls I'd be disappointing tonight.

Tiggy lifted my bag out of my bicycle basket and I followed her, apologizing to everyone for being late. I tried to temper their expectations as I poured my ingredients into the bucket of my ice cream maker. The girls had been so keen on last week's vanilla, and I would have loved to make them another batch of it. But sugar rations had been cut yet again and my mother forbade me to even open her pantry.

So I'd spent the whole afternoon trying to sweeten the cream with something other than sugar. I tried raw honey, apple juice, even shavings from one of our victory garden carrots. I'll admit, I enjoyed the challenge, experimenting, churning and tasting small batches, each one a step closer. That is, until time ran out and I needed to get to the lake. I wasn't sure the concoction I'd settled on would even be edible.

The girls didn't seem to care one way or the other, which would have been a relief, had I not cared so deeply. More than I ever expected to.

2   **siobhan vivian**

Normally, those of us who got letters from our boys read them aloud while we took turns on the crank, though I casually suggested skipping them this week, knowing Marcy's family hadn't heard from her brother Earl in nearly a month. Marcy insisted, even managing a weak smile. It amazes me how good we're all getting at pretending to be strong even when we're close to hanging it up.

Luckily, Dot went first and had us in stitches. I honestly can't get over how fresh James Pearson is. His mother would turn red as a beet if she knew how James begged Dot to send him a picture of her in her slip.

I read Wayne's latest letter. In it, he promised that the boys in his unit are as heartsick as we girls are back home. And he's glad to know we're keeping busy with our ice cream nights because being miserable and lonely will make the time we're apart pass more slowly.

I felt sorry as I folded his letter back up. Though I kiss each one I send to him and spray the envelope with what I hope is enough of his favorite of my perfumes to

last a trip across the world—I go through
a $7.50 bottle of Beau Catcher every few
weeks—I do write Wayne such boring things.
About my ice cream recipes or complaints
about Mother, who is intent on turning our
wedding into the social event of Sand Lake
the minute the war ends.

Maybe I should send Wayne a picture of
me. Not in my slip. For that, he'll have to
wait until our wedding night. But it might
lift his spirits to have a photo of me in my
bathing suit. With my hair curled and
pinned like Betty Grable.

Anyway, after the letters, and after we'd
aired our dirty laundry for the week—fights
with parents, the scarcity of pretty dresses in
stores, the latest newsreels—Tiggy brought
up the idea of my selling ice cream at the
Red Cross fund-raiser her mother was
organizing. I shot her a look because I had
already told her it wasn't a good idea. It
wasn't just that sugar rations were getting
smaller and smaller. I liked that our ice
cream nights were just for us. Ignoring me,
she asked the girls to suggest ideas for what
I might put on a banner, since each food
table needed one, and that went on until the
ice cream was ready to eat.

siobhan vivian

I wasn't listening. My stomach was in a knot as I unscrewed the cap and pulled off the crank. Though the thought did occur to me that if this batch of ice cream tasted terrible, Tiggy's idea of my selling it might disappear.

Tiggy crawled over and dipped her spoon right in, helping herself to the first taste. Her eyes rolled to the back of her head and she made "mmMMmm" sounds that had the girls squealing and huddling up for a taste. They'd never had anything like it, they said. What was in it? What was this flavor? Their eyes were wide, smiles big.

I figured they were being polite until the ice cream finally came back around to me.

But it really was terrific.

The best I've ever made!

The girls were clamoring for seconds and thirds and fourths, telling me that I just had to sell this. I'd make a fortune, guaranteed. And it would be such a help to our boys.

Tiggy made a joke then, reaching for yet another taste. "Boys? What boys? I've got

everything I need right here," she purred, and
naughtily licked her spoon.

The girls giggled, but I gasped and put
my hand on Tiggy's leg. "Tig, that's
it. My banner could say 'Ice Cream
So Sweet, You Won't Miss Your
Sweetheart.'"

Everyone went quiet. I closed my eyes.

I could paint the words in pink on some
muslin.

I'd have the girls wear their white
graduation dresses and curl their hair.

We'd set the ice cream out in rows, perfectly
round scoops in thin china. Mother wouldn't
want me using her good dishes, but I knew I
could make her feel guilty enough to let me.
I'd bet the other girls could persuade their
mothers too.

How much could we get for a dish?

Thirty cents?

Fifty?

siobhan vivian

Just as there's a moment in the churning when you first feel the cream and sugar thicken, I could sense the potential of what this could be take hold. I felt happier than I had in months, until the sound of sniffling made me open my eyes.

Tiggy and the rest of the girls were in tears.

"I'm so sorry," I told them, my face burning. "Please forget I said that." Ice cream was supposed to be our distraction from thinking about the war.

Tiggy wiped her eyes with her handkerchief. "Don't apologize. It's perfect," she said, taking my hand in hers and squeezing it. "I think this is going to be big, Molly."

If it were only Tiggy saying so, I'm sure I wouldn't have believed her. Not because she's a liar, but she's my best friend. But the other girls crowded around me with their spoons, wiping their tears and reaching for more.

CHAPTER  ONE

AMELIA VAN HAGEN IS KNEELING ON THE FLOOR IN her bra and a pair of khaki shorts, brown hair neatly split into two fishtail braids, a polo shirt draped over her lap. She smooths it, then gently plucks off a tiny fuzz ball and flicks it away.

When Frankie Ko gave her this Meade Creamery polo on her very first day, it was the exact same shade of pink as a scoop of strawberry ice cream. Now, four summers later, and despite the dim morning light of her bedroom, she sees that the pink has faded to a much softer hue, a color closer to cotton candy.

There are lots of summer jobs for the teens of Sand Lake and each comes with its own perks. Being a lake lifeguard means your tan lasts until October. The mall is air-conditioned and employees get a discount at the food court. Babysitters can make serious cash, especially if they get in good with the tourists. But

Amelia always dreamed of being a Meade Creamery girl.

The Meade Creamery ice cream stand has employed all girls and only girls since it opened, way back in the summer of 1945. And though the draw of the place is solely the ice cream, each time her parents would take her, and as soon as the line would bring her close enough, Amelia would lift up on her toes and study the girls working inside. Though the faces changed each summer—as the oldest ones left for college and the newbies struggled to keep up with the pace of things—the vibe between the girls stayed the same. Amelia liked how they talked to each other, a mix of codes and inside jokes, how gracefully they moved in such a cramped and frenzied space. How much fun they seemed to have, despite the heat and the crowds, despite their crappy radio with the foil-covered antenna.

Amelia pulls the pink polo over her head. It sort of *feels* like cotton candy too, soft and light from what probably adds up to a billion trips through the wash between her very first day and this one, a Meade Creamery girl's endless fight against the speckling of caramel dip, of hot fudge, of the bright red juice that the maraschino cherries float in. What hasn't paled, not even four summers later, is the thrill she gets from wearing it.

Frankie Ko handed this very shirt to Amelia four years ago. Frankie was Head Girl that summer, and she had been lying on top of one of the picnic tables, sunning herself while she waited for the newbies to arrive. Her shiny black hair was as long as her perfectly frayed cutoffs were short. She wore ankle socks with little pink pompoms at the heels and she had four, maybe five, woven string friendship bracelets tied around each wrist. She was half Korean, impossibly beautiful, effortlessly cool. That's how every newbie feels about the Head Girl her first summer, but Frankie, Amelia's sure, broke the mold.

Amelia cringes, remembering with embarrassing clarity how she herself looked four years ago, getting dropped off by her dad, lips slick with the peachy lipstick she'd bought to match her eighth-grade dinner dance dress, hoping it would make her seem older and cooler. Funny that it never occurred to her to remove her retainer, which she was so dutiful in wearing that most of her classmates hadn't yet realized she'd gotten her braces off.

A few weeks later, Frankie pulled her aside and gently suggested that cooler tones might flatter her skin more. She presented Amelia with a new lipstick—a berry red called All Heart—which was a freebie that had come with Frankie's recent Clinique purchase. Frankie helped Amelia apply it, too, taking twice as long to do it as Amelia did when she put it on herself, and the other girls working that shift nodded in approval.

Frankie Ko had made seventeen look the way it does on TV shows—a flower blooming with confidence and beauty and wisdom. Straightening her collar in the mirror, Amelia wonders what this summer's newbies will see when they look at her, because it feels impossible that she's as old today as Frankie was then.

But prom is over—and graduation, too. Amelia's opened every Hallmark card from her relatives and put the cash away for textbooks and a cafeteria meal plan and a real-deal winter coat, one that can stand up to the New England nor'easters people keep teasing will probably kill her.

Earlier this week, Amelia got an email from her future roommate at Gibbons—Cecilia Brewster, an English lit major, from Connecticut, on a partial tennis scholarship, with a long-distance boyfriend until further notice. After the introduction, Cecilia let Amelia know that she had already bought them a mini-fridge for their dorm room, and so it would be great if Amelia could get them a microwave (see helpfully provided links for style and color suggestions).

Amelia's reread this email so many times. Cecilia seems fine, way better than some of the dorm mismatches she's heard about when former stand girls drop by for a visit and a free waffle cone. Though she's drafted some potential replies, she hasn't sent one. It feels like the starting gun for a race she doesn't want to run.

Unfortunately, Amelia's last first day at Meade Creamery is undeniably the beginning of the end.

"Amelia?" Cate Kopernick emerges from a heap of blankets and pillows on the floor. Her long blond hair is looped in half with an elastic and it hangs over her shoulder like a golden lasso. She makes the screen on her phone light up and, after wincing at the glow, casts it aside. "You're going in already?"

"I couldn't sleep. I'm too nervous."

"Nervous?" Cate laughs. "Come on. Seriously?"

"I know, I know." Amelia says it as quickly as she's moving now, standing up, taking her tote bag off the back of her desk chair, wriggling her feet into her Keds.

"I heard you downstairs last night."

"I was baking blueberry muffins."

"At two in the morning?"

"I thought it'd be nice to give the girls something to eat before I start assigning chores."

Cate rolls her eyes. "Don't worry about being likable. Every-one already knows that today and tomorrow are going to suck."

siobhan vivian

She yawns again. "Just give me ten minutes to shower, and I can drive—"

"I'll ride my bike. It'll help me clear my head. Really. Please go back to sleep. I'll see you in a few hours."

"Hold up. Where's your pin?"

"I guess I forgot to put it on." Amelia blushes because she is a terrible liar and makes for the bedroom door.

Cate grabs her ankle. "Amelia! Quit acting weird!"

With a halfhearted shrug, Amelia goes to her jewelry box. Inside, mixed in with her nicer jewelry and the tassel from her graduation cap, is a gold flower pin the size of a Snapple cap, a clear rhinestone anchoring the petals. She hasn't touched it for nearly a year, not since it was given to her last August.

The girls were celebrating the end of the season with a sleepover down at the lake, a Meade Creamery tradition. Amelia was standing next to her half-set-up tent, having temporarily given up on putting it together in favor of using bits of broken sugar cone to scrape out the streaks of chocolate from their last remaining drum of ice cream.

Heather, who was Head Girl last summer, had just picked up the final paychecks from Molly Meade's farmhouse and was handing them out. She paused when peeling Amelia's from the stack, a funny look on her face. Then she shook the envelope so Amelia could hear the clinking inside it.

Amelia froze. A drip of chocolate rolled down her forearm.

"Amelia," Heather said. "Put the ice cream down and get over here!"

Stiffly, Amelia did as she was told. She chased the drip with her tongue, put the bite into her mouth, and forced a swallow. Setting the cardboard drum in the sand, she snuck a look over to the campfire and watched Cate, in a baggy sweatshirt worn over her bikini, toss on another log, sending up a burst of sparks. The other stand girls huddled around her, faces glowing.

Amelia opened the envelope. Inside were her check, the flower pin, and a key to the ice cream stand.

"Are you sure this is supposed to be mine?" Amelia asked, incredulous. "Did Molly say anything to you?"

Heather looked surprised at the insinuation. "Amelia, I haven't spoken to her all summer. Like, not once. Last week she left me a note to turn in my pin. I had no idea who she was going to pick." Heather shrugged, then gave Amelia an encouraging shoulder squeeze. "The envelope has your name on it. And you did have a fifty-fifty shot, right?"

Though it may technically have been true, it didn't feel that way to Amelia. Ever since their first summer at Meade Creamery, Amelia had believed Molly would choose Cate as Head Girl when the time came. Definitely Cate. A thousand percent Cate for a thousand and one reasons. And Amelia wasn't alone. She could see it in Heather's face, the surprise at how this was playing out, because Cate was the fun one, the girl everyone loved being around.

Cate must have realized what was going on while Amelia was talking to Heather, because she came sprinting over and wrapped Amelia in a big, bouncing congratulatory hug.

Amelia still doesn't know how long it took Cate to come to terms with not getting the Head Girl pin, but it pains Amelia to think of Cate hurting over it, even if only for a millisecond. And yet Amelia finds Cate's excitement for her right now only slightly less excruciating, as Cate leans forward, her chin in her hands, waiting.

siobhan vivian

"How about I wear it on opening day? That way, it won't get messed up," Amelia says, hesitating.

With a groan, Cate rises to her feet and takes the pin from Amelia's hand. "You're not officially the queen until you put on the crown." Amelia averts her eyes as Cate examines the pin for a second before she feels a tug on her collar. "There," Cate says, pleased. "Now it's official."

Amelia starts to protest, "It should be you," the way she has countless times since getting the pin. Cate's usually good about letting her get this perceived injustice off her chest, and Amelia always feels better afterward. Like she has voiced a truth that, deep down, they both know.

This time, however, Cate shushes her. "Not today, Amelia." And she guides Amelia back to the mirror. "What do you think?"

Amelia glances over her shoulder at Cate. For the rest of Amelia's life, she knows she will never find a friend better than Cate Kopernick.

Using Amelia's braids like handlebars, Cate steers Amelia's head so she's facing the mirror. "You look amazing," Cate says, stepping aside so she's out of the reflection. "Just like Frankie Ko."

Amelia laughs, because again, *yeah right*, until, finally, she looks, focusing not so much on herself as on the pin. Though it's small, it really does sparkle.

CHAPTER TWO

MEADE CREAMERY DOESN'T LOOK LIKE MUCH, AND especially not in the off-season, when the two service windows are boarded up with plywood, the picnic tables are brought in, and a heavy chain closes off the parking lot from the road. Really, the ice cream stand is a glorified shed, a white-shingled minia-ture of the farmhouse looming in the overgrown fields behind it, electricity zipping in from three thick wires sprouting off a nearby utility pole. But to Amelia, and most other people in town, it's one of the most special places in the world.

Amelia hops off her periwinkle three-speed cruiser and lifts the chain up and over herself as she passes underneath, then turns at the beep of a horn. A glossy black SUV pulls off the road and parks alongside the chain, roof rack strapped with luggage, a license plate from another state. These vacationers are passing through Sand Lake, headed down Route 68 toward other, larger lakes farther on—ones that permit Jet Skis and speedboats, ones where the waterfront is rented by the week.

The music lowers and the window unrolls, revealing a woman with big sunglasses perched on the top of her head. "Excuse me, sweetie! I know it's a little early in the morning for ice cream, but we've been dreaming about this since last summer!"

Amelia grins. The anticipation is something she feels too. She can't wait to taste the four made-from-scratch flavors they sell—vanilla, chocolate, strawberry, and the best-selling, wholly original, nothing-else-like-it-in-the-world Home Sweet Home. "I'm so sorry, but we're not officially open until Saturday!"

The woman beckons Amelia closer. "Well . . . is there any chance you could make an exception for us? I can make it worth your while." Her three kids eagerly look up from their phones in the backseat. Same for her husband on his tablet in the passenger seat.

If Cate were here, she would say something crazy, like *fifty bucks*, just to see what would happen. Amelia shakes her head. "I'm really sorry, ma'am. I would like to help you all out but I just can't." And she even adds, "I don't want to get fired," as if Amelia weren't herself Head Girl.

The woman isn't mad. She nods, understandingly, approvingly even, as if Amelia has confirmed some thought she already held about this place and the girls who work there. "Can't hurt to ask, right?" she says jovially, before lowering her sunglasses. "We'll see you girls on Saturday!"

Watching the SUV ease back onto the road, Amelia knows the woman means it, too. From the first week of June until the last week in August, there'll be a line for Molly Meade's homemade ice cream, out-of-towners and locals alike, a quarter mile of cars parked half in the rain ditch, stretching in either direction.

There are exactly two days until opening day.

As she turns back to the stand, Amelia's nerves give way to a new feeling—determination. She notes some of the obvious chores: mowing the lawn, weeding the crevices in the walkway, giving the stand a fresh coat of paint. She has a few hours before the other girls arrive, so she might as well get started. Anything Amelia's able to tackle on her own will make the vibe more relaxed and be less she'll have to delegate after everyone gets a blueberry muffin.

Slipping the key out of her pocket, she walks around the side of the stand. It surprises her to find the door already propped open with a brick. A few steps more and she sees Molly Meade's pink Cadillac parked, the trunk lid lifted. Amelia stops, wipes her hands on her shorts, makes sure her polo shirt is tucked tight into her waistband.

Though Molly Meade continues to make the ice cream every summer, nobody in Sand Lake sees much of her anymore, not even the girls who work for her. Molly replenishes the ice cream only when the stand is closed, and if she needs something, she'll call down and ask to speak with the Head Girl. This is generally regarded by the stand girls as yet another perk. They basically have the run of the place—no adults looking over their shoulders. At Meade's, the girls are in charge.

Amelia tiptoes over. There's a fuzz of bright yellow pollen across the hood like an afghan, as if the car hasn't been driven much all spring. She peeks inside the open trunk and finds it's in the middle of being unloaded—a lot of empty space on the left and six cardboard drums of Molly's homemade ice cream

siobhan vivian

on the right, each flavor marked with Molly's shaky, old-lady handwriting.

Amelia checks her phone for the time. Molly wouldn't have expected any stand girls to show up this early. Would Molly prefer Amelia make herself scarce until she's done unloading? Or would she appreciate help carrying in the ice cream drums, which aren't exactly light? Maybe Amelia should let Molly know that if she needs anything this summer, anything at all, Amelia would gladly be of service. Molly could surely use the help at her age. Though what if Molly found Amelia's assumption offensive and ageist?

Amelia rubs the back of her neck. She's been Head Girl for a few hours and she's already in over her head.

Biting her finger, Amelia decides that, at the very least, she owes Molly a *thank you*. After all, Molly Meade is inextricably, if indirectly, responsible for the best summers of Amelia's life.

She reaches in and lifts out a drum of Home Sweet Home, but the cardboard sides unexpectedly flex from the pressure of Amelia's hands, sending the lid popping off like a cork. A wave of pale yellow crests over the sides of the drum, coating both of Amelia's hands, and nearly the entire trunk bed, in thick, melted, lukewarm ice cream.

Amelia winces and gags as the smell hits her, an unpleasant sourness spiking the sweet. As if these tubs of ice cream have been sitting out in the sun for hours.

Maybe even days.

Amelia's heart fills her throat. She glances back to the open stand door as she sets the sticky drum down in the dirt.

Then she runs.

CHAPTER THREE

AMELIA RUSHES INSIDE, CALLING OUT FOR MOLLY.

Once her eyes adjust from the sun, she sees the cobwebs in the corners of the doorway, the floral bedsheet covering the toppings station, and another, different floral bedsheet hanging over the scooping cabinet. Boxes filled with waxed paper sundae cups, plastic spoons, and paper napkins are stacked neatly against the wall near the closed office door.

The stand looks the same as it does at the start of every season.

Another two steps, though, and she discovers one big difference: Molly Meade, in an old peach housedress and the no-name navy canvas slip-ons sold at Walmart for five bucks a pair, is lying on the floor.

Amelia's hands fly up to her mouth, stifling her scream.

This is the first dead body she has ever seen, and yet Amelia is positive Molly Meade is dead, even as her babysitter first-aid training kicks in and she crouches down and takes hold of Molly's wrist, hoping for a pulse—but finding skin that is cold to the touch.

Amelia rises back up and steadies herself against the wall and closes her eyes. Her head suddenly feels like an unripe tomato, too light.

Was Molly sick?

Cancer or something?

Or maybe, Amelia wonders, it was her broken heart that finally did her in?

She glances up at the one photograph of Molly in the stand, framed and hanging near the price list. In it, Molly is wearing a fuzzy sweater and a plaid wool skirt, her hair in soft bouncy curls, an army hat jauntily askew on her head, lips glossy and reflecting the autumn sunshine. She has one hand to her forehead in a playful little salute, the other outstretched, showing off an engagement ring. Her knees are turned in, and she's up on the toes of her saddle shoes in a pool of fallen leaves. She looks like the kind of girl painted on the cockpit of a fighter plane.

Next to Molly stands a young man, movie-star handsome, in his army uniform and trim haircut. Though he is facing the camera straight on, his eyes have drifted left toward Molly, and a wry, flirty smile is spread across his chiseled face.

Her fiancé, Wayne Lumsden.

Amelia has told the story of how Meade Creamery came to be thousands of times, repeating it to every out-of-towner who asks. It feels less like real life than a movie script: teenage Molly making ice cream to cheer up her lovesick friends because nearly every boy in Sand Lake, including her fiancé, Wayne, was off fighting in World War II. When the war ended and Wayne was declared missing in action, no one in Sand Lake thought Molly would make ice cream again. But the next summer, she reopened Meade Creamery with a full staff of girls. And it has been open every summer since, because making ice cream kept her hands busy, her life sweet, and her hope—that Wayne might one day find his way back home—from melting altogether.

A tiny cry startles Amelia as a black-and-white kitten rises sleepily from Molly's side. He cracks open his glossy red mouth and lets out another cranky mew.

Amelia clicks her tongue. The kitten doesn't seem to want to leave the bed he's made in the folds of Molly's housedress. He's not a stray—there's a white plastic flea collar around his neck— but he's clearly an outdoor cat. Nettles cling to the fur along the ridge of his back where his tongue can't reach.

Amelia lifts him straight up by the scruff, careful not to disturb Molly's body. He's a baby; he fits easily into her hand, and she can feel his tiny bones underneath his fur.

Then she notices a drum of ice cream that Molly must have carried into the stand and set down on the floor before she died. It's seeping pink across the white penny tile, a strawberry puddle creeping closer and closer to Molly's dress. With the tip of her finger, Amelia guides the hem so it's clear of the growing spill. Then, on unsteady legs, she flees into the office, sets the kitten on the desk, and picks up the heavy black handset of the landline.

"9-1-1. What's your emergency?"

Amelia peeks around the doorway and sees the toes of Molly Meade's slip-ons pointing to the ceiling. She answers, her voice trembling. "I . . . I don't think this *is* an emergency, exactly," she says, trying to clarify. "It *was*. Only not anymore."

siobhan vivian

After hanging up, Amelia debates calling her mom at the bank, but decides instead to text her dad, knowing his phone doesn't get much reception when he's fishing in Sand Lake.

Hey Daddy. Molly Meade passed away. I found her when I got to work this morning. I'm okay. Handling things here. Just wanted to let you know.

Next, she calls Cate. "Pick up. Pick up. Pick up," Amelia whispers.

It takes a few rings. "Hello?" Cate's voice is groggy, though once Amelia tells her the news, she sounds instantly, fully awake. "Wait, hold up. Are you for real?"

"Yes."

Amelia hears Cate swallow. "And you're there with her dead body right now?"

"I'm hiding in the office. I just called the police."

"Jesus," Cate says, and lets out a long breath.

Amelia lets out one too, and then notices an envelope on the desk, addressed to her in Molly's handwriting. "Cate, I should go."

"Do you need any help? Is there anything I can do?"

"No, I don't think—"

"What about the other girls? Should I let them know not to come in?"

Amelia doesn't say what she is suddenly thinking, the *ever again* part, because it is too sad. "I'll do it, Cate. You should go back to sleep."

"Amelia, there's no way I'm falling back asleep now! Please, I've got it. You're going to have enough to deal with there."

"Okay. Thank you. You're the best."

After hanging up, Amelia carefully opens the envelope.

Dear Amelia,

Happy First Day of Summer.

The walk-in freezer is fully stocked, as are all supplies. I tested the three waffle irons yesterday and found that one wasn't heating up properly, so I ordered a replacement. Hopefully you can manage with two until then.

Please don't hesitate to ask if you need anything or have questions. You Head Girls never seem to, but I am here if you do.

And thank you for working so hard for me over these past four years. I always loved seeing your polo tucked in so neatly. It's a little thing, but it speaks volumes about the kind of girl you are.

Stay sweet,
Molly

Amelia feels the back of her shirt as sirens wail in the distance. Being chosen wasn't arbitrary or accidental, the way Amelia had assumed. Somehow Molly had known her. Seen her. Believed in her.

The paramedics burst in. Careful to keep the kitten corralled in the office, Amelia slips out and watches as one calls out Molly's name, as if she might suddenly wake up, while another checks her neck for a pulse. It takes less than a minute before they radio for the coroner.

Amelia slinks backs to the office and closes the door.

A policeman arrives next, and double-checks with Amelia if there's anyone he should inform that Molly has died. There isn't, Amelia confirms, assuming his question is more a matter of procedure. Everyone in Sand Lake knows that when Molly's parents passed away, the farm was left solely to her. Though she had two brothers, she outlived them both. Molly Meade never married, never had kids. There's no next of kin, no anyone. Aside from the kitten pawing at Amelia's shoelaces, Molly Meade was alone in the world.

A little while later, the local funeral home arrives, trades some paperwork with the policeman, and takes Molly Meade away.

Then it's just Amelia.

Underneath the window is a love seat, a floral pattern on sun-bleached goldenrod velvet. Though it's threadbare in certain places—the center of each cushion, the top of each armrest—Amelia finds it beautiful. It's like a couch that might be for sale in a fancy shop, purposely distressed in that perfect way.

She lies down on it, her head propped against one armrest, her feet dangling over the other. She wonders how many girls over the years have sat on this love seat. Girls wanting to be consoled over fights with their boyfriends or their best friends or their mothers, girls hoping to spill the beans on terrific first dates, or giving the unvarnished truth of what it was like when they lost their virginity. Girls cooking up plans for a random adventure. Or simply trying to catch a few minutes of sleep during a shift break.

Amelia herself learned many lessons on this couch, like which teachers were good and which to avoid, how to lie to her mom and get away with it, and ways to protect her heart from being broken. Could she have survived high school without them? And what a shame to not have this sacred place to pass that knowledge along.

Not to mention that Amelia planned to spend a big part of this summer on this couch with Cate. Since Amelia was Head Girl, she could ensure they worked every shift together. They'd take their meal breaks here, maybe fit in a quick game of Boggle, depending on how the younger girls were handling the lines. All their plans would have hatched on this couch—what parties, what movies, what day trips. They'd include the other stand girls in most of their exploits, but Amelia also hoped there'd be a few special adventures just for the two of them while they still both lived in Sand Lake.

Amelia senses these intangible things, her every hope for her last summer, slipping away as the sun shines through the lace curtains and drifts across the office, landing on the filing cabinet, then the desk, then her feet, then the floor.

A fly hums near her cheek. Another lands on her arm. Another hovers near her ear. She swats them away, rolls off the love seat, and walks back into the main room of the stand. Flies swarm the pool of melted strawberry ice cream on the floor. Quickly, Amelia props open the stand door and aims the office fan to help shoo them out. She fills a bucket with warm soapy water and mops up the pink from the floor.

And then she continues cleaning, as if they were still opening in two days, because it's easier for her to pretend Molly's death won't change anything than to acknowledge that it will. She wipes

siobhan vivian

down the marble counters, and the white subway tile backsplash, and vacuums away the cobwebs. After carrying the rest of the spoiled drums to the dumpster, she takes a second bucket of water outside and scrubs out the trunk of Molly's pink Cadillac.

By the time she's finished, she's sweating through her polo. She knows just what to do to cool down. She heads back into the stand, passing the purple ski jacket that hangs on a hook, and wrestles with the door of the walk-in freezer, trying to break the seal. Where the ski jacket originally came from is a mystery. The girls put it on when the walk-in freezer needs to be reorganized. When it's too hot to think straight, they'll go inside for a few seconds without it.

A few tugs and the seal unsticks. An icy fog billows out.

It's just as Molly said in her letter. There wasn't one single scoop left to sell at the end of last summer, but the walk-in freezer is completely restocked, save for the few gallons that spoiled in Molly's trunk. Every shelf is packed tight with cardboard drums of ice cream, maybe a hundred total, each one marked in Molly's handwriting. *Vanilla, Chocolate, Strawberry, Home Sweet Home.* Molly's been at this for weeks, maybe even months, getting her ice cream stand ready for opening day, the way she has every summer since she lost her true love.

A sadness hangs on Amelia. Though Molly's ice cream was beloved and though her business ultimately became a success, surely she would have traded everything to have Wayne come home.

"Amelia?"

Amelia steps out of the freezer and sees Cate at the open stand door. Cate's not wearing her Meade Creamery polo. She's in a denim mini, a striped tank top, and flip-flops. Her blond hair is wet from the shower, split down the center of her head in a straight part.

"You haven't answered any of my texts!" she says. "I was worried!"

Amelia pats her empty pockets. "Sorry. I left my phone in the office."

Cate bites her bottom lip as she tentatively glances around. "Did . . . they take her away already?"

"Yeah, she's gone," Amelia says, dazed.

"Come on, then. Let's get out of here."

Amelia follows for a step, then stops. "Wait. I can't leave. The newbies are going to show up any minute to fill out applications." This happens on the first day back. A handful of recently graduated eighth graders descend, hoping to claim the spots of the departed. Despite her overall nervousness about being Head Girl, Amelia has been looking forward to this part—to trying to find herself and Cate in a pile of applications, giving two new girls the chance to build what she and Cate have with each other.

"So put up a sign."

"Saying what? That Molly Meade is dead?"

"Um, no! Definitely not. Just . . . keep it vague. *No Applications Today*, something like that."

Amelia goes into the office to make the sign. This time, the black-and-white kitten comes right out from under the desk. She makes the split-second decision to take him home with her, even though her mom is allergic.

While Cate struggles to lift Amelia's bike into the back of her pickup truck, Amelia closes the stand door, clicks the padlock shut, and hangs the cryptic sign. With the slightest hesitation, she pushes her key underneath the door.

siobhan vivian

She didn't get to use it, not even once.

On the way to Cate's truck, the kitten must realize that Amelia is trying to kidnap him, because he stops purring and starts wriggling in her arms. She tries bringing him close to her chest, but he flexes his claws and tears the inside of her arm in four red stripes. As Amelia flinches, the kitten leaps free, crashing through the tall grass of the fields, splintering it until he—like Molly—is gone too.

CHAPTER  FOUR

AMELIA WATCHED CATE ACE HER DRIVING TEST FROM A bench outside the DMV. Cate could have been a model out of a driver's ed handbook, her back straight, her hands at eight and four, making complete stops, checking her mirrors.

These days, Cate likes to tuck her left foot up underneath her body as she drives. She steers with one hand and holds the wheel down at the bottom, exactly how they say not to. With her free hand, she fiddles with something—the radio, her phone, her hair, Amelia's hair. And she treats posted speed limits around Sand Lake as mere suggestions.

Amelia would normally chastise Cate for any or all of these behaviors, but she doesn't say a thing about Cate's driving today. Instead, she rolls down the passenger window for the breeze and watches as the green graduation tassel hanging from Cate's rear-view mirror twists and spins. At the end of August, she won't be riding in Cate's truck anymore. Cate will be taking it with her to Truman University. And Amelia will be up at Gibbons, an airplane ride away.

Eventually Cate reaches over and rubs Amelia's shoulder. "Are you feeling okay? You look pale."

Amelia flips down the visor. Cate is right. There's no pink in her cheeks, and even when she pinches them, the flush slips away fast. "I guess I forgot to eat." Amelia holds out her hands in front of her. They quiver.

"What about your blueberry muffins?"

"I gave them to the police officer to bring back to the station."

"Pizza Towne might be open."

"Honestly, I'm more tired than hungry. I should probably go home and rest."

Cate frowns. "You seriously don't look good. Let's get a quick slice." She pulls a U-turn in the middle of the road. After a silence, she glances over at Amelia and says, "I'm trying to remember the last time I saw Molly Meade. I think it was at the bank."

Amelia nods. "Same for me. The day you bought the truck."

It was late last fall. Amelia had gone with Cate to take the truck for a test drive. Cate's neighbor was the one selling it, and though Cate felt the price was fair and withdrew exactly that amount from her savings account, she still planned to try and talk him down a couple hundred bucks for the rust and the lack of working AC.

They were in the outside lane of the bank drive-thru waiting on Cate's money, Amelia looking at something on her phone while Cate begged Amelia's mom through the intercom to send them two lollipops. That was when a pink Cadillac pulled into the drive-thru lane beside them.

Cate elbowed her and Amelia looked up, and together they watched Molly like they'd spotted some kind of rare, beautiful bird. Molly's hair was curled; she had makeup on, and earrings, and a fashionable, if slightly dated, gabardine wool coat. She looked the way people did when they dressed up for church, except Amelia never saw Molly Meade at church.

Molly handed Amelia's mom a deposit bag and waited for a receipt. Amelia silently willed her to look toward them, though she wondered if Molly would even have recognized them if she had.

Cate says now, "It seems weird that she got all dolled up just to hit up the bank drive-thru. Maybe Molly had a hot date."

Amelia rolls her eyes. "Stop."

"What! She was a good-looking lady! She totally could have shacked up with some handsome widower."

"She probably had a doctor's appointment. Or maybe lunch with a friend." Except, as far as Amelia knew, Molly never had company. Certainly Amelia never saw any cars, besides the mailman and the Marburger Dairy truck, head up her driveway. Amelia remembers her grandmother complaining that the worst part about getting old is outliving all your friends.

Cate pulls into a spot in front of the darkened windows of Pizza Towne. "Do you want to go somewhere else?"

Yawning, Amelia says, "Sure, wherever." She kicks off her Keds and puts her bare feet up on the glove compartment.

Cate decides on Starbucks, where they each get an egg and cheese sandwich and an iced mocha, and she refuses to let Amelia pay. "See? Don't you feel better?"

"Yes," Amelia says. "And sorry if I'm being a downer."

"You found a dead body today! You're forgiven."

Amelia nods, though she knows it's more than that. "I knew Molly would die eventually, but not this summer. Not *our* summer." Cate's profile blurs as Amelia's eyes flood with tears.

"Hey!" Cate says, turning toward her. "Amelia, it's okay. It was Molly's time. Please don't cry."

Except crying is exactly what Amelia does. Even though she knows it's stupid, because it's just a summer job, and she didn't even know Molly Meade, not really. "The walk-in freezer was full of ice cream, Cate. Ice cream she made with love that no one will ever get to eat. And I'm sitting here trying to remember what Home Sweet Home tastes like. I've probably eaten that ice cream a million times, nearly every summer of my life." She rubs her tongue against the roof of her mouth, swallows. "But I can't remember. It's . . . gone. And in a few weeks, you and I will leave—"

"Amelia!" Cate says, startled. "Stop it!"

Except Amelia can't hold back the tears now. Can't even try to. She keeps talking, pushing as many words out as she can between hysterical gasps. "We'll leave Sand Lake and go off to college and everything's going to be different. I know that. But I thought I'd have this summer to get ready. One last summer where it's you and me, the way it's always been."

"Okay, all right," Cate says, and rubs Amelia's back. "Let it out."

Amelia cries some more, quietly. She's aware that Cate's a bit uncomfortable by where Amelia has just taken things. Not that they wouldn't have had this conversation eventually. She's just unprepared to have it right now. "Sorry."

Softly, Cate says, "You don't have to say sorry. I know exactly how you're feeling, Amelia. Believe me."

Cate pulls into Amelia's driveway. Amelia's family doesn't live on the lake. Her house is tucked back in the woods a ways, a small, pretty colonial with wood siding painted butter yellow and a robin's-egg-blue front door. From Amelia's bedroom window, you can see a bit of the glittering lake through the trees.

"What are you going to do for the rest of the day?" Amelia asks Cate.

"Oh, I don't know. Maybe go down to the lake." Cate lowers her head to see the sky from the windshield. "Though it's suddenly too cloudy to tan." She shrugs. "I'll call you later and check in." Cate leans across the cab and gives Amelia a big hug.

Amelia goes inside and up to her room. She folds the blankets Cate slept in and puts them back into her closet. Next, she takes off her Head Girl pin and returns it, as well as Molly Meade's note, to her jewelry box with her other obsolete treasures, like friendship bracelets from long ago, which are too stretched out to be safely worn but that she can't imagine ever throwing away.

Flopping on her bed, she checks her phone and finds several missed messages. The stand girls want to know what happened. If everything's okay. It dawns on her that Cate didn't tell the girls that Molly had died, only that they shouldn't come in today.

Though she doesn't want to, Amelia dutifully starts a new text to the six girls who were supposed to return to Meade Creamery this summer, and then adds the stand girls from summers past that she has saved in her phone, thinking they would want to know what happened too.

Sad news. Molly Meade passed away. I think it happened sometime yesterday. I'm sorry I don't have more details. Honestly, I still can't believe it's true.

siobhan vivian

She hits Send, plugs her phone into the charger, and goes into the bathroom to swallow some Advil. When she returns, she sees a text back from Frankie Ko.

Amelia smiles. The last she's heard, Frankie graduated college somewhere in Florida, not FSU, another one, then moved down to Costa Rica to study sea turtles. She wonders what Frankie will say when she hears that Amelia was going to be Head Girl this summer. She hopes Frankie will be proud. Amelia feels bad for losing touch with her. Not that they became super-great friends, but because Frankie will always hold a special place in her heart. Amelia wants to tell her that. Before it's too late, because you never know.

The text says ERROR. INVALID NUMBER.

Amelia sets her phone down. As soon as she does, it begins to buzz again.

She leaves it on her nightstand and crawls under the covers.

CHAPTER FIVE

WHEN AMELIA LIFTS HER HEAD, WARM AGAINST HER pillow, she knows she's been asleep for a long time. Hours. She feels it in her body, the heaviness, and her room is shadowy. Rolling onto her back, she finds her phone and glances through the texts she's received from the other girls at the stand. It's a blur of sad emojis, virtual hugs that she can almost feel.

She changes out of her polo and into a big T-shirt—the one from Project Graduation night—and a pair of leggings, undoes her fishtail braids, and combs her fingers through the waves they've left behind.

Downstairs, she finds her mom and dad sitting together at their kitchen table, their plates pushed off to the side. Dad has his school papers spread out in front of him—he teaches math at the high school, and summer school starts next week—and

Mom is scrolling on her phone. A baseball game is on the radio. Someone gets a hit and they look up at each other and smile.

"Hi."

They glance over at her, startled, and then guiltily at the remnants of dinner. Her dad explains, "We thought you were out with Cate."

"It's okay."

Her mom winces and quickly clears their things from Amelia's normal spot at the table. "Would you believe we even told each other tonight is a chance to train ourselves for how lonely it's going to be around here in September?"

"Please don't make me more depressed." Amelia falls into her seat.

Amelia's dad offers a gentle smile. "How are you holding up?"

"It's hard to believe. This wasn't how I was expecting today to go, you know?"

"No, I suppose not." He reaches across the table and ruffles her hair. "You sure you don't want some steak? It'll only take me a couple of minutes to get the grill going."

"I'm sure."

Amelia's mom gives her shoulder a tender squeeze. "It's not easy to do what you did today. We're proud of you."

"I didn't actually do anything. I just walked in and found her." Amelia slouches in her chair and picks a tomato from the salad bowl. She appreciates their trying to cheer her up, but really, it was the bare minimum.

"You took charge," her dad insists. "You acted like a manager!"

"Head Girl," her mom corrects.

"Yes, right. Head Girl."

"And thank goodness you did, Amelia! Could you imagine

if this happened in winter? Poor Molly would have been lying there dead for months and no one would have known."

"Mom!"

Her mother's eyes go wide. "I'm sorry. That came out wrong."

"Very wrong," her dad adds.

Amelia's phone rings. "It's Cate. Do you mind?"

They nod, maybe even a bit gratefully, excusing her.

"Hey, Cate." Amelia leaves the kitchen and sits on the stairs.

Cate tsks. "I was hoping you'd sound better but you don't sound better."

"Well, my parents just tried to cheer me up by saying I prevented Molly's corpse from mummifying."

"That's . . . an interesting strategy."

"It was. It really was."

"How about I take a shot? What do you say? Up for it?"

"Sure."

"Cool. So I'm going to need you to walk out your front door right now."

Amelia flinches. "Huh?"

"Walk out your front door," Cate repeats, a playful teasing in her voice, and then hangs up.

Amelia rises to her feet and does as she was told, a smile already lifting the corners of her mouth. Shielding herself with the curtain, she peeks out the window of her front door. Cate's standing in her driveway along with the six other returning Meade Creamery girls—juniors Sophie and Bernadette, sophomores Mansi and Liz, and last summer's newbies, Jen and Britnee.

At least, that's who Amelia assumes they are. She can't be sure because each girl is wearing a dark-colored sweatshirt with a hood pulled up to hide her hair. They stand in a whispering huddle,

siobhan vivian

which breaks apart at the creaking sound of Amelia opening the door. But their buzzing energy is palpable, the way it always is at the start of the summer, when the returning girls reconnect and catch up after the school year, like bunkmates at a sleepaway camp.

"What's everyone doing here?" Amelia asks with a laugh.

Cate lunges forward, takes Amelia's hand, and pulls her away from the house. "Shhhhhh! You're going to blow our cover!"

"Cover for what?"

Jen tosses Cate a sweatshirt, which Cate then hands to Amelia. "Put this on." It's a navy one from Truman University, turned inside out. "I've been thinking about what you said today. How there's all that ice cream left in the stand. I can't come up with one good reason why we, *the last-ever Meade Creamery girls*, shouldn't be the ones to eat it."

"Seriously?" Amelia lifts up on her toes. "But what if someone sees us?"

"What could they say? We're still legally employees." Cate looks at the rest of the girls, almost daring them to disagree with her, which of course no one does. "Plus, you still have your key, so it's not like we'd be breaking—"

Amelia smacks her forehead with her hand.

"What?"

"I pushed it under the door before we left today."

Cate laughs good-naturedly, like this was to be expected somehow from Amelia. "No big. We'll figure it out."

To the other girls, Amelia says, "You all sure you want to do this?" They nod back at her, excited, burdened by none of the sadness Amelia carries. Though, when Amelia thinks about it, that sadness is mostly gone now, replaced by the feeling that her heart is about to burst in the best way.

. . .

Amelia and Cate ride together, with Cate's truck in the lead. The rest of the girls squeeze into two other cars belonging to Sophie and Bernadette. Amelia opens the passenger-side window and sticks her head out to watch the cars turn onto Route 68. With their headlights on, and the random celebratory beeps of their horns, they resemble something between Sand Lake's Homecoming Parade and a funeral procession.

Cate pats Amelia's leg. "You're not going to cry again, are you?"

"No!" Amelia says, turning to face front. "I'm really excited!"

"Me too!" Cate's cheeks are flushed and she speaks quickly. "So here's what I'm thinking. I'll get one or two of the girls to stand lookout, and the rest of us will go in and grab some ice cream. Then I thought we could drive down to the lake and eat it there. It'll be like our end-of-summer party. A chance for us to say a proper goodbye."

"Thank you for doing this. I can't believe—" Amelia cuts herself off because she *can* believe it. That Cate would organize this whole expedition for her. This is Cate. This is exactly why she would have made a terrific Head Girl. It's a shame Molly never noticed.

siobhan vivian

CHAPTER  SIX

THE GIRLS PULL INTO THE DRIVEWAY OF MEADE CREAM-ery, stopping just short of the parking lot chain, then climb out of their cars.

"Whoa. Someone moved Molly's Cadillac," Amelia remarks. She stands on her tiptoes and tries to see if it's parked up at the house. Only she can't. The grass is too high. And it's dark.

"Maybe it was towed away," Cate says.

"By who?" Amelia asks, her trepidation slowing her.

Cate doesn't answer. She's already moved on. To the girls behind her, she says quickly, "Okay. I need a couple of you to get down on the ground and shine your phones underneath the door so I can see where Amelia's key is."

Amelia and Cate both lie on their bellies in the dirt. With the help of the cell phone lights, Amelia can see her key a few feet inside on the floor. Cate asks someone to find her a long stick, which Jen races off to do. Then, after a couple of tries with it, Cate exclaims, "Got it!"

The girls jump up and down. Amelia, too, is excited. They'll likely be the last people in the world to ever eat Molly Meade's homemade ice cream. Amelia has a feeling in her chest that this is exactly what Molly would have wanted them to do tonight.

After clicking open the padlock, Cate hands Amelia back her key. Now that it's in her hands again, it suddenly feels like something she should keep.

A car passes on the road.

And then another, but this one slows down slightly. Or maybe it just seems that way.

From behind her, Amelia hears one of the girls whisper, "What if we get arrested?"

"Don't worry. Cate will get us out of it," another answers.

And though Amelia believes that is very likely true, she decides it would be best to get in and out of the stand as quickly as possible. "I'll run in and get the ice cream," she offers as Cate pulls open the door.

But Cate is already ushering all the girls inside, telling them to take one last look at the place. And Amelia thinks, *What's the harm?* This is their chance to say goodbye too. Every one of the girls has her own memories, her own experiences, her own friendships because of Meade Creamery.

They don't turn the lights on. Instead, they use their phones to see. Even in the dark, Amelia remembers so clearly where Molly's body was, and she's careful to step around the spot. Maybe it's a good thing that the stand is closing. Amelia doubts she can ever come here and not think of that moment.

siobhan vivian

"Ooh! I want to take a milk bottle!"

"Grab one for me, too!"

Amelia spins around and watches Britnee try to climb on Bernadette's shoulders. The rafters are full of these bottles, relics from the old Meade Dairy days.

Back then, the Meade family's primary business was milk, and their dairy was open year-round. But production stopped long before Amelia was born, the cow pastures left to grow in wild and shaggy. Molly continued making her ice cream though, sourcing her ingredients from Marburger Dairy, and selling it only a few weeks each summer.

Sometimes Amelia finds the original Meade Dairy milk bottles on garage sale tables for twenty five dollars, an inflated price jacked up for vacationers who might never come back. None of the locals buy them; they don't need to pay twenty-five dollars for a piece of Meade Creamery history as long as the stand is around. Though maybe now that will change.

Cate tells the girls, "No. We only take ice cream." Amelia is grateful. She's not sure who this stuff belongs to, but it's definitely not theirs. "Grab however much you want, Amelia."

Though it had crossed Amelia's mind to take a drum of each of the four flavors Meade Creamery offers, because they're all special in their own way, it feels suddenly too greedy. There's no way the eight of them are eating twelve gallons of ice cream tonight. So Amelia opens the walk-in freezer and settles on a single drum of Home Sweet Home.

Mansi calls out nervously, "Yo. There's a bunch of lights on up at Molly's."

Everyone runs to the office and stares through the window up at the farmhouse. There are, indeed, lights on. A dark figure steps out of the brightness of the front door, stands on the steps, and appears to look down toward the stand.

"Shit," Cate says, but her eyes are bright and excited. "Run!"

They make for the stand door at once, a stampede. The last to go, Amelia quickly closes the lock. A million fears grip her, the girls getting arrested, Cate losing her scholarship to Truman.

It would be because of her.

The girls hurdle the parking lot chain, dive into their cars, and speed back out onto Route 68.

"Who was that up there, do you think?" Amelia asks, turning around in her seat to look out the passenger window.

Cate's breathless and gunning it, her old truck straining. "Maybe the police?" she muses giddily.

"Why would the police be up there?"

"I don't know! Maybe it's those companies who clean out dead people's houses."

"This late at night? Plus, who would have called them?" Turning back around, Amelia sinks low and glances at the side-view mirror to see if they're being followed.

Thankfully, they aren't.

"Put the ice cream down there," Cate says, pointing to Amelia's feet. "It'll melt faster on your lap."

Ten minutes later, they arrive at an unmarked path splitting the dense piney woods. Cate drives down the sandy stretch and parks her truck. There's another swimming area on the other side of Sand Lake, one with a proper parking lot and picnic tables and a paved path to the beach, but the spot on this side is used primarily by teens.

The cove is horseshoe shaped. The shore is sandy, like the

ocean, and by the time it gets thick with underwater plants, most people can't touch the bottom anyway. The water in Sand Lake is crystal clear, though it's too dark to see that now.

The girls build a fire with sticks from the woods, one bigger than they would make at the end of the summer, because tonight the air still has a bit of that late-spring chill. The girls smooth out the blankets they brought, the blue-black lake gently lapping the shore. Amelia tips her head back. It's as if every star in the galaxy has come out for them.

They sit in a circle. Amelia hands out plastic spoons while Cate pulls the cap off the drum of ice cream.

"You should get the first taste, Amelia," Cate announces. "After all, this night was inspired by you. And you're our Head Girl."

Amelia appreciates Cate's saying that, though it's strange, how meaningless the distinction suddenly feels.

"It's okay, someone else can go first," Amelia says, because she's embarrassed, but the girls insist and pass the ice cream drum to her. Amelia dips in her spoon and finds that the ice cream has warmed to a perfectly scoopable temperature. Colorwise, it could be mistaken for vanilla, though it's far more buttery yellow.

Amelia closes her eyes as she brings the spoon up to her lips. Flipping it over, she uses her tongue to pull the egg-shaped taste into her mouth. Instead of swallowing, Amelia holds it on her tongue, letting it melt, cream filling the hollows of her mouth. Though the taste of Home Sweet Home is hard to describe, Amelia is desperate to commit some language about it to memory.

For the first few seconds, her brain simply rules out the typical flavors one might expect to taste in ice cream. It's not chocolatey, or nutty, or fruity. It's the least sugary of the Meade Creamery ice creams. There's a warmth and a depth to whatever makes it sweet, yet it isn't sticky like honey. It has a freshness and a brightness and a cleanness, nearly lemony, except not.

The best Amelia can do is to say it tastes like summer, like Sand Lake itself. Not the water but the feeling of sliding into it on the hottest, most humid day. Of everything and everyone she loves. And that, unfortunately, must be good enough. The truth is that no one knows exactly what's in Home Sweet Home. And no one ever will.

Amelia passes the ice cream drum to Cate next, and silently mouths *Thanks*.

The girls make small talk in between spoonfuls. Loose plans form to go to the county fair together. There's talk of a weekly lake day, maybe a monthly movie night. Though the girls no longer have the place that will bind them, they have good intentions of not letting each other go.

By twelve thirty, the fire has died out and everyone is full of ice cream. They fold up their blankets, pour water on their fire, and walk back toward the cars.

Amelia and Cate bring up the rear of the pack. It's so dark Amelia can't make out the three girls in front of her, only hear their whispered conversation.

"Do you think Molly had a will?"

"Doubt it. She didn't have any family."

"She had to be rich, though, right? With how popular the stand was?"

"Oh my God, what if Molly left the stand to us?"

"Huh?"

"Like a stipulation in her will. *Whichever girls are working for me when I die will inherit my stand and all my money.*"

Cate, staring into the glow of her phone, rolls her eyes.

Amelia has a moment of fun thinking about the possibility. Better, anyway, than what is likely the reality—that there will never be another summer at Meade Creamery. That tonight is truly goodbye.

CHAPTER SEVEN

WHEN AMELIA ANSWERS HER PHONE THE NEXT MORN-
ing, Cate is undiluted cheer and brightness. "Since we don't have
work, let's spend the day at the lake!"

It strikes Amelia as funny to hear Cate put it that way
because it's not like this is a normal day off. Everything about
their summer has changed. Amelia rolls over and looks out her
window. It's sunny with a cloudless blue sky. A perfect lake day.
"Great idea," she says, because really, it would be a sin not to
enjoy a day like this. "I'll make us sandwiches."

She makes turkey and Swiss with mayo for herself, lettuce
and cucumber and Swiss with mayo for Cate. There's one Coke
in the fridge, which is fine; they'll split it.

Back upstairs, she digs in the bottom of her underwear
drawer for her bathing suit. She puts it on, slides on a cotton

sundress over top, and pulls her ponytail through a Gibbons baseball cap.

Then, as she waits on her front steps for Cate to arrive, she sends a text to the other girls, letting them know that she and Cate will be at the lake, in case anyone wants to join them. A few say they'll try to make it. But then the group conversation shifts to what the summer will hold for the girls now that the stand is no longer around. They talk about which stores at the mall would be cool to work at. Sephora seems to be the consensus, that or Barnes & Noble.

Amelia can't blame them for moving on. Maybe she'd be excited for something new too, if this weren't her last summer here. If she hadn't been the one to find Molly's body. If there weren't already so much change on the horizon for her, with college just around the corner. She will have to get a new job, for sure. Her Meade Creamery salary went straight into her college savings account, but her tips funded her summer fun—money to chip in for Cate's gas, clothes, movie tickets, and Starbucks.

Before heading to the lake, Cate stops at the gas station to fill up and buy a pair of cheap sunglasses. They walk inside and wave hello to Peyton Pierce—a junior who was in Amelia's Spanish II class—working behind the register.

Peyton, Amelia remembers, orders either a vanilla cone with chocolate sprinkles or a cup of Home Sweet Home with peanuts, and he reliably throws his change into the girls' tip jar. It's never very much, maybe sixty cents, but Amelia appreciates the gesture. Kids their age hardly ever think to tip. She wonders if Peyton, or anyone else in town for that matter, knows that Meade Creamery is closed forever.

"Hey," Cate says from behind the sunglasses display. "Did you ever write back to your roommate at Gibbons? *Whatsherface?*"

"Cecilia Brewster."

"Cecilia and Amelia," Cate repeats with dramatic flair, and has a good chuckle.

Amelia winces. "Ugh. How did I not notice that before?"

"Well . . . did you?"

"Not yet."

"Amelia. She's going to think you're weird. Write her back."

"Okay, okay."

While Cate tries on sunglasses, Amelia takes out her phone, intending to respond to Cecilia. But she gets distracted by the rack of newspapers. She flips through the *Sand Lake Ledger*, looking for a mention of Molly Meade's death. A knot tightens inside her when there isn't one.

"Should I have written an obituary for Molly?"

Cate looks over the top of some mirrored aviators. "No one could think that's your responsibility, Amelia." She spins the plastic rack. "That's like . . . a family's job."

"Yeah, except she doesn't have any family."

"Fine, it's at least a friend's job. You didn't even know her!"

It stings Amelia a little, even though she knows Cate doesn't mean it that way. "All the summers we worked there, when did you ever see friends at Molly Meade's house?"

"I bet someone from the newspaper does a story on her." Cate takes off the aviators and tries a pair of turquoise knock-off Ray-Bans. They make her hair look extra blond. "These ones," Cate says, smiling at her reflection. "Right?"

Amelia nods. "Love them."

As they walk up to Peyton's register, Amelia passes a small

selection of cat food. Five cans for five dollars. Okay, so an obituary isn't her responsibility. But what about Molly's poor kitten? Who will feed him now that she's gone?

Amelia picks cans in a variety of flavors—Salmon Feast, Whitefish, Roast Chicken, skipping Turkey and Giblets because gross—then stands behind Cate in line. Cate glances back at her, confused.

"Don't ask," Amelia says, unzipping her purse. "But can we please stop by the stand quick before we head to the lake?"

Cate's truck hops the lip of the road. They don't need to bother with the parking lot chain, just make a wide turn and pick up Molly's driveway. She points across the cab and out Amelia's window. "Your newbie sign is still up."

"I wonder how many girls came yesterday," Amelia says, wistfully. "You know what's crazy to think about? Even after everyone in Sand Lake finds out that Molly Meade is dead, vacationers will be stopping by here all summer."

"Probably for the next few years," Cate muses.

Amelia shakes her head. It's beyond depressing—the thought of people driving past this place year after year, seeing it slowly decompose, rotting until it falls over, the way some other properties in town have, when there isn't anyone around to care for them.

Up at the farmhouse, things are quiet, which is a relief to Amelia after last night. She gets out of the truck and clicks her tongue for the black-and-white kitten. There's no sign of him.

Someone did move Molly's Cadillac up here. Amelia looks inside. The keys are on the dashboard. It must have been the police here last night, she's sure of it now. They probably swung by to move Molly's car and make sure the property was secure. Amelia wonders what will happen to the stuff inside the farmhouse. The things Molly Meade collected over her lifetime.

On her way up the front stairs, Amelia steps around a chipped teacup half full of brown triangles of cat food. She opens the cans she brought and sets them down on the steps. Despite her being picky about flavors, they all smell horrible.

While Cate tries to find better music on the radio, Amelia calls the local Animal Control to see if someone can come to the farmhouse with a trap. As the line rings, she leans over the railing. The front window is curtained with a sun-bleached bedsheet. There's nothing to see besides a couple of dead ladybugs lying belly-up on the sill.

She's starting to leave a message when Cate gets out of the truck, shielding her eyes from the sun—forgetting, Amelia guesses, about the new sunglasses perched in her hair. She hops up the stairs, passing Amelia, and opens the screen door.

Amelia covers the phone. "What are you doing?"

With a devious smile, Cate reaches for the doorknob.

For a second, Amelia can't breathe.

Cate pulls a couple of times, hard, and the door shakes on its hinges. "Locked," she announces, glum. "But could you imagine?" She backs down two, three steps and gazes up at the farmhouse. "I would love to see what Molly's got inside there. What she did with all her money. Maybe she's got a crazy fine art collection. That house could be full of Picassos or whatever."

Amelia seriously doubts that, though she would love to look inside the farmhouse too. As much as everyone in Sand Lake knew Molly Meade, she was also a complete mystery.

After leaving a message, Amelia hangs up and pulls Cate back

siobhan vivian

over to the truck by her arm. "Let's get out of here before someone sees us."

There are already plenty of kids from their high school at the lake, blankets and towels spread out in the same groups found during the school year in the cafeteria, a catwalk of sand in between clusters. Amelia expects someone will ask about Molly Meade, wondering why she and Cate are at the lake and not at the ice cream stand getting it ready to open tomorrow, but no one does.

They claim an open spot away from the tree line and spread out their towels. Cate's bikini is dark green with fuchsia trim and the tanner she gets, the better it looks on her. Amelia's wearing her favorite bikini from last summer—light blue gingham, high-waisted, with a demi-cup top. She feels like a glamorous old-time movie star when she's wearing it. It's also great because she doesn't have to be nearly as dutiful as Cate with her bikini line.

The girls coat their bodies with coconut oil. Amelia puts sunscreen on her face to keep it from freckling and Cate sprays her hair with another bottle that will eventually turn it white blond. Cate stretches out long and lean and lets out a happy sigh.

"How great if we could do this all summer? Just be beach bums until we leave for college."

Amelia settles in too, tipping her baseball cap so it's sitting on top of her face. "Maybe if I got a scholarship like you, I could."

"My scholarship isn't going to cover everything. College textbooks are hella expensive."

"We should try job hunting together. Make us a package deal."

She hears Cate sit up. Cate lifts the cap off Amelia's face. "Umm. So I have something to tell you. I already got another job."

Amelia sits up on her knees. "Wait, what? When?"

Guiltily, Cate says, "Yesterday afternoon. While you were sleeping."

"Why didn't you tell me last night?" As soon as Amelia says it, she knows. The real impetus for the impromptu trip to the ice cream stand was Cate's guilt.

"I don't know. I guess . . . I knew you were already upset about Molly and I didn't want to make it worse."

"Where are you working?"

Cate hides behind her hands. "JumpZone."

JumpZone is a newish business that opened near the Walmart. It's a place full of huge inflatable bounce houses and slides that people rent out for little-kid birthday parties.

"Are they still hiring?" Amelia asks, desperate.

Cate peeks through her fingers. "I don't think?" After rubbing her face, she drops her hands and reveals a hangdog pout. "Anyway, you don't want to work there. It's going to suck. Super-early mornings, inside, screaming kids."

Amelia feels like she's been punched in the gut. She lowers herself back onto her towel.

Cate returns Amelia's cap and then takes a sip of their shared Coke. "Don't be mad. You know I hate the thought of us not working together but I need the money."

"It feels like summer's already over."

"We wouldn't be having this conversation if you'd applied to Truman."

"Cate, please. I never would have gotten in." Truman is one of the best universities in the country. It's incredibly selective. Of course Cate got in. She got in everywhere she applied.

"Come on. You got into Gibbons! And that was your reach!

Which you also wouldn't have applied to if not for me."

This is true. Amelia was accepted to a few small schools, all close to home. But when Gibbons, a much better school that Cate had basically forced her to apply to, said yes, going seemed like a foregone conclusion. Her parents were thrilled, and so was Cate. Amelia was too, though she still, even now, has a hard time imagining herself living so far from Sand Lake.

Cate turns her head. Amelia sees a pack of gangly young girls, eighth graders, timidly approaching them.

"Can I help you?" Cate asks.

"Are either of you Amelia Van Hagen?"

Cate snickers and returns to her magazine.

"I'm Amelia," Amelia quickly answers, with a touch of nervous laugher. "Do you girls need something?"

"You're the Head Girl of Meade Creamery, right?" Amelia nods. "We wanted to know if it was true. If the stand really is closed for the summer."

Cate flips a page.

"Yes," Amelia says. "I'm very sorry to say that it is."

The girls exchange disappointed looks. "Oh, okay. Thanks for letting us know."

"I'm sure you'll find other great jobs!" Amelia calls after them. She keeps watching until the girls reach their beach towels. Then, to Cate, she wonders aloud, "Did we ever look that young?"

Cate has her magazine up in front of her face. She's not even looking when she says, "Nope."

"Do you think we would have been best friends if we hadn't worked at the stand together?"

"I don't like thinking about that."

"Why not?"

"Because it makes everything feel fragile when it's actually solid. And anyway, what does it matter? We *are* best friends, and we always will be."

Amelia flips over onto her stomach and closes her eyes. Before she got to know Cate, Amelia couldn't imagine being friends with her. Cate was one of the girls who took a limo to the eighth-grade dinner dance. And now that they are best friends, Amelia can't imagine life without her. Lots of things change, but thank goodness, that never will.

CHAPTER  EIGHT

AMELIA MAKES THE SALAD WHILE HER DAD TENDS TO the chicken on the backyard grill. She likes making the salad, because he always cuts the onions too thick.

When her dad comes in, Amelia asks him, "Do you think that if Mom had died when you were young, you would have married someone else?"

He takes a dish of marinade and a brush from the utensils drawer. He's not being evasive by not answering. He's taking his time, really thinking about what he wants to say. "I've been in love with your mom for nearly all the years I've been alive. It's hard to say what I would have done back then if I'd lost her, but at this point, I doubt that my heart knows how to beat without her."

"You've never once gotten your heart broken," Amelia says.

"Don't hold it against me!"

"I'm not. It's just . . . I don't know. Like a miracle."

"Never thought about it like that before, but I guess you're right. With the drama I've witnessed in the high school hallways, I guess I should be thankful."

There really is something special to that kind of love, Amelia thinks—when teenagers fall in love and stay together—that kind of closeness, of really knowing a person. Her parents have it. And Amelia always hoped she'd have it too. But it didn't work out that way for her.

There have been a few boys over the years, and always during the school year. Ty Straub was her first kiss, during the eighth-grade overnight field trip to Washington, DC. Jeb Browning took her to the movies last Valentine's Day, Wyatt Barnes the Valentine's Day before that. And there was Andy Farkas, who she would stress-French after SAT prep classes. Andy was also a great prom date, very careful about pinning on her corsage, always making sure she had something to drink when she came off the dance floor. But there's been no one permanent, no boy who made her feel like she might be falling in love.

Cate's even more cautious with her heart, though she flirts more and has kissed double the number of boys as Amelia.

Maybe because it's been drilled into their heads by older stand girls not to expect much from high school boys. It's the science of puberty. Girls develop faster, emotionally and physically. How can any girl expect a high school boy to give her the moon and the stars when he's basically an overgrown testosterone gland with legs? Better that you wait until college, or maybe even graduate school, before you really let someone into your heart. It was different in her parents' day, and definitely when Molly was her age. Amelia's not sure why, but back then, it seemed like boys were more earnest, more devoted, more ready to be in love.

A few minutes after six, Mom comes through the back door. She's dressed in her work clothes—a pencil skirt, blouse, and scarf—and removes a manila folder from her briefcase before setting it down at the door. Like Amelia's dad, she had studied math in college, and was pursuing a master's degree when she got pregnant with Amelia. She switched gears when Amelia was born, becoming a full-time mom until Amelia entered kindergarten. Then she took a job as a teller in Sand Lake, a career choice that felt more manageable and would keep her close to home. However, it wasn't long before she began rising up the corporate ladder, and her job became more and more demanding. She now manages services at several branches around the area.

She kisses Amelia's dad. "Hey there."

"Hi."

She gives Amelia's ponytail a playful swat as she passes by her seat. "I have a bit of good news to share." Amelia's reaching for a napkin when her mother says, "Specifically for you, Amelia."

"Oh?"

"Yes." Her mom sets the folder down in front of her. "I found out today that we're hiring a new teller at the Sand Lake branch."

Amelia takes a long, slow sip of her lemonade. "They hire high schoolers?"

"You're a college girl now, Amelia."

"Oh. Right."

"It's a good job," her mom says. "Pays well. Air-conditioned.

And a terrific résumé builder. I wouldn't be your direct supervisor," she clarifies, and then, with a smile, adds, "but your boss would work for me."

"I'd have to dress up," Amelia hedges. She can't imagine having to wear a skirt and heels every day. She still has some sore spots from the strappy sandals she wore to prom. She slipped them off about halfway through the night, but the damage had already been done. "Also, I suck at math, Mom. You know this. Dad knows this."

"You *would* need to dress up, yes. And, lest you forget, you're the one who chose not to attend a state school, so you'll do what you need to. And it would be genetically impossible for you to suck at math! Anyway, everything's automated. There's very little math you'd have to do."

Amelia flips through the materials in the folder and tries to imagine working there. It won't be Meade Creamery, but maybe if she can work the drive-thru lane, it will feel similar. She imagines herself on top of her steel stool, elbows on the counter, chin in her hands, gazing listlessly out of the bank's large drive-thru window. When a car pulls up, she can send out the little tray and get a whiff of fresh, non-air-conditioned air.

"Mom, can you feel the sun through those drive-thru windows? Or is it too thick because it's bulletproof?"

"You know, I never noticed one way or the other. You can see for yourself on Tuesday. Your interview is at noon."

"Tuesday? But I might have to help clean out the stand or something." Amelia has no reason to suspect this, of course, but she says it anyway.

Mom reaches across the table and takes Amelia's hand. "Meade Creamery isn't your responsibility anymore, Amelia."

It isn't said to wound her. Amelia knows her mom is right. But it still hurts to hear—the definition of a painful truth.

The next morning, Molly's obituary is in the paper.

MEADE, Molly Anne—died of natural causes on Wednesday. She was 88. The only and beloved daughter of the late James Meade and Erin (Kelly) Meade, sister to Liam Meade and Patrick Meade (both deceased).

Ms. Meade was a lifelong resident of Sand Lake and a graduate of North High School. During WWII, she sold her homemade ice cream at the Meade Dairy Farm stand. Her signature flavor, Home Sweet Home, was reportedly created when war rations depleted available sugar. After a fire destroyed the barn, her parents retired, and Ms. Meade took up operations. She relaunched the business as Meade Creamery and focused solely on the production of ice cream until her passing.

There are no known surviving relatives.

A memorial service will be held on Sunday at 2:00 PM at Holy Redeemer Catholic Church on Poplar Street in Sand Lake.

CHAPTER  NINE

"YOU'RE GOING TO MOLLY'S FUNERAL THIS AFTER-
noon, aren't you?"

"Why, hello and good morning to you, too, Cate," Amelia
groans. She's lying on top of her neatly made bed in her bra and
undies, a towel wrapped around her head.

Cate laughs hard into the phone. "I'm right, though, aren't I?"

Amelia lets out a long exhale. Across the room are three outfit choices her mom said would be good choices for her bank
interview on Tuesday. They also happen to work for a funeral, an
irony not lost on Amelia. She rolls over onto her stomach and
presses her face into her pillow. "If you want to know the truth,
I'm trying to talk myself *out* of going, so it's a good thing you
called. You can tell me how silly I'm being."

"Why would I do that?"

"Because, like you said, I didn't even know her," Amelia admits.

"That's true. Also, to that excellent point, I'd add that although you found her dead body, it doesn't mean you must personally shepherd Molly Meade into the afterlife. Plus, you've never been to a funeral before. They aren't romantic like you're thinking. They're mad boring." The phone is muffled for a second as Cate switches from one ear to the other. "Actually, when I die, make sure and tell my mom I don't want any of that stuff. I want a party. With expensive champagne. And dancing."

"Sure thing. For the record, I don't think funerals are romantic. I think they're sad. But these are very sound reasons to skip it. Thank you."

"You're welcome. Though I think you should go."

"Why?"

"If you don't, you'll feel terrible. That's just who you are, Amelia. You're a good person."

Amelia smiles for the first time that day. "So what are the chances I can convince you to come be a good person with me?"

"Somewhere in the range of impossible to totally impossible. I have to be at JumpZone for training. Apparently, there's a whole protocol about how to disinfect an inflatable if a kid pees or pukes. Which, as the newest employee, I'm sure is a responsibility that will fall to me."

"You could work at the bank with me!" Her mom said only one teller position was open, not two, but maybe if Amelia begged, she could get it approved.

"Ewww. I'd have to dress up. Also, you know I love your mom, but I can't imagine working for her. It's one thing when I show up late to your house for dinner, but if I'm late to work?" Cate starts cracking up. "Oh my God, Amelia. Imagine if your mom had to fire me. How awkward would that be?"

"It was worth a shot."

"Hey, text me after the funeral. If the timing works, I'll come pick you up."

Amelia goes with the black scoop-neck bodysuit and pale pink pleated skirt and her gray suede ankle booties with the low heel because she plans to walk over to Holy Redeemer. It isn't far, maybe a mile, and riding a bike feels unsuitable. She does a braid crown that wraps around her head and pins the end behind her ear with a bobby pin. Just a little makeup, tasteful, some blush and mascara and a glossed lip. On her way out the door, she doubles back, pulls a few tissues from the box in the foyer, and stuffs them into her purse. There's no way she's getting through this dry-eyed.

Holy Redeemer is a small church, but even with a handful of people in every pew, it still feels sparse, especially when compared to the normal Sunday mass crowd. There are the old people who probably come to anything church related, a few of the regular customers, Sand Lake's mayor. The first pew has been left open for family. But Molly Meade doesn't have any, so it's empty.

Amelia looks around for any other stand girls who might have shown up. She thought about sending a text out, but she didn't want to make the girls feel bad if they weren't planning to go. And apparently, no one else was. She's the youngest person there by far. She takes her seat in a row halfway between the altar and the door. People around her whisper.

"No one has seen her for so long. I wonder if it'll be open casket."

siobhan vivian

"I doubt the farmhouse is worth much."

"The property it's on could sell for a pretty penny to one of those housing developers."

Mrs. Otis takes her place at the piano and begins to play. Amelia flips through one of the hymnals simply for something to look at. She never, ever sings.

After two somber songs, the doors at the back of the church open and everyone stands up. Amelia gets nervous that there won't be anyone to wheel in the casket, except there is no casket. Only an urn, which Father Caraway, despite being ninety-something years old, carries up the aisle himself. For that, Amelia feels both relieved and sad.

Father's head is completely bald except for his eyebrows, which are white and bristly like two caterpillars. He positions himself behind the lectern, then with a shaking hand, pulls a pair of smudged reading glasses out from the folds of his robe and anchors them on the pink bulb of his nose.

"*Ice Cream So Sweet, You Won't Miss Your Sweetheart.*" Father looks up and smiles tenderly. "I'm sure you're familiar with Meade Creamery's original slogan." The entire church nods. "A similar adage might be *When Life Gives You Lemons, Make Lemonade.* Or *Every Cloud Has a Silver Lining.* This is how Molly Meade lived her life."

Amelia's attention begins to drift. Father comes to the stand once a month in the summertime, in his black clerical shirt and white tab collar, black pants, and a fraying Panama hat that looks about as old as he does. Father's regular order is a single scoop of chocolate with hot fudge and a cherry, which he tries to pay for with a handful of change. The girls never take his money, but he'll put however many quarters he's brought in their tip jar.

Father lifts his head, removes his glasses, and slides them into the folds of his robe. After a chest-rattling cough, he says, "I happened to be with Molly Meade the night she became engaged to a fellow named Wayne Lumsden."

At this, Amelia leans forward in the pew, elbows on her knees. She knows well the tragic story of Molly and Wayne, or, more specifically, the *ending*. But nothing about happier times. When it all began.

"I was a newly ordained priest around the time of the war when I arrived at this parish." Father dabs his forehead. "There was no time to get comfortable, no chance for me to ease into things. Not when every week, another family was sending their boys off, boys only a few years younger than myself."

Father went on. "It was customary in those days for the priest to visit the family, bless a final meal before they departed, and lead a prayer asking for the boy's safety. As you can imagine, this was generally not a festive occasion. There would be so much wonderful food, prepared with love, that nobody felt like eating.

"I shared two meals with the Meade family in a year, one for each of Molly's brothers—Patrick and Liam. The third time I was asked was the following fall, because a fellow named Wayne Lumsden was shipping out at the end of September. Wayne didn't have much in the way of family. When he passed through Sand Lake looking for work, the Meades essentially took him in and gave him a job at their dairy, which speaks to the sort of generous, kind Irish Catholic family they were."

Amelia realizes this must be the reason why over the years she's heard plenty of anecdotes about Molly Meade and never much about Wayne Lumsden. He wasn't actually from Sand Lake.

"Now, the good Lord sprinkled Molly and Wayne with the

siobhan vivian

same stardust he must use to make movie stars." Father's face spreads into a smile. "And to the surprise of no one in town, they fell deeply in love."

There are a few polite chuckles.

"I'd heard countless sad stories of men at war, of people lost and hurt and killed. In a way, this seemed almost sadder. That these two youngsters, in the prime of their lives and very much devoted to each other, were about to be ripped apart." He takes a sip of water. "When Mrs. Meade brought out a chocolate cake, I was trying to come up with an acceptable excuse to pass on having a slice. But then Wayne pulled a diamond ring out of his pocket and asked Molly for her hand in marriage. Molly said yes immediately. And a melancholy night became one of celebration."

Amelia can see it playing in her head like a movie: Young Molly, her handsome boyfriend down on one knee, maybe even in his uniform. Her laughing and crying. Him sliding the ring onto her finger, shaking her father's hand.

At this, her mouth drops open. The photo hanging in the stand—of Molly and Wayne, her hand outstretched, fall foliage around them—was likely taken that day. Amelia takes a tissue from her purse and dabs her eyes.

"Now, Wayne, as you know, never made it home from the war, may God rest his soul. But God did not forsake His lovely child, Molly. Instead, the Lord bestowed on her the gift of making ice cream, which comforted her through this profound loss. He works in mysterious ways, and this, I promise you, is one of them. Despite her own suffering, Molly continued to do His work, bringing joy into the lives of countless others for all these years. And for that reason, I have faith that—"

The church doors open suddenly and three people hurry up the aisle, a man and a college-age boy, both in tailored navy suits, and a woman in a black dress and a chunky strand of pearls. Amelia has never seen them before.

Father Caraway clears his throat to refocus the churchgoers and gestures at the sky as he resumes. "I have faith that, because of her service, the Lord has rewarded Molly by reuniting her with her true love Wayne, up in heaven."

After the memorial, Amelia exits the church and exchanges a couple of quick texts with Cate, who says she can be there in fifteen minutes. As Amelia slips her phone into her purse, the boy in the suit passes her at a quicker pace than the other people emerging into the sunlight. He's on his phone, urgently tapping away with one hand, while the two people Amelia assumes are his mother and father trail behind him, speaking quietly with each other.

She keeps the boy in the corner of her eye, looking but trying not to be obvious about it. Amelia doesn't often see boys wearing expensive suits. It's the color—a deep, almost velvety blue—that gives it away. And it fits him perfectly. It suddenly strikes her how frumpy the guys looked at senior prom, rented tuxes too tight across their shoulders, dress shirts not pressed. Also, this boy's shoes are cool. Whiskey-brown wing-tip oxfords that he's threaded with bright orange laces. The leather is rich and shiny—not a scuff on them.

The boy looks up from his phone and scans the crowd. When his eyes land on her, Amelia smiles a polite smile. This is apparently enough of an invitation for him to walk over.

"Hey," he says. Like they know each other.

"Um. Hello."

siobhan vivian

Amelia hates that her cheeks are heating up. He is that handsome. Tall and lean, but still muscular, like the boys who become lake lifeguards. He's tan, with freckles, and his hair is brown, cut tight to the sides and left a little long on top, enough for it to roll into a soft curl. Father Caraway would definitely call him "movie-star handsome."

He undoes the button of his suit jacket with one hand. "Sad, isn't it?" he asks.

"Yes."

"Did you know her well?"

"I was one of the girls who worked at her ice cream stand."

"I figured," he says, lifting his chin, apparently pleased with himself. He glances around. "Are any of the other girls here too?"

"No. Only me." Amelia presses her lips together. "I'm sorry. Have we met before?" she asks, knowing they haven't. She would have remembered. But it seems like the most polite way to find out who, exactly, he is.

"No, I don't think so."

"Oh. Well. So . . . how do you know Molly?"

"She was my great-aunt, my grandfather's sister." He holds out his hand. "Grady Meade." Sheepishly, he adds, "I feel terrible that we were late to this, but we got held up with some legal paperwork."

"Oh my gosh! Wait. Really?" She cups his hand in both of hers. "We didn't know Molly had any living family!" A few people look toward them, and Amelia quickly dials back the enthusiasm in her voice to something more funeral appropriate. "I'm Amelia Van Hagen. I'm so so so very sorry for your loss."

"Thanks." He glances down at his hand, still wrapped inside hers. "Thank you."

Blushing, she quickly releases him. "I was the one who found her. And . . ." Amelia momentarily second-guesses saying the next part. But if it were her relative, she'd want to know. She lowers her gaze respectfully to the sidewalk. "I don't think she suffered. She looked peaceful. Like she just needed a nap." Her eyes begin to tear up and she fishes a fresh tissue from her purse.

He is taken aback by her emotion. "Um. Thanks. I'll make sure to pass that along to my family."

Amelia dabs at her eyes, recovering. "You're welcome."

Grady Meade scratches his head. "Can I ask you something, Amelia?"

"Of course."

"Are you one of the girls who broke into the ice cream stand on Thursday night?"

The directness of his question leaves Amelia feeling wobbly. No lies come to mind despite how desperately she tries to conjure one. "We . . . we didn't mean any harm. I promise. We wanted one last taste of her ice cream."

He leans in conspiratorially. "Hey, look. No worries. I totally get it. I haven't been out of high school that long. Me and my buddies used to pull the same kind of pranks. This one time, on Mischief Night, we broke into the cafeteria after hours and stole a box of five hundred frozen chicken fingers and Super Glued them onto the statue of our school's founder. The whole next day, Halloween obviously, he looked like he was getting eaten alive by birds."

For Amelia, there is no relief in being let off the hook. Rather, she is desperate to explain herself. Taking ice cream wasn't some juvenile stunt. They did it because the stand meant so much to them. They had only wanted to say goodbye.

siobhan vivian

She struggles to say as much, but Grady waves her off. "For real, though, I'm hoping one of you girls has a key to the stand. I haven't been able to find one at the farmhouse."

"I do. I don't have it with me right now, but I could run home and get it. I don't live far."

Grady seems to consider this, until he spots his mom and dad climbing into a black Mercedes. "We have to get back to our hotel. Can you drop by the stand tomorrow?"

"Of course. Absolutely."

"Great. Let's say eleven o'clock." Grady types this into his phone, returns it to the inner breast pocket of his suit jacket, and walks away. As an afterthought, he looks back and adds, "Thanks."

Cate pulls up to the corner in her pickup truck. "Who was that?" she asks as Amelia climbs in. "And you'll have to speak up, because I've suffered permanent hearing loss from four back-to-back children's birthday parties."

Amelia watches Grady slip into the black Mercedes. "He's a relative of Molly Meade. Her brother's grandson."

"What? No way!" Cate cranes her neck to see him better.

"Yes way." Amelia rubs her temples. "They were the ones up at her house that night. And by the way, he totally knows we broke in."

"Eek."

"He wants me to show up at the stand tomorrow and give him my key."

"Why are you bummed? He's cute!"

Amelia slumps in her seat. The idea that anyone would think badly of her is one thing. The reality that a descendant of Molly Meade thinks she would do something as disrespectful as stealing ice cream from a dead woman's stand is almost too much to bear.

"Do you think that's all he wants? For me to return the key?"

Cate shrugs. "I mean, I guess there's a chance he could ask you out. But it's not like he lives around here, does he? So what would be the point?" She checks her mirrors and drives off. "Is that what you were thinking?"

It wasn't. But the truth—that Amelia was hoping there might still be a chance for the ice cream stand—feels too embarrassing to admit.

CHAPTER  TEN

AMELIA BARELY SLEEPS. BY MORNING, SHE'S TRYING TO focus on the one silver lining in this terrible misunderstanding— that Molly Meade has family who will take care of her estate now that she's gone. That she wasn't as alone as everyone in Sand Lake assumed. Amelia is still mortified by what Grady must think of her and the girls for doing what they did, stealing ice cream from his great-aunt. Though, thankfully, he was cool about it, she feels their actions have tarnished the entire stand girl legacy, made them appear childish, immature. In this way, handing over her key to Grady almost feels like appropriate penance.

She pours herself a bowl of Cap'n Crunch, and though she should be looking over the materials from the bank before tomorrow's interview, she instead turns on the small flat-screen on the kitchen counter. She loves watching game shows. Her secret talent is guessing the prices of supermarket items, and breakfast cereal is her specialty. It's always more expensive than contestants assume it'll be. She's leaning against the counter, watching as a man celebrates winning his-and-hers Jet Skis, when her phone buzzes with a text from her dad.

Did you see the big news in today's paper?

Dad starts every day by reading the *Sand Lake Ledger* even though it's barely a real newspaper and doesn't offer much beyond high school sports scores, garage sale listings, and the local police blotter. Amelia spots it on the kitchen table, exactly where he left the copy with Molly's obituary for her a couple of days ago.

She carries her cereal bowl over. The newspaper is unfolded to a huge color photograph taking up the front page. It's of Grady Meade, smiling broadly in front of the Meade Creamery stand, hands clasped behind his back, feet spread shoulder width apart. He's wearing the same deep blue suit he had on at the funeral yesterday, but his tie has been loosened, his pants rolled up just above his ankles, and he's changed out of his wing tips and into a pair of black Adidas soccer flats. His sunglasses are off. His eyes are as blue as the sky.

The headline reads YOUNG ENTREPRENEUR TO TAKE OVER LOCAL FAMILY BUSINESS.

The spoon slips from Amelia's hand and plunks into her bowl. Splatters of milk pucker the page.

Grady Meade, 19, is a currently a sophomore business major at Truman University. His original plan for the summer had been to backpack across Europe with his fraternity brothers on an unlimited rail pass. When he discovered that Molly Meade had left him the Meade Creamery ice cream stand in her will, he decided the chance to put his education to use in Sand Lake was too valuable an experience to pass up.

Amelia lowers herself into her seat, blinking in disbelief. Molly Meade left her ice cream stand, her *all-girl* ice cream stand, to . . . a boy?

"It's an incredible learning opportunity. Better than a traditional internship, where you're just watching from the sidelines. I'll put the skills I've been learning at Truman into practice."

While the last few days have been something of a whirlwind for this Chicago native, one thing that didn't surprise Grady Meade was to learn that the Meade Creamery ice cream stand is a fixture in the lakes region, and he is keen to continue the legacy his great-aunt saw fit to entrust him with.

"Both my father and his father before him have been extraordinarily successful businessmen. Seeing what my great-aunt Molly has built only reinforces that the Meades are born entrepreneurs."

Mr. Meade is currently thinking of ways to bring the legendary ice cream stand into the twenty-first century. "Obviously social media is huge right now, and so I'd like to create an online identity where consumers can connect with the stand." One modern problem he claims to have solved already? "For the first time,

Meade Creamery will be a gender-diverse workplace."

And of course, there's the question that will be front and center in the minds of his customers—will the ice cream taste as good? To this query, Mr. Meade simply grins. "I'm well aware that my great-aunt's recipes are the most valuable thing I've inherited."

Meade Creamery will reopen this Tuesday.

Amelia reads the last line twice more before it sinks in. Tuesday . . . is tomorrow.

She takes a photo of the article and texts it to Cate, who's well into her shift at JumpZone. Amelia's phone rings a minute later.

Cate says, her voice competing with the screams of children in the background, "Well, clearly Molly lost her mind there at the end."

"Do you think?" Amelia is less sure. Remembering the note Molly left for her in the office, the state of the stand, she appeared completely on top of things.

"Why else would she hand over her business to a boy?"

"Who knows. But this could mean we have our jobs back! Right?"

"Unless Grady plans to use the stand as a satellite fraternity house. Invite his bros down to Sand Lake for the summer." Cate chuckles at the thought of this. "They could change the motto to *Ice Cream So Sweet, You Won't Cheat on Your Girlfriend*."

It's been hard enough for Amelia to come to terms with Meade Creamery closing for good. Her heart squeezes at the thought of the stand running without her or the other girls. "The article says his friends went to Europe. It's got to be us."

siobhan vivian

"Yeah, you're probably right. I'm just surprised you sound so excited about it."

"Why?"

"Because sure, we're likely getting our jobs back, but in what capacity? Are you still going to be Head Girl?"

"I . . . don't know."

"Here's what you should do. Tell Grady Meade that the only way you're coming back to work is if you're still the Head Girl. Nothing less."

Amelia blinks. It's easy to imagine Cate doing that. But could she?

Wistfully, Cate says, "I wish I could go meet him with you, but another birthday party just came in."

"I wish you could too."

"Just remember that you have the power! If Grady wants to open for business tomorrow, then he needs us more than we need him."

Amelia nods to herself. "Yes. Totally true."

"So quit thinking of this as some job interview where you need to prove that you should be Head Girl. Amelia, you already got the job! Think of this as Grady's chance to impress *you*. Feel him out, see if you think he'll be a good boss. If not, then I say forget it. Because it'll suck way worse to be a part of the downfall of Meade Creamery than it will be to walk away."

Normally, Amelia would roll out of bed and put on a pair of cutoffs and a tank top to run over to the stand when she wasn't officially working, but she decides she should look more presentable. She showers and opts for a floral romper and her tan leather sandals.

Before heading over, Amelia takes the stand key from her jewelry box and slips it into her white saddlebag. For a second or two, her eyes linger on the flower pin.

She kisses it for luck.

CHAPTER  ELEVEN

AMELIA DOESN'T EXPECT TO FIND THE ICE CREAM stand ready for opening day, because how would Grady know all the things he'd need to do? But as she climbs off her bike, it makes her uncomfortable to see Meade Creamery so *not* ready. The lawn hasn't been cut. There are dandelions growing out of every crack in the blacktop. The picnic tables are missing, the trash cans too. Cate is right. Grady does need them more than they need Grady . . . at least in the short term. But the idea of walking away from Meade Creamery, watching Grady stumble from afar as he tries his best on his own, makes her feel even worse.

She pulls the weeds she passes and flings them toward the woods and then crouches down to look at the pile of things people have been leaving in honor of Molly Meade. Flowers—

some bought, some clipped from gardens. Handwritten notes and condolence cards. The impromptu shrine cloaks her in a velvety warmth. She picks up a crayon drawing, obviously made by a child, of a frowning ice cream cone crying two streams of blue tears.

"That might be the saddest thing I've ever seen."

Amelia looks up. Grady is standing behind her, an empty cardboard box in his hands. When their eyes meet, he seems the littlest bit confused.

"It's Amelia," she says, reintroducing herself as she rises to her feet. "Amelia Van Hagen."

"I remember your name, Amelia. It's just"—he momentarily trails off, his eyes trying to untangle something about her, as if she'd been wearing a disguise at the funeral—"my little cousin always wears her hair braided, the same way yours was yesterday. You . . . look older with it down."

Amelia touches her hair, threading some of it behind her ear. It's still damp from her shower.

He stares at her for a beat too long, and then he clears his throat awkwardly. "Let me grab the last of this stuff." He bends down and begins putting the items into the box, equally careful with each object: a bunch of flowers, a photograph. He picks up a teddy bear and pats away some dirt from its fur. "This is already my third box. People keep coming."

Amelia is touched that so many have shown up for the stand and for Molly in this way, especially after the somewhat anemic turnout at her memorial service. Molly was clearly beloved. Amelia bends to pick up a photograph. It's of a family of five lined up in front of the ice cream stand, big to little, with each one holding a corresponding serving of ice cream. The dad has a

siobhan vivian

waffle cone with three scoops, the tallest thing on the menu; the toddler has a kid's cup. "This place means a lot to a lot of people," Amelia says, passing it to Grady.

Grady takes a good, long look before placing it in the box. "I'm planning to go through everything when things calm down. Maybe even frame a few things."

Amelia smiles. As far as first impressions go, Grady is off to a very good start.

While Grady continues his task, Amelia discreetly observes him. He's wearing a button-up chambray shirt with the sleeves rolled to his elbows. His dark fitted jeans are folded in big cuffs to his calves, and he has white canvas sneakers on his feet—bright white, as if they just came out of the box—and no socks, though he's got a significant tan line around his ankles.

Grady is handsome for sure, but Amelia tells herself she's intrigued mostly because boys do not dress like him in Sand Lake. Boys here wear their jeans loose. They only put on button-ups for church or school dances. They prefer boots, but if they do wear sneakers, they're dirty from a pickup game of football or a hike or a ride on a quad. Though it's not as if Grady comes across as any less masculine. If anything, he seems almost more self-assured.

When the last of the mementos are boxed up, Amelia follows Grady around the stand to the door. The other two boxes are stacked there, along with a messenger bag, which Grady hoists over his shoulder. Meanwhile, Amelia takes the key out of her purse. "This might be the first time a boy has ever stepped inside Meade Creamery," she says, smiling over her shoulder as she opens the padlock.

"Actually, I've been in plenty of times before. I spent a whole summer in Sand Lake when I was a kid."

Amelia blanches as she follows him inside. "Wait. Seriously?"

He doesn't hear her. He's spinning in a slow circle, taking everything in. "Wow. This place hasn't changed. Like *at all*."

"You say it like it's a bad thing."

Grady steps over to the punch clock, checks the time against his cell phone, and pats the top of it, as if the machine were a small dog that had just performed an adorable little trick for him. "Not at all. Nostalgia is huge part of the Meade Creamery brand identity."

"Brand identity," she repeats. Amelia has never thought of Meade Creamery as a *brand*. But maybe it is?

Amelia looks around too, noticing the work that will need to be done to get the stand ready for customers. The cleaning she did on the day she found Molly is barely a leg up. The toppings sideboard is empty, the scooping cabinet is unplugged. No paper cups unwrapped and stacked by size, no napkin dispensers filled, no waffle batter mixed up.

Grady moves into the office, rounds the desk, and sits down. Even though Grady says that he's been here before, the sight of a boy inside the stand is very strange to Amelia. And to see one behind the Head Girl's desk is completely bizarre.

He takes several copies of the *Sand Lake Ledger* out of his messenger bag and fans them across the desk. "Did you happen to see the newspaper this morning?"

"I did. I was surprised that you're planning to open tomorrow. That's . . . very ambitious."

Though Amelia has tried to say it like it might not be a compliment, Grady grins. "The reporter wanted a quick human-interest story on the stuff people have been leaving at the stand, but once I introduced myself and explained how I'll be taking over the business, it turned into free front-page advertising." Grady takes out his laptop and connects it to his phone with a white cord. He taps the space bar and a bluish glow brightens his face. "Just give me a quick sec to answer an email from my advisor and we'll get to talking."

"Sure." Amelia lowers herself into a seat that has not been offered to her. She makes sure to sit tall, folds her hands in her lap.

As he types, he explains, "I'm trying to get Truman to pony up some internship or independent study credits for the work I'll be doing here this summer." He groans, like this has been a hassle. "Truman likes to push kids toward alumni *Fortune* 500 companies, but those places don't let you actually *do* anything. Just sit in on board meetings, shake a bunch of hands, eat steak lunches, and make contacts. But here I've got the chance to really get my hands dirty, see what I'm capable of, bring what I've learned in the classroom to the real world." He eyes her, looking to see her reaction.

Coolly, Amelia smooths her shorts. But inside, she is lit up with the sudden understanding, one she learned how to recognize from the older stand girls, that Grady is trying to impress her.

After hitting Send with a bit of a flourish, Grady closes his laptop and slides it off to the side. He takes a legal pad out of his messenger bag and searches in the smaller pockets for something to write with.

She stops herself from telling Grady to check the top desk drawer, because of the tube of OXY and the collapsible selfie stick that are mixed in with the pencils and pens. And she tightens, remembering other girly things hidden around the office, like the tampons of varying absorbencies in the bottom drawer of their filing cabinet, the heating pad for cramps and the PMS tea, and, dear God, the box of condoms—donated by Heather, who preached that girls shouldn't ever depend on a guy to bring protection—filling one whole cubby of the credenza. The space is more like a shared bathroom for a family of sisters than it is a traditional office, because they never imagined that a boy might be in here.

Grady says, "Aha," and, to Amelia's great relief, pulls a pen from his bag. Leaning back in his chair, he clicks the top of it rapid-fire. "So. Amelia. I'll get right to it. I'd like to officially offer you, and the rest of the girls, your jobs at Meade Creamery back."

Amelia tries to channel her best Cate and not look too eager, but she is very, very happy and relieved to hear Grady finally say this. "Thank you."

"Tell me . . . how many other scoopers are there, besides yourself?"

Amelia feels her smile slip, and it takes a few blinks before she can force it back on her face. She doesn't think Grady meant it condescendingly. And *scoopers* are essentially what the girls are. Still. There's something flip about the term.

"We typically have ten employees each summer," Amelia answers. She decides to say *employees* instead of *girls*, even though they've only ever been girls. The Meade Creamery girls.

Grady writes a number 10 down at the top of the page. "Great. And how much do scoopers get paid?"

There he goes again with *scooper*. Is he doing it on purpose, Amelia wonders? To make her feel insignificant?

She lifts her chin as high as Grady's. "Fifteen dollars an hour."

"You're kidding me. That's like twice minimum wage." Grady's mouth opens, then shuts, then opens again. "You're telling me that you girls make fifteen dollars an hour. For a high school summer job making sundaes."

Amelia feels herself begin to sweat. "I'm not sure if this falls under *brand identity*, but our customers expect a certain level of service when they come to Meade Creamery. The girls who work here are the nicest in Sand Lake. They are dependable, too. It's rare for anyone to call out sick. We've had several honor students over the years. In fact, my friend Cate is going to Truman this fall on scholarship. Mansi, who'll be a junior next year, was just named editor of the high school newspaper. Liz does student government and Britnee started varsity on the girls' basketball team, even as a freshman. Bernadette—"

"These are the same girls who broke in here with you, right? Who stole ice cream?" Grady doesn't sound put off so much as like he's trying to find a position from which to negotiate with her.

Amelia stiffens. She knows she needs to counter somehow, take a little power back. "Also, you should know that your great-aunt promoted me to Head Girl at the end of last summer. That's what we call the manager," she clarifies, hating that it sounds childish. "Head Girl gets seventeen dollars an hour. And I will personally vouch for every single girl on our staff."

Grady looks at her suspiciously. "What is *Head Girl* in charge of, exactly?"

Amelia takes a deep breath. "Well . . . Head Girl processes payroll, tallies shift receipts and prepares bank deposits, evaluates the newbie applications and does the interviewing, hiring, and training. Head Girl also is the stock manager, makes the weekly schedule—"

"Talk to me about the schedule. How many girls on a shift?" He fires off the question like this is an oral pop quiz.

"That depends. On weekdays, three girls can typically handle the first shift. Weeknights, things get busier, so normally we have four girls on. That way, there's one girl for each of the two windows, one can focus on making waffle cones, and one can float, stocking supplies, emptying the trash cans, cleaning. On weekends, we put four girls on both shifts. Unless it rains. If it rains, we can get away with two." She taps her chin with her finger. "There are other factors to consider, and those change every week, like when summer school is in session, the Little League schedule, holidays . . ." Amelia takes a breath, surprising even herself by how long she's gone on, considering she's never made a single schedule before. These are things she's picked up over the years, watching and learning from the older girls.

She knows a lot. And she can hardly hide her smile.

"Let's talk ice cream," he says, his voice low and conspiratorial.

"What do you want to know?" she replies, ready to spout off prices, rank flavors and toppings for him in terms of sales, the average number of scoops in a three-gallon drum.

Before Grady can ask a follow-up, there's a knock at the office door. Grady looks up and Amelia turns in her chair.

Grady's mom pokes her head inside. She's in a pale blue tunic with little mirrors and beads stitched to the collar, black capri leggings, and gold leather flip-flops, with an armful of gold bangles, and a huge black leather purse hanging from the crook of her elbow. "Sorry to interrupt your meeting, but we're leaving for the airport, sweetie. Come say goodbye."

Grady takes a deep breath once his mother leaves. To Amelia, he says quickly, "Fine. I'll pay the girls fifteen dollars an hour.

siobhan vivian

It's utterly ridiculous, but whatever." He stands up, checks his reflection in the mirror on the stand door. "But I'm the manager of Meade Creamery moving forward, Amelia. I hope that's not a deal breaker for you working here this summer, though I'll understand if it is. I'll give you a minute to think it over." He grabs two *Sand Lake Ledger*s from the top of the stack and hustles out the door.

Amelia whittles down her pinkie nail with her teeth.

It would be a deal breaker for Cate, absolutely. She would walk away from this place with zero regrets.

But can Amelia?

One thing she knows for sure—it's now or never. Springing into action, she leaps out of her chair and flies around the room. Her purse is small, but she manages to stuff all the condoms and tampons inside. The PMS tea will have to stay, though she takes the tea bags out and buries the box—along with the OXY—underneath some paper towels in the trash can.

"Did either of you see this at the hotel?" comes Grady's muffled voice through the stand walls. "I bought extra copies in case."

Amelia goes to the window and moves the curtain just enough to see outside.

Grady, his father, and his mother stand around a black Mercedes with tinted windows, the same one that was parked outside the church. The engine is running.

Grady's dad is handsome too. He's tall like his son, fit and clean-shaven. His hair is cut short, the white bits at his temples sparkle in the sun like the gold buttons on his navy blazer. His posture is stiff, his blue-and-white-check button-up crisp, and his black driving moccasins buttery soft.

Grady's mom reads the newspaper article out loud, pausing at the end of every paragraph to smile proudly. Meanwhile, Grady's dad pops the trunk, pulls out one of those huge European travel backpacks, and drops it on the grass. Then he takes out his phone and scrolls until Grady's mom finishes reading.

It makes Amelia's stomach hurt.

Grady kisses his mom on the cheek, walks over and stiffly shakes his dad's hand, then steps back as they each open their doors. His father takes one last long look up at the farmhouse before he climbs into the driver's seat. Grady waves until they pull onto the road and the car disappears.

Amelia hustles back to her seat and opens one of the newspapers, just beating Grady, who returns with his backpack on his shoulder. He sets it down near the door with a thud.

"Your parents aren't staying here with you?"

"No. They're going back to Chicago, and then on to New Zealand for some golfing trip for my dad. This is the one vacation he'll take all year."

Pointing at his backpack, she says, "And you gave up a Europe trip with your friends to stay here and run the stand." There's something admirable about this decision that Amelia glossed over when she first read the article this morning. This place must be important to him, to pass on something like that.

"Yeah. Basically."

But is it important enough to Amelia for her to give up Head Girl?

Grady crashes into the seat behind the desk and glances down at his legal pad, spinning the pen between his fingers like a mini-baton. He lets out a tired sigh. "I'll make you a deal,

Amelia. If you can promise we'll be ready to open by tomorrow, you can continue as Head Girl."

"Really?"

"I'm counting on you to convince the other girls to come back. We'll need all hands on deck. My newspaper interview is going to make for a huge opening day."

Amelia doesn't tell Grady that the lines on opening day always reach the road—even if it rains. And she doesn't say that it's going to be almost impossible to get everything done in one morning, when it usually takes the girls two full days to set up. Instead, she promises him from the bottom of her heart, "I will do my very best."

CHAPTER  TWELVE

JUMPZONE IS IN THE SAME SHOPPING PLAZA AS THE Walmart, along with a McDonald's, a Five Below, and the ten-screen movie theater. JumpZone used to be something else, but Amelia can't remember what. Maybe a Staples? She knows for sure, though, that it's much hotter out here than where Meade Creamery is. The blacktop amplifies the heat tenfold.

She locks her bike to the rack outside Walmart, then dances her way through customers perusing items set out on the sidewalk—huge backyard grills, boxes of foam pool noodles, bags of potting soil, and plastic lawn chairs stacked higher than her head. Other people's definition of *summer essentials*.

JumpZone's storefront has floor-to-ceiling windows that are painted with images of balloons, a pyramid of presents, and an enormous cartoony birthday cake. The cake has been drawn with arms and legs but no face, and Amelia finds this slightly unsettling. Huge colorful letters spell out JUMPZONE BIRTHDAY PARTIES! BOOK YOURS TODAY! in a font best described as *Friendly Graffiti.*

The lobby is practically a video arcade, with ten or so coin-operated games blinking and flashing. Farther back, Amelia sees basketball free-throw machines, a Whack-a-Mole station, an air hockey table, and a few of those scammy claw cranes filled with off-brand stuffed animals.

Kids run from machine to machine, banging on the buttons of games they haven't paid to play. Their parents sit on couches in the corner, tapping on their phones. There's a whiteboard next to them on an easel, and a boy in a JumpZone T-shirt and soccer shorts erases *Milly* and *11:00 AM* from *Happy Birthday Milly—11:00 AM* and replaces it with *Daniel* and *12:00 PM* before returning to the front desk, where Amelia now stands.

"Welcome to JumpZone. Which party are you with?"

Amelia shakes her head. "I'm looking for Cate."

"Faith?" The boy glances at his clipboard and checks the clock on the wall behind him. "Faith's party started at ten, so her group should be just about ready to head into the Pizza Room."

"Not Faith. *Cate.*" Amelia speaks more loudly this time.

The boy pulls something out of his ear, an orange foam plug. "Sorry. Did you say *Cate?*"

"Yes. Long blond hair. She just started working here."

"Cate," he says, drawing out the *a* sound, and Amelia knows it has clicked because of the bashful look suddenly on his face. "Cool, cool. Here you go." He pushes a paper and pen toward her. "Sign this, put your shoes in an open cubby, enter there, and hang a left." The boy then points toward two large doors underneath a sign that says GET YOUR JUMP ON! "She's working the Moat."

"Oh, I'm not going to jump. I just need, like, two seconds to talk to her."

"Everyone who enters JumpZone needs to sign a waiver," the boy says, his voice monotone. *He must say that a lot,* Amelia thinks sympathetically, the same way she's always telling tourists that the stand doesn't accept credit cards.

The boy pushes the earplug back inside his ear. Amelia squints to read the fine print, but she's too excited about giving Cate the good news. She scribbles a quick signature, slips off her sandals, and heads inside.

The noise in the next room is far worse than in the lobby. It sounds like the belly of an airplane. In a space that's maybe half the size of a high school gym, there are several massive inflatables, each with an industrial fan whirling full speed. Each one has a JumpZone employee assigned to it. Amelia passes a classic mesh-sided bounce house, a huge slide, and an obstacle course where kids try to knock each other down by swinging inflatable punching bags. And then, taking up an entire wall is the biggest inflatable of all. Amelia assumes it must be the Moat.

The Moat is an enormous ball pit with a platform on either side. Cate is standing on the right and a very tall guy with freshly buzzed peach fuzz is on the left. Amelia's dad wears his hair the same way, as he has his entire life. It's the kind of style that doesn't ever seem to go out of fashion for the men of Sand Lake.

The guy is helping kids, one by one, climb up onto his platform. At Cate's direction, each kid takes a running jump and dives elaborately into the pit. On the other side, Cate holds up

siobhan vivian

what look like homemade score cards to rate the jumps from 1 to 10.

Every girl scores a 10. The harder a boy tries to impress Cate, the lower the score she gives him.

And the kids *love* it.

This is Cate. Cate has the magical ability to make fun wherever she goes, even at a crappy job like JumpZone. She brings that energy. She always has. And with all the work that will need to get done tomorrow before opening, Amelia knows that Cate's presence at the stand will be essential.

"I lost my shoe!" one of the girls complains, climbing out.

Nodding, Cate cups her hands and says, "Jordan!"

"Ugh, again?"

"Yup. She thinks it's over here somewhere," Cate tells him, pointing to her half of the ball pit. But Jordan is the one to jump in, and even if he's a little put out, he does a swan dive, to make Cate laugh, which she does, and she also claps when he resurfaces, a pink high-top in hand.

Another door opens off to the side and a JumpZone employee, this one a girl, blows a whistle. "Okay, everyone here for Faith's birthday, come on into the Pizza Room!"

The kids and their parents empty out, but Amelia hangs back. Jordan tries to pull Cate into the ball pit with him, but she squeals and throws colorful plastic balls at his head. The girl who announced that it's pizza time flings a pizza crust at them before disappearing behind the closing door. Except for the fans, it becomes quiet.

Amelia hears Cate and Jordan talking as she gets closer.

Jordan says, laughing, "You robbed that one kid. A two for a double backflip?"

"La di da," Cate says, and then fakes a yawn. "That was nothing compared to the girl who did that flying karate kick."

"She was amazing," Jordan concedes. "We should have given her a prize."

"Wait, I want a prize!" Cate whines. "I spent my entire break plus five bucks in quarters trying to win that warped-looking Care Bear knock-off in the claw machine."

"What would you say if I told you I have the key to the claw machine? I can open it up and get you that ugly-ass bear right now."

"Seriously?" Cate shrieks. She's about to climb down the ladder when she spots Amelia.

"Hi!" Amelia says awkwardly. She didn't want to seem like she was eavesdropping, but also didn't want to interrupt their conversation.

"Hi!" Cate says back, hopping down and giving her a big hug. "Jordan, this is my best friend, Amelia. I told you about her."

"Hi," he says, climbing down after them. He looks embarrassed, likely because he was caught flirting.

Cate playfully asks Jordan, "I thought you were going to get me my bear?"

He talks while he walks backward. "Okay, okay, but if I get fired—"

"Don't worry. I'm Employee of the Month, remember? I'll put in a good word for you with Lou."

"He's cute," Amelia says, stepping closer to Cate.

"Eh. I mean, he's nice. But he's a little *Donnersville*," Cate says, referring to two towns over, a place with more farms, where boys get their permits to drive tractors. She scratches an itch on the back of her arm. "That said, it's kind of fun working with boys for a change. Flirting makes the time pass way faster." Her eyes suddenly widen. "God, I'm so sorry, Amelia! I should be asking you how it went with Grady!"

"Wait, you're already Employee of the Month? Have you even worked here a full week?" As ridiculous as this seems, Amelia finds it unsurprising.

Cate wrinkles her nose. "Long story. But you go! Tell me everything!"

"Okay." Amelia has trouble containing her excitement. "Cate ... it went amazing! I did exactly what you said. I was confident, I was assertive. I got everything I asked for. And the crazy thing is, I walked out of there feeling like I know way more about being Head Girl than I ever thought I did. For the first time, I believe I can do this. And I have you to thank for it."

Cate smiles. "So, what's Grady like? Because I got to be honest. I reread that article during my break and I'm worried he's going to ride our asses all summer."

"I didn't get that impression, exactly. He's definitely taking it seriously."

Cate frowns. "That's what I mean. I'm kind of loving how chill it is here. Truman is going to be stressful enough. It's sort of nice to not work super hard." She lets out a long exhale. "I just want to have fun this summer."

Amelia swallows. What would she do if Cate didn't come back? Could she manage the stand, manage Grady, on her own?

"It'll still be fun!" Amelia says. "It'll be me and you! Remember, I make the schedule, so we'll always get to work together!"

"I know, I know," Cate says, not exactly sold.

"Oh! And speaking of Truman! Cate, you should have seen his eyes light up when I told Grady you were going on scholarship." At this, Cate flushes, and even though her conversation with Grady didn't exactly happen like this, it strikes Amelia that Grady and Cate will probably get along famously. Both are driven and smart. In a brain fast-forward, she imagines them meeting, falling in love, getting engaged after they both graduate, serving Home Sweet Home at their wedding, their very cute baby in a little Truman onesie.

Cate examines her manicure, indifferent. "I guess it would be cool to be friends with someone before I even get to campus."

"Exactly." And though Amelia is glad she can see things shifting in her favor, it also dawns on her that Cate doesn't have any hesitation at all about leaving Sand Lake for Truman. Not like she does.

Jordan returns with the teddy bear. It is absolutely terrifying, with an off-kilter eye and cheap fur that makes it seem like it has a kind of stuffed-animal mange. Jordan hands it to Cate, who doubles over laughing. Then Jordan says, "I think you dropped something, Amelia." He bends down and picks up a red wrapper.

Cate gasps. "Is that a condom?"

Startled, Amelia looks down and sees that her purse has unzipped. As she takes it off her shoulder, a bunch more tampons and condoms spring out and onto the floor like a weird drugstore piñata.

Of course, Cate makes Amelia tell them both the story, and soon the three of them are in hysterics.

"I love that you thought to do that," Cate says. "Protect our honor." She turns to Jordan and says, "This is why I love her." And then she breaks the news to him that she is quitting Jump-Zone and going back to Meade Creamery.

siobhan vivian

Jordan looks sad, legitimately bummed to be losing Cate. Amelia, of course, doesn't blame him. Cate tells him that the next time he comes to Meade Creamery, she'll hook him up. And, as it is with most disappointments, the promise of ice cream makes things a little bit better.

CHAPTER  THIRTEEN

ON THE RIDE HOME FROM JUMPZONE, AMELIA TYPES A quick text to the rest of the stand girls to share the good news and ask that they report to work tomorrow at six a.m. She reads it aloud for Cate before sending.

Cate has feedback.

"I think it should sound more fun. Like an invite to a party."

"So . . . more exclamation points?"

"Think ice cream humor. Maybe something about having a *sweet scoop on some summer jobs.*"

"Ooh. That's cute. You're good."

"Or maybe *I scream, you scream, we all scream . . . because I got us our jobs back?*" Cate shakes her head. "Okay, no, I like the *sweet scoop* thing better. But add a winky face, otherwise the girls might not get that it's a joke. And follow up with the six a.m. thing separately to each girl after they've already said yes. Because if you'd told me that before, I'd still be working at JumpZone." Cate preemptively ducks, knowing Amelia is going to swat her.

By the time they get to Amelia's house, Amelia has received yeses from five girls. The sixth response is a no that comes in later, after dinner, when Amelia and Cate are upstairs in Amelia's room.

"Apparently Britnee is loving her new job at Sephora." Amelia sets her phone down, stunned. "That's a bummer."

"Can I be honest?" Cate bites her bottom lip. "I never loved Britnee."

"Really? Why?"

"Last year, she got super-weird about the newbie chores, as if cleaning the bathroom was some personal slight against her."

"How did I not hear about that?"

"No idea. But it pissed *a lot* of girls off, especially Heather. During the last week of summer, I swear, Heather was one eye roll away from straight-up firing her." Cate shrugs. "I say good riddance. We'll get way more hustle out of hiring a third newbie."

Amelia can't imagine anyone getting fired from Meade Creamery. She's also reminded that she didn't mention the need to hire newbies to Grady yesterday. Obviously tomorrow it will be way too crazy to try and train any new girls. But now it can be more than an abstract conversation, because she knows for sure that they're down three girls, instead of the two Amelia thought she'd have to replace. Three girls adds up to an entire shift.

Amelia brought up a plate of snacks with her earlier—some Cracker Barrel cheddar cheese and Ritz crackers—but Cate hasn't touched anything, and the ice is melting in her glass of

Coke. "What are you doing over there all secretive?" Amelia sits on her knees and tries to peek at Cate's phone screen.

"Oh, just a little recon on one Grady Patrick Meade."

Amelia freezes, her glass of Coke just underneath her nose, the fizz tickling her upper lip. "And?"

"I haven't found much yet. His accounts are set to private, friends only." Another tap or two and Cate says, "Ooh. Wait up. This could be something." And then Cate and holds her phone high in victory. "Yes! Jackpot!"

Amelia sets her Coke down and, trying not to look too eager, crawls over, asking, "Anything interesting?"

"I did a little research on Truman's fraternity chapters. Alpha Kappa Psi is the business one and Grady's in some of the party pictures." Cate winces at the screen, laughing. "Okay, he's still hot, but this is the dorkiest thing I've ever seen."

Cate flips her phone around to show Amelia a photo of Grady Meade standing with five other guys in a line, arms slung around each other's shoulders. Grady is the tallest and the tannest one. The thinnest, too. He doesn't seem skinny in real life, but the other guys are beefy, like rugby players or something. Anyway, they're wearing matching pastel button-up shirts, madras plaid bow ties, short khaki shorts, and docksiders.

Amelia curls up to Cate and takes a closer look. To Amelia, Grady seems so much more relaxed here than he was at the stand with her.

"Isn't it funny, to think of me going to parties like this?" Cate says. "Full of these rich, fancy people?"

Amelia studies the picture. The boys are in someone's backyard, a fancy one, with topiaries and a pergola and a huge in-ground pool. Someone who looks like a waiter stands in the background, balancing a tray on one hand. "Not at all. I feel like this is your destiny." Cate has always had her sights set on something bigger than Sand Lake. She was the one who advocated tirelessly for their senior class trip to go to New York City. In those three days, Amelia's pretty sure Cate never slept. Even at night, when the teachers would put tape over their hotel room doors, Cate would stay awake, watching the city streets from their hotel window.

Cate smiles appreciatively. "I'm actually required to take a bunch of business classes for my science degree. The thinking is that one of us might invent some crazy new medicine or diagnostic tool that could, with the right investors, make us millionaires, or whatever. I should get Grady's take on which professors are good and which ones suck."

Amelia sees this as another thing Grady and Cate have in common. They both are able to take a totally intimidating situation and see opportunity for themselves.

Cate swipes to another photo, one of Grady at the same party. He's now stripped down to just his swim trunks, in the beautiful pool, riding a huge inflatable swan. He's wearing his classic Ray-Ban Wayfarer sunglasses and beaming a bright and toothy smile to the camera. A girl in a metallic bikini clings to him, her head resting against his back, eyes closed.

"So that's his girlfriend," Amelia deduces. The girl is extremely pretty. Tall like a model, with perfectly polished red nails and a cloud of thick black curly hair. Amelia feels a heat prickling inside her rib cage.

"She very well could be, I guess," and Cate wags her finger at Amelia. "She's also the president of the Truman Future Business Leaders Club. I found these pictures through her page."

"Oh," Amelia says, mortified.

"It's okay. Biases are strong as hell, right? But girlfriend or not, I'm sure Grady will try to get with one of our girls this summer."

"Do you think? I mean . . . he's our boss." Anyway, that's the line in the sand Amelia's tried to remind herself of.

Cate shakes her head, like Amelia is naive. "You can't let a fox into the henhouse and not expect some carnage, Amelia. That's why we'll need to make it crystal clear to the younger girls that Grady's completely and totally off-limits."

"Yes. Completely and totally off-limits," Amelia echoes, and hearing herself say it aloud, like a pledge, comforts her. This new rule isn't emotional, it isn't personal. It's simply a sound and solid reason to smother any burgeoning interest she may have for Grady, beyond, of course, his ability to successfully run Meade Creamery.

They watch a movie and paint each other's nails. White, with little flecks of color, to look like sprinkles. Cate showers first, Amelia second, so they won't have to do it in the morning. Cate knows what drawer Amelia's pj's are in and she helps herself to a matching set of a floral cami and boxers, which Amelia realizes, come to think of it, might belong to Cate. Cate burrows into her nest of blankets on Amelia's floor while Amelia props herself up with a pillow and begins a to-do list in a notebook.

"There's no way I'm going to sleep this early," Cate says. "I don't think I've fallen asleep before ten since I was in diapers."

"It's important we get our rest!"

"Then put your notebook down!"

"I'm trying to figure out how we're going to get everything done tomorrow. We'll only have five hours."

"We won't get everything done," Cate says, matter-of-fact. "And so what? It's not like Grady will know the difference. Plus, we can always catch up after opening day."

"That's true."

"And you know, if you think about it, some of the chores we had to do to prep the stand were kind of bogus. Like rake the dirt? Seriously? I mean, don't get me wrong, I would totally rake dirt, no complaints, if Molly were still alive. But it's not like Grady will know one way or the other." Cate braids her hair and smiles slyly. "We should really think about how to use that to our advantage."

Amelia looks at her chore list and tries to think about what else could or should be changed. She's sure there's something, though nothing jumps out at her. She puts down her notebook, clicks off the light, and closes her eyes.

Despite her protests, Cate's out quickly, and if they didn't have to be up super early, Amelia might poke her awake and make a joke about it. Amelia wants to fall asleep herself but has the sense she won't anytime soon. It probably wasn't smart to think about the stand before bed. It's got her all anxious.

She picks up her phone. After turning the brightness down on the screen, she does a little digging on Grady Meade herself. Purely from a business standpoint, of course.

She finds an article in the Truman alumni news featuring Grady and his dad. There's a picture accompanying it, and it's the complete antithesis of the ones Cate found on the fraternity account. This shot is sober, corporate, constructed. Grady is wearing a white collared shirt and a Truman blue tie knotted tightly around his neck. He's standing next to his father, who's behind a huge mahogany desk inside a rich-looking library, wearing the same tie but a different shirt. Neither smiles.

Recalling the awkward exchange between them outside the stand, Amelia suspects *this* is the reason why Grady's social media is on lockdown.

The article states that Grady's father is a big-time business-man and one of Truman's most famous and successful alumni. His career took off when he was barely twenty and he began constructing his own billboards out of scrap lumber and placing them on his parents' property. He'd sell advertising to local businesses, use the money to lease more land on neighbors' property, and sell more ads. When asked whether retirement might be in his future, his answer is "I don't think that's going to be possible. Everywhere I look, I see the potential to make money. That's the lens I'm always wearing."

In a closing sentence, there is a mention of Quinn Greenfield-Meade. Amelia cuts and pastes the name into a new search. Before she can stop herself, she's scrolling through Grady's mom's photo stream, looking at different birthdays (never a homemade cake, always celebrated at a restaurant) and holidays (St. Patrick's Day seems big for them, which isn't surprising) and vacations (several ski trips, one Hawaiian resort, what looks like an Alaskan fishing cruise, the Harry Potter theme park) all going back to when Grady was seven years old.

Quinn's pictures are mostly of Grady and herself—many shots don't include his dad, even on Grady's high school graduation day, which took place around this time last summer. There's a selfie of Quinn tucked underneath Grady's arm in his cap and gown. She's done up beautifully, in a white sheath and matching white cardigan with pearl buttons, her hair perfectly blown out in soft, bouncy curls. Grady looks all Meade DNA. Amelia doesn't see much of Quinn in him.

She squints and brings the phone screen closer.

Maybe the brows. They both have great brows.

siobhan vivian

CHAPTER  FOURTEEN

IF AMELIA COULD WARN CATE'S FUTURE COLLEGE ROOM-mate about anything, it would be that she's the absolute worst at mornings. Once Amelia's awake, she's ready to go at full power. But the earlier Cate is dragged out of bed, the more time she needs to ease into things. Amelia has learned over the years that waking Cate up is a process. You have to give her ample time and space to look at her phone, to slowly join the living. Rushing only makes her crabbier and slower.

Today, that means setting a series of alarms, every ten minutes, beginning at five in the morning.

Eventually, Cate arches her back in a deep stretch. "Grady better be grateful. The only time I wake up this early is for Black Friday sales."

"I still can't believe you got your laptop for a hundred bucks."

"Just call me Door Buster," Cate says with a yawn.

Amelia sits on the edge of her bed, already dressed, Cate's Meade Creamery polo and shorts on her lap. She tosses them to Cate as Cate strips out of her jammies.

"Don't forget your Head Girl pin," Cate says. "I can't believe I have to keep reminding you."

They share the sink, brushing their teeth, washing their faces. Amelia pees upstairs while Cate uses their downstairs bathroom. And then Amelia's pushing Cate out the front door. Once outside, Cate hides her eyes from the sun and digs in her bag for those gas station sunglasses.

"You'd better not sign up for any classes before noon," Amelia warns. "You'll lose your scholarship."

"Maybe we should register for classes around the same times. Then you can be my wake-up call! I mean, we're already going to be talking to each other every day."

It's honestly not a bad idea, except they won't be in the same time zone.

Cate pats herself down for the key to her truck. "How about we grab breakfast somewhere? Starbucks drive-thru?"

"Nope," Amelia says, climbing into Cate's truck and pulling the door shut.

"We have fifteen minutes!" Cate whines.

"We have twelve minutes." Amelia doesn't mind if they aren't the first to show up, but she doesn't want to be the last.

"I'll never make it through the day. You know I need sustenance."

"I saw you grab a granola bar out of our pantry!"

Cate pouts. "That was a breakfast appetizer."

Amelia snaps her fingers. "Ugh! I forgot to bake a new batch

siobhan vivian

of opening day blueberry muffins." Maybe if she hadn't been so focused on stalking Grady, she would have remembered.

"After you get everyone started on chores, send someone out for bagels and cream cheese."

Though Amelia hasn't eaten anything, she doesn't feel the emptiness in her stomach. It's her nerves, she's sure. Once things calm down, she'll be starving too. "Good idea."

Despite its being so early, there's a lot of hugging and bouncing and happiness as the girls arrive at the stand. Though after a few minutes and a head count of seven, Amelia wonders when Grady might make an appearance. He will surely want to make a speech to the girls before they get started. He seems like that kind of guy. Also, Amelia thinks, it will be nice to have his help carrying out the picnic tables, which are solid wood and unbelievably heavy. Not that the girls can't handle it themselves, they do every year, but it'll be faster with Grady, and today, every minute counts.

Amelia turns around and realizes she's standing off by herself. Or, rather, the rest of the girls have drifted a few feet away from her, continuing to chat and talk and laugh. She recognizes this as the deference always shown to the Head Girl, but it feels weird, it being paid to her. Uncomfortable.

She walks over and finds Cate midconversation with the youngest girls.

"He's completely and totally off-limits, okay? Don't go out of your way to be nice to him, because he might interpret it as flirting. And if Grady flirts with any of you, or makes you feel uncomfortable in any way, I want you to come and tell Amelia or me ASAP." Amelia wants to assure them that it will be fine, that Grady seems like a good guy, but the girls look grateful for the protection of the oldest girls looking out for them.

And, really, the only thing that matters right now is that they get the stand ready by eleven o'clock.

But 6:15 comes, then 6:20, and there's still no Grady. What little time they have is slipping away. Amelia wanders past the stand and a bit up the driveway, as if staring at the farmhouse might make Grady appear.

"Can't you text him?" Cate asks, following her.

"I don't have his number."

"Well . . . I wouldn't wait much longer."

They walk back over to where the girls are standing around waiting for direction. Borrowing a hair thing, scratching a bug bite, touching up some lip gloss, yawning.

Amelia opens her notebook and tries to find the least-annoying chores to divvy up first. Except they're all annoying, in their own ways. Amelia has never gotten mad, or even remotely upset, at being asked to do something. Even the more stupid, hazing-ish stuff that newbies are sometimes made to do, like separating the sprinkles by color. But she suddenly feels weird about dictating who should be doing what, especially remembering what Cate told her about Britnee. And the fact that there are no newbies, at least not yet, means no one is here to pick up the slack on the least-liked chores, like cleaning the stand bathroom.

"Is it possible to be the boss without being bossy?" she asks Cate in a low voice.

"What's wrong with being bossy? You're the boss!" Cate laughs. "Here. Watch and learn." Cate claps her hands for their attention. "Girls! Listen up! Amelia's going to start delegating chores. Meanwhile I'm off to get us bagels, and anyone who isn't busting serious ass when I get back is going to be forced to eat the Pumpernickel Bagel of Shame." Cate winks at Amelia, as if to say *See? Easy.*

Amelia sticks out her tongue. Joking aside, though, she wishes she had Cate's confidence, and she's in awe at the ease with which Cate can straddle the line between being fun and calling the shots. Basically all the stuff that Amelia agonizes over just comes naturally to Cate.

The girls turn to Amelia. And the best she can do? Apologize after she calls out each task listed in her notebook.

The girls shrug, unbothered. They stand shoulder to shoulder, ready to work. Because they love this place as much as she does. Thank goodness.

Soon the stand is busy with activity. Mansi pushes the lawn mower across the grass. Liz wields the weed-whacker around the perimeter of the stand with her earbuds in. Sophie and Bernadette work together to carry out the picnic tables, moving each one just a few inches at a time, because they're so heavy. Jen lines each of the trash cans with a black bag before topping it with a bright pink plastic shutter lid to help minimize the inevitable bee situation. And no one, thankfully, comes close to being awarded the Pumpernickel Bagel of Shame.

Every task that isn't essential to being ready to sell ice cream by eleven a.m. will be left for another day. There's no time for a fresh coat of paint on the stand. The bee traps won't get set until Amelia can track down a recipe for the syrup they find so irresistible. Taking down and dusting the empty milk bottles, too. Even omitting those chores, there's still an enormous amount of work to do, and only a couple more hours to get it done.

Just after nine o'clock, Amelia hears someone calling her name. She's on her hands and knees, pulling weeds from the cracks in the pavement with Cate. They both sit up and watch Grady sprint down from the farmhouse as fast as he can run in his flip-flops. His hair is sticking up in the back, dented from his pillow. He has on a fraternity T-shirt with a hole in the shoulder and a pair of Truman University sweatpants.

"Sleeping Beauty has awakened," Cate whispers.

Grady crouches on the ground near Amelia and says in a low, urgent voice, "I can't believe it's after nine. Why didn't you knock on the door?"

"She did," Cate answers. "Twice, actually."

This is not true. Amelia shoots Cate a look. Grady doesn't notice. He's too agitated.

Amelia calls out, "Everyone, this is Grady Meade!"

Grady gives them a quick wave and then shields his eyes from the sun as he surveys the scene.

Cate stands up and extends her hand. "Hey, Grady. I'm Cate."

"She's the one going to Truman on scholarship," Amelia says quickly. "Cate's been here as long as I have and—"

"Hey, is that where the picnic tables usually go? Wouldn't they'd be better off to the side where there's some shade?"

Amelia squints to see where he's pointing. "That puts them under the trees and into a potentially volatile bird poop situation."

He spins 180 degrees. "What about the plywood? When does that come down? People driving by will think we're closed for good."

"That's typically the last thing we do, right before we open," Amelia says. "Otherwise people will start to line up now." She notices Cate's deepening frown.

Grady scratches his chin, contemplating the garbage cans. "We only have two of those? Is that enough?"

"We don't get a ton of trash," Amelia explains. "And we're good about emptying the cans several times during a shift." She gestures to Cate. "Anyway, we're all so proud of Cate. Truman is lucky to have her."

Finally, Grady seems to get it, and focuses his attention on Cate, who is standing off to the side, arms folded. "Hey, sorry, Cate. It's good to meet you. I'm a bit distracted this morning."

"No problem."

"So . . . what are you studying?" he asks earnestly.

"Chemistry," Cate says, still a little icy, but warming. "I'm considering a minor in math, though I'm not sure. I don't want to be a complete academic hermit."

"Well, you must be smart if you scored a scholarship. They don't hand those out to just anyone."

Cate shrugs, like this is no big deal. "It's not a full ride."

"It's basically a full ride," Amelia chimes in.

"Cool, cool," Grady says, distracted by the picnic tables again. He makes a *hmmm* noise. "I really think we should try shifting them a little away from the stand, so people can see it from the road."

Cate clears her throat, and when she has Amelia's attention, she discreetly flicks her hand as if shooing a fly away. Except she's shooing Grady.

Amelia nods and tries leading Grady toward the stand with a hand gently on his back. "You know what, Grady? I totally hear your point about the picnic tables, but I need Bernadette and Sophie to get working inside the stand. We've got a lot to set up in there still."

Grady checks his watch and groans. "I can't believe this happened. I set two alarms last night, but I get like zero signal out here and it sucked my battery dry. The girls probably think I'm some kind of slack-ass. What can I do to help?"

Amelia might be more annoyed if it weren't clear that Grady is annoyed with himself. And, honestly, it's not that big a deal. The way he's acting right now, so panicky and brimming with questions, it's better that he's been out of their hair. "We've got this under control."

He shakes his head. "Come on. Please. I need to help." Right then, the lawn mower sputters to a stop in a patch of high grass. Mansi tries pulling the cord a few times to restart it, but it's dead.

Grady cups his hands around his mouth and says, "I'll take a look!" Before he darts off, he spots the bag of bagels. "Thank God. I'm starving." He reaches inside. "Anyone got dibs on this last one?"

"Have at it," Cate says, grinning mischievously.

He puts the pumpernickel bagel between his teeth, and the girls have to do everything they can to hold in their laughter as he jogs over toward the lawn mower.

Amelia whispers to Cate, "He's really stressed."

Cate rolls her eyes. "I love how he comes down here and questions everything we're doing. As if he knows better than us." Thankfully, she doesn't seem *that* annoyed. If anything, she's charged up. "He really is cute," she concedes begrudgingly. "I bet he normally gets away with this crap all the time. But he's about to have a rude awakening because that's not going to happen here."

An hour later, Cate's inside the stand with several open cardboard boxes at her feet. She's filling up the sideboard with

siobhan vivian

toppings—sprinkles, crushed-up Oreo cookies, and chopped candy bars. She's got the radio on, singing and shimmying as Amelia makes trips in the purple ski jacket between the storage freezer and the scooping cabinet, stocking it with two drums of every flavor. Amelia's so tired, they feel twice as heavy as they normally do. Then, after the last trip, she sheds the jacket, closes her eyes, and stands for a second in the cold, hoping it will jolt her awake.

Next, Amelia fills a bucket with warm water at the slop sink and carries it outside and around to the bathroom. On her way, she sees Grady sitting underneath a tree, the lawn mower in pieces on the ground, his brow furrowed in concentration, a smear of grease across his cheek.

Through the bathroom walls, Amelia can hear Cate singing along to the oldies station—"My Boyfriend's Back," "Chapel of Love," "Mr. Sandman." Amelia has her hands inside a pair of yellow rubber gloves, her bare knees on a folded piece of paper towel. Whoever cleaned the bathroom last August (probably Britnee, now knowing what Cate said about her) didn't do a very thorough job. There's a ring of grime inside the porcelain toilet bowl, and Amelia scrubs it with a piece of steel wool with all the elbow grease she can muster.

The bathroom is the least-favorite chore of Meade Creamery girls. It would be one thing if it were just *for* the girls, but it's used by customers as well, and it boggles Amelia's mind how careless they can be about making sure paper towels find their way into the trash can. At the very least, to be a human on earth, people should wipe up their own pee from the toilet seat.

Amelia sits back on her heels and wipes her brow. The bathroom really should be cleaned, at least superficially, once a day.

That rarely happens. It's a chore specifically for the newbies, so a newbie has to be on shift, and even then, they have to be *explicitly* told to do it. And that, Amelia knows, is why it was the last job left up for grabs. Today, she's fine to clean it herself. It's her way to thank everyone for busting their butts.

After the toilet shines, she snaps off her gloves and checks her phone. Less than one hour until they open. She steps outside, dumps out the water in the dirt, and heads back toward the stand.

Grady notices her and bounds over. "Lawn mower is fixed and I cut the rest of the grass. I'm going to run up and grab a quick shower, if that's okay with you."

"Sure."

"You look tired, Amelia," he says.

"Thanks?"

"Wait, no. What I meant is that I know you've been working hard. I'm sorry if I was freaking out before," he says quietly. "I didn't mean to get in anyone's way. I just want today to go well."

"That makes two of us," she says.

At the very least, there's that.

CHAPTER FIFTEEN

A FEW MINUTES BEFORE ELEVEN, AMELIA FEELS A RUSH of anticipation, the same way she has on every opening day. Peeking around the door, she sees that the line for ice cream is out to the road. There are couples, packs of kids straddling their bikes with their allowance tucked into their socks, teens looking down at their phones, families on vacation with fresh sunburns, a group of women in hospital scrubs, even four old men listening to a baseball game on a small handheld radio.

Grady is in the office, filling the two register tills with cash. He's showered and dressed up in a pale-gray cotton blazer over a white oxford shirt and tan chinos that are snug to his legs.

Cate hooks her chin on Amelia's shoulder and whispers, "It looks like he's dressed for a yacht christening."

Amelia covers her mouth to keep the laugh in.

Though he doesn't look up, Amelia senses that Grady knows they've been talking about him. His cheeks flush pink.

Sheepishly, Amelia retrieves a cordless drill from the supply closet and presents it to Grady. "Would you like to do the honors and take the plywood down?"

"Yeah, okay. Thanks."

It's tradition that the most senior girls work the windows on the first shift of opening day, with two girls standing by behind them to assist in making the orders. Amelia and Cate take their positions. And as the clock ticks over to eleven, they high-five, hip-check, slide their windows open, and take their first orders of the season.

No matter how fast Amelia and Cate scoop, the line doesn't seem to get any shorter. It's partly because everyone who comes to the windows wants to talk, saying things like "I was so worried the stand would close forever!" or "It wouldn't be summer without Meade Creamery!"

And for the first time, Amelia doesn't feel sad when she thinks of Molly's death. In fact, she hopes Molly is up in heaven, somewhere in that perfect blue summer sky, sitting with Wayne Lumsden on a fluffy white cloud, looking down on her stand, able to see all the happy faces and hear the compliments.

Meanwhile Grady walks the line, snapping pictures and shaking hands. Even the mayor shows up, with her husband and new baby, and introduces herself to Grady. He brings them straight to the window and benevolently instructs Amelia and Cate to, for the rest of the summer, put whatever the mayor orders on his personal tab. Mayor Heller looks embarrassed, and politely declines Grady's offer for freebies and the chance to cut the line.

"That was awkward," Amelia says quietly to Cate.

"His *personal tab*?" Cate snarks back. "What a cheeseball." And then she pokes Amelia in the side, making Amelia bend and squeal; however, she manages to keep the top scoop of strawberry on her sugar cone from rolling off.

She and Cate do this a lot, see if they can get each other to mess up an order. They'll banter with each other's customers, joking with them that they picked the wrong window, teasing that they'd have put way more sprinkles on a cone than the other would have, two cherries instead of one on the top of a sundae. Both of their tip jars fill up fast, more dollars than change by a long shot. The younger girls see it and are in awe. Happy awe, because tips get split equally at the end of every shift.

Amelia feels her most confident here next to Cate—the best, shiniest version of herself. Today the summer feels long. She won't let herself think of the opposite of this day, in August, when they'll be close to saying goodbye.

Instead, she serves their friends, former teachers, neighbors and cousins and old babysitters. Cars zip by on the road and people honk and wave. Little kids spin around the picnic tables on a sugar high. Parents teach their sons and daughters the proper way to lick a cone, from the bottom up.

"I don't ever remember it being this busy," Cate says from her window. "This is like Fourth of July plus Labor Day weekend times a heat wave." She calls out for one of the girls to bring another drum of Home Sweet Home from the walk-in freezer.

She's right. Thankfully, it's not disgustingly hot, the way it'll be come July. The zip of cold air that hits her every time she opens up the scooping cabinet keeps her cool.

The next man at Amelia's window has on a purple paisley

shirt and a porkpie hat. He's an older gentleman, but the people he's with are younger and fashionable and snapping pictures of the place.

"I like your hat," Amelia tells him.

"Thank you!" He orders two scoops of Home Sweet Home in a waffle cone.

His friend pops up next to him and asks Amelia, conspiratorially, "So what's the deal with Home Sweet Home? Can you *really* not tell us what's in it?"

"I don't know myself."

"What if I'm allergic?"

"We tell people that if they're concerned about any potential allergens, they should order something else."

"He's not allergic to anything!" one of the girls says, swatting him with her woven clutch.

"He's just nosy," another says, and the whole group laughs.

The man in the hat tells them, "Order a waffle cone. They're homemade and they put little mini-marshmallows in the bottoms to keep the ice cream from dripping out!"

Amelia punches his order into the register. "That'll be five dollars, please."

The man turns to his friends. "Can you believe how cheap this is?"

This always seems to happen with city people. Amelia isn't sure why. Do normal things like ice cream really cost so much more there? She hands the man his order and, after dropping a five into the tip jar—for which Amelia gives him a heartfelt thank-you—he takes a lick of his cone.

"Oh my God, this takes me back." He closes his eyes, and Amelia can see him work the ice cream around in his mouth before he swallows. To Amelia he explains, "I grew up not too far from here. Chesterfield."

Amelia smiles. These are her favorite customers. The locals who've long since moved away, who take one lick and are transported back to a particular summer, a moment, a feeling. She's sure that's why the ice cream stand becomes the center of the universe during summers. People wanting to find, even in the smallest taste, something they've lost.

Maybe fifteen minutes later, Grady pops into the stand, equal parts excited and concerned. "I can't even see the end of the line. Can we pick up the pace? Maybe do a little less of the chitchat? I don't want anyone to give up and go home."

"We're moving as fast as we can," Cate says, like he's a cloud passing over her sun.

"Okay, okay." And then he calls out, "Girls, I just want to say thank you. You ladies are killing it."

Amelia ushers Grady away and motions for another girl to take over her window. This, she realizes, will be part of her job this summer. The good thing is that Grady will need to be up at the farmhouse soon, making the ice cream the way Molly used to.

"Hey, Grady, before you go," Cate says, and Grady stops. "I'm not sure if Amelia mentioned this or not. . . . It's tradition that Molly Meade bought us pizzas on the first day of the season." The other girls, including Amelia, raise their eyebrows because this isn't at all true. But Cate is smooth. She reaches down into a tub and keeps scooping. "Call Pizza Towne. It's on Main."

Grady, to his credit, doesn't hesitate. "No problem. Everyone cool with pepperoni?"

"Liz and Jen and I are vegetarians," Cate informs him.

"Okay, one plain, one pepperoni. I'll get some sodas, too."

Though she swats Cate, Amelia only feels relief as Grady steps outside and places an order. Between the two of them, they can manage Grady and also the stand. Everything's going to be just fine.

Amelia spends her break going through the register tape. She'll do a full accounting when her shift ends, but she's curious to see how much business they've done. She's never been the most senior person on a busy day, like opening day or the Fourth of July, so she has no idea what to expect.

There are two shifts per day, and each one averages anywhere from six hundred to eight hundred dollars. On weekends, they'll do double that. But today they've already gone through four drums of Home Sweet Home and three of everything else. It might just be a record breaker.

Grady comes in with the pizzas. "I feel like a celebrity out there in that pink Cadillac. Everyone's waving at me." He comes around the back of Amelia's chair. "How it looking?"

Amelia punches some numbers into the calculator. She almost can't believe what comes up. "We've already done over fifteen hundred dollars and we've still got two more hours to go on the first shift."

She looks up to share a prideful smile with him, but Grady is staring into his phone. "Fifteen hundred dollars," he says, typing it out. "Don't wait too long. Pizza will get cold."

Glumly, she puts the calculator away and stands up. "I'm going to empty the trash cans first."

Hearing this, Grady rushes to finish his text and then darts over, deftly putting his body between Amelia's and the door. She finds herself suddenly standing so close to him, she can almost feel the vibrations of his cell phone buzzing with a text back, now that it's tucked inside his blazer pocket. "No," he insists, almost parentally. "You haven't taken a break yet. Eat first. What kind do you want?"

"Plain."

He opens the box and surveys. "Okay, you want your slice more on the saucy side? Bigger crust? Those burnt cheese bubbles?"

"Saucy and big crust, no burnt cheese bubbles."

He selects her slice and delivers it to her, then starts ripping off sheets of paper towels and folding them up. "Enjoy."

Cate walks in and grabs a piece of pizza. Between bites, she says, "Grady. We have napkins. This is an ice cream stand, remember?"

"Right." Grady seems to sense the coldness. To Amelia, he says, "Hey . . . So, you're going to stay through to closing?"

Amelia checks the face on the punch clock. By the time the first shift ends, she will have worked eleven hours. She's already planned to stay a little later. But the way Grady asks, it feels less like a question and more like an expectation.

"Yes."

"And can you text me more frequent updates on the registers? Hourly, if you can?" He takes out his cell phone. "I should have asked you for your number yesterday. What is it?"

Amelia tells him and she feels embarrassed, even though it is clearly a work ask.

Once he's gone, Cate says, "Don't let him guilt you into staying until closing. The juniors can handle it. They closed plenty of times last summer."

"Yeah, but I figure I can knock out the schedule for the rest of the week and that sort of thing. You should totally go home, though."

"I'm not in any rush. I'll stick around for a while," Cate says. "But before we do anything"—she comes to sit next to Amelia—"we're eating more pizza."

Second shifts feel different from first shifts for a few reasons. Things get quiet around the dinner hour, between four thirty and about seven, but then it'll be busy until closing.

And once the sun goes down, the stand turns into a stage, and it's impossible to see past the floodlights mounted under the awning. You can't tell who's next in line until they reach the window. It's less families and more couples. For the last hour, ten until eleven, it's nearly all teens.

Amelia texts Grady the hourly register updates he asked for, and he doesn't show his face again. She fills out time cards for all the girls and then gets to work on the weekly schedule while Cate lies on the love seat. She stayed a lot longer than Amelia thought she would, though mostly she's been hanging out here in the office. Not that Amelia minds. She likes having Cate's company.

"Don't you dare put either of us on first shift tomorrow," Cate says with a yawn. "We deserve to sleep in. Otherwise, our seniority is worthless."

"Cosigned." Amelia opens the top desk drawer and takes out three keys that open the stand. These copies are hers to divvy out to the most senior girls, who'll also be opening and closing. She tosses one to Cate. "Catch!"

"Why do I need one? Won't I be working every shift with you?"

"Yeah, absolutely. I just thought you might want one anyway." Cate shrugs, and Amelia thinks back to last summer. It's not the key Cate wanted. This one doesn't come with the Head Girl pin.

"Give it to Mansi or Liz," Cate says, tossing it back.

"Oh. Okay. Sure." Amelia decides to make the girls flip a coin for it. So it'll be fair.

At eleven on the nose, they lock the service windows and flip off the outside lights, releasing the moths that have been trapped in their glow. The girls cover the open ice cream drums in plastic wrap and move them from the scooping cabinet back into the walk-in freezer.

There are other chores that everyone is expected to do at closing time. Windex the service windows so they aren't smudgy with fingerprints, restock the toppings, empty the trash cans. The whole circuit, with four girls on, can take as little as fifteen minutes.

Amelia's about to get started, but Cate tells her and the other girls, who look like zombies, "Let's not even worry about it."

Amelia hesitates for a second, but everyone's so beat, and already walking out past her. Anyway, it's not like the place is trashed. She follows the girls out and flips off the lights.

That they didn't have any newbies on changed the feeling of the first day. There was no impromptu little ceremony when new pink polos were passed out, no going over the rules, no challenging the newbies to try and do a dip-top and let them think they'll be fired when their scoop of ice cream inevitably falls into the vat. Which it always, always does. These rituals aren't just for newbies. They make all the girls feel like they're part of something bigger than just a summer job.

But there was so much anticipation leading up to today; they didn't know if they would even get to open on time, let alone have such a banner day. The girls came together and accomplished something huge, something practically impossible.

Amelia sends a text to Grady.

All closed up. I'll bring the deposit bag up in a sec.

He responds almost immediately.

Don't worry. I'll come down and get it.

The younger girls are already scattering. Amelia clicks the padlock shut. Cate leans against the stand, picking away some peeling white paint.

A car pulls in. Amelia's mother.

"Am I too late for a cone?"

"Any other day, I'd say no, Mom. But today, the answer is yes."

Now that Amelia has a ride, Cate says with a yawn, "Peace," and climbs into her truck. Amelia's a little relieved that Grady doesn't appear until Cate's pulled out onto the road.

"Oh. Hello." He leans down into the window of Amelia's family car. "Are you Amelia's mom?"

"Yes."

"Nice meeting you. I couldn't have done this without her today. She's invaluable."

Amelia's mom beams at the compliment. Amelia blushes shyly.

She steps a few feet away and hands him the deposit bag. "We did it."

"I kind of got the feeling that the girls were uncomfortable having me around."

Amelia feels bad. There were a lot of laughs at Grady's expense today. She keeps it simple. "It's just not what they're used to. Molly pretty much left us to our own devices."

"I want to give you girls your space, but I want to be a part of this too."

Grady's earnestness catches her off guard. She quickly nods. "Of course. Totally."

He nods, grateful. "Okay. See you tomorrow."

Once they're in the car, her mom says, "He's quite handsome."

"Is he? I hadn't noticed."

"Ahem. Well then, I'm happy to report that I was able to schedule another candidate for your interview slot at the bank today, even with your last-minute notice. We had several terrific applicants, actually. Not that you were worried about leaving me high and dry," Mom says playfully.

Amelia presses a finger into her left bicep. Her scooping arm is tender to the touch. The soreness makes her smile.

Her mom is right. She wasn't. Not one little bit.

CHAPTER SIXTEEN

THE SIGN ON THE ROOF OF THE ICE CREAM STAND IS A
large rectangle made of plywood, painted white with a pink
frame border, MEADE CREAMERY spelled out in thick pink
script. The paint is weathered and peeling in places from being
out in the elements year-round.

The entire stand gets a fresh coat of white paint at the start of
every season—Amelia figures she'll work that into the schedule
maybe next week—but painting the rooftop Meade Creamery
sign is a special chore reserved for the most senior girls.

Amelia remembers Frankie Ko climbing up on the ladder that
first summer, with Celeste and Johanna following right behind
her. When they reached the top, the three of them stretched
and took deep breaths, as if the air smelled better, fresher, just a
few feet up off the ground. From their elevated vantage point,

Frankie supervised the rest of the chores, tossing Starbursts down to the girls for jobs well done, waving to friends who drove past the stand and beeped.

Painting the sign doesn't take much time at all, but the older girls always milked it, rolling the sleeves of their polos up so their arms would get tan, playing music on one of their phones, using small paintbrushes to make sure the line work was super crisp.

It seems to Amelia like a perfect way to start the day.

Cate's not exactly brimming with excitement at the idea, but she perks up some when Amelia suggests Panera for lunch, her treat.

The girls working the first shift are surprised to see Amelia and Cate there an hour earlier than scheduled. The stand seems to be running fine, though the toppings sideboard is a bit of a mess—cookie crumbs scattered everywhere, peanuts low, rainbow sprinkles sprinkled on the floor. Amelia probably should have cleaned it last night. Anyway, the three girls are quick to apologize, but they had back-to-back summer camp buses pull up in the last hour.

Amelia nods sympathetically.

As Amelia and Cate hang up their things on the hooks near the walk-in freezer, they hear Grady inside the office talking to someone. Or, rather, listening to someone talk. The voice is deep, so Amelia figures it's Grady's dad, and she wonders what time it might be in New Zealand. He must want to check in on Grady, she thinks, make sure he's settling in okay.

Cate holds a finger up to her lips and she and Amelia tiptoe closer to the office door. It's open a crack and they peek inside. Grady's sitting behind the desk, holding up his phone,

FaceTiming. He's freshly showered and dressed up again in a button-up blue shirt and a skinny black tie.

"Did you get the pictures I sent? Of the line? Dad, I even got to shake hands with the mayor. And she said if there's anything I need from her, I should call her office directly."

Amelia and Cate share a look at what a big deal Grady assumes this is. He's clearly not from a small town like Sand Lake, where everyone has a touch on the mayor.

But if his dad is impressed, he doesn't show it. "Have you calculated your overhead?"

"I started going through her books last night."

"You need to do a full audit. Taxes on the property, maintenance, supplies, equipment, payroll."

"I know, Dad."

"Well, you keep talking about how great yesterday's take was, but without an accurate picture of operating costs, it means nothing. Without a P&L, you could be underwater, for all you know. You could be *losing* money."

This strikes Amelia as dead wrong. It seems to strike Grady that way too. He argues, "Dad, this place is incredibly popular." She's heartened to hear him defend the stand. "I mean, my guess is that it could bring in—"

"I'm not interested in your guesses, Grady, especially not any hunches formed in under forty-eight hours on the job."

"Yeesh," Cate whispers, shaking her head. "This is why kids at Truman are so stressed out! They've got these alpha parents pushing them. I've heard like over half the student body is on Adderall. I feel totally lucky. My mom could have died a happy death the day I got my Truman acceptance email. Anything else I accomplish is the cherry on top." Cate heads outside to find the paint supplies and get the ladder from the shed.

Amelia closes the office door to give Grady some privacy, and as it closes, he glances up at her and gives a grateful smile. But the office walls are thin. She can still hear them inside talking and she can't help but linger and listen.

"Your priority right now should be business school, not this ice cream stand."

"I'm getting independent study credit for it. My advisor signed off on everything this morning. Between this and my other online classes, it's almost a full semester course load."

Grady's dad lets out a heavy sigh. "Grady. If you're serious about this—"

"Is it not obvious that I'm serious? Dad, this is a huge opportunity for me. This could be the same kind of start for me as the billboards were for you. Did you know the Ben and Jerry's empire began with one shop? Don't worry about my classes. I'll get the work done."

"If you're serious," his dad reiterates, not conceding an inch, "then you need to get a business plan together, get a handle on your operational costs, and look for ways you can maximize profits. If the numbers don't work, shut it down, sell the property, and cut your losses."

Amelia steadies herself against the wall. Sell Meade Creamery?

"I am serious," Grady stresses again. This time, his voice is much quieter.

Amelia doesn't want to hear more. Thank goodness Grady isn't entertaining that thought. And the stand is *already* successful. His dad will figure that out eventually.

She looks for Cate so they can start painting the sign but sees that she's busy chatting up one of their middle school English teachers in the line, so Amelia decides to clean up the toppings sideboard.

Grady comes out of the office, rubbing his temples. He glances at the schedule and then at Amelia. "You're here early."

"Yeah. Cate and I are going to paint the roof sign before our shift. Is, um, everything okay?"

He works hard to smile. "Yup."

Though she doesn't want to press Grady, Amelia doesn't believe him. But she does feel bad for him. And she knows just the thing to cheer him up. "Hey, do you want some ice cream?"

"Nah, I'm good."

"Really? I mean, this should be one of the biggest benefits to owning an ice cream stand, right? All the ice cream you want, whenever you want it? Come on. What's your favorite flavor?"

"I don't know that I have one."

"I thought you spent a whole summer here as a kid."

Something flickers across his face as he swallows. "Yeah, but that was a long time ago."

"Well, then I'm bringing you a taste of all four. A taste test. You can call it market research."

"Market research, huh?" Grady laughs. "I guess I haven't eaten breakfast yet."

"Wait here," she says.

Amelia heads up to the windows and squeezes in between Sophie and Liz, who are both helping customers. She pushes the lid open on the scooping cabinet and gets a generous scrape of each of the four flavors on four white plastic spoons.

Grady has hopped up on the desk to wait for her. He's scrolling on his phone when she walks in with the samples.

"Customers say the flavors in our ice cream are more intense than any other kind they've ever had," she announces, and presents the ice cream spoons, two in each hand, with a little bit of a flourish, like a game show hostess. She holds vanilla up and takes a whiff of the rich, sugary smell.

"Vanilla," she announces, and presents Grady with the spoonful of white snow. "Don't look so excited."

Grady doesn't look up. "It's vanilla. Vanilla, by its very nature, is vanilla."

Amelia would be more annoyed if she weren't completely confident in what she's holding. If anything, Grady's cockiness will only make her victory sweeter. She holds the spoon closer to his face and she can tell he smells it by the way he perks up. He puts his phone away and takes the spoon from her, examining it skeptically.

Grady says, "Vanilla can't ever be a ten. The best vanilla in the world is, like, a six, max."

"What an ignorant thing to say. Now, close your eyes. I want you to concentrate on the flavors."

Grady barks a laugh. "Wow, you're bossy today."

"Don't be sexist."

His cheeks glow. "Sorry. I was kidding." He closes his eyes.

Amelia hands Grady the spoon and watches intently, brimming with excitement, as he takes his first lick. "Huh. That's pretty good." His eyes flutter open as he takes a second taste. On his third, he cleans the spoon. "It's, like, infinitely more vanilla-y than the fro-yo place on campus."

"Duh. Fro-yo is basically frozen chemicals. *This* is ice cream." She takes the used spoon from him and tosses it into the garbage can, pleased that his bad mood has already vanished and there are still three flavors to go. "Now, would you please look at this color!" she says, holding up the chocolate. "It's like tar."

"Marketing tip. Think *aspirational. Tar* is not a good descriptor for something you want people to eat."

"Okay, it's like"—her eyes brighten—"fudge at midnight."

"Yes! That! Exactly!"

She hands him the spoon. "Hurry up before these melt."

This time, Grady closes his eyes and goes right in, taking the whole bite at once. "Whoa. That's intense. It's almost . . . bitter." He rubs his chin thoughtfully. "Not in a bad way. It's really sophisticated."

"Next is strawberry," Amelia says, but Grady shakes his head.

"I want more chocolate." Peeking at her, he opens his mouth to be fed.

Amelia feels her heart speed up. Ignoring him, she hands him the next spoon. "Our strawberry," she announces, "is the most beautiful shade of pink. Not pale, like the weak stuff you get from the grocery store. Deep. Lively. Also, you'll never bite into an icy chunk of strawberry. It's completely incorporated."

Grady's eyes go wide as he tastes. "Holy shit."

"No cursing in the stand, please. But I know, right?" she says. "And this . . . this is Home Sweet Home," Amelia says, putting the spoon in his hand. She's surprised how nervous she feels. She wants Grady to love it as much as she does.

"Ahhh yes. You know, that reporter guy told me this might be the biggest unsolved mystery in Sand Lake," he says, examining the spoon.

"Last year, a guy offered me fifty bucks to tell him."

"Did you?" he asks, grinning.

Amelia cocks her head. "Uh, no." After all, how could she? The only one who knew the recipes was Molly.

And now, Grady.

"Come to think of it," he says, "I should probably require all the girls to sign NDAs."

"What's an NDA?"

"A nondisclosure agreement. It means if they tell anyone our recipes, I can sue them for damages." He pops the spoon into his mouth.

"That's a bit overkill, don't you think? None of us know—"

She quiets, watching Grady's strange reaction. He blinks a few times, almost stunned by what he's tasting. Then his jaw sets, his brow furrows, and he forces a swallow after a most unpleasant battle of his will. Once he gets it down, his face is totally unguarded, because he's been blindsided. He can't even pretend to hide what he's feeling—an emotion Amelia never would have expected.

Sadness.

"Hey, Amelia? You ready to paint?"

Amelia spins as Cate enters the office, and she takes a giant step away from Grady; until this moment she hasn't realized how close she's been standing to him. Grady hops off the desk and hustles out.

"Market research," Amelia tells her, answering a question that Cate hasn't asked in too loud a voice.

Cate cocks her head. "Uh-huh."

Amelia grabs the Panera bag with the sandwiches, nervously passing Grady on her way outside. She isn't sure if he looks at her, but she sure as heck doesn't look at him.

As Cate climbs up the ladder with the paint cans and the brushes, Amelia notices something from her vantage point on the ground. Certain boards—the ones higher up—are peeling white paint faster than others.

"Throw me up the sandwiches!" Cate instructs.

Amelia tosses the bag and climbs the ladder, pausing at the top to inspect that wood. More paint flakes away when she touches it; it's barely sticking. Underneath, the wood is damp and soft with rot.

"Holy crap, Amelia. You have to see this."

Amelia hoists herself up and over the lip of the roof.

At first, she thinks Cate is talking about the view. Because, on her tiptoes, she can make out a bit of the lake, see the green trees and the rooftops of a few houses, see up and down Route 68 for miles. She knows in her heart that Sand Lake is the most beautiful place in the world, even though she's never really been anywhere else.

"Not out there! Look down."

She does, and at her feet are signatures in pink paint, hundreds of them. The names of the girls who've worked at Meade Creamery over the years cover the entire roof. Some are faded, some fresh, and plenty are illegible because the shingles have shifted or chipped, the broken pieces clogging the gutters with last fall's leaves. She bends down, wishing she had time to put the puzzle back together.

They pop their paint cans and get to work, adding another coat of white on the sign and pink for the letters. Though before they do, Amelia uses the handle of her paintbrush to scrape away an abandoned, flaking wasps' nest from the bottom of the sign. No wonder they had so much trouble with them last summer.

They play music, shout hello to some friends in line, sit back and lazily eat their sandwiches. "Do you think you'll come back to Sand Lake next summer?" Amelia asks.

"Amelia! Why are you already thinking about next summer? We've barely started this one."

"I'm just saying that I definitely want to come home," Amelia says, a tad defensive. "I already miss it here."

"Just make sure you keep yourself open to other opportunities. You could score a killer internship somewhere."

"Maybe." Amelia shrugs. Though that feels like a remote possibility, considering she even doesn't know what she wants to study. "You're coming home for Thanksgiving, right?"

"If I didn't, my mom would kill me. Christmas, too. Those holidays are mandatory."

"Gibbons doesn't go back from winter break until the middle of January. What about Truman?"

Cate shrugs. "No clue."

They find a spot to paint their names. Right next to each other, where the roof tiles still seem in decent shape. Cate adds a heart surrounding them, and also the last two numbers of the year. It's how she signed everyone's yearbooks.

When they finish, they lie down next to their names and take a few selfies together for posterity. They have fifteen minutes before their shift when Amelia starts packing things up. Cate says, "Let's hang out here for just a little while longer," and pulls Amelia back down.

Amelia rocks into her. "See? Aren't you glad you didn't stay at JumpZone? You would have never known about this roof. Your name wouldn't have been here with the other girls who've worked here. Now we're officially a part of this place forever."

"I was never going to stay at JumpZone!"

"Okay, okay."

"But you're right. This is pretty cool. I'm glad I didn't miss it." And together, they use their hands to help fan the paint dry, so nothing messes up their place in Meade Creamery history.

CHAPTER SEVENTEEN

BY THE END OF THE FIRST WEEK, THINGS AT MEADE Creamery feel mostly back to normal.

Mostly.

On the whole, and to all the girls' relief, working for Grady isn't much different from working for Molly, because he's hardly ever around. He spends the bulk of his days up at the farmhouse. He assumes he's untangling Meade Creamery's financial picture, as his dad instructed him to do, and tackling his schoolwork. That's all in addition to, obviously, making Molly's ice cream.

Amelia suspects his distance might also have something to do with whatever happened between them in the office, during her ice cream tasting. Though it seemed to Amelia like they had been getting along well enough before that moment, their interactions feel more formal and stilted now. When Grady pops down at the stand—usually around five o'clock, when he stops in to grab any packages that have been delivered and to check the register totals—he barely speaks to her.

Not that she minds. It's better this way.

And she reciprocates in kind, careful not to be too friendly or chummy, even the times she's encountered Grady around Sand Lake—he was studying at the public library when she dropped off some checked-out books on Wednesday, and then again on Thursday, at the lake. Though she didn't *actually* see Grady there, just spotted Molly's pink Cadillac parked on the public beach side as Cate drove past.

The only way Grady seems comfortable talking to her is by texting . . . which he does plenty of.

Day and night, Amelia has been answering his random questions about the business. The girls get paid on Mondays. No, there is no premade waffle cone that might compare with the ones we make fresh. We average about one supersized container of sprinkles a week. So many questions that Amelia has taken to keeping her phone on silent, with no vibrate, because Grady often texted her when she was off the clock and doing other things, like on Saturday afternoon, when she was helping Cate weed her closet of fall clothes that looked too explicitly *high school*, or on Sunday night, when all the stand girls went to the movies together after closing.

This is, in part, because even when Grady's visits to the stand are brief, Amelia notices there's still a shift in energy that starts when he walks in and lasts until he leaves. Conversations get quieter, the girls less playful. Like on Monday, when a few of the girls were chatting with each other during a shift change, the topic of conversation was Liz and a guy she had a crush on.

Grady was in the office with Amelia, and they could both hear everything that was being said outside the door. Cate was doing most of the talking, pumping Liz up, giving some advice on how to act if the guy came to her window that night.

Amelia raised her head, pausing from the cardboard she was breaking down to see if Grady was listening. He seemed focused on prying their old punch clock from the wall. Grady had found a payroll app—one that had been created by a guy in his frat and that made him an insta-millionaire—and had all the girls download it onto their phones. It would make payroll easier for sure, but there was something sad about the punch clock getting the heave-ho. Amelia almost wished Grady would leave it, even if they wouldn't be using it anymore.

Still, Amelia got the sense that she should say something to the girls, let them know Grady could hear them. They probably didn't know he was there. But before she could, Grady walked to the office door, the punch clock under his arm.

"Hey. Here's my two cents. If a guy likes you, he'll call you. It's really as simple as that." He smiled, like he was being helpful. The girls stared at him blankly until he realized he'd majorly overstepped and hastily made his exit.

At least, as Cate said later, it provided her with a teachable moment about mansplaining.

Grady's made a few other changes too, besides the time cards. Meade Creamery is now on all social media platforms, and he's been talking about creating some kind of Instagram-friendly wall on the side of the stand, to encourage more online traffic. Last check, they had a measly sixty-four followers. Grady has asked the girls to share his posts, though none of them have, either because they don't love the photos he's taken (Amelia's eyes were closed in one shot on opening day) or because he's gone embarrassingly overboard with his hashtag game (#you-knowyouwantit, which, ugh).

Grady's also ordered two credit card readers, but he hasn't gotten Wi-Fi installed, so they aren't usable. For the time being, they live on the shelf near the radio. And the stand is now offering nearly double the toppings it did in summers past—a difference made up almost entirely by sugary breakfast cereals. It has made their already cramped sideboard area even tighter, but Grady thinks customization is a thing consumers expect, and it helps to give their four-flavor menu some depth.

For the most part, the girls have been accepting of, if slightly irritated with, these changes. Despite her own misgivings, Amelia has decided to pick her battles with Grady carefully.

Her first opportunity came this past Monday.

She'd just gotten to the stand when Grady texted Has there ever been another Meade Creamery storefront? Like somewhere on Main Street?

Nope. Just this one.

Before she could put her phone down, Grady texted back. This was unusual. He'd always taken her answers at face value. But not this time.

Mistake.

Amelia stared at the word. How so?

Main Street would be a way better location. We're in the middle of nowhere.

Amelia shook her head. With her top lip curled, she typed, This is where everything started. And then added, Also, you've probably noticed that people don't have any trouble finding us out here.

siobhan vivian

Amelia waited for Grady to answer back. When he didn't, she was a little bummed. She wanted to keep arguing with him. Or at least, that was what she thought, until he suddenly came in through the back door.

"Don't get defensive, Amelia. It's just an observation."

"I'm not," she said, even though she could feel her pulse in her throat. She'd been fine with changes and helping Grady wrap his head around the business. But she wouldn't let him imply that Molly Meade didn't know what she was doing. "Part of what makes this place special is that it isn't close to other things. It's a pilgrimage."

"All I'm trying to say is that she could have been making more money. Imagine if she had a place down near the lake!"

"There are no shops at the lake."

"I'm just brainstorming here," he sourly informed her, lowering himself onto the yellow love seat. "And when brainstorming, you're not supposed to shut down ideas."

"I'm not shutting you down. I'm telling you the facts. There's nothing around the lake but trees. So it seems silly to think about how much better business would hypothetically be if you moved the business to a location that doesn't *actually* exist."

After getting up, he chastised, "You have to dream big if you want to succeed in business, Amelia. Look for green lights, not stop signs."

As Grady walked out, Amelia caught the eyes of the other girls in the stand. They were beaming at her, and Cate licked her finger and pretended to touch Amelia with it, making a sizzle sound. But while Amelia felt happy to have stood up for the stand, their conversation was more proof that any friendliness between her and Grady had chilled since she'd given him the ice cream. Now, even when they did talk, they argued. Something had happened in that moment, she just wasn't sure what.

The next day, one week since the stand opened, Grady pulled up in the pink Cadillac, beeping his horn long and hard. He was being followed by a tow truck, yellow rooftop lights flashing. Hitched up to the truck's hook was an old white van.

"Holy crap," Cate said. "Is that a food truck?"

Amelia, Cate, and the other girls ran out.

The shape of the thing immediately betrayed its age. It was boxy, with plenty of dents and nicks. There were hinges on the side, for a fold-up awning and a fold-down counter. An old logo had been painted over hastily.

Grady hopped out of the Cadillac and directed the tow truck driver to park the food truck behind the stand. "Ain't it a beauty?" he said, stuffing his hands in the pockets of his khakis. "I found it on Craigslist last night. It's been in someone's garage for the last three years."

Cate, to Amelia's surprise, looked just as excited. "Yo, this is going to be so awesome! We can park down at the lake!"

Grady nodded and pointed. "Yes. Exactly. So what do you think, Amelia? Now that I've made the impossible possible."

Cate gave Amelia a nudge. "Come on, Amelia, it would be so much more fun to work at the lake! We could go for a swim on our break."

Amelia climbed aboard. The inside of the food truck wasn't in much better shape than the outside. And it definitely wasn't set up for ice cream. There was a long grill, and underneath, two old propane tanks. Also mouse poop everywhere. Everything that had been chrome was now rusted. The exhaust fan over her head was thick with fuzz. She touched one of the walls with her

siobhan vivian

finger. It felt slick, yellow with old grease, like honeycomb wax.

Cate followed her inside. Her head flinching back slightly, she said, "Grady, I hope you don't think we're cleaning this thing."

But Grady didn't respond. His eyes were on Amelia, and his expression betrayed his disappointment in her lack of excitement.

"How much did you pay for this?" she asked.

"Not *that* much," Grady insisted, though he avoided her eyes as he said it. "And it was the only one for sale in the state!"

"Does it even run?"

"The guy who sold it to me said he's pretty sure all it needs is a tune-up." Amelia saw, over Grady's shoulder, the tow truck man roll his eyes. "It's a good idea," Grady said to Amelia, trying to get her on his side. "You'll see." He held out his phone to the girls. "Can someone take my picture? I want to send this to my dad."

By that afternoon, two mechanics had already been over and given Grady estimates. He crumpled them both up and threw them in the office trash can, saying he was sure he could do better.

Amelia expected to feel more victorious than she did.

Other than those disruptions, the traditions of summers at the stand are back in full force. Different games and pranks, always done in good fun, passed down through the years. One that began while Amelia was here—if not last summer, then the one before, she's not positive—is that if there's a closed door, there's a good chance someone is hiding behind it, waiting to jump out. Last summer, Cate nearly killed Heather when she sprang up from the backseat of Heather's car, but then Heather got her back that very same night, jumping off the roof when

Amelia and Cate were closing. Sometimes scares happen in front of customers. Amelia once tucked herself into an empty box on the floor near one of the service windows, and when Britnee was about to hand over two cones, she sprang up and screamed. Britnee smashed both cones into the closed service window.

Amelia hopes that's not why Britnee chose to stay at Sephora.

Since there are no newbies yet this summer, some chores are falling by the wayside. Namely, the cleaning of the bathroom. But no one has stepped up to pick up the slack.

That's why, on Wednesday, Amelia is on her hands and knees, wearing yellow rubber gloves, cleaning the bathroom for the second time since the stand opened this summer. The big mop bucket holds the door open. Cate walks up, leans against the doorframe, and folds her arms. "Well, here's something I never thought I'd see."

"What's that?" Amelia says, wiping down the toilet.

"A Head Girl cleaning the bathroom."

"I don't mind. . . ." Or, more truthfully, Amelia doesn't feel comfortable asking Jen, last year's newbie. She already put in her time. She isn't a newbie anymore.

"You can't give yourself bathroom duty all summer. I won't allow it. Has Grady said when you can hire newbies? We're down three girls! That's a whole shift!"

There's something to what Cate is saying. Yes, they need to hire more girls. But in the meantime, everyone should be required to take a turn.

The fairest way Amelia can think up?

A chore chart.

She makes one on her break that day. A Sunday-through-

Saturday grid with separate Post-it notes for each girl, so she can rotate the names around. This way, everyone knows who's responsible for what newbie chores each shift. And Amelia won't have to personally seek the girls out to let them know when it's their turn.

When she hangs up the chore chart, Cate is not thrilled.

"Come on, Amelia. Are we twelve?" Cate whines, and tries to grab her Post-it note and take it off the chart. "Plus, we're seniors! You and I shouldn't have to do this at all."

Amelia sees the girls on the windows quickly busy themselves, but she knows they're listening. Rather than fight about it, Amelia takes Cate's Post-it, shifting all the other girls up and putting herself and then Cate last in the order. Hopefully they'll have newbies in place before her turn comes up.

It's around eight thirty in the evening, and she's just scraped the last scoop of Home Sweet Home out of the drum in the scooping cabinet. It's been drizzling for most of the evening. There's no one in Amelia's line, and Cate's not too busy either, leisurely chatting up a couple visiting from out of town whom she's already served scoops of chocolate in waffle cones. Amelia closes her window, drops her scooper into the wash well, and jogs out back to throw the empty drum into the dumpster.

Walking back in, she puts on the purple ski jacket, grabs the tally clipboard, and heads into the freezer, intending to grab a new drum and also do a quick stock check. The girls should be keeping up with this every time they take out a new drum— marking what's being taken, as well as shifting everything to the right to create empty space on the left for the new tubs, so that nothing is sitting too long in the freezer. Every few days, Molly would come and grab the tally sheet, so she knew which flavors she needed to restock.

No one kept track on opening day. It was so busy, the girls were bringing new tubs out of the walk-in and moving them into the scooping cabinet almost every hour. But over the week, only a few marks have been made on the clipboard, which means only some of the girls are remembering this responsibility. So Amelia now plays catch-up, organizing and straightening, and counts a total of fifty-one drums gone. When she shifts everything to the right, nearly half the walk-in freezer is empty.

"Whoa," Cate says from behind her. "I've never seen it like this. Why hasn't Grady brought us down more ice cream?"

"He probably never thought to check. I'll let him know."

"Do you think he's started making it?"

"I hope so. There's probably going to be a bit of a learning curve."

"Hopefully not too big." Cate knocks into her playfully. "And, while you're at it, talk to him about us hiring newbies!"

"I promise I will." Amelia already has a running list of things to discuss with Grady. The staffing situation, the missing tiles on the roof, the rotten wooden slats, and now ice cream. She goes into the office, straightens her shirt, and undoes the braid in her hair, because of how young Grady had said it makes her seem.

Hey, Grady. We are running low on ice cream down here, just FYI. Also I have a few managerial issues I'd like to discuss with you.

Cate leans over her shoulder. "Make sure you're assertive with him about the newbies. If you sound like it isn't a big deal, like we're managing okay, he'll blow you off. Remember, his dad told him to maximize profits."

"You sure you don't want to have this conversation?" Amelia's only half joking.

"You're Head Girl, not me. Remember? And anyway," she adds, flopping onto the couch, "I'm on my break."

Amelia can see Grady writing back.

Sure. Come on up. I'll leave the door open.

She glances up at Cate. "Oh my God. He's inviting me inside the farmhouse."

Cate tries grabbing on to Amelia's arm. "Wait! I'll go! I need Grady's advice on my dorm application anyway!"

Amelia wriggles free and darts past her, laughing. "Enjoy your break!"

CHAPTER EIGHTEEN

AMELIA FOLLOWS THE DRIVEWAY UP TO THE FARM-house. The sun has started to set, filling the sky with shades of pink, and the damp air has the slightest whiff of honeysuckle. Molly's Cadillac is parked at the top of the driveway, a week's worth of crumpled fast-food bags tossed in the backseat.

As promised, the front door has been left open for her, but she still feels the need to knock politely on the screen door as she opens it.

"Look out!"

A hand grabs Amelia's arm and yanks her inside. She falls into Grady's chest as the screen door slams shut behind her.

Pushing off, she says, "Jeez, Grady!"

He's wearing a pair of gray mesh shorts and a Truman T-shirt. It's the most casually she's ever seen him dressed, aside from opening day when he overslept. "Sorry." He crouches down and the black-and-white kitten comes darting over. "Little guy was trying to make a run for it."

Amelia squeals and takes the kitten into her hands. "I wondered what happened to him! He was with your great-aunt Molly when she passed away." Amelia twists her arm, but the scratches the kitten gave her have healed.

"He's my new study buddy. He keeps me from going crazy up here by myself." The kitten crawls from her arms to his. Grady brings him close and rubs his cheek against the kitten. "Right, Little Dude?"

"You didn't name him that, did you? That's a terrible name." Amelia scratches between the kitten's ears and he works his head into her palm, purring like crazy. "You should call him Moo. In honor of the dairy."

"What do you think?" Grady asks the kitten. "Little Dude or Moo?" Moo crawls back into her arms. "Moo it is, then."

Amelia cuddles Moo for another few seconds before he wriggles to be put down. He starts pawing and mewing and crying at the door. "Grady, you know he's trying to get outside because he's an outdoor cat."

"Yeah, I kind of assumed. But I'm afraid he'll get run over by a car. It's safer for him in here with me." Grady picks up Moo by the scruff of his neck and lifts him so they're eye to eye. "We'll both get used to being in captivity, right, Moo?" Then he sets Moo down and uses his foot to nudge the kitten deeper into the house. Then they share in an awkward pause, without Moo as a buffer, and Amelia wonders whether or not things will go back to being contentious between them. "Sorry it's so hot in here. Turns out Great-Aunt Molly did not believe in air-conditioning. But if I close my eyes"—which he does, to illustrate—"I can almost imagine I'm on a beach in Barcelona with my fraternity brothers."

It is hot. Stuffy. And though the house appears tidy, Amelia sees hints of Molly's age. Some cobwebs on the lampshades, dust bunnies where the walls meet the floor; both are likely too faint for old eyes to see.

Amelia follows Grady into the main hallway. Ahead of him, she sees Molly's kitchen. It's a classic farm style: white cabinets, big white porcelain sink, a noisy fridge, and a window that frames the back fields. Amelia knew the Meades owned a ton of land, but she's had no sense of how much until now.

Grady takes a left into the formal living room, with a striped couch, two matching Queen Anne chairs with floral backs, and a coffee table. This seems to be where he is spending most of his time. His laptop is open, perched on a tall stack of college textbooks. Several pairs of his pants are draped over the backs of chairs, his shirts buttoned up on hangers that have been hooked on the fireplace mantel, on the lip of the bookshelves, on the wooden box of a grandfather clock. Molly's financial records paper the coffee table, three emptied bank boxes' worth. There's also a blanket and pillow smushed up on the couch.

"I tried sleeping in the spare bedroom upstairs," he explains, "but it's twice as hot on the second floor as it is down here. I can't get any of the windows to open."

She walks over to the mantel, where there's a line of framed family pictures. In a large silver oval is Molly's high school senior portrait.

Amelia is pretty sure the photograph has been artificially tinted because it has a watercolor-y look. In it, Molly is wearing

siobhan vivian

a red blouse, and her strawberry-blond hair loops in soft bouncy curls over her shoulders. She's smiling a closed-lipped smile, red and juicy, her shoulders angled ever so slightly, blue eyes sparkling. She is gorgeous.

"Did you know she was elected homecoming queen *and* prom queen two years in a row?" Amelia asks Grady. "Supposedly a man from Hollywood once slipped Molly's dad his business card because he wanted to bring Molly to California and put her in movies." Amelia's been told stories like these over the years, by the older customers who show up less interested in placing an order than they are in sharing memories of the Meades.

Grady blinks.

"You don't see it? She absolutely could have been a movie star!" Amelia is suddenly annoyed at Grady for being so handsome. He doesn't deserve his good looks if he doesn't care about where they came from.

"It's not that," he says, defensive. "I just feel weird calling my great-aunt hot." He points out another photo, this one of the three Meade siblings standing in height order on the stairs. "I think this guy's my grandfather," he says, pointing to the one on the top step, tall and wiry, in slacks and a boxy button-up. "Patrick. I never met him, but I've seen his picture. And that's for sure my dad's nose."

"Your nose," Amelia says.

"You think?" He runs a finger down the slope. "Sometimes I wonder if my dad and I are actually related. Anyway, that would make this other guy my great-uncle Liam," he says, pointing to the shorter and stockier of the two Meade brothers. "He died in a car accident a couple years after making it back from the war."

To Amelia, it seems unfair, how much tragedy has befallen

the Meades. She scans the other photos. The last one on the right was taken in front of the stand, and it seems to be the most recent. Molly is laughing jovially at the camera. Next to her, a tall woman in cutoffs and a white linen shirt is smiling at a little boy, who's bawling because he lost the top scoop of his cone.

Grady.

"That's my mom," he mumbles.

Amelia leans closer, trying to match this woman up to the one she first saw at Molly's funeral.

"So, ice cream," Grady says, backing up.

"Um. Right."

Grady leads her down a hallway, past the kitchen, to a black wooden door with a glass knob. It opens to a narrow stairway, walls decorated with a dustpan and broom, some shelves of canned goods. He descends first and Amelia follows, every step getting darker until they reach the bottom. Then Grady walks off and a few seconds later flicks a light switch.

Amelia's hand goes straight to her mouth.

It's less of a basement and more of a teenager's hangout from another time. The walls are pasted with faded magazine clippings of fashionable girls in beautiful outfits alongside images of dairy cows, and the juxtaposition of these subjects makes Amelia smile. A few small windows are up near the ceiling, each one with a set of cute, home-sewn curtains made from pink ticking-stripe fabric with white eyelet lace at the hem. There are a couch and a club chair that exactly match the yellow love seat down in the stand, only not nearly as faded and worn.

Most amazing, though, is the kitchen. This part of the basement is like something out of the future: sterile, clean. There are two large industrial freezers and a stainless steel table that wouldn't be out of place in a doctor's office. Underneath the table are stacks of nesting bowls, and hanging from S hooks are several sets of silver measuring cups and spoons. Waist-high containers marked as sugar and powdered milk, each with a huge scoop. A stainless steel vat, large, like a witch's cauldron with general temperature gauges.

Finally, Amelia notices a silver rectangle sitting on a second table all by itself, unsurprising as it isn't a friendly-looking contraption. It's about the size of three microwaves stacked on top of each other. There are a couple of unmarked knobs and gauges, and one big triangular spout in front. It's old. You can tell by the way the metal is stamped with the company name EMERY THOMPSON AUTOMATED MACHINE.

Grady pats the top of the ice cream maker like a used-car salesman. It seems to be in good shape, not a dent or a scratch on it. It's like peering under the hood of a classic vintage car, all shiny chrome.

Amelia makes a slow spin, trying to take it all in. This was Molly's sanctuary, but thinking of her working alone down here for so many years tugs at Amelia's heart.

"So what are we looking at, in terms of restocking?" Grady asks.

"We're down almost fifty gallons. I've got the exact breakdown of flavors here." She takes out the stock sheet, unfolds it, and hands it to Grady.

There's an awkward silence as he glances at it. He folds the paper and hands it back to her. "Was there something else?"

This confuses her. Maybe Grady has a photographic memory? "I noticed earlier this week that some of the wood on the back wall is rotten. And there are a lot of broken shingles on the roof."

Grady yawns and stretches. "I try to stick around here in the mornings, in case my dad calls from New Zealand, but I'll check on it tomorrow after lunch."

She takes a moment to steel herself. "There's one more thing. We need to hire more girls. Three more, to replace Heather and Georgia, who graduated last year, and Britnee, who decided to stay at Sephora."

"Let's table that for the time being. I'm still trying to explain to my dad why I agreed to pay you girls so much for scooping ice cream." He quickly follows up with "I don't mean *you*, of course. You've been a huge help."

Agreed? But that's what they've always gotten paid. Amelia shakes her head, tries to refocus. "The problem is that three girls make up an entire shift. Without them in the rotation, the rest of us have only one day off a week."

"I'm still sorting through Molly's financial stuff. It's going more slowly than I expected. Her books are a mess. I don't know if it's going to work."

"Okay, but . . . we've always had ten girls on staff. So it obviously *does* work."

He gives her a thin-lipped smile. "Anything else?"

Amelia feels unsteady. She was not expecting to be shot down so quickly. She knows Cate is going to be angry. And when Amelia goes over the conversation with her, Cate is going to find a hundred different ways that Amelia could have been stronger, more articulate, more firm.

"All right then . . . ," Grady says, without waiting for her to answer, and walks toward the stairs.

"Wait a minute."

Glancing over his shoulder, Grady says, "We can connect

tomorrow on anything else you need to talk about, Amelia. I've got a paper due for one of my summer classes that needs to be up by midnight."

Amelia shakes her head, incredulous. "But I need ice cream. Remember?"

Finally, he stops. And when he turns toward her, confusion twists across his face. "So make whatever you need. You're not going to bother me."

Amelia nervously laughs. "I don't know how to make ice cream. Only Molly knows the recipes. Everyone in Sand Lake knows that. Molly . . . and now you."

Grady presses his palms into his eyes. "Amelia. I'm seriously too tired to be messed with right now. When we first sat down, you told me that you helped her make the ice cream."

"I never said that."

"Then you implied it!"

"No. I didn't!"

"I distinctly remember you saying that, as Head Girl, you were in charge of managing the stock."

Amelia puts her hands on her hips. "Which is why I am here now, telling you that we need more ice cream."

"I asked you, *What about the ice cream?* And you said, *What do you want to know?*"

"I never said I helped make ice cream," Amelia says again, though this time, her voice is shaky. "If you had asked me that specific question, I would have said so."

Grady bites his fist to muffle a curse.

"Whatever, it's fine," she says, uneasy. "I mean, I'm sure I can do it. Just give me her recipes and I'll figure it out."

"I don't have the recipes."

"You said in the paper that the recipes are the most valuable things you inherited! So go get the recipes *you inherited* so I can try and figure out how to make ice cream."

"I meant that in a general sense! How would I know where the recipes are?"

"Have you looked for them?"

He's pacing, pinching the bridge of his nose. "Why would I have looked for them? After our interview, I figured you knew. Either where they were or . . . I don't know, by heart." His breathing is getting faster and faster, leaving Amelia to worry that he's about to hyperventilate. "How much ice cream do we have? How long will it last us?"

"We have about fifty more drums. They could last us another week. Maybe a week and a half if it rains?"

"How can I run an ice cream stand if there's no ice cream?" He startles, surprised at the volume of his own voice.

Amelia gets a text from Cate.

How's it going? Can I put out the newbie applications yet?

Amelia doesn't write back. It's nine thirty p.m. An hour and a half until closing. It wasn't busy when she left. Cate and the other girls can hold down the fort.

Something about Grady freaking out makes Amelia feel super calm, like she has to keep it together because he's losing it. And right now, keeping this ice cream stand open is important to both of them. She convinced the girls to come back. She can't let them down.

"Okay, there's no need to panic," she says. "I'm sure the recipes are here somewhere."

Amelia wanders over to the kitchen area, thinking they would most likely be kept where the magic happens. Grady lurks not far behind her, more watching over her shoulder than helping. Amelia pulls open the drawers, which contain mismatched, bent silverware. Next she checks the cabinets. Strangely, each one is filled with plain glass vases, the cheap kind that come with floral deliveries. Amelia opens the refrigerator and finds it half full of expired milk and eggs and cream from Marburger Dairy.

Grady's phone rings. He mutes it, but almost immediately, it rings again.

"Is that your dad? Should you answer?"

"If it was my dad, I'd *definitely* answer. It's my friends trying to FaceTime. They got to Amsterdam today, which means they're high." He puts his phone down and it starts ringing yet again. "Don't give me that look. It's legal there, Amelia."

"I'm not giving any look!"

Across the room is a large wood cabinet with gold mesh fabric across the front. Amelia walks over. Half the top of the cabinet is lifted up, revealing a record player inside. Amelia peeks inside the other hatch. It's full of old records. Hundreds of them.

The phone rings yet again. "Ugh. They're not going to give up." With a groan, he flicks off his baseball cap and answers. "Yo, dudes. It's a very bad time for me."

Five, maybe six guys scream at once.

"You should be here with us, Grady!"

"Dude, screw your dad! Get on a flight!"

"Yeah, tell ol' Paddy Meade to ease up! He hasn't canceled your credit cards yet, has he?"

Grady gives a quick glance at Amelia. "I'll hit you guys up later." He hangs up and tosses the phone aside. "My friends are complete idiots."

"Forget them and help me."

They continue to search the basement, silent and focused. Obvious places are checked again and then checked a third time. When they come up empty-handed, they exchange a brief look and start searching weird places, like inside the books on a bookshelf, underneath the couch cushions.

Amelia does discover a few ingredients that shine a light on Molly Meade's process—containers of vanilla beans marinating in a dark syrup, gallon jugs of homemade fudge sauce. There are jars of homemade strawberry jam too, maybe a hundred, tucked inside a small cabinet underneath the basement stairs. The lids are marked with the current year, which means Molly prepared them this past spring. "Grady, I think this is how she got the strawberry so perfectly integrated." This discovery amuses Amelia no end. She sits back on her heels and holds a jar up to the light. It looks like liquefied rubies.

"Amelia, not to be a complete jerk, but the only things I care about you finding are the recipes." Grady lets his head drop into his hands. "Which are totally not down here."

She's disheartened too, of course. In the back of her mind, a niggling thought takes hold, wondering if they aren't hunting fool's gold. After all, Molly had been making her ice cream for so long, it's not like she'd need to consult a recipe. Amelia pushes this thought aside. It's too early in their search to be pessimistic. Instead, she chooses to hope. Because why would Molly bequeath her stand to Grady without also leaving him her recipes?

Amelia hears three long beeps outside. She checks her phone, shocked to see that it's already eleven thirty. The stand's been closed for a half hour. She glances out the basement window and sees Cate's truck, here to pick her up.

"Grady, I'm sorry but I have to go."

"Damn. Me too. I haven't even started my paper yet."

"I'll be back first thing tomorrow morning."

He beams a grateful smile. "Oh, really? Wow, great, thank you so much." Then his long legs take the stairs two by two. Amelia follows. "Please don't tell any of the girls about this," Grady says. "We don't want anyone to panic. Or word to get out to the customers. Or that newspaper guy."

Amelia avoids answering Grady's request directly, because of course she will be telling Cate. Like, the second she gets outside. But she does want to help him. "I'm sure we're going to find them tomorrow. We've only searched one room. There's a whole house to go through yet."

Grady walks Amelia to the door.

Cate calls out her open truck window, "What have you guys been doing up here all night?"

"Amelia's helping me with some paperwork," Grady lies, almost too easily.

"Oh? That's cool." Cate tosses Grady the deposit bag and the day's receipts. As Amelia climbs into the truck, Cate whispers, "What the hell, Amelia! I was about to come up and make sure you weren't being murdered!"

Buckling up, Amelia whispers back, "I'm sorry. I lost track of time," and she gives Grady a small wave goodbye. Through her teeth, she says, "Just drive and I'll explain everything."

Once they're on the road, Amelia lays it out. "Grady doesn't have the ice cream recipes. He has no idea where they are." She tells Cate the whole story, including how she may have potentially, inadvertently misled Grady during their first meeting.

Cate is having none of it. "Amelia, this is so not your fault."

"You weren't there, Cate. I could have been more direct. I—"

"Even if you accidentally led him to that conclusion, which I know you didn't, it's still Grady's responsibility to be up to speed on all things Meade Creamery. It's his fault for assuming. This is *his* problem. This is *his* stand. We're just the employees."

Amelia knows this is true, even if it doesn't feel that way. "Well, I don't mind helping him find them. We're on the same team."

"Grady isn't Molly. He's not some sad old lady trapped in a farmhouse, making ice cream to ease her broken heart. He's smart. He's savvy. If he makes you feel bad or like you have something you need to prove to him, it's because he's playing you."

"Playing me? What do you mean?"

"Let me guess. I bet he dropped his boss routine real quick and acted all grateful and nice to you, so you'd stay up there and help him tonight."

"He *was* grateful," Amelia says. Though how can she be sure it wasn't also, simultaneously, a guilt trip? She doesn't even know the guy. Not really. But she's nervous when she admits to Cate, "I told him I'd go back tomorrow morning to help him look some more."

At this, Cate is silent, but when she reaches the next stop sign, she puts her truck in park and turns to face Amelia. "I'm not saying don't help him find the recipes. Just remember you don't owe him anything. At the end of the day, this is his problem to solve. Don't let him use you."

Amelia fiddles with the flower pin on her collar. She knows that Cate is probably right. This is Grady's problem. And hopefully, sooner rather than later, he will solve it.

siobhan vivian

CHAPTER  NINETEEN

AMELIA RIDES HER BIKE TO MOLLY'S FARMHOUSE AND arrives by nine o'clock, two hours before the stand opens, dressed in one of her newer, brighter Meade Creamery polos and a pair of white twill shorts. Grady answers the door in running shorts and no shirt, his hair wet from a shower.

"Hey, Amelia. I didn't expect you here this early." He holds the door open with his foot.

"I'm on the schedule for first shift and I don't want to leave the girls shorthanded," she says flatly, and quickly averts her eyes, though she can almost feel the heat of his tanned skin as she passes him in the doorway. "Can you please put a shirt on?"

"Oh. Sorry. Of course," he says, though Grady doesn't seem embarrassed to be half-naked in front of her. Amelia remembers walking through a coed dorm on a campus tour of Gibbons;

when the group stopped to look at a study lounge, a boy walked out of the bathroom dressed only in his boxers. He excused himself, completely unselfconsciously, while passing between Amelia and her mother to cross the hall, and his body wasn't even half as good as Grady's. Maybe this is what dorm life does to you?

He holds out a plate balanced in his hand like a waiter. "You hungry?"

"I'm fine," she says, because she's there to work, not hang out, though his eggs do smell good. They're fluffy and cheesy, just how she likes. White toast, too, glistening with melted butter.

"You sure? Eggs are my specialty."

"Boys who can't cook always say that." That's what her home ec teacher used to say, anyway.

"Well, I'm also ace at doctoring up cafeteria ramen. Just give me access to a half-decent salad bar and some hot sauce and I can make ramen magic happen."

"I'd rather we get started."

"Suit yourself." Grady shovels the eggs into his mouth in three bites before setting his plate on a foyer table.

She clears her throat. "Did you get your paper in last night?"

"Yeah. About a minute before midnight." He grabs a T-shirt hanging on a doorknob and slides it over his head. Then he claps his hands once. "I think it's safe to say that the recipes are not in the basement. So let's start clearing the first floor room by room. Cool?"

"Cool."

Amelia begins in the kitchen. She checks every cabinet, empties two junk drawers. She shakes out every cookbook. She drags one of the kitchen chairs over to see the top of the refrigerator.

Nothing.

Meanwhile, she hears Grady rummaging around in the back bedroom. He emerges more disgusted than disheartened.

"What's wrong?"

He almost can't make the words, like he's got a mouth full of sour candy. "Doing a granny-panty raid in my deceased great-aunt's room is not exactly what I had in mind for this summer. Have you finished in here?"

"Almost," she says, stepping down. "I still need to check the pantry."

He opens the pantry door and gasps. "Hells! Yes!"

"What?"

After a fist pump, he reaches in and removes a tin box marked RECIPES. "Boom! We're back in business!"

He pops the lid off and dumps all the index cards onto the table. Amelia joins him and they begin checking each one, front and back, like some kind of matching game. One that, after a minute, they lose.

Grady slumps into a seat. "I really thought . . ."

"Come on. Shake it off," Amelia says. "Where do we try next?"

Amelia follows him into the living room but splits off at the foyer, diligently searching places she is 99.9 percent sure the recipes won't be, like in the pockets of the coats hanging in the hall closet, and tries not to feel disappointed when she comes up with nothing but loose change and lint.

Then she joins Grady, sitting cross-legged on a rug, pulling books out of the bookshelves and fanning through the pages while Grady paws through the drawers of a writing desk.

On the second floor, the air is hotter, drier. By the time she reaches the landing, Amelia can feel the back of her hair sticking to her neck.

Grady quickly reveals what's behind each of the closed black doors they pass as they make their way down a white hallway. "That's the guest bedroom, that's my grandpa's old room, a bathroom, linen closet." At the end, the roof is angled, coming down in two sharp peaks, with one door in the center. "That's Molly's bedroom."

Amelia wrinkles her nose. "I thought you said she slept downstairs."

"She did. This is the one she had when she was a kid. I'm putting you in charge of going through it, for the underwear situation I previously mentioned."

"Whatever you say," she says breezily, though excitement is fizzing inside her. She has the doorknob half turned when she hears Grady open a different door.

"But let's start in here," he says. "I think this is where we've got the best chance."

The room is small and stuffed to the ceiling. There's a desk on top of an oblong braided rug, and a fireplace that's been filled in with red brick. Stacks of cardboard file boxes—the same as the ones Grady had open downstairs—cover every other available bit of space.

"This was her office," Grady says. "Though I don't know how she worked in here, seeing as it's ten degrees hotter than in any other room in the house."

Amelia approaches the desk and pulls on the lower of the two drawers. It's packed tight with green folders. She's not sure she could squeeze in a single piece of paper more if she tried.

"They have to be in here, don't you think?" Grady says, the desperation in his voice obvious. "I mean, clearly she kept everything." He wipes his forehead with his sleeve as he walks

siobhan vivian

toward the one window. "Let me try this again," he says, thrusting his hands upward against the window frame to try and pop it open. The harder he tries, the more embarrassed he gets. "Dammit!"

Amelia comes over with the intention to assist but gets distracted by the perfect view the window provides of the ice cream stand. She checks her watch; it's already a few minutes before eleven. One of the girls, ant-sized, is sitting on top of a picnic table, waiting to be let in. Cate's truck isn't there yet.

Even though it's hot as an oven, Amelia shivers, thinking about Molly Meade standing in this very spot, looking down at them. It had felt, on some level, like the place belonged to the girls, the Meade Creamery girls, since Molly herself was never around. Now Amelia sees how foolish that was. She'd been watching them the whole time.

"Grady, I've got to go and open the stand."

"Doesn't Cate have a key?"

"No." Amelia doesn't say any more. That Cate hadn't wanted hers.

"Well, I have to go to the bank, so why don't I let them in, and give them the heads-up that I'll need you up here for a couple of hours. On my way home, I'll swing by Walmart and grab us a fan for up here. I'll try to be back as quickly as I can."

Amelia nods. "Okay."

Grady hurries down the stairs, and a few minutes later, Amelia hears the engine of the pink Cadillac turn over. From the window, she keeps her eyes on Grady, now back to his classic handsome in jeans and a navy-and-green-striped polo shirt, as he races down to the stand and unlocks the door. Cate pulls in right then, ten minutes late, and the two cars pass each other,

Cate and Grady pausing to talk for a moment, before Grady pulls onto the road and Cate parks.

Amelia pulls herself away from the window and returns to the job. She opens a closet and finds more boxes, and potentially the promise of slightly better organization. At the very back, on the bottom, is one box marked *1945*.

The first year of the Meade Creamery stand.

Amelia wrestles it out, hope fluttering inside her heart. Inside are lots of scraps of paper, old time cards from the punch clock, invoices, a receipt for Molly's Emery Thompson ice cream maker, which cost her eight hundred dollars. Amelia is surprised it was so expensive—weren't movies like fifty cents back then?—but clearly the machine was worth every penny.

But no recipes.

Amelia does, however, find a photo—black and white, scalloped edges—of the girls from that first summer, posed in front of the ice cream stand, flexing their scooping muscles, big wide smiles. They must have been excited, on the cusp of something new, lined up in crisp white blouses instead of the modern polos.

Amelia's phone rings. It's Cate.

"How's it going up there?" she asks.

Amelia slumps backward, against the wall. "I don't know when I'm going to be down today. Do you want me to call one of the other girls? Get someone to cover for me?"

"It's fine. If we get swamped at lunch, I'll text you. Where are you right now?"

"Sitting in Molly's office, sweating my butt off. Hold on." Amelia puts the phone down and peels off her Meade Creamery polo. It's way cooler in just her bra.

siobhan vivian

"Are you having fun? I'd think you'd love going through her stuff."

"I'm too stressed to enjoy it." Suddenly the air on the line sounds weird. "Cate?"

Amelia's phone rings again, but this time, not with a call: a video chat. She slides her finger across the screen and sees Cate in the stand office, her feet up on the desk.

"Is that some kind of new uniform Grady's having you try out?" Cate cackles.

"Shush up! I just took it off. I told you, it's a million degrees up here!"

"Relax, I'm just teasing. Come on. Show me something."

"Like what?"

"I don't know! I want to see her house!"

Amelia reverses the camera and pans the office.

"Boring. What else?"

Amelia almost doesn't say it. "Well, her childhood bedroom is across the hall."

"Why are you holding out on me?"

Amelia bites her finger. "Okay, hold on." Aiming the camera in front of her, she walks down the hall. She turns the knob and pushes the door wide open.

"Holy crap," says Cate.

It's a big, dreamy space with six-paned windows on both sides of the sloping ceiling. One has views of the roadside and the other overlooks the back fields. Molly clearly got the best room in the house, likely because she was the Meades' only girl.

Amelia walks over to the vanity. It's neatly arranged with dozens of thick glass bottles, ceramic tubs, a tortoise comb. A square gold compact with pink pressed powder sits next to a bottle of Mavis talcum powder. There are two Revlon lipsticks in colors named Rosy Future and Bright Forecast. That had to be, Amelia thinks, some marketing strategy for the girls left at home during World War II. She picks up a pineapple-shaped glass bottle of deep amber liquid with a tiny pink bow fastened just under the nozzle. The name sends her eyes rolling—*Vigny's Beau Catcher*—though she's curious enough to take a sniff. The scent is warm and sweet. Orange blossoms and honeysuckle and sandalwood.

"What's that on her vanity mirror?" Cate asks. "Pictures?"

Amelia sets the perfume down and aims the camera. Wedged into the mirror frame are more black-and-white photos. Molly and her girlfriends at the lake. Molly holding a baby calf.

"Any of that hottie Wayne Lumsden?" Cate asks.

"No. Maybe because it was too painful to see his picture," Amelia reasons.

"Closet, please!" Cate says.

Inside are the most gorgeous clothes. Silk and satin party dresses with billowing skirts, day dresses in crisp cotton, tea-length skirts, soft blouses. Wedge sandals and pointy high heels. A woven straw sun hat.

"Anything else?" Cate asks, a little bored.

Amelia spins around and walks toward Molly's four-poster bed. It's twin-sized, with one pancake pillow and white sheets with yellow scalloped edges that are hand-sewn. Her quilt is gorgeous, a checkerboard of pastel squares that make flower shapes and sunbursts on white backing. Next to that is a nightstand, white wood, with one pull drawer and a pink glass knob.

"It's kind of weird, don't you think?" Amelia muses. "This looks like the room of someone who died during high school, not who lived until she was almost ninety."

"Hey, Amelia, try lifting up her mattress!"

"Why?"

"Because that's where girls keep their secrets!"

Amelia turns her phone around so Cate sees her. "What secrets do you keep under your mattress?"

"Wouldn't you like to know!" Cate says coyly. "Come on! The recipes could be there!"

Amelia sets the phone down on the carpet and kneels on the floor next to the bed. The mattress is heavy, but she manages to lift it a few inches.

"Anything?" Cate asks.

Amelia stares down at a pale pink and clothbound book, the word DIARY stamped in gold script on the cover.

"Nope," Amelia says, letting it fall. And then, quickly, "Hey, Cate, I should go. The sooner I find these recipes, the sooner I can come back down. Text me if things get busy."

"Don't forget to put your shirt back on before Grady gets home," Cate teases.

The diary has that old-book smell that's hard to describe. Amelia flips through it without reading. The paper feels brittle against her fingers. The pages were probably white once, but they've turned something closer to khaki. The handwriting is a neater, crisper version of Molly's familiar old-lady cursive.

Amelia knows she shouldn't. Molly Meade was so private. But Cate's right, Molly's diary may be the key to finding the recipes. Curiosity tugging at her, she turns to the first page.

September 22, 1944

Every other boy was already on the bus, hidden behind fogged-up windows, though some had wiped space off for a last goodbye wave to their families. The bus driver had one boot up on the tire, one boot on the street, while Tiggy tried to make small talk with the driver, bless her, to give Wayne and me a few seconds more together.

"You know, the sooner I leave, the faster I'll be back." He said it as a joke, but I started to cry. He was ready to go. Eager to fight. And I didn't want to let him.

"Promise me," I said. "Promise me you'll come back."

"Of course I will, Moll Doll," he said, taking my face in his hands, wiping away my tears with his thumbs. He kissed me on the lips, then brought my hand to his mouth and kissed it, almost on top of the engagement ring. Though I didn't realize it at the time, this was a trick to make me let go of him.

And then, suddenly, I was cold. I closed my coat and watched Wayne bound onto the

siobhan vivian

*bus, giving the driver a chummy clap on the
shoulder as he passed.*

*We walked home. Tiggy had to lead me
because I'd forgotten the way. She kept
saying it would get easier, but never easy.
On some level, I knew it. My brothers have
been gone a year already. Tiggy's brother
nearly two. But this time, it's different.*

This is my love.

The realness, the rawness of the emotion have Amelia shaking like a leaf. She looks up from the page. Would Molly have wanted this? Some stranger, in her bedroom, reading what would turn out to be the most painful experience of her life?

No. Absolutely not. No girl would.

Except . . . what if Molly wrote the recipes inside? There is a good chance of this. The timing is right.

Amelia carefully thumbs through the entire diary, gently, scanning each page. Not reading, but allowing her gaze to land lightly here and there, a word, a number, something recorded in a way that resembles a recipe or a list of ingredients. If she finds something, she'll pull out the relevant pages, show Grady only what he needs to see and maintain Molly's privacy.

When she reaches the end, she goes back through once more, just to be sure.

But no, there's nothing.

And yet she can't bring herself to put the diary back under Molly's bed.

CHAPTER TWENTY

GRADY AND AMELIA SPEND THE REST OF THE DAY DIG-ging through Molly's office. The fan he's bought doesn't provide relief so much as a disappointingly warm wind, but she is grateful that Grady locks it so it blows primarily in her direction.

At the end of first shift, Cate texts Amelia and lets her know that she and a few of the other girls are heading to the lake, and does Amelia want to come with?

Ugh. I should stay and keep looking. But hopefully I can meet you guys there in a bit! Amelia knows it's a stretch. It's not as if they seem any closer to finding anything. But she is trying to remain hopeful.

She readies herself for a bit of pushback from Cate. Maybe a guilt trip that Cate had to work the whole shift without her, or a bit of teasing.

But Cate doesn't even respond.

Amelia has been attacking the oldest files, Grady the newest.

Grady moves with assembly-line speed, setting aside any-thing he thinks might be helpful for his business plan, send-ing everything else through his brand-new shredder, which he picked up with the fan at Walmart.

Amelia winces every time the shredder's blades whirl. This takes care of any lingering remorse she might feel about slipping Molly's diary inside her tote bag.

But Grady is making better time with the job, that's for sure. Amelia's pace is far slower, in part because her boxes contain more mementos and ephemera, especially the ones from the late 1940s and early 1950s, when Molly was just starting out. She's tempted to read everything. And Amelia can't determine what, if anything, she should shred. An ad in the *Sand Lake Ledger* from 1947? A certificate of recognition from the Sand Lake Chamber of Commerce?

And what about all the photos? Of summer picnics at the farmhouse, of the girls at the county fair, and what seems like an annual tradition of the stand girls posing in front of Meade Creamery, their scooping arms flexed, exactly like they had the first year in business. *Why did that end?* she wonders, and examines the faces in each one, looking to spot town residents, noticing how hairstyles changed, in curls one summer, up another, then cut into bobs. Eventually, she sets them aside in a separate, neat pile. Grady might throw them away eventually, or shred them, but she's not going to be the one to do that.

While she tries to lose herself in the work, her thoughts drift back to Molly's first diary entry. Her goodbye kiss with Wayne. Even though Amelia doesn't think she ever actually heard

Molly's voice, she can imagine it now, somewhere faintly inside her, urging him to promise to come back to her, with no idea that it would be the last time she ever laid eyes on him.

Amelia's eyes begin to tear, her throat tighten. A tear rolls down her cheek.

It is so tragically romantic.

"Whoa," Grady says, his blue eyes intent on her. "You okay?"

"Ugh. It's so dusty in here," she complains, dabbing at her eyes with her sleeve and shifting the direction of the fan, and only then does she peek over at Grady to see if he's bought her performance. Only he's not watching her anymore.

Grady's got a bundle of papers in his lap.

And from his stunned blinking, Amelia assumes they are *something*.

"What did you find?" she asks, crawling toward him.

He glances up, startled. And as Amelia nears, he seems to want to hide whatever's in his hands.

"Grady?"

"These are letters my mom sent to Molly."

Amelia sucks in a breath. "Whoa. I bet she'll get such a kick out of seeing them. You should send them to her!" Grady lowers his head and rubs the back of his neck, which makes Amelia feel suddenly unsure. "I mean, maybe wait until she's home from New Zealand. I don't know how much international postage costs. Probably a lot."

He wets his lips. "These are from my *real* mom," he explains. "She died when I was six. My dad married Quinn a year or so later. That's who raised me, basically."

Avoiding her eyes, he passes over a stack of envelopes held together by an old rubber band. They're addressed to Molly

Meade. The return address is from a Diana Denton-Meade.

"Oh."

"She got cancer. The summer she and I spent in Sand Lake was her last one."

She passes the letters back to him. Maybe this, and not the heat, is why Grady's confined himself to one room of the farmhouse. "I'm so sorry."

"It's fine. I've tried not to think too much about it."

Except Amelia knows he has thought about it, at least once. The moment he tasted Home Sweet Home. The sadness she saw in those lake eyes.

Grady sets the bundle on the mantel and goes back to flipping through a bank ledger. Maybe he'll read them once she's gone.

Or maybe he won't.

By the end of the night, what sounds like a thousand crickets are chattering away in the dark, and they still haven't found the recipes. Grady says, tiredly, "I'll drive you home."

Outside, it's much cooler. Almost cold. The girls have already placed the evening deposit bag with the receipts in the mailbox. Grady sticks it in his waistband, then loads Amelia's bike into the trunk of the pink Cadillac while she climbs into the passenger side. The seats are deep and made of smooth tan leather.

On the way down the driveway, Amelia says, "We should probably check the stock. See how much the girls sold today."

Grady doesn't slow down. "I'd rather not."

So Amelia directs him to her house. His mind seems to be elsewhere, but he does make the correct turns. He pulls up to the curb and she asks him, "Have you asked your dad? Would he know something about the recipes?" Grady shakes his head nervously, as if answering both questions at once, and puts the car in park. Amelia tries again. "Well, maybe he'll have some advice for you about what to do."

"Come on. You don't need a business degree to know that an ice cream shop can't stay open without ice cream to sell."

"Right, but—"

"Here's the thing, Amelia. I can't fail." He leans back, his hands in his lap, and stares at the roof of the Cadillac, his shoulders sagging like he already has.

It's clear Grady has a weird relationship with his dad. And he has his own emotional ties to Meade Creamery. But do those things add up to this level of anxiety? Because Grady's making it seem like Meade Creamery going under is on par with the end of the world.

She thinks of Cate's warning. Grady could be trying to play her.

"I don't want the stand to fail either. This place is as important to me as it is to you." Amelia is almost sure their reasons are different. But what does that matter now?

He rolls his head toward her. "So what do we do?"

She closes her eyes and takes a deep breath. "How hard do you think it is to make ice cream?"

He shrugs. "I wouldn't know."

"It's not like Molly had any formal training. We have her whole setup. And most of the ingredients. Her strawberry jam. Her fudge sauce. The vanilla beans she has soaking in that random syrup. Maybe we can find ice cream recipes that use those ingredients and see how close we can get."

"What about Home Sweet Home?"

"Home Sweet Home will probably stay a mystery," she con-

siobhan vivian

cedes, getting out of the car. "But three out of four flavors would be enough to keep the stand in business. Meanwhile, we keep looking for the recipes. We'll find them eventually."

Calling after her, Grady says, "You're making this sound easy."

She calls back, "Look for green lights, not stop signs, remember?"

For the first time that day, Grady laughs. "What idiot told you that?"

Amelia's mom is still awake when she comes through the door.

"Oh. You waited up?"

"No. I was coming to get some water. Cate dropped you off?"

"Yes," Amelia lies, because she doesn't want to get into it right now. She glances at her phone. There's still no text from Cate. Not since her afternoon invitation to the lake. "Well . . . good night."

Upstairs, Amelia gets ready for bed. She texts Cate Sorry I never made it and then brushes her teeth.

Cate's response comes as Amelia moves on to flossing. Any luck?

No. Hopefully tomorrow.

Amelia carries her phone back into her bedroom, watching as Cate types a response. And then Cate stops. It takes another few seconds—until Amelia climbs into bed and pulls the blankets up to her chin—before Cate types again.

K.

Amelia sets her phone down. Cate's clearly annoyed with her, probably because she was abandoned for an entire shift today. And since she just volunteered to try making ice cream tomorrow, there's a good chance Amelia won't be around for that shift, either.

The best thing that could happen, on all fronts, is that Amelia finds the recipes ASAP.

Though she's tired, she opens Molly's diary and begins reading.

November 29, 1944

I've been trying to help Daddy with his chores, not that he lets me do any real work, even though everything is falling behind without Liam and Pat and now Wayne around. He threw me out of the barn yesterday—that's how much he did not enjoy the sight of his only daughter dripping with sweat during the first dusting of snow, shoveling a knee-deep pile of dung in the cow stalls. I can't say I enjoyed it either, but he needs help and I desperately want to do something. Being physical did ease some of the heartache for me, calluses aside.

But no, Daddy says my job is to be a comfort to Mother.

I would really like nothing more. Except Mother steeps herself in her sadness like her tea, never lifting the bag out, letting the hot water go black and bitter and cold. I don't blame her. She has so many worries. My brothers and Wayne. The business. Daddy. Me.

siobhan vivian

The only time she is happy is when she's making wedding plans for Wayne and me. Tiggy thinks I'm a fool because I've let her take the reins on pretty much everything, but if I didn't, I don't know if she'd ever smile.

Amelia turns the page, intending to read the next entry, but her eyes can't quite focus. Her Molly Meade history lesson will have to wait until tomorrow.

CHAPTER  TWENTY-ONE

AMELIA'S NOT SURE IF IT'S AN OMEN OR A SIGN OR what, exactly, but she skids her bike to an abrupt stop about half-way between the stand and the farmhouse, sure as anything that Molly Meade is gazing down on her right this moment.

The wild grasses on this stretch of the driveway grow nearly as tall as Amelia, and as dense as a thicket on both sides. Blossoming among the tall grass are hundreds of wildflowers in a rainbow of colors and textures and sizes. This, she's seen many times over the years, but never as it is in this moment.

It's just after seven, and the morning dew still clings to every-thing, a sparkling coat refracting the sunshine like the dust of a thousand diamonds.

Goose bumps prick on her arms and legs.

Amelia sees now why Molly brought flowers for the girls each and every time she brought new ice cream down to the stand. How could anyone pass this and not try to capture some of the beauty? Of course, by the time the girls rolled into work at eleven, the dew had long disappeared, and they were left with pretty blooms arranged for them in a mason jar—a simple thank-you from their boss.

She puts down her kickstand and walks toward the brush, finding the most beautiful flowers and pinching their stems. She makes a bouquet of pink and yellow cone flowers, and foxtail lilies and bee balm. It's too much to hold and try to steer her handlebars, so she leaves her bike where it is.

She doesn't bother turning on the lights. She finds the mason jar on top of the filing cabinet, fills it with water, and arranges the bouquet inside. On the back of a paper napkin, she writes,

Have a great day, girls!
Xox,
Amelia

Grady has left the inside door of the farmhouse open, and Amelia steps though the screen door gingerly, careful not to let Moo out. There's music coming up through the floor.

She descends halfway to the basement and sees Grady at the sink, one of Molly's frilly aprons tied around his waist. The record player is spinning, the volume turned up loud; some old crooner is singing in rich tones that fill the basement.

Grady hasn't heard her come in, so she watches from the stairs. He's shimmying, dancing in a modern way, almost a pop and lock, to the old music. It is, quite frankly, adorable. She bets Grady would be a fun date at a dance. Hardly any boys from her high school danced at prom. Never to any fast songs, and even for the slow ones, they had to be dragged to the dance floor.

Grady's got a big stock pot on Molly's stove, the blue gas flame turned up high. There are grocery bags at his feet, filled with gallons of milk and cream. Amelia watches as he cracks an egg and slides it into the smoking cream stew.

He is making ice cream.

The record ends and the needle begins to click as it continues to spin. Grady looks up from his pot, wanting to change it, but his hands are full. Amelia decides then to reveal herself, and takes a couple of steps down.

"Nice apron," she teases.

"I'm hoping it will bring me luck."

"When did you get all this stuff?"

"I drove to Walmart after I dropped you off last night," he says, and Amelia flushes, realizing just how persuasive she'd been last night. "Thought it'd be nice to take a break from the book-keeping this morning and do something fun."

"You don't find bookkeeping fun? I figured that was manda-tory for a business major."

He pulls a face. "Um, no. No one does." He holds up his phone. "Now, this is a recipe for the 'Perfect Vanilla' ice cream, accord-ing to the *New York Times*. Figured that'd be a good place to start. I mean, if it's in the newspaper, it's got to be fact-checked."

Amelia leans over the side of the big stock pot as Grady cracks another egg. It is filled to the brim. "Should it be bub-bling that much?"

"Shit." Grady turns down the flame.

"I'll head back upstairs and keep searching."

"Great." He licks the back of a spoon and smiles, proud of him-self. "Maybe I'll get good at this and I can create a brand-new

siobhan vivian

flavor! We can launch it this summer. Come up with a cool name."

"I admire your confidence," Amelia says.

Moo follows Amelia up to the second floor. The letters Grady found yesterday sit unopened on the mantel. There's a big stack of boxes still to go through, but Amelia lies down on the braided rug, kicks off her Keds, and begins to read Molly Meade's diary, planning to read one or maybe two entries before she gets started.

An hour later, she's read though Christmas, then New Year's, and is approaching Valentine's Day.

> *February 13, 1945*
>
> *I've never spent Valentine's Day alone before. Of course, I'd rather be with Wayne—he went all out last year, candy, flowers, a pair of earrings—but I am excited about going to the movies with Tig. Coney Island with Betty Grable finally made it to Sand Lake.*
>
> *There's no pressure. No need for a new dress, to put on makeup or a girdle. We're going to eat all the popcorn we want.*
>
> *Hopefully the line will be long enough that I miss the newsreel. If not, I guess I'll just close my eyes.*

Sand Lake used to have its own movie theater? It had to be on Main Street, but where? Amelia's only ever seen movies at the thirteen-screen megaplex in Beaumont. Amelia loves that theater—they have a whole wall of candy you buy by the pound—but it would be so cool if Sand Lake still had a single-screen theater. In fact, she might prefer it, because she and Cate could walk there, and parking at the megaplex is always a zoo.

She reads on, and winter turns into spring.

April 1, 1945

On Sunday, Holy Redeemer had a tag sale for the war effort. Mother wanted to hunt for things for my trousseau, and I dragged Tiggy along with us.

We'll receive presents from the guests, of course, but Mother wants to make sure I have the essentials covered, everything Wayne and I will supposedly need to start our lives together when he comes home.

It's funny. I used to dream about this moment. One of my favorite games to play growing up was "house." I'd drape two tablecloths over the dining table and then I'd select things of Mother's as if I were shopping in a department store. I always took the candy dish from the living room, always her apron with the embroidered strawberries, the gold hand mirror on her dressing table, the iron. When Daddy would come in for his lunch, he'd eat his sandwich

siobhan vivian

in there with me, and I'd keep his coffee cup full like a doting wife.

Mother had me by the elbow for most of the afternoon, holding things up for me, asking my opinion, debating what was most essential. I felt as if we were asking for something bad to happen, tempting fate, but to be agreeable, I said yes to everything, which really annoyed her. I'm not sure why. And I don't know how strong one's opinions could be about a bathroom scale.

Eventually, things got so uncomfortable between us, Tiggy pretended to have left her purse on one of the tables and the two of us broke away and walked around by ourselves for a while.

I found an ice cream maker, a deep wooden bucket with a metal cap and a large handle you crank in a circle. When I asked Mrs. Finch if it still worked, she pinched my arm and said it takes a lot of cranking, and warned me to go easy on it. I wouldn't want to surprise Wayne looking like an Atlas Man when he came home.

Tiggy thought my idea of playing around with it was a bit wacky, but the truth is that

I can't bear the thought of sitting home for
one more miserable Saturday night. Our
friends have the same trouble. Going out
for Coca-Colas or to see a movie only
makes us feel guilty that we are here
while the boys are over there. I don't
have this problem with Wayne, of course,
but everyone's deathly afraid to be seen
by the parents of their sweethearts having
anything that resembles fun.

Maybe we can churn away our loneliness.
And even if we can't, at least there'll be
ice cream.

Amelia rubs her fingers across the page, feeling the grooves from Molly pressing her pen tip against the paper, collapsing the distance between then and now.

This is the day when Meade Creamery began.

She can't turn pages fast enough, reading about those early ice cream nights on the lake, how every week more and more girls showed up. Molly wasn't thinking about starting a business, only an excuse to be with her friends. It's amazing how little has changed between then and now. Meade Creamery, in whatever form, has always been a place where girls come together, support each other, thanks to Molly.

Eventually, Amelia reads an entry from May 3, 1945, about a month into Molly's ice cream nights. Molly writes about a new recipe with unconventional ingredients to substitute for the rationed sugar, and it's a huge hit with the girls.

siobhan vivian

This has to be Home Sweet Home.

Amelia's so close, yet heartbreakingly far. Molly didn't leave a clue, not a single hint, of what she put in that batch.

She lays the diary down and texts Cate. It's right around the start of Cate's shift. How's it going down there?

Great! I stopped at Rite Aid and bought a lipstick that I saw in Elle. It's supposedly a "universally flattering pink" so we're putting it to the test.

Ooooh! Lemme see!

Cate texts Amelia a picture that could be an advertisement, the three girls cuddled together. Cate's holding up the lipstick tube, and the shade is bright, a couple of notches away from electric. On Mansi, it's a shiny shade of coral. Bern's lips look perfectly bee-stung. Cate is prettiest of all, sandwiched in the middle, her blond hair unbraided and mussed, her lips a deep glossy rose.

Amelia feels a sudden ache in her chest.

What brand is it?

She waits a minute for Cate to text back and then goes to the window. The line of customers is long. This gives Amelia an acute sense of dread. The more customers they have, the quicker their ice cream stock will go.

And then, slowly, as if awakening from a dream, Amelia becomes aware of Grady calling her name, his footfalls on the stairs. She has barely a second to hide the diary in her tote bag before he bursts in.

"Amelia! I've been shouting—come help me downstairs! And grab every towel you can find in the linen closet."

"Grady, your feet!"

His black Adidas are covered in thick white glop. Moo jumps

down from the desk and licks the footprints he's left in the hallway.

Amelia does as Grady has asked, filling her arms with towels, and follows him as he speeds back down to the basement, where Molly Meade's Emery Thompson ice cream machine is spurting like a fountain, a geyser of half-frozen white ice cream spewing out from the top hatch, the spout, pretty much anywhere there's an opening.

Grady has set an empty cardboard drum underneath the spout, but it has long since filled, and as the ice cream continues to flood out like soft-serve, it splashes down in a frothy white cascade onto the floor.

"Shit! My phone!" he says, slipping as he lunges toward the counter. He fishes a dripping rectangle out of the spillage on the counter, which is oozing down the front of the cabinets and making a pool on the floor.

"Turn the machine off!" she shouts. The spill is icy on her feet. Like stepping into a slushy winter puddle with bare feet.

"I did, but it won't stop coming!"

Amelia reaches over and pulls the plug. A few more chugs, a few more spews, and the machine comes to rest.

Grady shakes his head, stunned. "I followed the recipe exactly, except I upped the quantities to make three gallons' worth. But I double-checked my math. I don't know what happened."

"Grady! When you freeze something, it expands. Three gallons of liquid in won't be three gallons of frozen ice cream out!"

After a pitiful breath, Grady takes a taste of the ice cream with his finger. He winces and gags. "That's maybe the worst thing I've ever tasted."

Amelia carefully carries the three-gallon drum, full to the brim, over to the sink. She tips it in and runs the hot water.

siobhan vivian

"Don't help me clean up. Just go back upstairs and keep looking."

Amelia swallows. She hasn't done much today besides read Molly's diary. "It will go way faster if I help you."

It takes the better part of an hour to get the kitchen back to decent shape.

"Is there a manual for this thing?" Amelia asks. "I wonder how you're supposed to clean it."

"If there is, I haven't found it."

Amelia Googles Emery Thompson, hoping she can find some instructions online.

She finds better. It turns out that Emery Thompson has been making ice cream machines for over a hundred years. And their website is full of useful information: recipes, video demonstrations, and troubleshooting Q&As.

Grady gathers up a full trash bag. "I have to go upload some discussion questions for one of my summer classes, but then I'll start over." He shakes his head, like that's the last thing he wants to do. "My friends rented scooters and are tooling around Milan tonight on a guided street food tour. And instead I'm here, destroying a business that's been in my family for generations."

"Why don't I try making the next batch?"

He looks sincerely grateful. "By all means." He places a hand on her shoulder and playfully says, "You can't do worse than I did." As he lifts it off, his fingers graze her neck every so slightly, and Amelia finds herself holding her breath. She doesn't exhale until he's gone.

She sits down on the couch and cues up a video from the Emery Thompson website called Ice Cream 101. Just as it starts playing, she gets a text from Cate.

Hey. Any chance you can come down here for a sec?

Shoot. Terrible timing. Amelia presses Pause and types back Why? Are you slammed?

No. I want you to try this lipstick!

Amelia doesn't feel like she can tell Cate no. So she slips out and hurries down to the stand.

She's a few feet from the door when she hears the girls squealing and laughing and singing along to the radio. Amelia's relieved everything's okay, though she feels a little pang of jealousy, at how much fun they're having without her.

But her heart sinks as she steps inside. Cate has the stand radio turned up loud enough that customers have to shout their orders over the music. The trash can is overflowing, the order windows are greasy with fingerprints. No one is looking at her chore chart, that's for sure.

Amelia could stay down here and clean up the mess before returning to the farmhouse. But she did just promise Grady that she'd get to work on the ice cream. That's just as important, if not more so, than what's happening down at the stand. Isn't it?

Thankfully, none of the girls even noticed Amelia come in.

Or, just as quickly, slip back out.

CHAPTER  TWENTY-TWO

AMELIA TWISTS HER HAIR INTO A TIGHT BUN AND secures it with an elastic. She selects one of Molly's aprons, a peach cotton one with tiny embroidered strawberries running along the edges, less for the mess and more for the luck it might bring her.

She begins with a simple batch of vanilla. With the help of the ice cream videos, she can see where Grady's attempt went wrong, aside from his measuring.

A few places, actually.

He slid in the eggs too fast, into cream that was too hot. And he didn't allow his base to properly chill before running it through the machine.

Whether she'll do any better remains to be seen.

Her hands are shaking as she measures out the ingredients

she'll need, but she's comforted by the fact that Molly Meade didn't know what she was doing at first either. Amelia knows this for sure. She read it in Molly's own words.

Sugar, skim milk powder, and fresh milk go into the saucepan. The last time she touched a whisk, she was making cupcakes for Cate's birthday from a boxed mix, but she grabs one and has at it while the mixture froths and bubbles.

When she thinks everything is well blended, she whisks hard for another minute longer, just to make sure. Next comes the cream, next one vanilla bean she fishes out from the sticky brown syrup with her fingers. She stares at a thermometer, waiting for the thin red needle to rise until it hits 110 degrees. The eggs get whisked in a separate bowl, and she uses a little dollop of the hot cream mixture to warm them. She slides the eggs in and brings up the heat, then swiftly removes the saucepan from the stove.

One of the videos recommended steeping this mixture—the base—for at least twenty-four hours for maximum flavor, but there's no time for that. Anyway, this is just a test. She's pretty sure it won't be anywhere near good enough.

From another video, she learns that there's a difference between the two refrigerators in Molly's kitchen. One is a blast chiller, which cools down the bases after they've been pasteurized; the other is a deep freezer, basically a smaller version of the walk-in down at the stand, which hardens the ice cream up after the base is run through the machine. Amelia never knew there were so many complex intricacies to making ice cream. Molly Meade was practically a scientist.

Since Amelia is making a small batch, just to see if she can even do it, she doesn't think she needs to leave it in the blast chiller for the full hour the video recommends. Instead, she sets an alarm on her phone for thirty minutes. She puts on one of Molly's old records, the Andrews Sisters, counts the grooves, and lines up the needle with "Rum and Coca-Cola," a song she knows from the oldies station. She dances while cleaning up her mess, loving the nostalgic crackle it has. The songs after, she's never heard before. "Let There Be Love." "I'll Be with You in Apple Blossom Time." "Last Night on the Back Porch."

When she finishes cleaning up, there's about ten minutes left on the timer. She goes upstairs to Molly's office.

She could, and probably should, sort through the contents of one more banker's box. But her mind hinges back to the diary.

May 27, 1945

After V-E Day, everyone in Sand Lake is cautiously optimistic that the war will end soon. But fear still darkens me most days.

Here are my three greatest worries.

1. Wayne will die and we will never be married.

2. One or both of my brothers will die and my family—my mother in particular—will never recover.

3. Our dairy will not survive.

On a good day, I can mostly push them out of my head. But lately, it's been harder. And this week, I've been in a sheer panic.

I haven't gotten a letter from Wayne since the beginning of May.

The girls go out of their way to tell me what a mess the mail service is over there, with the boys getting moved around so much. Or how Sylvia Schur hadn't heard from Neil George for weeks, only to get a bundle of five letters at once.

I have kept writing to him anyway. That's the only thing I can do. I write my brothers, too, every Sunday, even though they never write me back, just Mother.

Making ice cream for the girls is my only relief right now. When I'm not, I'm sour as a lemon. And I know I've been terrible to Tiggy. Bless her, she lets me have my moments.

If I get a letter, everything will be OK.

Please, God, send him home to me.

When the batch is done, Amelia scoops a ball into a teacup and brings it upstairs. Grady is back at work in the living room, intensely

siobhan vivian

typing on his laptop; his brow is furrowed, and he's muttering quietly to himself. He reminds her of how her mom and her dad look every year around tax time. Like they are having no fun at all.

"I have something for you to try."

"Hey!" He shuts his laptop. "Is that what I think it is?" His blues brighten as he bolts up, hurdles the coffee table, and races over to her.

"Please don't be excited. I mean, it's edible. But it's not very good."

He takes the spoon. "Amelia! What are you talking about? This is great! You've conquered vanilla!"

"It's not," she insists. "Take another taste, but this time, rub the ice cream against the roof of your mouth." Grady does as instructed. "Do you taste those little waxy pieces?"

"Yeah."

"That means I let it churn too long. Also, it barely tastes like vanilla. Molly's vanilla was like . . . *pow*. Mine is a whisper." She sighs. "I want to cook up another batch, but I need more ingredients."

"I'll head to the store right now," and his enthusiasm makes her laugh. "Anything else I can do?"

"Keep looking for the recipes when you get back," Amelia says. "And pray for rain."

CHAPTER TWENTY-THREE

TURNS OUT THERE ARE LOTS OF WAYS TO SCREW UP ICE cream. Turns out it's not easy to make something not just good, but deliciously good. Molly's ice creams, Amelia realizes now, are deceptively simple. There's chocolate and then there's *chocolate*, like comparing a Hershey's Kiss with a Godiva truffle. And though her failures gives her a newfound respect for Molly, it's also incredibly frustrating, because she is so painfully far from getting it right.

Still, she keeps at it for the rest of the day, batch after batch, cycling through all aspects of the process, cooking up a new base with ingredients slightly tweaked from the last, while another batch cools in the blast chiller, while another one churns inside the ice cream maker. Repeat, repeat, repeat. Her arms feel heavier than after gym class push-ups, and her lower back aches from standing. And yet, time passes like magic. Hours feel like minutes, minutes feel like nothing.

If the learning curve weren't so steep, Amelia might believe she was getting somewhere.

There is no eyeballing, no freestyling, the way her dad likes to in the kitchen, a pinch of this, a glug of that. Making ice cream isn't cooking, it's chemistry. Unfortunately, Amelia got a B in chemistry her sophomore year, unjustly she believed, and she never forgave Mr. Dunlap for it, returning his hellos with a frown for the rest of high school once she got her report card. Now she knows a B was too generous. Cringing, she thinks about apologizing to him the next time he comes to the stand, maybe even paying for his order out of her tips.

Take chocolate. Add too much of Molly's homemade fudge sauce and the ice cream is thin and runny. Too little, and the chocolate flavor is nothing but an undertone, muted by other ingredients. Or it might taste decent as a finished base out of the blast chiller, but once it goes through the ice cream machine, the flavor is cloudy.

And that's just the flavoring. If the measurement of *any* ingredient isn't just right, the ice cream comes out gritty, or buttery, or eggy.

Timing is also a huge issue. Churn it too little in the ice cream machine and it pours out a slushy mess that won't ever firm up, no matter how long you put it in the deep freezer. Churn it too long and the ice cream comes out solid as a brick, hard enough to snap a plastic spoon in half.

It's an almost-impossible puzzle that Amelia must solve three different times, for vanilla, chocolate, and strawberry.

And Home Sweet Home? She doesn't even know where to start with that one.

The clock is ticking, and the remaining stock dwindling.

Grady comes down looking somber. "I have bad news."

"What?" Amelia doesn't take her eyes off the whirling ice cream machine, like a kid too close to the television. The batch she's churning now is the closest she's come. Good dark color, good depth of chocolateyness when the base went in.

"I've gone through all the boxes upstairs. No recipes." His voice is almost toneless, resigned.

It's all on her now.

Amelia pushes the lever and a stream of ice cream comes sliding out the chute.

Grady asks, "Can I try?"

But Amelia sees something she doesn't like. The color is . . . off. She takes a taste and knows immediately. It's tainted. "I forgot to clean the machine out from the last batch of strawberry I ran."

"Chocolate and strawberries go together, though, right? That's a thing!" Grady says, trying to be helpful.

She bites her lip and stares up at the ceiling, hoping to keep the tears in her eyes from spilling down her cheeks. She made a dumb mistake because she's tired. But there's no time for dumb mistakes. She takes the entire drum over to the sink and turns on the hot water full blast so the ice cream breaks apart and sinks down the drain.

"Amelia, wait! It could have been good—"

"No. I screwed it up."

He softens his tone when he sees how near to tears she is. "At this point, I think we give up on *right* and aim for *good enough*."

Amelia shakes her head. "I don't know if I can do that."

The front doorbell rings.

siobhan vivian

Jogging upstairs, he says, "You can't let this get personal. It's business."

Amelia leans her hands against the counter, stretches her back. Everything about this business is becoming very personal to her.

"So this is where the magic happens." Cate comes down the stairs.

Amelia rushes over and almost tackles her in a hug. "Cate!"

"I've been texting you all afternoon." Cate squeezes her back, then peels away, concerned. "You're soaked."

Amelia glances down at herself. There are sweat marks on her shirt, from her armpits down to her waist.

"No air-conditioning." She feels woozy and leans against the refrigerator. It's cool against her skin. "What time is it?"

"Six thirty." Cate's tone is clipped. "Have you had dinner yet? Or even lunch?"

"I'll order us some pizza," Grady volunteers, having only made it halfway down the stairs before he pivots and heads back up.

"She might not want pizza," Cate calls back, snippy. And then, to Amelia, "You've been working for how long today? Have you taken even one break?"

"Nine hours? Ten?" Amelia says. "And no, not yet."

Grady descends the basement steps, uneasy. "Pizza's on the way. Cate, do you want to join us?"

"I don't think so," Cate says.

"Oh, and Amelia, I can drive you home tonight, whenever you want to call it quits," Grady offers.

Cate gives a thin-lipped smile to Grady. To Amelia, she says sharply, "Walk me out?"

It feels disorienting to be outside after spending hours in Molly Meade's basement. Amelia takes a deep breath, enjoying the fresh air and the pinkish evening light. "Thanks. I think you're right. I needed this to clear my head."

"Is something going on between you and Grady?"

Amelia startles. "No. I'm . . . just trying to help the stand."

"How do you see this ending?"

"I haven't thought about it."

Cate takes her by the shoulders. "Well, maybe you should? Before you get trapped up here, making ice cream day in and day out like Molly Meade."

"That's not going to happen."

"I know you. You're sensitive, you're caring, and you'll do anything for anybody. Those are the things I love best about you, Amelia, but they also make you vulnerable to getting taken advantage of. You are so invested in this ice cream stand and helping Grady be a success. And you've known him for what? A couple of weeks?"

"I . . . want to figure this out."

Cate shakes her head. "If I'd known it would be like this . . ."

"Like what?"

"Let me ask you something: Is this the summer you wanted? Because I gotta be honest. It's not the one I wanted. I mean, sure, I'm having fun with all the girls, but I wish you were with me."

A lump rises in Amelia's throat. "I know. I do too." Has she let Grady take advantage of her niceness?

"We've worked one week with each other this summer. One. Week. We're short-staffed, I'm picking up all your slack, trying to keep everyone happy and having fun for no thanks, no extra pay. And the reason why I came back was so that we could hang out together! I mean, that's how you said it would be."

"I'm sorry," Amelia whispers.

"What are you even doing down there? Just, like, Franken-steining a bunch of random recipes together?"

"Basically."

"That sounds miserable."

"Except it's really not. Sure, I'm tired. I'm frustrated. But I'm having fun trying to solve this puzzle."

"It's sounds like you have Stockholm syndrome."

"I think I'm getting close."

"To Home Sweet Home?"

"No. I haven't even attempted that one. I'm talking about chocolate. Less so on strawberry. Every batch comes out icy. And with vanilla, I'm still—"

"Will you please listen to yourself? You sound ridiculous!"

Amelia gazes down at her Keds. Yes, she looks terrible. And yes, she was just crying. But this is important to her, and she doesn't understand why Cate's dismissing that. "If I can't get this right, Meade Creamery is going to close. All the girls will be out of jobs."

"When Molly died, I got another job *that same day*. We can get other jobs. So who cares?"

Amelia nods like she concedes Cate's point, even though she does care. She can't explain why, but she cares so freaking much.

Cate continues, "And to be honest, I doubt any of the girls will want to come back after this summer. The freezer is almost empty. You're totally MIA. They know something's up. I'm doing my best to keep Grady's secret, but there's a major undercurrent of *what the hell is going on here*."

Amelia's phone alarm begins to chime. Another batch is ready to go into the ice cream machine. Another chance, hopefully another step closer.

"I promise I will make this up to you! And all the girls, too!" Amelia says, backing away from Cate. But making amends will have to happen later.

Back in the basement, she finds Grady waiting for her, wringing his hands. "Is everything okay?"

"Yeah. It's fine."

"You don't have to stay. I know this is my problem. And I don't want to cause trouble between you and Cate."

"I want to stay," Amelia says. And it feels good to tell someone, even if it's just Grady, that tiny truth.

siobhan vivian

CHAPTER  TWENTY-FOUR

AMELIA LETS HERSELF IN THE NEXT MORNING. SHE'S halfway to the basement door when Grady grabs her hand. "Hey. How about some breakfast? You'll see I wasn't lying about being good at eggs." He pulls her one, two steps toward the kitchen, with a friendly smile.

Amelia imagines Grady in the Truman dorms, the morning after a frat party, making the same pitch to get a girl to cut class and watch TV in his twin bed.

In the next second, she imagines she is that girl.

The thought is intoxicating but also scary. Having that freedom, no parents around watching to make sure she's sleeping in her own bed at night.

But Grady is off-limits. And if there's any line that Amelia absolutely, positively cannot cross, it's that one.

"I'm good, thanks. I'll be downstairs if you need me."

Before starting up another batch, Amelia opens Molly's diary and consults the last entry she read before falling asleep the night before.

June 5, 1945

One of my mother's bridge friends told me about a trick yesterday afternoon. You know you've got a real diamond in your engagement ring if it'll scratch glass.

When I told Tiggy, she said, "Maybe you should check yours."

And I said, "Wayne Lumsden would never propose marriage to me with a fake diamond."

"So, try it," she teased. "Unless you're scared."

The only thing that scared me was how much Tiggy seemed to want my diamond to be fake.

I shouldn't have been surprised. The truth is that Tiggy and Wayne have never gotten along.

Tiggy thinks Wayne's cocky. She's not wrong. He is. But I've always loved his

siobhan vivian

confidence. He seems so much stronger than any of the boys in our grade. I think it's because of what he went through in his family, left to fend for himself at such a young age. When it's just me and him, he's sweet as a kitten, but I've seen him get hot-tempered plenty. Since he shipped out, I've come to think of this as a blessing, because I know Wayne can handle whatever comes his way over there.

But boy oh boy, does he love to tease Tiggy. I wish I'd never told him that it bothers her, because once I did, he seemed to enjoy doing it even more. Sometimes he'll even rib her in the letters he sends to me, knowing I read them out loud to the other girls. Near the end, he'll write something like, "Tell Tig I've been passing her picture around to the single guys in my unit. So far, no takers besides our cook. He's sixty and only has three fingers, but beggars can't be choosers." I am always careful to skip over those parts.

I honestly think they're a bit jealous of each other. Which is silly. I can have room in my life for a best friend and a husband. Anyway, Tiggy wouldn't let it drop, so I slid the ring off my finger and went to the basement window. But before I made a *scratch, I told Tig that, real diamond or not, Wayne and I were getting married.*

And in my next letter, I'm telling Wayne that Tig's agreed to be my maid of honor.

If I get my way, the three of us (plus Tig's future husband, whoever he may be) are going to live Happily Ever After, here in Sand Lake, for the rest of our days.

Setting down the diary, Amelia pulls back the curtains on every basement window until she finds the etching on the glass. *Mrs. Wayne Lumsden.*

There's a loud rumble. Amelia shifts her focus from the scratches to the horizon, thinking it might be a storm rolling in. But the sun is out, there's not a cloud in the sky. Then she realizes the rumbling is Grady's feet on the floor above her, louder as he runs from the living room down the hallway and pulls open the basement door.

Amelia lets go of the curtain. She doesn't have time to hide the diary before Grady's hopping down the stairs two at a time. It's in plain sight, right on the couch.

Luckily, he's too frantic to notice.

"Amelia, I need your help right now." He takes her hand and pulls her back the way he just came.

"What's wrong? What's going on?"

"I just got a text from my dad. He's back in the States. He's on his way over here to check up on me. And if he thinks I'm not doing a good job, he's going to make me sell the place."

siobhan vivian

Her stomach lurches. "Are you serious? I thought your family lived in Chicago."

"He's part of this private jet club. He can go anywhere at any time!" He shakes his head, panting, "Everything needs to be perfect. And I need to look like I'm in charge."

"You are in charge," Amelia reminds him, pointing to the misaligned buttons on his shirt.

Grady gives her a pained stare. "Please help me. If he finds out about the ice cream, that we're days from going out of business . . ."

Amelia wants him to finish. But he's so panicked, her own heart starts to race.

Grady and Amelia grab all his papers and textbooks, shove the pile into the Cadillac, and together they drive everything down to the stand. He can't bear to look at the jalopy of a food truck, still parked in the same place it's been since the day he bought it.

Cate's in the office, her bare feet up on the desk, painting her toenails. She's so startled, she flinches and the bottle almost topples over. "Jesus!"

Luckily, Amelia grabs it just in time. She caps the bottle, opens the window, and tries to waft the smell out. "Grady needs to be in here."

"What?" Cate says, indignant. "Why?"

Grady pushes into the office. "Someone very important is coming." As soon as Cate stands up, he sits down at the desk. He takes out his laptop, spreads out some papers and his textbooks, and smooths his hair, which he has wet and combed down in a way Amelia has not seen before. After frantically assessing the desk, he pulls out the calculator and a pad, then jumps up and grabs the morning receipts, which have already been calculated, but then spreads them out as if they haven't. Sitting back down, he swings a skinny navy necktie around his neck and ties it faster than Amelia would have thought possible.

Cate is watching all this, her back pressed up against the wall, dumbfounded. Still, she manages to keep her freshly painted fingers and toes carefully spread.

"Amelia, make sure everything in the stand is neat and orderly, okay? And that the girls look like they're working hard."

"They *are* working hard," Cate says incredulously. "We always are."

Amelia guides her out, grabbing the mason jar of now-dead flowers on the way and mashing them down into an overflowing trash can. "Just hurry. I'll explain." Glancing around the main area of the stand, she sees that the service windows are both smudgy. She lunges for a bottle of Windex and her feet nearly slip out from under her. "There are sprinkles all over the floor," she says, disappointed. "When was the last time someone swept in here?"

"Seriously?" Cate howls. "It's the middle of a shift. And I'm on my break. Also, I'm not the boss here," she says, pointing to Amelia's flower pin. "You are."

Jen and Bernadette, the two other girls on this shift, are frozen.

"It's okay, everything's fine." Amelia tries to reassure them while simultaneously straightening up and wiping, a tornado of stress. "But Cate and I are going to take over the windows for a little while. Jen, can you please go empty the trash cans? And sweep up these sprinkles, and"—she glances behind her—"Bern, I know we're okay on waffle cones right now, but could you get some more cooking anyway, to get the place smelling yummy?" She takes a deep breath. "And please make sure all of you have your shirts tucked in," she adds, taking her own advice.

"Who the hell is coming?" Cate says, doing the same. "The president?"

Amelia combs her fingers through her hair and glances out the window. "Grady's dad is on his way here," she announces. "So everyone, please . . ." Amelia blanks on how to end her sentence. Because what is she asking them, really? ". . . be on your best behavior."

Not a minute later, a black Mercedes pulls into the stand's driveway.

"Grady," she calls out. "He's here."

Grady pops up beside her and peeks discreetly over her shoulder. "Okay. I'm going outside."

The next few customers Amelia helps, she feels like she's drunk, she has so much adrenaline coursing through her veins. As she hands over a double-scoop cone, she catches a glimpse of Grady greeting his dad out of the corner of her eye. Grady extends his hand for a shake, and his dad obliges.

"How was your vacation?" Grady asks breezily as he leads his dad inside.

"Courses were beautiful. I shot very well." Grady's dad surveys the place down the tip of his nose. "You've been busy."

"I can't believe you came all the way here to surprise me," Grady says, his energy 180 degrees off from where he was a few minutes ago.

"I think you can understand why I felt compelled not to take your word for how well things are going."

Grady's cheeks burn. "Well, I'm glad you're here. I'm excited to show this place off." Except Grady does the opposite. He ushers his dad into the office and closes the door.

"Grady's dad is intense," Cate whispers.

Amelia whispers back, "He's here to spy on him to make sure things are going well."

"Then you'd better make sure he doesn't open our walk-in freezer."

Frowning, Amelia walks over and puts on the purple jacket. Maybe two drums of each flavor are left. "Cate, why didn't you tell me we were so low?" She grabs the clipboard to see, but no one has been filling out the stock sheet.

"Because I didn't want to upset you. And don't even say anything about the clipboard, okay? It's painfully obvious what we have left."

Grady calls out, "Amelia! Can you bring my dad a scoop of each flavor?"

"Coming!"

"Coming!" Cate singsongs, mocking her. "You sound like his secretary."

"I do not," Amelia says, knowing she does.

Amelia makes four junior-sized cups, careful that each flavor is a full, round, beautiful scoop. She stands at the office door, ready to enter, but there's a conversation in progress. She presses her ear to the door.

"What's it like up in the house?" Grady's dad asks.

"Hot," Grady says with a jovial laugh. "But I can take it."

"And the girls aren't distracting you too much?"

"No, no," Grady says. "They stay down here. And I'm up at the farmhouse, working, basically twenty-four-seven."

Amelia frowns. *That's not entirely true, Grady.*

siobhan vivian

"I worried this was going to be a party for you."

"Oh, anything but. Between my online classes and running the business, I don't have time for any distractions."

"And how are they taking to having a man in charge?"

"There've been some growing pains," Grady says with a laugh. "But they know who's boss."

Amelia shakes her head. *What the heck does that mean?*

After a pause, Grady says, "Sorry, Dad. I don't know what's taking her so long with your ice cream. Hey, Amelia!"

Amelia nudges the door open with her foot. "Here you go, Mr. Meade," she says. Grady's dad nods and then leans back, as if she were an inconvenient waitress, to allow her the room to place them on the desk in front of him.

"Frankly, Grady, you're doing better than I expected."

"Thanks, Dad."

"But now you need to be asking yourself how you can take things to the next level. I want you thinking *big*."

"How do you mean?"

"Like your email about raising prices. Your spreadsheet was solid, but you missed opportunities like, say, shrinking your scoop size." He peers into the cups Amelia arranges before him, and then up at her with a pressed smile. "How many ounces is this, dear?"

She bristles. "Four."

"See? Go down to three. You'll get however many more scoops per three-gallon drum, at a higher price."

"So . . . give them less and charge more?"

Every muscle inside Amelia clenches tight. Is he serious? She really, really hopes he is not serious.

Grady's dad clears his throat and his eyes roll from Grady over to Amelia.

"Um, did you need something, Amelia?" Grady asks her.

"No."

"Then would you mind closing the door on your way out?"

Stunned, Amelia nods obediently and backs out.

Grady's dad barely notices her. He doesn't say thank you. And he doesn't take a taste. Instead he leans back and says, "I have a buddy who's done some franchising in Chicago. I'll give him a call."

"Are you going to try the ice cream? It's really good, Dad. That flavor was Mom's favorite."

"Actually, I could really go for a coffee. Can you call that girl back in here?"

That girl?

"Amelia?" Grady calls out.

Cate puts her hands on Amelia's shoulders. Amelia hadn't known she was standing there. "Please," Cate says, raring to go. "Let me."

"Cate, don't."

"Don't worry. I'm not going to ruin anything."

"Hey, Amelia?" Grady calls louder.

Amelia positions herself behind the office door where she can peek in without being seen.

"Amelia's taking care of something," Cate says, entering the office. "Can I help you?"

"Oh." Grady is standing at their coffeemaker. "Sorry. I couldn't find any coffee."

"That's because none of us drink coffee," Cate says. She smiles sweetly at Grady's dad. "Can I make you a cup of tea instead?"

He doesn't look up from the spreadsheet he's holding. "Yeah, okay."

Cate runs hot water through the coffeemaker while Grady's dad flips through some more of the ledgers. "Mind if I take some of these with me? I'd like to look them over."

"No. Not at all."

"Here's your tea," Cate says, delivering a cup.

Grady's dad takes a sip. "Mmm. What is this?"

"An herbal blend."

"It's good," he says, surprised, taking a second, deeper sip. "Have some," he tells Grady.

"Do you want a cup?" Cate asks Grady.

Amelia can hardly keep from laughing behind the door.

Grady and his dad are sipping on PMS tea.

It's late when Amelia hears Grady open the front door of the farmhouse. Almost closing time. She knows he left the stand with his dad not long after she went up to the house. Cate texted her to say that the two of them had climbed into Grady's dad's Mercedes and roared off.

That was hours ago.

The day has been on rewind in her head; she's been replaying how Grady and his dad treated her. Grady's dismissive tone, his father's condescending attitude, calling her "dear." Grady didn't even bother to introduce her, or single her out in any way. And as Head Girl, she feels like a total failure for not standing up for herself. She's supposed to be a role model? Thank god for Cate's PMS tea clapback.

She ends up making a pretty great batch of chocolate. Not as good as Molly Meade's but pretty darn good. Could they sell this? Absolutely. But she doesn't feel happy. She feels humiliated.

Amelia hears Grady kick off his shoes; the floorboards of

the hallway creak under his feet. The basement door opens and Grady trudges down the steps. She doesn't say anything to him. No *hello*. No *How was dinner?*

Not that he notices.

Grady falls onto the couch like dead weight. "Well, that was completely exhausting. I swear, nothing is good enough for him. It's like, I think I've figured out how to make him proud, but then he immediately ups and moves the goalpost." He adjusts a pillow so it's behind his head and kicks off his shoes. "He never asks for my ideas, he never wants to hear what I think. The whole night was just him going on and on about all the things I should be doing with Meade Creamery. Bigger brand presence. Adding revenue streams. Sell the milk bottles. Sell the polo shirts."

"What?"

"Oh, yeah. He wants me to start selling your Meade Creamery polos for twenty-five bucks apiece."

Amelia drums her fingers in frustration. Only Meade Creamery girls get pink polo shirts. They aren't nearly as special if everyone can buy one. "And what did you say?"

"I didn't say anything. He doesn't *want* me to say anything. He just wants me to do it."

She spins toward him. "What about his idea for using smaller scoops? And charging customers more?"

"I don't love the idea, but it would buy us more time." Grady stretches, letting one long leg go to the floor. "You said you're close, right? I have faith in you." Amelia rolls her eyes. "What's that about?" he says, drawing a circle in the air with his finger.

"Nothing."

"Come on, say it."

Her hands go to her hips. "How come you didn't even intro-

siobhan vivian

duce me to your dad? I've been busting my butt to help you. You treated me like your secretary! When I'm Head Girl!"

He quickly sits up. "Wait, Amelia. Hold on a second. If it's not already obvious, I have a very weird relationship with my dad."

"No, that's clear, Grady. Super clear."

"I promise I didn't slight you on purpose."

"But you also made it seem like you're the one doing everything." She's embarrassed saying this, because it's not like any of this is hers. She's a secondary character, background in the Meade family saga.

"I can't have him thinking I'm not good at this."

"He's going to have that impression when you run out of ice cream," she points out. "Which is going to happen very soon."

"I'm hoping we figure it out before I have to tell him."

"You mean you hope *I'll* figure it out."

"Hold up. I was fine to keep trying. You're the one who volunteered to give making ice cream a shot. And I didn't stop you because it seemed like you enjoyed doing it. And, to be completely honest, it's been fun to watch you."

Amelia doesn't let herself soften. "I do enjoy it."

"So what's the problem?"

Amelia doesn't like how this is getting muddled. "I don't want you selling our uniforms! Make different shirts, if you want to, but don't sell these."

"Fine, Amelia. We won't sell the polos. And I won't raise the prices, and I won't use smaller scoops. I definitely don't want to make you upset."

Cate texts her. Ready?

"I'm not upset," she tells him, hooking her bag on her shoulder.

"You are. And I'm sorry if that's my fault."

"I'd rather you didn't apologize, honestly. It's business, right? Nothing personal?"

Grady lies back down and covers his face with the pillow. It looks like he might want to stay that way forever. "That was the idea," he says, muffled. "But I'll make an exception for you. Please. Just stay."

Amelia's heart races. This is the most overtly flirty thing he's said to her, something much harder to ignore, play off, look away from.

Unless he's saying it because of the ice cream?

Part of Amelia wants to know. A bigger part than she'd like to admit.

But Cate is the most important thing in her life. Not Grady. Not ice cream. Not Meade Creamery. And on top of all that she made a promise. So even though she wants to stay, she goes.

And if anyone would understand that, Molly would.

CHAPTER  TWENTY-FIVE

AMELIA IS AT THE SINK, DRAINING A POT OF SLIPPERY elbows from a late-night box of too-late-for-anything-else mac and cheese for her and Cate. Cate had to stop for gas if they were going to make it home from the stand, and while she filled up, Amelia ran into the mini-mart for snacks. Luckily, they had the good kind for sale, where the cheese isn't powdered. Instead, it's a creamy sauce that comes in a foil packet, which gets mixed in once the noodles are cooked. Amelia squeezes and rolls the foil, working dutifully to get every last drop out.

"You know what sucks?" Cate says, digging in the fridge for hot sauce. They both like to douse enough hot sauce on their mac and cheese to make their eyes water.

Amelia steels herself. She doesn't really want to talk about what happened at the stand today with Grady. She mentioned on the ride home that Grady apologized, but Cate seemed less convinced of his sincerity than Amelia.

"Amelia?"

"Sorry. What?"

"It sucks that Sand Lake doesn't do their own fireworks show anymore for the Fourth." Cate grabs utensils and sets two places at Amelia's kitchen table. "Remember that?"

"Totally. It used to be my favorite holiday."

The town used to set off fireworks from a barge in the center of the lake when they were kids. After dinner, everyone in town would walk down with picnic baskets, blankets, beach chairs, and coolers and wait for the sun to set. Amelia loved the way the lights twinkled in the sky and also on the water, a perfect mirror image. And the peppy songs the high school marching band would play from the parking lot. She isn't especially patriotic, but there was something about the way they matched the beat to the bursts that would make her feel a swell of pride.

"Anyway, the girls were talking today about their plans for the Fourth, and I was remembering the fireworks, and they looked at me like I was crazy. None of them remember going." Cate shakes some hot sauce into both their bowls, looks up at Amelia, who gives her a nod of encouragement. "Did we ever go together?" Cate asks, adding a bit more.

"Nope. It ended when we were in sixth grade."

Cate stirs her bowl. "Ahh, sixth grade BCA, *before Cate and Amelia.* I wonder why the town stopped doing them."

"I think because more and more people ditched Sand Lake for the better fireworks shows at the other lakes." It was true, their fireworks show was never as impressive as at some of the other nearby towns, where they actually charged people money, but it was a mostly steady stream for around fifteen minutes, explosions loud enough that Amelia would plug her ears.

"What do you think about doing our own fireworks show at the lake this year? For the girls."

"Oh my God, that would be so fun!" But Amelia's smile wilts as fast as it has bloomed. "I'm not even sure we'll have ice cream to sell in two days."

Cate gently asks, "Has Grady said what he's going to do when we run out?"

"No. I don't think there's anything he can do. I mean, we've searched the farmhouse top to bottom. Molly's recipes aren't there. I think he's just hoping I'll figure out how to make ice cream that's good enough to sell."

Cate slowly lowers her fork to the table. "But even if you manage to churn out some truly terrific ice cream on your own, it's not going to be *Molly's* ice cream. Customers aren't going to taste what's good about yours, only what's *different*. And they're going to be disappointed."

"Shoot. I never thought about it like that before." Amelia remembers the man she served on opening day, in the porkpie hat, how his eyes rolled back in his head with just one lick of his cone. How would his face have looked if he'd tried the ice cream Amelia made?

"I worry about the girls, too," Cate admits. "This summer's been one big bummer for them. That's another reason why I think you should start channeling your energy into making the Fourth of July night super fun."

Amelia slumps back in her chair. "So what should I do? Totally give up on making ice cream?" If she abandons Grady, won't that be dooming them all?

Cate makes her preference known. "You've tried your best to save Meade Creamery, but I think now it's time to come back down to the stand. When the ship finally sinks, I think you'll regret not being on it with us."

CHAPTER TWENTY-SIX

THAT NIGHT, AMELIA IS TORTURED BY DREAMS OF ICE cream, like a sugar-starved kid. But only during the few minutes she manages to fall asleep. Mostly, she is wide awake, tossing and turning in her bed, kicking at the sheets.

She does not ride her bike to the farmhouse the next morning. Instead, she drives with Cate to the lake. They aren't on the schedule today until second shift, leaving them a few sunny hours to tan and swim. Cate is already enviably bronze. Amelia sprays herself with extra coconut oil, hoping to catch up.

From their towels, plans for their Fourth of July party begin to take shape. There was never a Fourth party before, which seems like a startling error in retrospect, and Amelia suspects it could potentially become a new summer tradition, if Meade Creamery somehow survives.

Amelia types up a shopping list on her phone—food and fireworks, basically—and then she and Cate brainstorm a rough itinerary for the night. They'll start with a bonfire beach cookout. Hot dogs wrapped in crescent roll dough, then roasted on sticks, ears of corn smoked in their husks, gooey perfectly half-burnt s'mores. Once the sun begins to set, they'll hold a bunch of contests—prizes TBD—for things like the best interpretive dance using sparklers. And then the night will end with Amelia and Cate rowing a canoe to the middle of Sand Lake and setting off as many fireworks as they can afford to buy for the girls on shore.

The whole morning, Amelia keeps expecting to hear from Grady. A text, or maybe even a call. Isn't he curious why she isn't there like usual? Isn't he wondering where she's at with the ice cream?

Maybe he knows she needs a break.

Or maybe he's accepted that it's a lost cause.

When Amelia gets to the stand for her shift, she stays down at the stand and tries her best to pretend things are normal. She sings along to the oldies on the radio, she takes the lead on all newbie chores to give the other girls a break. It feels good to be back with them, and the girls are excited about the Fourth of July plans, but Amelia isn't able to lose herself the way she used to. She can't forget that the stand is in trouble, and it hurts her heart. But Cate is so clearly happy to have her back, signaling in a hundred small gestures—hip checks, hugs, ponytail swats—that Amelia's made the right choice.

At the end of the night, and without a word from Grady, she stoically brings the receipts and deposits up to the farmhouse. Deep inside, she's hoping to see him. Hoping he'll invite her in.

Grady has the lights off.

· · ·

On July 2, Home Sweet Home sells out.

On July 3, chocolate.

On July 4, Amelia takes the final drums of vanilla and strawberry out of the storage freezer and moves them into the scooping cabinet. The stand is only open for the first shift on the holiday. If it were a full day, they wouldn't make it to closing.

It's become so depressing, Amelia avoids working the windows. It wounds her when customers order flavors they don't have. Their *ohs* of disappointment feel like arrows shot into her heart, a constant reminder of how Amelia felt the day Molly Meade died, thinking she'd never get a taste of Home Sweet Home again.

The girls offer vague excuses about problems with production, promises that they're trying to get things fixed. They offer free toppings. Amelia doesn't want them to lie. Just apologize. But what does it matter, at this point?

To that end, Amelia wants tonight to be epic. Nervous that they don't have enough fireworks, Amelia sends Cate back to the vendor tent that's sprouted up in the Walmart parking lot with a whole week's salary. Cate's only supposed to be gone thirty minutes, but it gets to be almost two hours. Amelia wonders if Cate stopped in to say hey to the people at JumpZone. Maybe she's trying to get her old job back.

After Amelia closes up and sends Sophie and Jen home, she changes out of her uniform and into the festive clothes she's brought with her: a blue-and-white-striped tank, cherry-red shorts that tie in the front in a bow, and a pair of espadrille wedges. Amelia and Cate have planned to head to the lake straight from work to begin setting things up on the beach. The other girls will join them around six.

Where are you? Amelia texts Cate.

Sorry. I ducked into Walmart to get bug spray but the lines are crazy. Be back to the stand soon.

Amelia walks up to the farmhouse to hand Grady the deposits. They still haven't spoken. After putting the bank bag in the mailbox, she turns to walk away. But then she whips back and rings the doorbell, intending to inform Grady about the ice cream. How there isn't any more left. How it's really, truly over.

When he doesn't answer, she presses the doorbell again, and again, and again. She feels tricked by him. Grady swept her up into his frenzy, sucked her into his family drama. All that time they spent together, those risky, flirty moments. She sacrificed her summer and her relationships to help save something she thought was as important to him as it was to her. Molly Meade wouldn't have wanted that.

Grady doesn't answer, even though the pink Cadillac is there. Could he be in the basement trying to make ice cream? If he was, would she forgive him for ghosting her?

The house is unlocked. Amelia slips inside.

But the basement is quiet. It hasn't been touched. He's not in the living room, not up on the second floor. Amelia hears Moo mewing and follows the sound into Molly's office. Moo is sitting on the desk chair, contentedly scratching at the wooden armrest.

On her way out, Amelia notices that the letters from Grady's mother are no longer on the mantel. Her heart catches, remembering that sad look in his eyes. Did he finally read them?

No.

Grady hasn't touched them. He's only moved them over to the pile of papers that he's destined for the shredder. Actually, they'd probably be shredded by now if he hadn't jammed the thing.

The anger simmers inside her. Why wouldn't he want to read them?

Amelia's not sure why she herself is drawn to them. Maybe she can't bear the legacy of of another dead woman disappearing— of Grady's mother's words thrown away by her one and only son. She picks up the bundle and unties the string around them. She's somehow made a habit of reading things she has no business reading, it seems.

Most of them are letters, and there are a couple of greeting cards, too. A birthday card to Molly. A Christmas card with a school picture of Grady inside. He's wearing an annoyingly cute little sweater-vest, reindeer leaping across the red wool.

Then Amelia comes across an envelope that feels thicker than the rest. Amelia opens it up. It's an ornate thank-you card, silver foil with a white ribbon bow affixed to the front. Inside, there's a picture of Grady's parents and Molly Meade, standing in a posh reception hall.

Grady's dad looks so happy and young. Almost like Grady, only with slightly curlier, puffier hair. He might be only a few years older here than Grady is now, she thinks. There's something boyishly earnest about his smile. And Grady's mom, elegant in a white lace dress.

Molly looks beautiful too. Her hair isn't white, it's still some-what reddish. She's stylish, in a gold tweed dress with bell sleeves, a rose-colored silk bag. In the picture, she's squeezing Grady's mom's hand. And she looks happy in a way that Amelia wouldn't have expected. There's not a trace of sadness for her own doomed romance to be found.

Dear Molly,

According to current wedding etiquette, couples have one year from the date of their nuptials to send thank-you cards. I'm embarrassed it's taken the full year to write this note, especially when your present was far and away my favorite of all the gifts we received.

Molly, I'm honored that you would share your recipes with me. And that vintage ice cream maker is a work of art. Is it your original?

One upside to this card coming so late—I can share the news that I am expecting! The ice cream is coming in very handy in that regard. And being pregnant is the perfect excuse to have a scoop of Home Sweet Home each day!

It was lovely to get to talk to you at the reception, albeit briefly. I will check with Pat's secretary and find a time for us to visit this fall before the baby comes.

Love,
Diana Denton-Meade

siobhan vivian

Amelia gasps and calls out for Grady. But there is no answer. Only the quiet of the old farmhouse.

She runs into Molly's bedroom and checks the window that looks out on the back acreage.

She sees him, quite a ways off, out for a run, rising and falling in a steady rhythm along a path in the back fields, moving farther and farther away from her.

She tries his cell but it goes straight to voice mail, his cool professional voice instructing her to leave a message.

Instead, she flies down the steps—how to run in wedges is another thing Amelia picked up from stand girls—and out the front door. She hops on her bike and stands on her pedals to get around the farmhouse and into the fields as quickly as possible.

The farther away from the house she gets, the louder the sounds of nature get. The buzzing of insects, the breeze in the grass. She zooms past a large concrete pad, all that's left of the burned-down barn.

"Grady! Grady!" she shouts, coming up behind him.

He has his music on. But he must eventually hear her, because he turns and glances over his shoulder, and promptly stumbles and falls to the ground.

"Jesus, Amelia! You almost gave me a heart attack!"

As he picks himself up, she sets down her feet and tries pushing the card into his hand. It takes him a second to realize what it is. "I can't believe you were going to throw your mom's letters away."

"I already read through them."

"Grady, I know you're lying."

Grimacing, he checks his elbow. It's scraped raw and bleeding. "Can you please not look at me like you hate me?"

"I don't hate you, but please, you have to read this!" She presses the card into his hands. "Molly gave your mom the ice cream recipes. They were her wedding present to your parents."

Grady clenches his jaw. He rips out his earbuds, flings them over his shoulder, and begrudgingly takes the card from Amelia.

Her heart is pounding. "Do you remember seeing this ice cream maker around? Maybe in your kitchen?"

His eyes run back and forth, back and forth. "No."

"Your mom wrote that the recipes were very special to her. You don't think your dad would have kept them?"

Grady chews the inside of his cheek. He seems to be rehearsing what he's about to say before he says it. "Right after my mom died, Dad moved her things into storage. They're at our beach house in Dooley. I have no clue what he saved."

"Dooley. That's like, what? Two hours away from here? You could leave now—"

"Amelia. You just called me out for not reading my mom's letters. So what makes you think I'm going to want to dig through her things?"

"I don't understand. Your mom loved this place. And Molly Meade loved you enough to leave it to you. Don't you feel an obligation to them both to see this through till the end?"

Rubbing his hand over his face, Grady says, "Molly didn't leave the stand to me. She left it to my mom, and I guess she never updated her will. I only inherited it because all my mom's assets come to me. It's a technicality."

"You think Molly didn't know it would work that way?" Amelia shakes her head. "Technicality or not, it's yours now."

"Don't you get it? Knowing how important this place was to my mom only makes this harder. It's one thing not to please

siobhan vivian

my dad. I don't know if I ever will, and I'm starting to think I shouldn't even try. But I can't let down my mom. Not any more than I already have."

"Grady, you have to go and see if you can find them."

His eyes drop to the ground, where he kicks at the dirt. Amelia holds her breath until he looks up at her, eyes hopeful and needy, his hands twisting his headphone wires. "Will you come with me?"

"Grady, I can't."

"Please, Amelia. I don't mean to ask any more of you. That's why I haven't chased you down. This is my problem, not yours, and you've already gone above and beyond. But I honestly don't think I can go through her stuff myself. I'll show you where everything is. You can go through the boxes, see if you find them."

"I have plans tonight that I absolutely can't miss," Amelia says, though she suspects that if she gave Grady a night to sleep on this, he'd very likely change his mind. "What time can we get back?"

"Two hours there, an hour to search through her stuff, and then two hours back. So around ten?"

Amelia would miss the dinner, miss the interpretive sparkler dance contest. But she'd be back in time for fireworks. "Can you be ready to go in ten minutes?"

"Yes. Absolutely."

"You have to drive like the wind. A safe wind, but the wind."

"Promise."

They run back to the house together. Grady jumps into the shower and makes sure Moo has fresh food and water while Amelia heads down to the stand to see Cate.

She's never been more nervous in her life.

Cate has her fireworks haul spread out on the Head Girl's desk. "This was a great call, Amelia. You look so cute, by the way."

"Cate, I need to talk to you about tonight."

"What? Did something happen?"

Amelia takes a deep breath. "I found Molly's recipes. Or I think I did. The thing is, we have to go to Grady's dad's beach house to get them. It's not far. It's only over in Dooley. We're going to leave right now."

"You and Grady."

"I'll be back in time for fireworks."

"Amelia, I cannot believe you'd . . . Wait. Is something going on between you two?"

Amelia shakes her head quickly. "No!"

"Because we all said—"

"Cate, nothing is going on between me and Grady! I swear!"

"Then why can't you just go tomorrow?" Cate's lips press together in a thin line. "Why do *you* have to go at all?"

Amelia hasn't told Cate anything about Grady's real mom. She would like to, but now is not the time. She doesn't have *any* time. "I don't want to have any regrets."

"You'll regret missing tonight," Cate warns. Or maybe it's a threat.

"I won't miss tonight! I'll be back!" Amelia stresses again. "Save me a hot dog, okay?"

Cate's gaze flicks upward.

Amelia rushes forward and hugs her best friend goodbye, and she can feel Cate's disappointment. It almost makes her stay.

Almost.

CHAPTER  TWENTY-SEVEN

THEY PASS THROUGH CITY, INTO COUNTRY, INTO CITY, into country again before they make it to the coast—windows open, radio on low. Every few minutes, a car passes them on the highway, and the driver honks and waves.

"Note to self," Grady says. "If you ever have to go someplace incognito, do not drive a pink Cadillac." He looks toward Amelia for a laugh.

The best she can manage is a weak smile.

"You're regretting coming with me," he deduces. "Look. If it makes you feel any better, I'm regretting going." Grady wrings the steering wheel with his hands. Since leaving Sand Lake, he's only gotten more anxious, not less.

Meanwhile, Amelia is trying her best to preserve what little professional distance remains between her and Grady. She sits up tall in her seat, keeps her hands folded in her lap, eyes on the road. Though she hasn't technically broken her promise to Cate and the other stand girls—that Grady is off-limits—she doubts a defense of her actions thus far would hold much water in the court of public opinion. Of course, she could say that everything she's done so far has been for the good of the stand. But even that rings a bit hollow.

"You never talk about college. Where are you going again?"

"Gibbons."

"That's right. Are you excited?"

"I guess," Amelia says. "But I envy you and Cate. You both knowing exactly what you want to do with your life."

"Well, I wouldn't say I had much of a choice. It was always assumed I'd be going to school to follow in my dad's footsteps." Grady adds, "I'm incredibly lucky. It's like getting handed the keys to a corner office. The only thing I have to do is not screw it up."

"Good thing you love it."

"Right. Good thing." Grady cracks his neck. "Have you registered for classes yet?"

"Not yet."

"One good thing about being undeclared is that you can take all sorts of classes. My buddy Troy took a course about Food Culture Across the Romance Languages, and the class went out to a new restaurant twice a month. Oh, and Rob took a class called Poetry of the Songwriter, where they listened to music and analyzed the lyrics like poetry. He did his final on Pearl Jam."

"What about you? What cool classes do the business majors get to take?"

He laughs. "Business school isn't meant to be fun."

"Come on."

"I'm not kidding. I take stats and econ and that's basically it. All my classes are in these huge auditoriums. They're so big, the professors don't even bother taking attendance. You actually don't have to show up."

"Seriously?"

"I personally wouldn't *recommend* not going." He props his elbow up on the driver's-side door. "I pretty much failed out last semester."

"Are you serious?" Amelia twists her body so she's facing him.

"I had motivational issues, I guess. But so long as I pass all my online courses, which I'm on track to do, I won't be too far behind. Then all I have to worry about is my dad."

"What do you mean?"

Grady flushes. "Umm . . . He's basically threatened not to pay my tuition for next semester."

"Would he really do that?"

"He said his investment in me wasn't looking like a promising return."

"Wow."

"Yeah, so when the opportunity to run Meade Creamery presented itself, I jumped to take it on. I'm basically using it to prove myself to him, so I can go back to school."

"What if we don't find the recipes? What will you do then?"

"I don't know."

"I'm sure he won't let you *not* go back to Truman. I mean, he's seen how hard you've been trying. Right?"

"Like I said, my dad and I have a very weird relationship."

"So why didn't you reach out when I didn't come back to the house to make ice cream these last few days?"

"I wanted to, but not because of the ice cream. I . . . missed hanging out with you, Amelia. Plus, I was ashamed of the way I behaved when my dad came to visit." He shakes his head and lets out a long exhale. "I'm realizing that I'm more like him than I thought."

Though Amelia isn't sure exactly what Grady means, she reaches out to touch him, comfort him, but then pulls her hand back at the last second.

If Grady notices, he pretends not to. He keeps his eyes on the road. "We'll be there soon."

A little over two hours later, they arrive at a large iron gate anchored by a stately wall of tall hedges on either side. Grady rolls down his window, leans out of the Cadillac, and punches a code into a sleek little box mounted on a metal pole. After a beep, the gate slowly swings opens.

Grady pulls forward and a thudding fills the car. They are no longer on a paved road. This one is cobblestone and the pavers are beautifully laid, gray and white, in a chevron pattern.

They drive past a few smaller buildings. One or two cottages, and then a big garage with four barn-style doors. The driveway curves and then reveals an enormous house in the distance. It is the biggest, most opulent house Amelia has ever seen.

"*This* is your beach house?"

"Not mine, my dad's. And not for much longer. It's for sale," Grady explains. "He bought a place in Palm Beach that's near my stepmom's family two summers ago. He hardly comes here anymore."

As they climb the front steps, little motion-sensor lights click on. There are beautiful succulent plants and window boxes bursting with vibrant petunias and dripping in sweet potato vines.

They reach the front door, which is also oversize. Grady takes out his phone and taps some app, and it clicks open.

As they walk in, the lights around them automatically turn on. He types a code into another small panel. Window shades roll up, exposing floor-to-ceiling two-story windows.

Amelia slips off her espadrille wedges, leaving them by the door. It's a beautiful house for sure, but it has about as much cozy feeling as a hotel lobby. It's ornate, well decorated, but without a single homey touch.

She follows Grady into the open kitchen, which has a huge island topped by marble—swirling blue like ocean water—and a dining table with twelve chairs, crowned by a driftwood chandelier. Grady opens a cabinet door that camouflages a fridge. Inside, soda cans are lined up, and bottles of Snapple, too. There's also Gatorade, all orange, the flavor Grady drinks. There aren't any groceries, but below is a pull-out freezer full of frozen pizzas and burritos.

"Are you hungry?"

Amelia shakes her head no. She can't believe that the ice cream recipes might be here. This place is so unlike the Meades' farmhouse in every way.

She turns around and sees watercolor streaks of pinks and blues through the windows, the ocean shimmering, the caps of the waves dusted in the glitter of dusk. Grady pulls open a sliding glass door for her. The air is sticky and salty outside, thick and still hot despite it being evening. There's an outdoor shower and a hot tub and a wet bar, which they pass to get to the railing. Amelia focuses past the grassy dunes to the beach. No footprints on the sand, the lifeguard chair tipped over, an old man walking a small dog right where the waves break, and pipers poking their long thin beaks into the wet sand.

She has only ever been to the ocean once. Down in Florida, visiting a cousin of her father's. The waves scared her off from going in deeper than her knees. Aside from that, every summer has been spent swimming in the smooth, still waters of Sand Lake.

"Sometimes you can see dolphins out there," Grady says, pointing off toward the ocean.

"Grady, this house . . ."

"I know." Something tightens in his face. "My dad is really good at making money." His eyes move slowly across the horizon, as if trying to capture something, a panoramic picture. Then he turns his back to the water. "Far less successful at being a dad, unfortunately." He pushes himself off the railing and heads inside.

"It's okay. If you need more time."

"No. I just want to get this over with."

He leads her back through the kitchen, and then down a staircase. They pass a gym, a home theater. "Her stuff's in this room." He takes a deep, shivery breath. And then he shakes out his arms and legs, like an athlete psyching himself up for a race. He doesn't want to be here, doing this.

Though she feels excited, hopeful that they are so close now, she wishes it wasn't coming at Grady's expense.

siobhan vivian

CHAPTER  TWENTY-EIGHT

THE ROOM IS THE ONLY ONE AMELIA HAS SEEN THAT has no furnishings. There are no beachy decorative accessories, like glass vases filled with alternating layers of sand and shells, or starfish cast in silver.

No. The light is harsh, the walls lined with stacks of cardboard moving boxes, all the same size, four tall. Each one has a white sticker in the bottom left corner, the size of an index card, listing the contents. Printed out on a computer, not even handwritten.

Grady approaches the stack nearest to him. It's as tall as he is. He presses his hand flat against the topmost box, as if he's searching inside it for a heartbeat. The sticker reads: *Clothes: semiformal.* The one below that, *Fiction E–La.* Below that, *Handbags, hosiery, scarves, socks.* Below that, *Desk accessories, stationery.* Then the floor.

Amelia can see the redness creeping up his neck as he tells her, "We've owned this place for six years. Before that, he had them in our old beach house, which is maybe a mile away from here."

Amelia struggles to make sense of this. Clearly Grady's dad loved his mom. If he didn't, he would have thrown this stuff away years ago. "Well . . . he took a lot of care in packing it up."

Grady turns away from her. "He paid someone to do this. Probably one of his assistants."

Amelia says, "I'm sure it was hard for him."

"Yes, I'm sure it was," Grady says, every muscle in him tightening.

"Do you want to wait outside?"

He seems to be summoning something from deep within himself. "No," he says, jaw set. He shimmies the stack out so he can see the labels on the ones stacked behind it.

And that's how they go through the room, with Grady pushing, restacking, and shifting boxes until he finds ones to open. Amelia's not sure if his picks are because something on the label has him thinking the ice cream maker might be inside, or if something she can't account for piques his curiosity. Whenever it happens, though, she makes sure to turn her back to him, to allow him that little bit of privacy.

She only opens one box herself, one marked *Serving Pieces*. Inside is a sterling silver tea set, each tarnished piece cloaked in dark felt.

It takes only fifteen minutes before Grady finds the ice cream maker in a box labeled *Antiques 3*. It's a heavy wooden bucket with a cap that is clamped on. A white crank handle is attached to the top, and though the mechanisms are likely old, they still spin with ease.

Grady gives it a shake. Inside they hear papers fluttering around.

He holds on to the base while Amelia unscrews the cap. At the bottom they find a wedding card.

Dear Pat and Diana,

I hope you'll forgive a spinster for sharing some unsolicited advice on your wedding day, but this saying (a favorite of my father's) has proven itself true for me, time and time again.

The fruits of hard work are sweeter than the sweetest of nectars.

Though life may not always be easy, it still can be plenty sweet.

With love,
Aunt Molly

Folded up in the card is one oversaturated paper photocopy, the contrast turned up so high that every wrinkle and fold on the original casts a deep shadow on its duplicate. Just like the ancient photocopier at the Sand Lake Public Library, Amelia thinks. Four index cards have been copied onto the page, with Molly's handwritten ingredient amounts for her commercial machine. Not that it says so explicitly, but Amelia can tell by the measurements, which Molly has annotated in pencil, sizing them down for the hand-cranked ice cream maker.

Where are those cards? Still in the house somewhere? How could they have missed them?

There are no step-by-step instructions. That's okay, though, because Amelia's played around with the machine and read enough other recipes to know. She can see exactly how her experiments fell short. In Molly's vanilla, she used less white sugar and more of the barley syrup the vanilla beans are soaked in, which Amelia thought was used only to preserve them. Amelia came closest with the proportions of the chocolate, though she never allowed it to cure for the correct amount of time in the batch chiller. Amelia's attempts at strawberry were way off.

Her heart catches when she sees the card for Home Sweet Home.

Wild honeysuckle flowers, at least three handfuls, steeped overnight in cream

And it's as if the secret is now in her mouth, making immediate and absolute sense. Sweet, floral, like honey, but milder. All the honeysuckle growing wild in the old cow pastures.

It's the taste of home.

Amelia feels euphoric, but Grady is somewhere on the other end of the spectrum. It's as if all the adrenaline that propelled him this far tonight has burned off, run dry. He leans against a stack of boxes and gives a deep exhale.

She steps closer to him, puts her hand on his arm. "Do you want to stay awhile? Look through . . ."

He closes the boxes and begins to stack them back up carefully. Amelia helps. "I could just leave it a mess, he'd never know

I came in here," he says. But he continues to straighten them anyway.

"If you told him, would he be mad?"

"I honestly don't care."

She's not sure what she prefers—Grady's desperate need for his dad's affection, or this sudden icy detachment. Hopefully the latter is just temporary, a response to emotions being so raw. Amelia would hate to think she played any role in breaking a family apart.

Grady shuts the door to the room, turns off the lights in the house. Amelia slips her shoes back on at the door.

He must have so much going through his mind right now. But he doesn't share any of it.

Grady slides from one lane to the other and back again. Whichever lane they pick goes slower than the other. Holiday traffic. He lays on the horn.

It's a little after eight o'clock and they are barely halfway to Sand Lake.

Amelia's phone battery is almost gone. She tries sending a text to Cate, letting her know they're on their way back, but stuck in traffic. It dies in the middle.

Grady fiddles with the dial. Nothing comes in super clear on the old Cadillac radio, and the scratchiness gives the music a sort of faraway sound. Amelia tells herself not to fall asleep. Falling asleep is the worst thing you can do to a driver on a long road trip.

"Amelia."

She is curled up next to him. She sits up, slides over to her side of the front seat. They are finally back in Sand Lake. It's nearing midnight.

"Oh no!" Amelia says, breathless.

"Where do you want me to drop you off?" Grady asks.

She shows him the way.

The headlights shine in the trees, the car rocking over the sandy path, evergreen branches scraping at the sides. Amelia keeps waiting to see the back bumper of a parked car. Cate's truck, or one of the other girls. But it stretches, empty, all the way to the water.

Amelia climbs out. She can see where they built the fire. It's died out, just a pile of ash. The sand is smoothed from blankets, and there are shreds of colorful papers from fireworks lit and exploded.

Grady's out of the car. He shoves his hands in his pockets. "I'm sorry. I drove as fast as I could."

"I know you did." Amelia presses her lips together. This isn't Grady's fault. Amelia made the choice to go with him. She will have to deal with the consequences.

"Should I take you home?"

Amelia nods. "But I need to make a quick stop first."

Grady parks the Cadillac but leaves it running, headlights on. Together, in the bright beams, they pull honeysuckle flowers off the bushes. Amelia holds out the hem of her shirt and they fill it like a basket.

"How much do you need?"

"Three handfuls." The smell is intoxicating, wafting up directly into her nose.

He holds a blossom up to the headlight beam. "This looks like your pin."

Amelia looks. Five petals, exactly the same size as the Head Girl pin. The secret was in plain sight all along.

Her parents have waited up for her. They are watching *Independence Day*—her father's favorite movie—each with their own bowl of popcorn, because Dad likes butter and Mom doesn't.

"How'd your fireworks show go off?" Dad asks.

"With a bang," Amelia teases, and kisses them both on the cheek. She doesn't want to lie. But she doesn't want to get into it either. Though, as she kisses each of them on the cheek, she feels lucky. Lucky that she has always had their support, their trust, and their love.

In her bedroom, Amelia plugs her phone into the charger and waits until it come back to life. It is now close to one in the morning. As soon as it has enough juice, she texts Cate.

I'm so sorry.

Cate doesn't write back immediately. Amelia puts her phone down on the bed, watching the screen as she changes into her pajamas.

Did you find the recipes at least?

Yes.

There's another stretch of lag time. Amelia takes the phone into the bathroom with her to brush her teeth when Cate finally responds.

What's the secret of Home Sweet Home?

For a second, Amelia hesitates, her mouth full of minty foam. Should she tell? But to not share this with her, Cate of all people, feels like a betrayal. She spits, bites down on her toothbrush, and uses both hands to text.

Honeysuckle. Molly picked them in her fields and steeped the flowers in the ice cream base overnight.

Cate doesn't text back, and Amelia doesn't expect her to. But she hopes that as things at Meade Creamery finally get back to normal, she and Cate will get back to normal too.

July 5, 1945

The Red Cross benefit is in two weeks. I'm so grateful for all the help I'm getting from the girls. They are a talented bunch. Painting the banner for my table, sewing us all matching aprons. Martha even decorated a tin box to keep the money in. They've taken care of everything.

All I need to do is make the ice cream.

It will sound terrible to write this, but I've always thought of myself as unremarkable, even though I've been told all my life how beautiful I am. But now . . . I wish I knew how to put it into words. When I'm making ice cream . . . I . . . feel as if I have found my whole self.

CHAPTER  TWENTY-NINE

AMELIA WAKES UP TO A TEXT FROM GRADY.

No cereal this morning. ☺

And when she arrives at the farmhouse, he is already holding the screen door open for her, Moo cradled in his arms. He has made them both a full breakfast of scrambled eggs and toast, crispy bacon, sliced banana. He's even dressed up, a madras plaid shirt and a polka-dot tie.

"You *are* good at eggs," she admits, taking a bite.

"Told you," he boasts.

They eat quickly, excited to get working, and descend the basement stairs.

"I called Marburger Dairy and asked them to resume the deliveries Molly used to get. They should come by later this afternoon."

"What if I don't get it right?" Amelia asks, tying an apron around her.

"I have complete faith in you."

She quickly ducks her head in the refrigerator to hide her blushing cheeks. Inside is a large plastic container of the Home Sweet Home base that she prepared last night. The honeysuckle flowers have floated to the top.

"Grady, can you help me? I don't want to spill any." Even though he just got comfortable on the couch, he jumps right up. "I'll hold the strainer," she tells him, unhooking a huge silver conical sieve from the side of the worktable and grabbing an empty plastic tub. "Take this tub and pour the base through the strainer into this."

He does exactly what Amelia says. The cream is tinged a soft yellow. The strainer holds all the bruised flowers of honeysuckle, coated with the cooked cream. She selects a blossom and pops it into her mouth, sucking it clean. It tastes deliciously, delicately sweet.

Amelia walks over to the ice cream maker, clicks it on, and sets the time and the temperature to what Molly Meade indicated in her recipe, which Amelia has hung on the refrigerator door. She also took a photo of it with her phone as a backup. Just in case.

She flips up the silver hatch at the top of the machine and pours the base in.

"Eight minutes," she says.

"Okay." Grady flops back down on the couch and taps his foot.

Amelia is so nervous, she can hardly handle it. She stands next to the machine and listens to it churn and spin.

"I could put on a record," Grady offers.

"Yeah, sure."

siobhan vivian

He picks one out. The Mills Brothers. Four African-American men in white suit jackets and bow ties. "These dudes look cool."

"I'm pretty sure I've seen you in that same outfit."

"Hardy har." He puts the needle down and a jazzy harmony kicks in. Grady sits on the couch and taps his foot along with the beat. "I can't believe you figured out how to use that thing," he says, pointing at the huge silver vat of the pasteurizer.

"It wasn't hard," Amelia says. "It's actually just like a pot on the stove. Except you have more control over the temperature, and you can obviously put more in it."

He appears to be glancing at the album cover, but Amelia has the sense that he's watching her. She grabs one of the cardboard ice cream drums and opens the ice cream maker's latch to check on the consistency of the ice cream. Immediately, Grady is behind her, peering over her shoulder, wanting to see every step.

When the consistency seems right, Amelia opens the latch full throttle and the ice cream comes pouring out of the spout. She works quickly, turning the cardboard tub every few seconds so the ice cream pours in evenly, tapping it against the table to make sure there are no air bubbles inside. Molly's measurements are perfectly precise. There's barely any overrun.

Grady is grinning. "You make it look easy."

She's barely listening, up on her toes, peering into the drum. Her heart is beating faster than it ever has for any boy. "The color's good. And it has the right smell."

Grady rubs his hands together. "Can we try it?"

Amelia reaches for a spoon, slides it into the drum, and hands it to Grady. "Here, I'm too nervous."

He takes the spoon, but immediately turns it around to feed her. "Close your eyes, Amelia. So you can concentrate."

She closes her eyes and thinks about that night down at the lake, when she and Cate and all the girls said goodbye to Molly Meade. She feels the spoon under her nose, smells the sweetness of the cream, feels the chill radiating off it. She opens her mouth.

Her eyes pop open. "It's . . . perfect!" She reaches for another spoon. "Here, you try!"

Grady has a similar reaction, though his joy is considerably muted. Maybe he will never be able to disassociate the experience of losing his mom from the taste of Molly Meade's ice cream. He swallows, and lifts his eyes to hers, and he is beaming. "You did it!" He wraps his arms around her waist and lifts her up in the air.

"Okay, okay!"

Laughing, he gently lowers her. But when her feet hit the ground, Grady doesn't let her go. Instead, he pulls her even closer to him. There is a warmth in his eyes; his chest fills with every inhale, collapses with every exhale.

Her cheeks burn. "Grady—" she begins, but she has no idea what to say next.

Not that it matters.

They are kissing.

Even though Grady is off-limits.

And, technically, her boss.

And she told Cate there was nothing between them.

The idea that she is falling for a Meade is ridiculous.

All these thoughts are in her head somewhere, but really, what she wants to concentrate on are his lips on hers, how he can't seem to get close enough to her, how his curls feel softer than she ever imagined. Amelia and Grady are fizzing like two shook-up soda bottles, a summer's worth of tension uncapped.

siobhan vivian

Together they shuffle toward Molly's couch, not allowing any space to bloom between them, and lower themselves onto it. Grady rolls so he's on top of her, fitting between her legs. His hands rub her from ankle to knee and she prickles in goose bumps. He leans forward to her ear, nudging her head gently to the side with his nose, kissing that tiny space between her earlobe and her neck. Amelia opens her eyes . . . and sees the goldenrod yellow of the couch.

Cate.

What is Cate going to say?

Amelia already knows. Cate warned them all on opening day why the girls should be careful around him, why there should be boundaries.

But Cate hasn't spent time with Grady the way Amelia has. She has come to know him in a way the other girls don't.

Does it matter?

Or has she chosen Grady over the girls in a way that is now inexcusable?

Amelia pulls away. "This isn't a good idea."

"Really? Should I stop?"

She doesn't want him to. "I'm working. I'm officially working right now. And you're my boss."

"Amelia. I hope you don't think I'm trying to work some kind of power dynamic thing over you. Because that's not what this is at all." He shakes his head, resolute. "I've always been so intimidated by you. At first, because I thought you were pretty. But then you turned out to be smart, too."

"That doesn't change how it'll look to people."

"By people, you mean the girls."

"Yes. I do." She sits up. "I care about what they think."

He takes her hand in his. "So what do you want to do?"

She thinks. "No one can know about this. Whatever this is."

"Okay."

"And I don't think we should kiss during work hours. At least not when I'm on the clock." He makes a pouty face that Amelia finds unfairly cute. "I'm serious, Grady. I take my job very seriously."

"I know you do."

"And as soon as I get our stock levels back up, I'm working at the stand again with the other girls."

"Absolutely understood."

"Okay."

"Aren't you supposed to take at least one fifteen-minute break per shift? That's labor law."

She grins. "I can work with that."

He wags his eyebrows. "So . . . break time?"

"Break's over. I want to bring the ice cream down and let Cate taste it. And the other girls too."

Grady threads a stray lock of her hair behind her ear. "Can I come with you? I want to see them freak out when they taste how great this is."

They both roll off the couch, grinning and goofy and suddenly shy with each other. Amelia smooths her hair, makes sure her shirt is tucked in tight. Grady does the same, picks up her drum of ice cream, and holds her hand until they reach the front door. There's a pause where a kiss might go, but they smile at each other instead, owning this secret.

CHAPTER THIRTY

IT'S A QUARTER TO ELEVEN AND A LINE IS FORMING. Cate has not arrived yet, but the other girls who are on shift— Jen and Mansi—sit by the stand door, waiting.

"Oh! Hi!" Amelia says. She passes the drum to Grady and takes out her key. "I didn't realize you were waiting. I can let you both in."

They barely manage a smile for her.

Cate being upset with her is bad enough. But all the stand girls disappointed in her? It makes Amelia's heart hurt.

A voice behind her says snarkily, "Already at it, huh?" Amelia turns and sees Cate walk in and hang her purse on one of the hooks. "I'm not late," she announces defensively. "It's not eleven yet."

"No one said you were," Amelia says.

Grady can clearly sense the tension. After clearing his throat, he calls out, "Hey, girls! I want everyone in the office for a second. Amelia's got some great news to share!" He nudges Amelia, as if to remind her of the happiness she felt moments ago.

Cate and the other girls flop onto the love seat. Amelia races off to the main room of the stand and returns with plastic spoons.

"I . . . found Molly Meade's recipes last night. That was the reason I missed the party," Amelia tells Mansi and Jen. "And this morning I made my very first batch of Home Sweet Home. I think it came out pretty okay."

"Okay?" Grady pops up. "Don't be modest! You girls won't be able to tell the difference."

"If she's using Molly Meade's exact recipes, why would we?" says Cate.

"Because there are a lot of variables," Grady says. "Making ice cream isn't an easy thing to do. Trust me, I know."

Amelia makes eye contact with Cate, tries to draw Cate's focus away from Grady. "I'm excited for you to try it." She hands Cate a spoonful. And Jen and Mansi too. They all taste at the same time.

Jen and Mansi don't react. They both look at Cate. As if they need her permission.

"Are we done here?" Cate asks.

Amelia knows Cate's trying to be hurtful, because Cate's hurt. She tries to shake it off. "I should be able to get a couple more batches done today. And after this sits in the freezer for fifteen minutes, it'll be ready to scoop. We can take the *Sold Out* sign down."

"So now you'll be at the farmhouse, making ice cream for the rest of the summer," Cate says icily.

"For now, yes," Grady interjects. "But once we're caught up, Amelia will be back down here with everyone."

"It shouldn't take me long," Amelia says.

Cate checks her phone for the time. "It's after eleven. I need to open."

Amelia nods. "Right. Sorry."

Jen and Mansi scurry out past Grady. He closes the office door. "Hey, Cate, hang back for a minute, okay? I'd like to talk to you about something."

Cate makes a big show of sitting back down.

Amelia tries pulling Grady aside. She doesn't want him inserting himself into their friendship drama. She knows he's trying to help, but it'll only make things worse.

He gives her a quick thumbs-up, which frankly only makes her more anxious.

Stepping around the desk, he says, "First off, I'd like to personally apologize to you for last night."

Cate glances over her manicure, seeming bored. "You don't owe me an apology, never mind a *personal* one."

"Well . . . it's my fault that Amelia missed out on her plans with you and the other girls. She didn't want to go with me to the beach. She wanted to be with you. The last thing Amelia would want to do is let you down."

"Grady, if you want to talk with me about the business, cool. Otherwise, I'm not interested in discussing my personal life, my relationships, with you."

Amelia feels a tightness in her chest, seeing Cate model the way Amelia could have dealt with Grady from the get-go.

"But this has to do with business," Grady insists. "Cate, you brought up a good point earlier. For the time being, Amelia will have to concentrate on production. I don't want things falling through the cracks here because she's focused on making ice cream. I said as much to her on our ride back to Sand Lake, and she suggested that I promote you to Head Girl."

Cate's mouth opens, then closes. "Wait. Are you serious?" She turns toward Amelia. "Really?"

Amelia, as surprised as Cate is, smiles back, because she's happy to see Cate happy. Happy like someone switched a light on inside her.

Grady goes on. "Amelia's constantly telling me what a great job you're doing down here, how protective you are with the younger girls, and how much you've been picking up the slack. I know the circumstances have been challenging, but I'm hoping we can move forward from here and have a great rest of the summer."

Amelia keeps a smile on her face, remembering the ways Cate cuts corners sometimes. But Grady's probably right. It has been a challenging summer. Cate hasn't had the incentive to step up her role. Maybe that will change now.

"And I'll get the Head Girl pay raise too. Right?" Cate asks.

Grady nods. "I'm shifting all of the Head Girl responsibilities onto you. Making the schedule, supply orders, stock—"

"I know, I know," she says to Grady, almost like she's annoyed, like he's ruining this, and then she turns her attention fully to Amelia. Cate's eyes are sparkling. She's happier than Amelia would ever have expected her to be, because Cate always played like being Head Girl was no big deal. "Amelia, are you sure?"

"Absolutely. I always said you'd make a great Head Girl." These words are 100 percent true, and yet it does hurt Amelia to say them. Maybe because she knows that, this time, Cate's not going to argue with her. And she doesn't. She wraps Amelia in a spine-cracking hug.

"Okay, I'm going to let you girls hash this all out." He nods. "Glad this worked out so well."

Cate watches him go. "Ugh, I thought he'd never leave." Amelia laughs nervously as Cate pulls her onto the love seat. "Gah! This is so crazy!" Cate drums her feet on the floor.

Amelia nods. "Totally crazy." She squeezes Cate's hands and then lets them go.

"C'mon! Let's do something to celebrate! At least a Starbucks run!" And then, with a laugh, "That's an order."

"I should really get started on another batch."

"Wah. You're no fun."

Amelia scoots forward, her behind perched on the edge of the couch cushion. "The thing is . . . I want to do it. I like making the ice cream. I'm good at it." It feels freeing, to admit at least this much to Cate.

"Well, then I'm glad you found what you were looking for." And Cate holds out her arms for another hug.

Though Cate is still probably a little annoyed with her, and would definitely *not* hug her if she knew Amelia had just kissed Grady, Amelia wraps her arms around Cate anyway and squeezes her as tightly as she can. It's a miracle, really, that they were able to get to this place after how contentious things were between them just a few minutes ago. It is, Amelia thinks, a testament to their friendship.

Amelia stands up. "Cate? I'm sorry again about yesterday. I really didn't want to miss it."

"Don't worry. There will be other chances. *Plenty* of other chances." Amelia is halfway out the door when Cate clears her throat. "Hey, before you go . . . ," Cate says, and Amelia turns back. "I want to ask you something, but I don't want it to be weird."

Amelia swallows, thinking of Grady. Could Cate sense something? "Of course."

"Can I have the Head Girl pin? I mean, you're in this new position now, and it's like, the girls are down here at the stand with me. I think it will be good for morale if they know something's really changed."

Amelia feels a pang. Her ice cream victory has been all but eclipsed by Cate's promotion. But maybe Amelia deserves that for being too much of a coward to tell Cate about kissing Grady. It's pretty clear by the way this summer has gone that she wasn't Head Girl material after all.

"You don't have to do it now," Cate says quickly, sensing that this might be a delicate subject. But Amelia removes the pin from her collar and hands it over. Cate takes it to the mirror, puts it on, and beams, brushing her hair off her shoulder on that side, to get a better look.

siobhan vivian

CHAPTER THIRTY-ONE

AMELIA MAKES ICE CREAM FOR THE REST OF THE DAY. Mixing up new bases, pasteurizing them, letting them steep, putting them in the blast chiller, running them through the Emery Thompson. But unlike when she was blindly trying to replicate Molly's secret recipes, she feels much more confident, much less stressed. It's blissful.

Grady brings her lunch—a chicken salad sandwich, a Coke, and a bag of chips from the local deli. And he apologizes to Amelia for springing that Head Girl stuff on her today. "I just knew you were upset because Cate was upset. And I wanted to help you because you've done so much to help me."

"It was a good idea," Amelia says. "I do want to concentrate on this."

"Okay, good. If you want some company, I could bring my schoolwork down here."

"Sure. That would be nice."

She does enjoy Grady's' company, of course. Though they don't kiss, per Amelia's decree, they find plenty of times to touch each other, his hand on her knee, her knocking into him. Grady hooking his chin on her shoulder. Amelia likes him, more than she wants to admit to herself.

But the work?

She *loves* the work.

When Grady heads upstairs to take an online exam, Amelia returns to Molly's diary. She doesn't need to find the recipes anymore. And maybe she should feel guilty for continuing to read it. But she doesn't. She feels only kinship.

July 15, 1945

I sold clear out of ice cream at the Red Cross benefit. The dishes went faster than the girls and I could churn. There was always a line, people waiting for more. And once I ran out, people in town asked if I'd have more for sale at our dairy stand.

I just about sprinted home to Daddy and found him on the porch with his pipe.

He's been so down lately. He's struggling with all the work, and the dairy is barely breaking even. He tries to hide it from

Mother, but I can see it on him. When I told him about the benefit, he was so proud of me. And he laughed harder than he has maybe all summer when I told him how I raised the prices by another fifty cents for the last ten dishes.

He said the apple doesn't fall far from the tree.

"Let me help you," I said. And I told him my plan. That I could sell ice cream at our farm stand. I could bring in money, money we need, using the milk and cream we aren't selling.

"Could you really churn that much in that little bucket of yours?" he asked me.

"No, but I can get a machine for eight hundred dollars," I told him. "It'll churn faster than I ever could. I could make way more, and have more control over it too."

I saw an ad for them in one of Daddy's dairy catalogues, and spent more than an hour on the phone with one of the Emery Thompson salesmen, asking him all sorts of questions.

Right away, Daddy said we don't have that kind of money. I told him we do, because that's the budget for my wedding. I overheard Mother say so to Mrs. Duluth two weeks ago.

Mother must have been eavesdropping, because she pushed outside in her nightgown and said absolutely not and she forbade me to use my wedding money for anything other than marrying Wayne.

Daddy explained that this was the first he was hearing about it and he hadn't made a decision yet one way or the other. I let them go back and forth for a while before I finally put my foot down and said if they didn't let me do this, I would refuse to marry Wayne, I'd become an old spinster and never give them any beautiful grandchildren (Tiggy's idea of a last-ditch threat)!

And that was the end of that.

Now I'm in bed, too excited to sleep. It seems almost sinful to be this lucky. So on Sunday, I'm going to put a little something extra in the collection plate and pray a few more rosaries than I normally do. That way, God will know how very grateful I am.

siobhan vivian

. . .

Near the end of the evening, a little before eleven, Amelia has four gallons of strawberry, chocolate, and vanilla completed, as well as several bases of Home Sweet Home steeping. They'll be ready to put through the machine tomorrow morning.

She goes upstairs to see if Grady can give her a ride down to the stand with the new stock. It's been quiet, and she wonders if she's going to catch him asleep on the couch. She actually hopes she will, just to scare him, because it will be funny.

But Grady isn't asleep. He's on the floor, with his back up against the couch, his mother's letters spread out in front of him.

Amelia tiptoes backward, but he looks up. "Hey."

"Sorry. I didn't mean to disturb you."

"No, you're not." He beckons her closer. She sits next to him, leans against him.

He has opened every one.

"I was so little when she died," he tells her. "I don't have that many memories of her beyond that summer I spent with her here. It's been nice learning about her, in her own voice."

"Tell me."

He does, pointing out some small thing in each and every letter: his mother's terrific penmanship, how she was funny, quick to make a joke, smart. There's never a clunky sentence, or a half-formed thought.

Also, she loved her son. Every letter had some proud mention of him—how alert he was as a baby, how early he started to walk, how much he enjoyed being read to at night.

"And I was going to throw these away," he says, almost in disbelief.

Grady's mother also dropped plenty of delicate hints of

tension in her marriage to Grady's father, mentioning how hard he worked, how his desire for success often left her and Grady in the shadows. She made excuses as to why plans to visit Molly evaporated for one reason or another—a new acquisition, a meeting that couldn't be rescheduled. He wanted to give his family the world, provide for them, but it came at a cost.

"I'm nineteen years old. And do you know I've barely had one conversation with my dad about my mom? Like, how screwed up is that?"

"It doesn't sound like he made it easy on you."

"Oh, he definitely didn't. Talking about my mom made him uncomfortable, but that shouldn't have stopped me from doing it. My stepmom wouldn't have cared. For a while, she was the one who'd remind me when it was my mom's birthday." Amelia can see the anger building in him, a little pulsing vein in his neck, fire reddening his cheeks.

He picks up a letter. "He knew my mom was sick when she and I came to Meade Creamery that summer before she died. I thought he didn't. I thought he found out after and that's why he couldn't come with us."

"Oh, Grady. I'm sorry."

"I mean, does he regret that? Knowing his wife was sick and not being with her? Not stepping away from work?"

"You could talk about it with him. Tell him what you found. It might start to change things between you and your dad."

"Maybe," he says, gathering up the letters, though Amelia isn't sure he believes it.

Amelia gets a text. It's Cate.

Are you working late?

No.

Then can you come down for couple of minutes? I can give you a ride home.

On my way!

Grady helps Amelia pack up the Cadillac with the ice cream, and then he drives her down to the stand. Popping open the trunk, he pauses, taking it in.

"Where were those boards you said were rotting?"

Amelia had forgotten about the repairs the stand needed. Things have been so crazy. "Over here." She has to use the light of her cell phone to show him which ones.

"And there was something else, right?"

"The roof tiles. A bunch of them are loose and broken. But if you do anything up there, please don't throw any away."

"Huh?"

"You'll see."

"Okay. Whatever you say." Grady's phone rings. It's his dad. He puts it to voice mail. "You sure I can't drive you home? I really don't mind."

"Cate's got me tonight. But I'll see you tomorrow."

He helps her carry the ice cream inside. All the girls are in the office. Not just the ones on shift. All of them. They're laughing and talking, though when they see Grady, things get hushed.

"Thanks for the help," Amelia says.

"Of course." He looks like he wants to kiss her, and of course she would love him to. Instead, he gives her hand a quick squeeze.

Amelia walks into the office.

Cate says, "Ugh. Is he gone?"

Amelia's heart lurches, but she tries not to let it show. Though lots of things are changing, Grady is still their enemy. "Yeah. What's going on?"

"Staff meeting. Girls only." Cate claps her hands. "Okay, girls! I know we've had quite a rocky start to this summer. The ice cream drama, Grady . . . and, of course, Bern's unfortunate sparkler incident last night."

At this, all the girls crack up, and Bern acts indignant but then joins in. Amelia smiles, even though she doesn't know the story.

"But some big, breaking news today. Amelia has taken over ice cream production." Cate gestures to Amelia, and there's a smattering of applause. "And"—Cate flicks her hair off her shoulder, so that the Head Girl pin is visible—"I'll be taking over down here."

The girls gasp and rush over to Cate, examining the pin on her collar.

Amelia bites the inside of her cheek.

"To me, being a Meade Creamery girl has always been about hanging out and having fun with some of the coolest girls I've ever met. Yes, we busted our butts, we earned every penny in our paychecks, but we always had a blast doing it. So much so that it almost didn't feel like *work* at all, you know?" Cate sighs wistfully. "But that's the exact *opposite* of how it's felt around here this summer. In fact, I'm kind of shocked that none of you have quit yet."

A few of the girls laugh nervously, like they've been outed. Amelia forces down a swallow, though her throat and mouth are bone dry. Did it really come close to that? Girls quitting? It seems unfathomable to her.

Glancing around, Amelia realizes no one will look at her. Not a single girl.

Maybe she is to blame, Amelia thinks. By leaving them short-staffed all those shifts. By not throwing any parties, planning any adventures. Amelia never showed up with a cool lipstick for everyone to try. She was too busy pestering them to clean.

"But today's a fresh start." Cate looks over at Amelia and winks. "Today, we're taking our summer back."

Amelia thinks if the fresh start Cate's promising will help hit the reset button on everyone's perception of her, then she's all for it. So when she sees her chore chart crumpled in the trash, Amelia makes herself look somewhere else. Anywhere else.

CHAPTER THIRTY-TWO

WHEN IT COMES TO MAKING ICE CREAM, AMELIA IS getting better, faster, more efficient. Like this morning, instead of plucking individual honeysuckle flowers, she's in the driveway using a pair of pruning shears to snip blossom-laden branches, putting those glass vases inside Molly Meade's cabinets to good use.

"Amelia! Can you come here for a sec?" Cate is standing half out the side stand door, waving her hands.

Amelia sets down her bundle and heads to the stand.

She's thinking maybe Cate has a question for her about something stand-related. She's probably diving into the things Amelia has been neglecting. "How's it going?"

"Terrific!"

Amelia looks at the tip jar. It's bursting with money. "Looks like you're killing it today."

"Customers are happy again, now that all the flavors are back." Cate smiles, pleased, and dumps the jar out on the desk. "You should talk to Grady. However long he's going to have you up at the house, you're losing out on tips." She starts smoothing out her bills.

"That's true," Amelia says, though she has no intention of talking to Grady about that. She has been happy working up at the house. On the corner of the desk, she notices a stack of papers.

Newbie applications. There are maybe fifty, filled out.

"I put them out yesterday," Cate says, and then winks. "Word travels fast."

"You're hiring newbies? But summer's half over."

"Um, yeah! How else is the legacy supposed to go on? You want Bern or Sophie to have to hire and train five girls next summer?"

"That's true."

Cate peels the top application off the stack. It's been flagged with a little pink Post-it. "Listen to what this girl wrote for why she wants to work here. *Mostly looking to up my tolerance for ice cream headaches. Also, cash money.*" Cate giggles. "You know she's going to be fun to work with."

"She sounds like a young you," Amelia says.

"That wouldn't be the worst thing. Double the big tip earners!" Cate shuffles some papers to the next one she's flagged. "And listen to this one." She clears her throat. "*I'm brand-new to Sand Lake and I have no friends. I don't have a boyfriend. I'll take*

any shift you've got. I've seriously got nothing else to do this summer."
Cate puts down the paper. "How great would this be for her? She'll meet people, she'll get to arrive at high school next year and have friends. This summer could change her life."

Amelia smiles. Cate's right. This is important. A job at Meade Creamery could completely change someone's life.

Cate picks a third newbie résumé out of the pile for a reason she does not share. Then she lifts the receiver of the black telephone.

"Wait. I'm just wondering if maybe you shouldn't clear these with Grady first." Cate frowns, and Amelia treads lightly. "I just don't want him to raise any objections after the fact."

Cate bristles at the suggestion. "That's not how it's ever worked. The Head Girl makes the call. And that's me."

"Okay, okay."

Cate dials her first pick. She uses a low voice to say, "Kimmy Fox, you have been chosen as a Meade Creamery girl. Get ready to have the best summer of your life."

Amelia can hear giggling and screaming on the other end.

As Cate phones her next girl, Amelia remembers when she got the call.

It came in as her family sat down to dinner. Amelia had gotten some texts from friends who'd just heard Cate Kopernick had been hired for one of the two openings.

If Cate was the kind of girl they were looking for, then Amelia knew she had no chance. But she still waited with hope during the next few minutes for her phone to ring, before slowly setting her hot dog down, nudging her dinner plate away, and lowering her forehead to the table.

Her dream, dashed.

"I guess it was naive of us to think she wouldn't start acting like a high schooler until September," her mom said, a bite of salad hanging from her fork. Her dad, who was turned sideways from the table so he could see the baseball game on the television in the living room, laughed.

And then *her* phone rang.

She pushed back hard from the table, knocking her mom's lemonade over. Amelia said *sorrysorrysorry* before bolting out the back door and across the lawn to the shed. Leaning against it, she took a deep breath before answering.

The girl on the other end didn't introduce herself, though Amelia knows now it was Frankie Ko. All she said was "You're in. See you tomorrow at eleven sharp." Then the line went dead.

Later that night, she got a text from Cate. Amelia still isn't sure who gave Cate her number. She was friendly with Cate, but no one would have called them friends. Cate was in the group of girls who took a limo to the eighth-grade dinner dance. But they texted the entire night, all caps and exclamation marks. Even if they weren't close, they knew that by the end of that summer they would be. That was the magic of Meade Creamery.

"You call the last girl?" Cate says, holding out the receiver.

"No, that's okay."

"Amelia! Come on. Don't you want to be a part of this?"

She does. And it is nice of Cate to include her. Amelia takes the phone while Cate dials.

"What's her name?" Amelia asks, but the girl picks up before Cate can tell her.

"Hello?" comes a small voice.

Amelia tries to hang up the phone, because she hasn't even

thought about what to say, but Cate pushes her hand away, laughing.

"Hello?" the girl says.

Amelia clears her throat and makes her voice low, but it gets stuck somewhere in her throat. "Hello. You've been hired at Meade Creamery for this summer." The girl on the other end sounds like she's going to hyperventilate. Amelia swears she can hear her smiling. "Be here tomorrow at noon o'clock." Noon o'clock? Amelia looks at Cate, who busts up laughing and tries to muffle it by pressing her face into one of the love seat cushions.

"Wait. Is this a joke?" the girl on the phone asks.

"No. Not a joke. See you tomorrow," Amelia says, back in her normal voice, and then quickly hangs up.

Cate is still dying. "Noon o'clock!"

"Oh my God, I suck!"

The pink Cadillac pulls in as Amelia's leaving. Grady has the trunk open and filled with lumber, the backseat with brand-new tools.

"What's all this?"

"I was up early, looking at the stand. It's actually in worse shape than you thought. It's kind of a miracle this place is still standing."

"What?"

"Don't worry. I'm going to replace all the rotting boards, seal the concrete, and try to figure out a fix for the roof that keeps those signatures in place. A Home Depot guy was talking about this water sealant I can try. And when I'm done, the stand will be good as new."

"You've got time for this? With all your schoolwork? And the stand stuff?" That said, she understands his urgency. Grady's avoided dealing with his mother's death for too long. Fortifying the stand is a chance for him to right some of those wrongs.

Grady's cell phone rings. He quickly puts the call through to voice mail, and the look on his face when he does it tells Amelia exactly who it is. "Yeah. This is important."

Later that day, Amelia makes herself a dish of ice cream and takes it out to the front stairs of Molly's house. The echo of Grady's hammer can be heard all the way up here. She opens the diary on her lap.

July 30, 1915

It's the night before I'll be selling the ice cream at our farm stand. I've tried my best to prepare, get familiar with my new machine, which only arrived three days ago. Tiggy stayed so late tonight, helping me to get everything set up. She's never worked harder in her life but she didn't complain, not once.

I love her so much.

Meanwhile, every time Mother sees my ice cream machine, she frowns. And she tells everyone exactly how expensive it was. If this ice cream thing doesn't work, I told.

her I'll sell it. She says I'll have to, or else
I'll be marrying Wayne in a Sunday dress
in the fields.

She says that to scare me, but if that's the
worst thing that happens, I think I'll be fine.

siobhan vivian

CHAPTER  THIRTY-THREE

AMELIA TRIES HER BEST TO KEEP MOLLY'S CADILLAC centered on the driveway as she drives down to the stand with a trunk full of ice cream, but this proves an unfortunately difficult task for someone who can barely see over the dashboard. The vehicle rocks over the lumpy dirt—an off-kilter pink tank—and every time the brush scrapes and claws like fingers against the doors, Amelia shrieks.

Grady has started keeping the car keys on the table near the entryway for her, so Amelia can use it when she needs to. She is surprised at how rusty she feels behind the wheel, though she probably shouldn't be. Amelia got her license this past spring but she hardly ever drives. She gets around fine on her bike, since her family only has one car. Plus, Cate's always around to drive them wherever they need to go. But the speed with which her heart races on these trips up and down the driveway, compared to the speedometer needle fluttering at just under five miles per hour, is probably a sign she should practice more.

Amelia parks alongside Cate's truck, but she doesn't find Cate in the stand with the other girls.

"Is she here?"

"Yeah," Jen says, thumbing outside. "She's waiting for the newbies."

Amelia walks outside to the front of the stand. And there is Cate, perched on the picnic table, her blond hair long and catching the breeze. She's wearing makeup—eyeliner winged, a touch of pink blush, cherry-red lip gloss—and her arms and legs are coated in her favorite vanilla bean lotion, the one that has a bit of sparkle mixed in. Her Keds are new and spotless.

"You look amazing."

"Thanks. You know, I've wanted to do this, to be this girl, ever since our first summer," Cate sheepishly admits.

"Do you need help with anything?"

"Nope," Cate says. "Though, if you could get Grady out of here, that'd be amazing. There are all these huge holes in the stand now. It's embarrassing."

Over her shoulder, Amelia watches Grady determinedly yanking off wooden boards with a crowbar. From a distance, he looks like he knows what he's doing, but Amelia knows better. He has Band-Aids on every finger. When she turns back, the three newbies are approaching. One comes by bicycle, and the other two are dropped off by a grandpa-type. She lingers, wanting to see Cate do her thing.

Cate tosses them each a polo shirt. "Okay, girls, I know I don't have to tell you how special this place is." Grinning, Cate leans back, resting her weight on her elbows. "But trust me that it's even more special once you're behind the counter with us. If you prove yourself worthy over the next few days, you'll never be a plain old customer again. You'll be a Meade Creamery girl. And that lasts forever."

Amelia is happy to hear Cate say it. Sometimes it feels like they don't hold Meade Creamery in the same regard.

Cate goes on, "We take care of each other in here, the way sisters do. No one risks sneaking off to text their boyfriend when a school bus full of campers might pull up. No one's going to wimp out and not empty the trash cans even if there are bees around. We may not always get along perfectly, but not one girl here would ever think of taking the last tampon out of the box in the office without dropping off a new box the next day, whether they were on the schedule or not. You know what I mean?"

The three girls nod like bobbleheads.

"We take pride in every aspect of this job. *Every. Aspect.* Even down to the sprinkles." Cate wets her lips. "You newbies don't know it yet, but there's actually a fine art to getting perfect sprinkle coverage on an ice cream cone. And I'm going to show you how right now."

The three girls look awkwardly at each other.

"Let's go! Chop-chop! Into the stand!"

"Cate," Amelia whispers. "This isn't *Lord of the Flies*!"

Cate looks pleased as punch. "I always thought the Head Girl could up the theatrics a little bit."

Amelia is cleaning up after a batch of strawberry when she hears Grady come into the house. He washes his hands, then comes downstairs. He's a little sunburned.

"How's it going out there?"

He hooks his chin on her shoulder. "Good. At least I feel useful." His phone rings.

"Is that your dad again?"

"Yeah."

"You've been avoiding him for days. Is that smart?"

"I don't know. Probably not. But it's not like he's calling to find out how I am or anything. He wants to talk business. He went through the books and he has all these new ideas for me."

"All bad ones, you think? Nothing that might be worth considering?"

"Good or bad, once he tells me them, they won't be optional."

"You're doing a great job. There's ice cream to sell; the girls are happy."

He kisses her neck. "What are you doing tonight? Let me take you out on a date."

Her eyes slowly close as she melts into him. "We can't."

"What if we went someplace far? Like a few towns over."

"Things are just getting back to normal with me and Cate. If word got back to her before I told her about us . . ."

"So tell her! Or I can tell her, if you want."

"I'll tell her eventually. Just not yet. Anyway, don't you have schoolwork you're neglecting?"

"Promise me we'll go on at least one date before the end of the season. Okay?"

She nods, but what happens after that? She doesn't ask Grady, in part because she's got ice cream to make, and also because she doesn't know herself what she wants the answer to be.

CHAPTER  THIRTY-FOUR

WHEN THE ICY CLOUD DISSIPATES, AMELIA SMILES AT the wall of cardboard ice cream drums. It feels good to see the walk-in freezer filling back up. A few more days of this, Amelia thinks, and she should be able to get back on the schedule rotation, working at the stand with the rest of the girls.

But life is pretty sweet right now, popping in for a little girl time at the stand when she has ice cream ready, then heading back up to the house to have lunch with Grady.

On this afternoon, Amelia hangs up the ski jacket and enters the office. Cate is there, applying lipstick on the three newbies, who are squished together on the love seat, lips pouted in preparation for their turn.

"Hey, Amelia! I never tried this on you!" Amelia comes over

and parts her lips. Cate draws the lipstick on and gives her a tissue to blot. "Oooh. That's a great MLBB on you."

"A what?"

"*My Lips But Better*. Go look!"

Amelia walks over to the mirror. It looks lighter pink on Amelia, like her actual lips, which is sort of anticlimactic. Then she sits down on the corner of the desk, watching Cate make over the newbies. Cate has already calculated the receipts for the first shift, but Amelia takes them and smooths them out and fastens them together a bit more neatly.

And then Amelia looks up. "Does something smell weird in here?" Since no one answers her, Amelia follows her nose, searching around the office. Underneath the credenza, she finds a crusty beach towel that stinks of a million gym lockers.

A few days ago, temperatures had crossed a hundred degrees. Amelia came down and saw that Cate had lined her truck bed with a tarp, filled it with water, and had the girls swimming between customers.

A moldy towel, a messy stack of receipts, and a schedule that never goes up on time. She takes a deep breath, reminding herself that she needs to be okay with these trade-offs. The other girls wouldn't ever complain about these things.

Though she probably could stay and hang out awhile, Amelia tells Cate she needs to head back up to the farmhouse. Better that, she decides, than let these little things bother her.

After throwing the towel in the dumpster, Amelia drives back up to the farmhouse in her lipstick, excited to show Grady. She's never wearing makeup around him, never in normal clothes. It *would* be nice to go on a date with him. There's a miniature golf course twenty minutes away. Sure, Grady plays golf, he's got his own clubs, but Amelia has never missed a putt through the spinning blades of the windmill. She thinks she can probably take him.

She's slipping inside the house when she hears Grady in the midst of a heated argument in the living room. He's so focused, he doesn't even look up. Her stomach sinks with every step down to the basement. Could Grady's dad have figured out they went to the beach house?

A few minutes later, Grady comes down hot.

"That didn't sound like it went well," she says gently.

"Yeah. My dad's not happy with our bottom line. The stand makes a decent profit, but a lot of the revenue gets turned back over into the business, cost of ingredients, payroll. So he's been talking to his buddy Rod, who works in restaurants, and . . ." Grady shakes his head. "I don't even want to tell you."

"What?"

"My dad thinks we should stop making homemade ice cream and start serving, like, Hershey's or whatever. Something we can buy in bulk from a distributor."

"What? That's crazy! The ice cream is what makes Meade Creamery special!"

"I know."

Amelia shakes her head, resolute. "No, Grady. You can't. Absolutely not." Molly Meade would roll over in her grave. "This is ultimately your stand, Grady. If you don't want to take his advice, you don't have to."

"That's what I tried to tell him. And then . . . we kind of got into a big fight."

"How big?"

"Huge." He drops onto the couch and stares at the ceiling. "I used to look up to my dad so much. I'd do anything to please him. But now I'm scared that I'm going to turn into him." He swallows and then turns his head to look at Amelia. "I actually said that to him."

Amelia's eyes go wide. "What did he say?"

"Nothing. He hung up on me."

Amelia can't get it off her mind for the rest of the day. The idea that Grady's dad would erase the best thing about Meade Creamery to make a few extra dollars. Thank God Grady drew a line in the sand. But she's no fool. She knows Grady's dad has the power here. Grady's Truman tuition is hanging in the balance.

Would Grady's dad really sacrifice his son's future to make a point?

Or maybe he secretly wants Meade Creamery to go out of business for the same reason his son wants to keep it open.

Grady's mother.

CHAPTER THIRTY-FIVE

THE NEXT TIME CATE DOES THE SCHEDULE, SHE GIVES herself and Amelia the same day off. "Now don't you think new-bies were a good idea?" she says, knocking into her.

"Yes."

The plan is to go shopping at the mall. Get some dorm essentials.

Amelia gets out of the shower and sees a text from Grady.

I miss seeing you this morning. Boo for days off.

Yay for days off! she writes back. I'm in real clothes!

I wanna see. he writes. And then, quickly, adds, Not in a creepy way!

Amelia takes a selfie in her baby blue off-the-shoulder peasant dress, blooming with hundreds of tiny embroidered red roses.

Man, you so cute. Aren't you going to ask what I'm wearing?

Amelia grins and types. Is it a blazer?

Grady sends back a photo of himself . . . in a pink Meade Creamery polo. Amelia doubles over laughing.

Take that off, imposter!

I'll do whatever it takes to take you out on a date, Amelia. For real.

And then her phone starts buzzing nonstop.

Will you please go on a date with me?

Will you please go on a date with me?

Will you please go on a date with me?

Grinning, she puts her phone on silent. Would this be how they'd do it, if they tried long distance? There might be something nice about it. She'd get her space and have a boyfriend, too. The distance almost takes the pressure off, in a way.

But what to tell Cate?

The truth, obviously. She must tell her the truth. Sooner rather than later.

She goes downstairs to eat a quick bowl of cereal. Cate's supposed to pick her up in fifteen minutes. She finds her parents waiting for her in the kitchen.

"Can I borrow a credit card? I'm going dorm shopping with Cate."

"Amelia, we need to talk," her dad says soberly.

"Okay." She slides into her seat.

Her parents share uncomfortable looks with each other, like neither one wants to go first.

"You guys are scaring me."

Her mom places her palms down on the table. "We stopped by the stand yesterday for an ice cream."

"You did?"

"We were hoping we'd surprise you. But . . ."

"What?" She thinks they're going to say something about her being up at the farmhouse with Grady. Or, even worse, about the ice cream not tasting right. She takes a taste of every batch, to make sure it turned out okay, but maybe she missed one. Sometimes it is hard to concentrate, with Grady around.

"The service was . . . bad," her dad says with a heavy sigh. "Bad, Amelia. It was as if the girls didn't care anymore. I couldn't believe it. The lines were so long, but they didn't move like normal. And the girls seemed distracted, talking to each other and joking around. I know you girls have a good time there, but it was like we were an afterthought."

"We waited at the window for a good five minutes while the girls inside finished up a conversation with each other."

"Oh."

Mom says, "And I mentioned something at the bank and . . . well, our experience isn't an isolated one."

And Dad adds, "We thought we should tell you, since you are Head Girl."

"I'm actually . . ." Amelia pauses. "Cate's taken control of things down at the stand."

"Oh. Okay. Well, then maybe check in with her. She probably has no idea. It could be girls slacking off when she's not around."

Or, Amelia thinks, it could be the fresh start Cate talked about.

Either way, it's not exactly a conversation she's excited to have. But better Amelia bring it up than Grady. If he did, Cate might just quit. And Amelia can see a scenario where the rest of the girls follow her out the door.

CHAPTER  THIRTY-SIX

AMELIA USED TO THINK THE MALL JUST OUTSIDE SAND Lake was enormous. It definitely seemed huge when she was a kid and she used to get her annual picture taken on Santa's lap. But over the years, it's as if the place has shrunk.

There are just enough stores to do a halfway decent back-to-school shopping trip: a Gap, a Macy's, a Victoria's Secret, a Sephora. But most girls in their senior class ordered their prom dresses online.

In Molly Meade's day, this wasn't here. Amelia's not sure what was. Probably just a field. The shops were all on Main Street. Molly bought a dress for her high school graduation at a place called Blauner's. It's now a Dollar Store. Miller's Pharmacy, now a Rite Aid, is where she'd buy cosmetics. One of the only places Molly wrote about that is still around is Corbet Jewelers, which is across the street from the post office, but Amelia almost never sees anyone going in and out of there.

She and Cate take the escalator down into the basement of Macy's with two coupons Cate clipped for them out of last Sunday's newspaper. There's already a sale going on for practically everything in the home department, but these coupons, Cate informs her, will give them an extra 20 percent off on new comforters for their dorm rooms.

Amelia feels oddly adult, surrounded by KitchenAid mixers, stacks of silver baking sheets, rows of decorative vases.

"This is cute, isn't it?" Cate says, pulling out a clear plastic bag with a pale yellow floral comforter stuffed inside. She turns it over, then puts it back. "Ideally, I want a whole look. Sheets, comforter, bed skirt, pillow sham. What about you?"

"I'm just going to get a comforter." Amelia knows she sounds glum, but she's dreading the thought of having to confront Cate about her parents' experience at the stand.

"Don't. Get a matching set, like me! It'll make your side of the dorm room look so much more pulled together." Cate laughs. "Though wait. You'll probably want to run your picks by Cece."

"Who's Cece?"

"Cecilia. Your roommate at Gibbons. Did you ever hear back from her?"

Amelia gasps. "Oh my God, Cate. I never wrote her back. I meant to, when you told me all those weeks ago!" It's crazy, how fast time is flying. It's practically August.

"Amelia!" Cate scolds. She grabs Amelia by the hand and drags her over to the mattress section so they can sit. "You are so worried about the ice cream stand, you aren't paying attention to what really matters. What if she asks for a transfer and you get stuck with some weirdo who never showers?"

Amelia pulls out her phone and searches for Cecilia's email. "I just don't know what to say. She wrote this whole long thing about herself."

Cate holds out her hand and Amelia passes her phone over. After reading the message, Cate says, "I'll do it for you."

"Okay."

Cate narrates as she types. *"Hey Cecilia. Thanks so much for getting us the fridge. I will totally handle the microwave, no problem. Sorry for not writing sooner. My summer job is madness—I'll tell you all about it in a few weeks. Anyway, a little about me—I'm undeclared right now, no boyfriend (What can I say? I like keeping my options open) . . ."*

At this, Amelia tries to take her phone back. "Don't write that!"

"Why?" Cate says, swatting her hand away. "Because of Grady?"

Amelia's whole body goes cold. "No. Why would you say that?"

"Chill, I'm kidding."

As Cate continues typing, Amelia realizes that, should Grady randomly happen to text her, the fact that she's been hiding him from her best friend will blow up in her face.

Cate narrates the rest of her email. *"Also, not sure what the style is yet of our dorm room, but if it's bunk beds, can I claim the bottom? I have this thing with heights."*

"I don't have a thing with heights. At least, I don't think I do."

Cate shrugs. "She seemed a little alpha in her last email. I want to push back on that a bit. I don't want her thinking she

siobhan vivian

can railroad you. Plus, trust me, no one wants the top bunk."

"Fine," Amelia says, anxious, and then takes her phone back.

Cate settles on a bed-in-a-bag, white with a blue ikat pattern, embellished with little blue tassels sewn around the edges. She buys a second set of sheets and a throw pillow.

Amelia ends up with a solid pink comforter made special by little ribbons of chenille sewn across it. She can't find the matching sheets, but the saleswoman says they're available online.

They're in the food court when Amelia finally summons the courage to ask Cate about the stand. The stand matters too much to her to let things slide any more.

"Did you happen to see my parents yesterday? They stopped by the stand."

"Oh yeah? I must have missed them."

"Yeah, they said the lines were super long," Amelia says, fingering the straw in her fountain Coke. "Like, longer than usual. Sounds like it was a little . . . chaotic." She's hedging, trying not to sound accusatory, giving Cate some room.

"It *is* chaotic. Grady's making a total mess of the place playing handyman. All his hammering and sawing. I had to throw out a huge vat of waffle cone batter because there was sawdust in it. I don't know why he doesn't just hire someone."

"I think he's enjoying the work."

"Well, he's making my life incredibly difficult."

Something rises in her. The desire to hold Cate accountable. "I totally get how that would be annoying," Amelia couches. "But I'm worried it isn't just a Grady problem." At this, Cate groans, and it almost derails Amelia from continuing. "I . . . I know you want the girls to have fun while they work. But it's a job, too."

Cate dabs at her mouth with a napkin. "I don't want to talk about the stand with you."

"But Cate . . ."

"I've caught you secretly looking over the stuff I do like a hundred times. And whenever you come down to the stand, I feel like you always find something negative to focus on, instead of how much better things are, how much happier everyone is."

Amelia sits back. She can't defend herself against Cate's charge, because it's true. And Cate doesn't even give her the chance.

Cate begins gathering her unfinished meal and places it on her tray. "If you didn't want me to be Head Girl, why did you tell Grady I should be promoted? Why did you give me your pin?"

Amelia bites her lip. She never actually said that to Grady. That was his idea, a way to smooth the ruffled feathers of their relationship. And it worked, at least temporarily. But the promotion clearly didn't solve their problems. Things are still weird between them.

"Forget it," Cate says. "I wanted to have a fun day with you."

"I did too!" Amelia calls out as Cate walks toward the trash can.

Instead of catching up to her, Amelia lets Cate walk ahead of her at a slight distance.

She was already anxious about the future. Now she's dreading it.

siobhan vivian

CHAPTER  THIRTY-SEVEN

AT AROUND THREE O'CLOCK THE NEXT DAY, THERE'S A knock at the basement side door. "That's got to be my delivery from Marburger Dairy," Amelia says. She's in the middle of a batch, so Grady gets up and opens the door.

It takes the man three trips with a dolly to bring in all the milk and eggs and cream. Just in time, because she's about through with last week's delivery. And, just like that, Amelia has more work to do.

She's grateful for the distraction.

Every time Amelia thinks back to yesterday's conversation with Cate at the mall, she gets angry. Amelia's made plenty of her own mistakes, but she's also shouldered the blame—probably more than her fair share, come to think of it—for the things that have gone wrong.

And no one could say that Amelia hasn't worked her butt off for this place.

So why did she let Cate blow off her concerns? Her *valid* concerns? Is it just because of Grady guilt? Or something deeper?

"Here's your invoice," the man tells Grady. "The credit card you gave us was declined, but I'm still delivering your order because your great-aunt was such a loyal customer. And just so you know, in more than fifty years, Molly was never once late with a payment."

Grady and Amelia share a look.

"That's weird," Grady says nervously. And to Amelia, he deduces, "It's probably all the stuff I've been buying at Home Depot."

"I can take a check," the deliveryman announces.

"Um, okay. Great." But his eyes bug out when he looks at the invoice. "This is a lot of money. Is this right?"

"It's the same as it's always been," the dairyman says, somewhat defensively. "You're paying for quality. All our cows are—"

Grady shakes his head. "I know you make incredible stuff. It's just . . . a bit of sticker shock."

"Grady," says Amelia.

"Don't worry. I've got it." To the dairyman, he says, "I'll be right back. My checkbook is upstairs."

Later that day, Amelia notices that Grady's put a FOR SALE— FOOD TRUCK sign on the roadside. Buying it never seemed like a good idea to her, but she hopes it will to someone else.

siobhan vivian

CHAPTER  THIRTY-EIGHT

THE COUNTY FAIR IS ALWAYS THE LAST WEEKEND IN July. It's not in Sand Lake, but in Plaistow, three towns west and way more rural. There are rides, music, livestock competitions, games. Business at the stand is usually pretty dead that weekend, and the Head Girl normally stacks the schedule so every girl gets one night off to go.

Amelia assumes that's what Cate will do too. But when Cate hangs up the schedule for that week, she's got a red line drawn through Saturday's second shift, as if the stand were completely closed.

Cate comes up behind her. "Don't say anything," she whispers, which is the most she has spoken to Amelia in a week. And it feels like a test of Amelia's loyalty.

Grady comes in a few minutes later, looking for the drill. He glances at the schedule. "What's up with Saturday night?" His eyes go right to Amelia for an answer.

Cate pipes up from the office. "Oh. I figured Amelia would have said something. Every year, Molly Meade would give everyone the night off for the fair. It was like a special thing she would do for all the girls. Like . . . for bonding."

Amelia tenses, thinking of Grady's declined credit card. Shutting down the stand, even for one night, means lost revenue. He said the stand is profitable, but can they afford it?

"Sounds fun. And you know what? I'll pay for everything. Rides, food, the works."

Amelia spins. "You don't have to do that," she urges.

Cate comes bounding out of the office. "That's really nice of you, Grady. I bet Molly would be proud." At this, Amelia's stomach turns over.

"Please," Grady says benevolently. "It's the least I can do. I used to be the social director of my fraternity. I'd plan outings and stuff to basketball games, a boxing match. I know how to do it up. Tell the girls to dress up. We'll meet here. Everyone can go over together."

Amelia pulls him aside. "Seriously, you don't have to do this." She wants to say more—that Cate's making the whole thing up, closing for the night isn't a real tradition—but she can't bring herself to throw Cate under the bus. Though things are fraught between them, Cate is still her best friend.

"It's worth it to take you on a date, Amelia. Here's my shot."

And so on Saturday, Meade Creamery closes at five o'clock.

Amelia shows up in a pink floral dress with buttons up the

front. She braided her hair after her shower that morning, and now it is all waves. Despite everything, she's excited for tonight.

Cate's in a silky green romper and a long gold locket. "You look pretty," Amelia tells her.

"Thank you," Cate says stiffly. "You too." And then, to the other girls milling around the front of the stand, Cate wonders, "Is he planning to drive us all over in the pink Cadillac?"

Grady comes down from the house. He's got on a dark denim shirt with the sleeves rolled up, a pair of light denim jeans, and his boat shoes. He's gotten a haircut. And Amelia can smell his cologne. Cedar and clove and orange.

"You look nice," he tells Amelia. His focus is solely on her as if no one else is there.

"Thanks." But she's quick to look around and add, "All the girls look nice tonight, don't they?"

"Yes they do." Grady shades his eyes and smiles at the road. "Ah, looks like our ride is here."

The girls cheer as a white stretch limo pulls into the stand driveway.

Amelia has never ridden in a limousine before. She was actually kind of disappointed when their group rented a party bus for prom. The man driving it comes out wearing a black suit and tie.

Grady claps his hands. "All right! Let's get our kettle corn on!" he says, and opens the limo door.

"Oh, wait." Cate stops, and laughs awkwardly. "I didn't realize you were coming with us, Grady. This is normally a girls-only night. I'm sorry. I thought I made that clear."

Fuming, Amelia whispers to Cate, "You do remember that this isn't an actual tradition, right? Just one you made up?"

Grady glumly stuffs his hands in his pockets. "Ah. Okay. Well, that makes sense."

Amelia quickly grabs him by the elbow. To the other girls, she announces, "Since Grady's paying, I think he deserves to be made an honorary Meade Creamery girl tonight, don't you all?" And instead of waiting for an answer, Amelia is the first to climb aboard.

The girls hang back as Grady approaches the ticket booth. Amelia stays as close as she can to him, watching out of the corner of her eye as one, then another, of his credit cards get declined.

Grady pulls out a third. "Sorry, but could you give this one a try?"

The boy at the booth slides it into the machine. "Sorry, man."

Amelia wraps her arms around herself. Though Grady played it off to her initially, it's clear now that this is a repercussion from his dad.

"Grady, we can pay for ourselves." She discreetly slides her hand into his and gives him a squeeze, whispering, "No date is worth this much."

"I have cash." He opens his wallet and hands every last dollar over, buying admission for every girl and as many ride tickets as he can. "I can get more rides and food if anyone wants," he tells them as he passes them. "I'll just need to hit up an ATM."

Amelia is just about to say thank you when Cate does something completely unexpected, snaking her arm through Amelia's and dragging her off like old times.

After all these summers, Cate and Amelia have their county fair routine down pat. Together, they lead the charge, herding the girls toward their personal favorite rides (the bumper cars, the Super Slide, the Tilt N Swing) bypassing the rides that make them sick (the teacups, the Zipper). They each get a corn dog and a fresh-squeezed lemonade, split a bag of rainbow cotton candy, and devour it all while watching three college-age girls in matching denim dresses harmonize a country version of a Katy Perry song onstage at the grandstand. They pet the baby lambs in the livestock pen. They even get their faces painted, just one cheek, the Best Friends Forever broken heart.

As good as it feels to be with Cate, Amelia hates leaving Grady at the back of their group. She tries her best to make him feel included, pulling him in on different conversations, smiling when she catches his eye, but she's also careful not to be too chummy with him either.

It kills her to do this. This night is for her.

Some of the girls want to get their fortunes read, and Cate leads the way to the striped tent. Amelia's following too, until Grady slips his hand in hers and pulls her to a stop.

"Will you ride the Ferris wheel with me?"

"Grady, I—"

"Come on. Get on quick, before they notice we're gone."

They hurry quickly into the Ferris wheel line, climb into a car, and swirl their way up to the top. It's dark, and the stars twinkle above them.

"What's going on with your credit cards?"

"Let's not talk about it. Not when I finally have you to myself."

"It's your dad. He's punishing you."

"Don't worry," he says, threading some hair behind her ear.

"What are you going to do about Truman?"

"I'll figure it out. So long as I have the stand, I've got something."

Their ride is coming to an end. As their carriage lowers to the ground, Amelia sees Cate and the other girls emerging from the fortune-teller tent, looking around for them. She squeezes Grady's hand tightly.

"It's cool," he tells her. "You can let go. I'm not offended. I knew what tonight would be like."

She eventually does let go, but not a second before she absolutely has to.

That night, as she snuggles into bed, Amelia reads a diary entry.

August 10, 1945

I don't quite have the words for how I am feeling tonight. Or what to put in my letter to Wayne.

Almost a month ago, I wrote to Wayne, overjoyed about how well my ice cream went over at the benefit.

He never wrote back.

And then, two weeks ago, I wrote to him again about what might be the happiest day in my life thus far. My first day selling ice cream at our farm stand.

Maybe that is the problem.

I've never been more tired in my whole life as I was that night, but I was desperate

siobhan vivian

to put the entire day down on paper, so I
wouldn't forget a single wonderful moment.
I knew I only had it in me to write it once,
with all the emotion I was feeling. But
instead of writing it here, in my diary, I
decided to put it down in a letter to Wayne.

It was my longest one yet, pages and pages
and pages. I wrote for more than an hour,
even though I had a burning cramp in my
hand from all the scooping. I didn't dare
stop, afraid some little thing might slip
away from me and be lost. The aprons all
the girls wore. How long the line got and
who was in it. Just wanting to get down
every single moment for Wayne, so he
could feel as if he were here with me, living
it with me.

I have been checking the postbox every day.
Waiting for his reply. Or for both my
letters to be returned. Undeliverable would
almost be better.

Today, his response finally came. A quick
note, just to say hello and that he loves me.
Nothing about my letters, even though I
know he at least received the last one, because
he casually mentioned one small thing I
had written about a friend of his—Paul

Hockey—who'd asked after him when he reached the front of the line.

No pride in me.

No excitement for what I had accomplished.

When I got to his signature, I burst into tears and ran straight to my room. Mother came right up after me and pushed open my bedroom door, convinced I'd received some sort of bad news about Wayne. She took the letter straight out of my hand and read it and was so relieved.

But it was bad news, to me.

I told Mother how upset I was, but she thinks I'm batty for caring this much about ice cream, especially in light of the things Wayne and my brothers are facing every day. She made a million excuses for him, that he could have been going off to battle, that maybe a second page of his letter had somehow not made it into the envelope.

She said, in all honesty, "How could he care, Moll? This is a hobby for this summer. Once Wayne comes home, you'll get married and start a family. And, God

siobhan vivian

willing, if things keep going well for our side, your brothers and Wayne will be home before you know it, and you can go back to being just Molly. And everything will be the way it was always supposed to be."

Mother said it to comfort me, but it did the opposite.

The war changes people. I've seen it in Sy Sampson and Harry Gund, who came back. I sense it in Wayne.

But I think the war is changing me, too. And I'm not sure I can go back. I'm not sure I want to.

CHAPTER THIRTY-NINE

"CAN YOU PLEASE STOP?" CATE ASKS HER, POKING HER head out of the office door, the same way she's already asked twice before. But Amelia hears something in Cate's voice now that has shifted. From playful teasing to straight-up annoyed. And so she puts down the broom and gets on one of the windows.

She's been back down at the stand for nearly a week now. And she's been very careful not to annoy Cate, especially after the county fair night, where it felt like they'd begun to patch things up. But even walking on eggshells, she seems to bug Cate every time she tries to do something that wasn't asked of her.

Grady's down at the stand too, doing the work that Cate has been complaining about. It's true, it's not the most conducive to business. The customers keep shouting *What?* over the bang of his hammer, and occasionally Grady lets out a frustrated curse.

Today, his focus is on the roof; he's trying to seal up the shingles with some kind of solution. The smell is pungent and sulfuric, and it's making the girls dizzy. Every so often, a gooey drip of it will fall through the ceiling and land on the floor with a splat. Grady's shoes are sticking to the roof. Every footstep sounds like ripping two pieces of duct tape apart.

"I can't hear myself think," Cate groans, and fans herself with a schedule she's been working on for the last hour. "I'm going to pass out from the fumes."

Amelia scrapes the last scoop from a drum of strawberry and then goes to the walk-in freezer to fetch a new one. She notices that something is wrong right away. She doesn't get goose bumps the way she normally does when she ducks inside.

"Has anyone heard this kick on lately?" she asks, ducking out.

The girls all shrug.

The scooping cabinet between the service windows is set to 5 degrees, so the ice cream is soft enough to scoop. But the walk-in freezer is kept at -10 degrees, and the ice cream that comes out of there is rock-hard. Amelia pops off the lid of a drum and drags her finger across the top. It sinks in deep, like into cake icing.

She shouts out to Grady, "Grady! We have a problem!"

And then she waits for him to answer.

When he doesn't, she calls out again, "Like an ASAP problem!"

"One second!"

She bites the inside of her cheek. She could move some of the ice cream up to the house, but there isn't enough room for all of it. She's completely replenished the stock.

Finally, Grady comes down off the ladder and checks out the situation. He's sweaty and frustrated. In the office, he puts his sticky hands on the desk and the phone, and Cate is groaning. He calls a repairman and begs him to come, agreeing to pay whatever it takes to get him out straightaway.

The repairman opens up an access panel and begins tinkering. After nearly an hour he says, "Haven't worked on one this old before. I replaced the fan and tried my best to clean the condenser coil. I got her running, but you're going to need to upgrade. If she makes it through the end of the summer, you'll be lucky."

"How much does a new freezer run?" Grady asks.

"You're looking at around eight to ten grand."

Amelia sees Grady wobble. He heads outside, beet-red and barely keeping it together. She wants to go to him, help him figure this out, but she can't.

Later that afternoon, Amelia is out in the field, gathering branches of honeysuckle. A storm is coming; the sky is getting darker by the minute and a mean wind whips her hair.

Grady comes up behind her. "Hi." His shoulders hang.

"Hi." She doesn't want to push him, but it's on her mind. "What are you going to do about the freezer?"

"I don't have that kind of cash liquid. Not even close." He spins her around. "But it's not your problem. I'll figure it out."

"You could try to talk to my mom. See about getting a small-business loan."

"I don't know what bank would give me any money. I don't have a credit history. All my credit cards are through my dad."

"But if we don't have a freezer, what are you going to do about next summer?"

Grady smiles thinly. "To be honest . . . I haven't thought much about next summer. I'm barely getting through this one."

It begins to rain. They stand in silence as the drops multiply.

"Come on," Grady says, taking her hand. "Let's head inside."

It's the perfect escape from what Amelia knows will be a difficult conversation. What does the future hold? For Meade Creamery, but also for them?

They look at each other at the same time and book it to the house, branches scraping at their legs as the sky opens up and the rain spills out.

Crashing through the back door, she's hot and cool all at once. And completely soaked. Her hair sticking to her cheeks, her shirt clinging to her body. Grady, too, is soaked through, his hair in clumps of wet curls, his chest heaving.

He pulls her close to him and kisses her. Their wet bodies stick together. His hands are pulling at her, peeling her shirt up over her head. Then she peels away his. And they are kissing and walking, heading toward the living room couch half-dressed, the rain blurring the view out of every window. The room is dark with the storm until a crack of lightning flashes, brightening everything up.

And then, there is Cate—wet as a stray cat, shivering in the hallway. "The roof is leaking," she says, annoyed. "I tried calling you like seventeen times, Amelia."

"I . . . I . . ."

Cate shakes her head. "Don't even try."

Cate waits in the foyer, impatiently tapping her foot, while Amelia declines Grady's offer of a dry shirt, wriggling into her wet one.

They all go down to the stand together. A few folks sprint

up to the windows, but they don't have many customers. Grady climbs up on the roof and, in the midst of the storm, tries laying down a tarp. The wind lifts it up on him a few times, snapping it. The reason the roof isn't fixed, Amelia knows, is all because she wanted him to salvage those signed shingles.

As Grady battles the tarp, Amelia scrambles to place containers on the floor to catch the drips. The other girls find rags to dry the floor, wipe down surfaces, pull the old milk bottles down from the rafters.

Cate is the only one not moving, just standing still in the middle of the frenzy, snorting with laugher.

"You seriously find this funny?" Amelia manages to ask, even though she's having trouble breathing. Will Cate out her and Grady to the rest of the girls? Would that be the worst thing?

"Yeah, I do. You're trying to catch drips when this entire place is falling apart. The freezer, the walls. One more rainstorm this summer and we're flooded out."

Amelia knows this is likely true. But it doesn't make her laugh. It makes her cry.

"Oh, lighten up, Amelia. It's just an ice cream stand."

She ducks outside so no one will see.

Looking back at the stand, and shielding her eyes from the rain, Amelia sees the tarp wrapped tight to the roof, raw lumber piled on top to hold it down, but there's no sign of Grady.

Cold and wet, feeling like a dog nobody wants to let in the house, she wraps her arms around herself and walks back up to the farmhouse.

She finds him pacing the length of the fireplace mantel. "I don't have the money for that freezer. I definitely don't have money for a new roof."

The stand wasn't as profitable as she thought, and Molly hadn't been taking care of the place. Amelia can't help but wonder if it even would have been around next summer.

"What are you going to do?"

"I'm going to have to ask my dad for a loan."

"Will he do that for you?"

Grady shrugs. "He might. He'd be in a position of power over me, which he'll enjoy. It's probably going to come with some conditions, though."

"Like . . . taking his ideas."

Grady nods.

Amelia, of course, is thinking about the ice cream.

Grady seems to read her mind. "I'm just going to get the money and then I'll figure it out the rest later."

Amelia nods. She's got the same plan for dealing with Cate.

Later.

CHAPTER  FORTY

GRADY AND AMELIA SIT SIDE BY SIDE ON THE BASE-
ment couch, heads close together, Grady's cell balanced on his
knee. They're splitting Grady's earbuds so they can both listen in
on the call. Jazzy hold music plays on the line.

"Can you hear my heart beating?" Amelia whispers to Grady.
It pounds in her ears, in her throat, in her chest.

He squeezes her hand. "If this is too weird, you don't have to
do it. But I like having you next to me for moral support. I don't
want to screw this up."

Amelia can hear how nervous Grady is. She wishes he didn't
have to make this call, go crawling back to his dad to ask for
money, but what other option is there? This conversation is
surely going to be about more than just a business loan. Hanging in the balance is Grady's ability to return to Truman this

fall, and maybe any chance there might be to repair something deeply broken in his relationship to his dad.

She squeezes his hand back. "I'll be right here."

The hold music ends abruptly. A secretary comes on the line and says, hurriedly, "Are you still there, Grady?"

"Yeah, Nancy. I'm here."

"Okay. Your dad just got off his conference call. I'm going to put you through to him now."

"Thanks."

Everything inside Amelia freezes as the line rings once. Twice. Three times. Then, the clunk of a telephone receiver lifting off its cradle.

"Grady."

At the sound of his father's voice, Grady immediately straightens. He lets go of Amelia's hand and wipes his palm on the leg of his pants. "Dad. Hi. Thanks for taking my call."

"I have something in ten minutes," Mr. Meade informs him. Amelia hears him shuffling papers around. She remembers the photo of Mr. Meade's office that accompanied the Truman article she dug up on Grady, his austere mahogany desk covered in piles and piles of work. "That leaves you six minutes. So. What can I do for you?"

It doesn't sound like a question. Or at least, that's how Amelia's ears interpret Mr. Meade's brevity. This is his opening jab in this negotiation and he's immediately put Grady on the ropes.

Grady takes a deep breath. "I want to apologize to you, Dad. I . . ." He glances at her, unsure of what to say. Probably because he isn't actually *that* sorry. "I let my emotions get the better of me the last time we spoke." Amelia nods approvingly. Perfect. "I'm sure everything I said came out of nowhere, but—"

Mr. Meade cuts his son off with a sigh. "I got an alert that you keyed into the beach house, Grady. So, no, it didn't."

"Oh."

"You went through your mother's things, I assume."

Grady bites his lip. "Yes."

And that's all Grady says. *Yes.* Even though there's so much more to the story. Amelia wants Grady to explain, tell his dad about the letters and the missing recipes they found. But Grady keeps his lips pressed together.

"While I appreciate your apology, this is exactly why I didn't want you to get involved with Meade Creamery to begin with. I knew you'd get emotional and lose sight of what's important."

Grady tenses up, leans forward. "Yeah, I got emotional. And Mom was—" He shakes his head, starts over. "She *is* important."

Amelia fights the urge to lay a gentle hand on Grady as a way to dial him back because she knows he needed to say it.

"Of course you miss her. And, whether or not you believe it, I . . . miss her too."

Hopefully hearing this simple declaration will help Grady. And his father's words do seem to soften him. Amelia watches his shoulders come down from his ears. He leans back against the couch cushions and Amelia leans with him.

Mr. Meade continues. "But your primary concern needs to be the solvency of the business you are attempting to run. Which, don't forget, is an endeavor you took on to prove yourself because you nearly failed out of Truman."

"I know."

"Grady, emotional decisions are never good business decisions. Like, say for example, telling off your father when he foots the bill for your clothes, your vacations, your tuition, your car.

siobhan vivian

Every single Starbucks coffee you drink. Every trip through the drive-thru for a cheeseburger and fries. You can't let emotion cloud your judgment. It's a recipe for failure. The reason I have a dollar to my name is because I've learned to separate my head from my heart. That's not a weakness, that's an asset."

Grady's cheeks flush and his jaw sets. "I would like to get to a place where I didn't have to rely on you for money."

"But that's why you're calling, correct?" There is no anger in Mr. Meade's voice. If anything, he sounds satisfied. After all, he set this trap for his son by canceling all his credit cards. "So quit beating around the bush. What do you need?"

"We've had a few operational setbacks at the stand."

"And you're out of cash."

"Yes."

After an excruciatingly long pause, Nancy comes on the line and informs Mr. Meade that she has his next call waiting.

"Grady, I do think we need to continue this conversation, but I'd prefer to do it in person. Why don't you meet me at Wyndham Sands for eighteen holes tomorrow afternoon? Nancy, are you there? Can you book us a tee time around noon?"

His secretary pipes up. "Of course, Mr. Meade."

Amelia can't believe she was listening in this whole time.

"Okay," Grady says.

"See you then," Mr. Meade says. And then the line goes dead.

Grady pulls out his earbud. "As much as I hate to admit it, my dad's not wrong. I shouldn't get emotional about this. I need his money, simple as that. He's got that over me, he always has. So I just have to play his game. I'm going to make this golf game as transactional as an ATM withdrawal."

"It won't be like that forever, Grady. You're getting a good education now, and you'll graduate and get a job—"

"Where my dad will also pull the strings," he says. He shakes his head, determined to push aside whatever melancholy is trying to take hold. "I don't mean to sound ungrateful. I know I've had every advantage possible in life. I'm better off than so many other people. I'm lucky."

Lucky is not exactly the word Amelia would use. But as she helps Grady pack, she tries to remain hopeful that this story will have a happy ending for both of them. He'll leave today, spend the night at the beach house, and meet his dad for golf in the morning.

For a moment of levity, Amelia asks Grady to try on his golf outfit. He ducks into the bathroom and emerges looking handsome in a gray-and-white-striped Nike polo made of superlight material, navy slacks with a little swoosh on the back pocket, a bright blue belt, and a white baseball hat that says NIKE GOLF.

"Are you sponsored?" she asks.

"Ha. No. But I'm actually pretty good. My dad's forced me to take lessons since I was a kid. I regularly kick his ass, which drives him crazy. Once, in Palm Beach, he got his ball stuck in a sand trap. I was cracking up until he drove off in our golf cart. I had to walk back to the clubhouse."

"Well, tomorrow, let him win." She sits down on the arm of the couch. "I wish I could do more to help you. Will you text me when you can? Let me know how it's going?"

"Sure. Wish me luck," he says, leaning down for a kiss.

"I wish you all the luck in the world," Amelia says, and she means it, every single word.

After Grady leaves, she stays up at the farmhouse, lying on the couch in the basement, listening to Molly's records, trying to figure out what to say to Cate about her and Grady.

Obviously her biggest transgression was kissing him in the first place. Grady was supposed to be off-limits to all the girls, and though she tried to keep their relationship purely professional, something did eventually develop between them. She should have told Cate right away after that first kiss, but she was too scared.

Why?

If Amelia's being honest with herself, it's because her kiss with Grady wasn't the first time she'd picked him over the girls at the stand. After all, that kiss came immediately after she missed their Fourth of July party.

All Amelia can do is hope that Cate will forgive her when she's had a chance to explain.

But how far will Amelia need to go back, in trying to do that? She'll have to fill Cate in on Grady's dead mother, and on the things she's read in Molly's diary, and admit the heat that clearly existed between her and Grady the very first time they met in the stand. It's a whole summer's worth of catch-up.

There's a lot she's been keeping from Cate.

Amelia can't help but wonder if this will be how their friendship is come September, when they're at different schools. And what about December? Will they continue to grow apart at lightning speed during the school year?

By next summer, they could be strangers.

Her stomach in a knot, Amelia walks down to the stand. The rain has stopped, thankfully, and the sky is a beautiful pinky red. She opens the door just as Cate is passing by. Cate gives Amelia the most fleeting of glances, and Amelia can barely get out a whispered "Hey, can we talk?" before Cate stalks into the office and shuts the door on her.

"I deserve that," Amelia says, as quietly as she can through the door. "Please let me explain."

She waits a minute for Cate to answer.

And then she turns around. Liz and Mansi are on the windows, and they quickly look away.

One of the newbies looks away too, and tries unsuccessfully to form a waffle around the cone mold, but it won't hold its shape. Amelia steps over and discreetly whispers, "You only have a few seconds after taking them off the griddle to wrap them around the mold. If they start to cool down at all, they won't hold their shape." She realizes as she's saying it that the waffle cooled because the newbie was watching and listening to her appeal to Cate.

The girl looks up at Amelia and whispers, "Thanks," gratefully and also nervously. As if she doesn't want to be seen fraternizing with Amelia.

Liz and Mansi don't acknowledge Amelia.

Sides have been taken in this battle.

Amelia steps away, embarrassed.

The stand looks like hell after the rainstorm. Amelia does her best to ignore the discomfort and awkwardness, focusing instead on cleaning, trying to get the stand back to the way it's supposed to be, appearance-wise anyway. She wipes down every surface, mops the floor, drains the milk jugs and buckets and empty ice cream drums of cloudy rainwater.

Cate stays in the office the whole time.

It's near closing when Amelia is finishing up in the bathroom. She's gone through an entire roll of paper towels and is well into her second. In the last hour, she's heard lots of whispering discussion inside the office, and she's hopeful that Cate will eventually call her inside to talk.

But those hopes are dashed when she hears Cate's truck start up outside. Amelia checks her phone for the time—it's barely a minute after closing. Ducking her head outside, she sees that the exterior lights have already been turned off and the girls are already in Cate's truck—Liz riding shotgun, Mansi and the newbie in the back.

She watches, almost dumbfounded, as Cate calls out to her, "Lock up when you're done, okay?" before driving away.

At Meade Creamery, Amelia's always felt like one of the girls, among her sisters. Now she feels like an outsider.

Or worse. A traitor.

Though it hurts, she knows that being left behind tonight is something she probably deserves. After all, Cate wasn't the only one she let down.

And, looking back, Amelia knows there were plenty of times when she could have been down at the stand with the girls and instead chose to help Grady. What good was trying to save the stand if she neglected the girls to do it?

One thing Molly said, over and over again in those early diary entries, was that it was never supposed to be about the ice cream. It was supposed to be about the girls.

How could Amelia have forgotten?

This is bigger than just her and Cate. If Amelia really wants to make things right, she's going to have to reckon with all the girls.

CHAPTER  FORTY-ONE

AMELIA IS THE FIRST ONE AT THE STAND THE NEXT morning. She arrives with a Tupperware full of sweet corn muffins, which she stress-baked the night before, a tub of butter, and a container of orange juice. Her plan is to call all the girls into the stand for a staff meeting and lay herself bare, tell them everything that's been going on, share Molly's diary with them. Try to explain her feelings for Grady and her reasons for hiding them. And, most of all, she'll voice her regret over losing sight of the most important tenet of being a Meade Creamery girl—that the relationships created here are the most important thing.

She already has the text written in her phone, but she needs the newbies' phone numbers, which she's hoping to find somewhere in the office.

As soon as she unlocks the stand door, a strange, foreign smell hits her. Like something's been burning. She worries at first that the walk-in freezer has shorted out, and she rushes in to check on it, knocking over something made of glass. She stoops and sees an overturned Meade Dairy bottle. Inside is a sludge of sooty water with several waterlogged cigarette butts.

Amelia flicks on the lights. Though she cleaned the entire stand yesterday, it's been turned upside down: couch cushions damp and in a circle on the main floor, pictures crooked, and the radio off the shelf, dangling upside down by its black cord.

She opens the bathroom and recoils at the smell of vomit.

Back outside, she lifts the heavy plastic lid on the dumpster. Inside is a pile of beer bottles and crushed beer cans.

She finds more beer cans inside the walk-in freezer. These were left behind, and they have exploded. Icy beer has splattered all over the drums of ice cream Amelia made earlier in the week. The whole freezer smells yeasty.

Amelia goes back into the office and pulls out her phone. She's shaking, she's so angry. After a bit of scrolling, she comes across several pictures from the party here. The girls having fun together. Playing cards on the office desk. A dance party in the stand. Running through the trees in the dark.

That last picture makes Amelia remember once coming home late from her grandmother's house on a summer night, when she was just a kid. It was past midnight; her mother was asleep against the car window. They drove past the stand, long closed to customers, but the girls were still there, sitting around the picnic tables, talking, their voices a streak of sound that came and went as the car passed by.

But last night's party was not just stand girls. There were other people here from the high school, too. Pictures of Dane

Zapotowsky and Christopher Win feeding each other ice cream straight from the scoop. A Boomerang of Zoe Metcalf throwing fistfuls of sprinkles in the air on repeat. Three of Cate's Academic Decathlon teammates lying stacked like a sandwich across the office couch. John Stislow sticking his hand straight into the vat of chocolate dip.

Amelia hears Cate's truck pull up outside. All three newbies are in her truck. They look totally worse for wear, green and unsteady.

Cate comes in. Amelia knows she's surprised to see her, because Cate avoids her eyes as she passes her.

"Looks like you had some party here last night," Amelia says, trying to keep her emotions in check.

"We had a great time." Cate stretches. "Sorry I didn't think to invite you. I figured you'd be busy with your boyfriend."

The newbies all snap to attention.

"Grady isn't my boyfriend," Amelia says, trying to project a little bit of confidence, because this is true, Grady isn't. "But yes. Grady and I have kissed. A few times." Turning to the newbies, she says, "I'm sorry."

Cate sneers. "I thought Grady was cute too, you know. I could have gone after him, but I didn't, because we had a pact." She rolls her eyes. "Meade Creamery has been open for how many years now? Drama-free? One summer, one boy, and it all comes crashing down, thanks to you, Amelia."

"That's not fair. You know the stand, and you girls, are the most important things to me."

"You chose Grady over us. It's as simple as that. And he's had you wrapped around his little finger all summer." At this point, Cate turns to walk into the office. "It's honestly pathetic but not surprising."

siobhan vivian

"So is that why you had a party here? To get back at me? Because you know there's not supposed to be anyone but employees in the stand. And newbies aren't ever allowed to drink." Amelia expects Cate to look at least a little bit guilty, but she doesn't. If anything, she's indignant, folding her arms across her chest.

"Isn't that convenient," Cate says. "I'm the one who has to follow the rules, but you don't."

Amelia tries to explain. "It just . . . happened." That's about all she can get out before she feels the tears come.

Amelia sees something soften in Cate when Cate sees her cry. "Look, I don't blame you. I blame Grady. He's been taking advantage of you from the second you met."

"That's not true."

"Why are you defending him? He's using you, Amelia!"

Amelia shakes her head. "No, he's not." If there's one thing Amelia is certain of, it's that.

"You're such a pushover."

She's reminded of how many times Cate has called her a pushover this summer. And it suddenly hits her: it's true—but it's Cate, and not Grady, who's always doing the pushing.

"What about you?" Amelia asks. "Are *you* sorry?"

"For what?"

"You're the Head Girl, Cate. That job comes with a certain level of responsibility."

Cate seems to wave this away. "Look. Last night started off as just us girls hanging out, but then some other friends dropped by. Dane had beer left over from his family's Fourth of July party, and they were drinking it. I'm not going to police the girls. They can make decisions for themselves."

"The place is trashed. And there are like at least twenty drums of ice cream that have been ruined in there by exploding beer cans."

"So take it out of my pay."

"Do you even care about this place?"

"Oh, here we go."

"Because you're always late, the stand looks like hell, everything's slipping. And now this? Throwing a party here and leaving the place trashed? I don't get it. I thought you wanted to be Head Girl."

"Of course I did. And we both know I deserved it."

"So why are you acting like you don't care about it? And when I try and talk to you about work stuff, you completely shut me down."

"Because it's not exactly easy doing things *my* way when I have you watching over me all the time! Judging me for everything I do because it's not the way you would do it!"

"You're right. I would have never, ever thrown a party like this. And I definitely wouldn't let newbies drink. They're barely out of eighth grade, Cate." The Head Girls didn't let Amelia and Cate drink until they were juniors, and even then, they kept a close watch on them.

Cate shrugs. "So what do you want? An apology? If anything, you should apologize to *me*, to all of us girls, for ruining our summer."

Amelia feels an apology bubble up. She does have a lot she's sorry for. But instead, she takes a deep breath and says, "Yes. I do want you to apologize. And I want you to promise that you'll try harder. That you'll do a better job. That you'll work hard and respect the traditions and take it seriously. Because this place is going to fall apart unless you do."

"Are you kidding me? Meade Creamery *is* falling apart, Amelia. Do you not remember that we almost got washed away during that rainstorm yesterday?"

"Is that a *no*? Because if it is, I don't think there's a place for you here anymore."

It's so suddenly silent that all Amelia can hear is the quiet wheezing of the tired, failing walk-in freezer.

Cate starts laughing. "Give me a break."

"Is that a *yes* or a *no*, Cate?"

"That's a *screw you*."

Her words do sting. But Amelia simply says, "Then you're fired."

"You don't have the authority to fire me. I'm Head Girl."

This may or may not be true. But Amelia doesn't blink. "Take your stuff and go."

Cate's laugh turns into a sneer. "I don't need this. I'll see you girls around."

Her adrenaline surging, Amelia says, "Wait. Give me the pin back."

When Cate turns around, her face is contorted into a pucker that Amelia has never seen before. A line in their friendship has been crossed that Amelia isn't sure she'll be able to get back over.

Cate takes off the pin and sets it on the desk. Then she peels off her polo shirt so she's in just a tank top, and drops it into the trash can on her way out, the door whacking against the stand so hard that one of the milk bottles tumbles off its roof beam and shatters.

The girls stare in stunned silence.

Amelia goes into the office. Pushing her muffins aside, she lays her head down on the desk and cries.

. . .

Amelia's not sure exactly how long she spends crying, but when she reemerges from the office, she has a splitting headache. But the three newbies are still there, having cleaned up the mess from the party. And not just them. All of the girls are there now.

Minus Cate.

Jen notices Amelia first, elbows Mansi. Then all the girls turn to face her.

"I'm so sorry," Amelia announces, her voice breaking. "I never wanted to fight with Cate in front of you, never mind fire her."

Liz says, "It's okay, Amelia."

Sophie says, "You were right. Cate wasn't a very good manager."

"She was super fun," Mansi adds.

"But not, like, good at the *job* part of the job," Sophie says.

"It was worse than you know, actually. Cate was always late with the schedule."

"She basically never did any chores."

"We seriously don't care if you're dating Grady. That's your business."

Amelia shakes her head. "No. I made a promise. And Grady is my boss. It's not right."

Bern shakes her head. "*You're* the boss of this place, Amelia."

Amelia manages a weak smile. It would be the ultimate compliment, if not for the fact of everything.

CHAPTER  FORTY-TWO

AMELIA IS STILL WAITING FOR WORD FROM GRADY when she climbs into bed for the night. And she's trying everything she can to relax until he reaches out. A scented candle flickers on her nightstand, and she's wearing a calming face mask that she'd forgotten to use before prom. But as she lies back on her pillow, eyes closed, the wet mask sheet clinging to her face, a lump bobs tight in her throat, making it almost impossible to swallow even the smallest sips of her chamomile tea.

The cruel reality is that, no matter how things go with Grady and his dad, Amelia has already forever lost the summer she'd hoped to have. One that would reinforce her friendship with Cate, make it strong enough to withstand the distance and change that college would bring. In fact, Amelia's not sure if she'll ever hear from her best friend again.

Yes, Cate was a terrible Head Girl, but had Amelia really been any better? Using Grady's promotion of Cate as a Band-Aid, hoping it would smooth over their problems so she wouldn't have to tackle them head-on. Amelia's letting things slide only made the problems worse. In that way, hadn't she set Cate up to fail?

After the mask is done, she dabs her face dry with a tissue and tosses it into her wastebasket. On her night table, next to the candle, is Molly's diary.

As Molly's entries have closed in on the end of the war, Amelia has hesitated to keep reading, knowing the terrible things coming. Both in the war itself—Amelia still feels sick thinking of her country dropping a bomb that instantly killed over 80,000 innocent people in Hiroshima—as well as the most painful parts of Molly Meade's life, the death of Wayne Lumsden. But tonight, she decides to read straight through until the very end, wanting to poke the bruise.

There is another gap in Wayne's letters, one that Molly attributes to their fight about her ice cream. Initially, Molly is indignant, filling the pages of her diary with news of how business is booming. As summer comes to a close, it's as if clarity returns to Molly.

August 14, 1945

When the news came in from the president on the radio—Japan unconditionally surrenders—every girl in the stand froze.

Tiggy and I had been scooping two cones. She dropped hers right on the floor, rushed

forward, and hugged me. The others pushed
out the door, screaming, crying, grabbing the
folks in line who hadn't heard. People in
the cars turned up their radios. Horns were
beeping, people sprinting.

Mother and Daddy came running down
not five minutes later. Mother lifted her skirt
and danced the jitterbug—which I didn't
even know she knew how to do—with Daddy
right there in the stand, and they kissed like
newlyweds.

Everyone rushed out to Main Street. All
of Sand Lake.

I've never seen the streets so full. The entire
town hugging and weeping and cheering in
the street. I had so many conflicting feelings,
all those innocent people killed, but the war
was over now. No one else would die. Our
boys will come home. My brothers and
Wayne back as if they never left.

I wonder when I will hear from Wayne.

Will he still want to marry me when he
gets back?

Or have I ruined things between us?

When the stand closes, at the end of August, Molly has nothing to occupy her mind. Every entry is full of worry about Wayne, regrets, and fears.

In her last entry, dated September 2, 1945, Molly described how she invited the girls for ice cream at the lake to celebrate the official end of the war. But the night was unseasonably cold and the girls were all worrying about their figures again.

On the back of that page, there is a newspaper announcement, neatly clipped and taped inside, dated almost exactly one year later. It is for a memorial service at Holy Redeemer in honor of Wayne Lumsden, war hero, declared missing in action. The rest of the diary's pages, nearly half of the book, are left blank.

The buzz of Amelia's phone wakes her up. Her room is dark. The candle has burned down to nothing.

It's Grady.

I'm turning onto your street. Can you come outside?

She texts back, It's two in the morning. If my parents catch me sneaking out, they'll kill me. Though Amelia recognizes that, in a few weeks, she'll have the freedom to do whatever she wants.

Please.

The waning hope in Amelia's heart twists into something tighter.

Okay.

She quickly pulls on a pair of shorts, then tiptoes downstairs in the dark. Her mom is in bed, but her dad has fallen asleep in the den, an infomercial flashing colors on the walls.

From the front window, Amelia watches the pink Cadillac creep slowly past her house and park on the other side of the street. Grady kills the lights. Opening her front door as quietly as she can, Amelia slips outside in her bare feet.

The asphalt still feels warm from the day.

Grady reaches over and unlocks the passenger door for Amelia. She climbs in, and before the interior lights click off, she sees the redness on the bridge of his nose, the back of his neck. "You're sunburned," she says, touches his arm gently with her fingertips.

"I was so nervous, I forgot to put on sunscreen."

But what is Grady feeling now? Amelia searches his face for any happiness, any relief, any glimmer of success. He manages a tired smile, which Amelia clings to as a good sign, and she asks him, "How did it go?"

"Everything was great for the first nine holes," he tells her. "I was basically doing exactly what my dad said, trying not to get emotional. I laughed at all his jokes, listened to college stories I've heard a million times over, and purposely screwed up almost every one of my putts. And he kept saying to me, *Isn't this nice?* and *Isn't this great?* and *We have to get out here more often!*" Grady wrings the steering wheel. Guiltily, he says, "I hate to say it, but it *was* nice, pushing everything aside and getting along with him."

"Believe me," Amelia says quietly, "I get it."

"Once we hit the back nine, I started making my pitch. Casually, you know? I explained the situation to him, told him that if he loaned me the money to cover the repairs and a new walk-in freezer, I'd be willing to implement all his business ideas—scoop size, price increase, salary cuts. And I promised I'd pay him back, with interest, basically double the sum and give him fifty percent of all the profits until then." Grady swallows.

"And the ice cream?"

"I said that was the one change that I couldn't entertain."

At this, Amelia impulsively leans forward, takes Grady's cheeks in her hands, and kisses him.

He kisses her back, his hands slipping up her neck and into her hair. When she tries pulling away, he leans forward, holding his lips to hers, extending the kiss for a second, two, three. Like he doesn't want it to end.

When they finally pull apart, Amelia learns why.

"He's not going to loan me the money, Amelia."

She's taken over by a helpless, shivery panic, not unlike the moment when the safety bar clicks down on a roller coaster and there's no getting off. "Because of the ice cream? I mean, what if you found another dairy? There has to be someone who'll sell you the ingredients for cheaper. Maybe—"

"No."

"Well, did you talk about your mom? Tell him how important this was to her? Did you tell him how you almost cried tasting Home Sweet Home?" She shakes her head. "You should have gotten him to eat some that day he came here. Maybe then he'd understand."

Grady is starting to look frustrated with her. "It's just not a good business decision. The profit margins are small, and there's so much work to be done on the building. There are other things I didn't factor in either, which my dad brought up. Like that no one is going to be living in the farmhouse all winter."

"So hire someone to take care of it! Or! Or you could rent it out!"

"And then what? I'm supposed to come back here every summer for the rest of my life?" He avoids looking at her when he says, "If Molly hadn't died, I'm not sure she could have kept this place going another year. In some ways, maybe it lasted as long as it needed to. As long as she did."

"Let me guess. Because you're listening to your dad, he's going to send you back to Truman and reinstate all your credit cards. Is that what you really want?"

"No."

"So the stand can be your freedom!"

"I know. I've . . . decided to sell the property."

All Amelia can do is blink. Grady left to try and save Meade Creamery. And he came back ready to sell the entire place.

"Look, I spent the whole drive back to Sand Lake trying to think of a way to make this work. I think I got so wrapped up in this place and with you, and proving myself to my dad, that I wasn't thinking clearly about the practicalities. I don't want to be a businessman."

"What?"

He seems to understand that she's whiplashed. "I'm going to sell the stand, and use that money to pay my *own way* to Truman. I'll go back on my terms. I'll be out of my dad's pocket forever. I'll be able to find something I love."

Desperately, she says, "But your mom . . ."

"My mom was not a Meade. And I know she would want this for me."

"So that's it. It's over. How much do you think you can get?" It sounds crass asking, as crass as it would be to curse.

"I'll get enough to cover me until I graduate and hopefully a little extra."

"When?"

"If I make a deal, it'll be for the end of the summer. The stand will keep running. I figure if the big freezer quits, we can use the one in Molly's basement and just run stuff down as needed." He looks up at her. "I wouldn't cut this summer short. I know how important it is to you."

Amelia puts her hand to her heart, needing to make sure it's still beating.

"Amelia, you have to know how sorry I am that everything worked out this way. I really wanted to save this for you."

"I know you did." She gets out of the car and slams the door, because he didn't, because if he really believed in Meade Creamery, he would never think of selling it off. And that's all there is to it.

CHAPTER  FORTY-THREE

AMELIA STANDS AT THE OFFICE WINDOW, WATCHING as Grady speaks with a local Realtor and another man drives a stake into the rain ditch running alongside Route 68, a FOR SALE sign. Grady turns and walks into the office.

"I need to go out for a while, but I left the front door open if you need to get in."

"Thank you," Amelia says coldly.

"Amelia . . ." But Grady doesn't say anything more. Because what is there to say?

Once he's gone, Jen knocks on the door. "Amelia? Someone's asking for the Head Girl outside."

Amelia stands up, straightens her shirt.

There's someone at the left service window. An old lady with a cane, dressed up in Sunday clothes, buttons and stockings.

Amelia walks to the window, unhooks the latch, and slides it open. "Can I help you?"

The old lady doesn't answer her. Instead, she looks past Amelia into the stand and clicks her tongue. "Not a thing has changed."

Not yet, Amelia thinks.

"I used to work here a long time ago."

"Oh. Well, welcome back." Amelia leans forward on her elbows, forcing a smile to her face. "I'm Amelia."

"I'm Theresa Wolff, but the girls used to call me Tiggy. I was Molly's best friend."

Amelia's mouth drops open. Tiggy? She's always assumed Tiggy was dead.

"Oh my gosh, it's so nice to meet you." She reaches out for a handshake. Tiggy's skin is loose and cold, and though Amelia tries to hold her gently, she clings to her with excitement. But as she lets go, that excitement gives way to dread. Amelia worries that Tiggy might not know that Molly has died. That she'll have to be the one to break the news. She forces a swallow. "I'm not sure if you heard, but—"

"Oh yes. My granddaughter sent me the obituary. I got ill and couldn't make the funeral. If I hadn't promised my friends here the best ice cream they ever tasted, I don't know if I could have gotten a ride out today." Amelia didn't realize before, but Tiggy's brought a nurse with her, a short man with dark hair and a mustache who is carefully and gently assisting her. And there's a white transport van from a nursing home parked off to the side, near the picnic tables, where a woman is standing watching them. She waves when she sees Amelia looking.

"I figured this might be the last summer of Home Sweet Home. Can I have a small cup?" Tiggy shuffles backward a little so she can take in all of the ice cream stand.

Amelia grabs her scoop and opens the dipping cabinet. Even though Tiggy asked for a small, she gives her two big scoops, and makes chocolate sundaes for both Tiggy's aides.

Tiggy tries to pay, but Amelia waves her off. "On the house," she declares. "And Tiggy, I hope you don't taste a difference. I've been making the ice cream myself since Molly passed."

Tiggy closes her eyes and takes a lick off the top. "It's like I'm seventeen again."

"I'm so glad."

"And you're Head Girl?" Tiggy asks.

"I am."

"Where's your pin?" Tiggy asks, suspicious.

"Oh," Amelia says, looking down at her collar. "I guess I forgot to put it on."

This is a lie. But Amelia didn't feel right, putting it on after firing Cate. As if that were the reason she'd done it, simply to take the power back.

"What a shame," Tiggy says.

Amelia thinks at first that Tiggy is referring to her missing pin, but then she feels something on her shoulder. Tiggy has lifted her cane and stuck it inside the stand. It rests on Amelia's shoulder, as if Tiggy were setting up a trick shot on a pool table. Turning slightly, Amelia sees that Tiggy's got the rubber tip lined straight up with the photo of Molly and Wayne.

"Yes, it's very sad," Amelia agrees.

"Sadder than you know," Tiggy answers cryptically.

Except Amelia does know. She's read Molly's diary, cover to cover.

"Well . . . ," Amelia says. "I'm glad you decided to come to visit. You heard right, I'm afraid. This is going to be the last summer of Meade Creamery."

"Well, you ought to take that picture down, now that Molly's gone."

"Do you want it? Nobody will mind if you take it."

Tiggy laughs heartily. "Me? Want that? Lord no." She looks over her shoulder to make sure no one is behind her. "Molly would kill me for telling anyone this, but I never forgave that son of a bitch."

Amelia's eyes go wide. And Tiggy's eyes, old and watery and cloudy as they are, twinkle. She leans in close. "Have you ever held on to a secret for so long that you nearly burst?"

"Yes," Amelia answers without hesitation. The fact that she is in possession of Molly Meade's diary.

For Tiggy, this seems to be the right answer. "The story of this place, of those two right there, it's not what you think it is."

Amelia feels unsteady. She knows the story. She knows it straight from Molly's own pen. So what could Tiggy be referring to?

Tiggy shakes her head, puts a finger to her lips. "I've already said too much. You shouldn't speak ill of the dead. But I've always hated that she kept his photo hanging up, after everything that happened."

"She did it because she missed him," Amelia answers automatically. "Because when she was making ice cream, it was as if . . ."

Amelia's rote performance comes to a halt as she sees Tiggy rolling her eyes, almost bored. "Yes, yes, dear. I know that story."

That story. As if there were another one.

"We didn't know her," Amelia says apologetically. "Not really."

siobhan vivian

"People knew what she wanted them to know. Being a war widow is very good for business."

It feels almost crazy to say out loud. "So . . . Wayne didn't die in the war?"

Tiggy looks around again, the secret almost on the tip of her tongue. "Aw, heck. I might not live to see another summer, and what good is a story this delicious if you don't share it?"

CHAPTER FORTY-FOUR

TIGGY ENTERS THE OFFICE AND SETTLES ONTO THE YEL-low love seat, rubbing both hands across the fabric. Amelia pulls up a chair close to her, and they sit across from each other, one of the first Meade Creamery girls opposite one of the last.

And as Tiggy relays the story, Amelia is easily able to picture it, playing like a movie in her mind. How, at first, Molly did think Wayne was dead. How depressed she'd been, how she blamed herself, how guilty she felt that they'd been fighting.

"The strange thing is that no official word ever came. But we thought it was only a matter of time."

But near Christmas, Tiggy and Molly had been together in Molly's basement, listening to records and wrapping presents. And Wayne came in through the side door.

"I don't know where he spent those months since the war

ended, but he'd clearly been injured," Tiggy says. "He was walking with a limp."

Molly was so shocked she clung to him. And Tiggy, even though she and Wayne had had their differences, rushed over to him too. But Tiggy could tell right away that something was wrong with Wayne. "He had wild eyes," she says.

When he saw Molly's setup in the basement, it was as if he'd caught her cheating. He told her in no uncertain terms that he wanted her to give up the ice cream stand. He wanted one normal thing back, the life they were supposed to have together.

Tiggy continues, "She thought he was joking at first. We both did. And Wayne took great offense at our nervous laughter. He said Molly didn't have to work anymore, now that he was back. Perhaps it was because he and Molly had been out of touch so long, but she told him *no* straightaway. She said, *No, I will not*, and I think he just about fell over because she'd never spoken in such a way to him before. There was more argument, and they were both struggling to keep their voices down, and eventually Molly stormed out."

Wayne followed her. Quick, like a hunter. "That's when I began to get scared," Tiggy admits. "I was grabbing him and begging him to please calm down. He lit a cigarette and they continued to fight and he threw his cigarette aside. A few minutes later we saw smoke. The barn had caught fire."

Molly screamed, "Wayne! Help me!" Because all the Meades' dairy cows were inside.

And Tiggy says Wayne just stood there, frozen.

"Do you think he did it on purpose?" Amelia asks.

She sighs. "I'm not sure. I ran up and put my hand on Molly's shoulder, to let her know I was there. *Come on*, I said, pulling her back to the house, saying we needed to wake her dad and her brothers, even though I knew it was already too late. And Molly looked at Wayne and said, *Go.* And that's just what he did."

Amelia holds herself. She can imagine how scared Molly must have been. But also, she's in awe of Molly's strength. Her presence of mind.

Tiggy stares off, unfocused, for a second or two. "I once asked Molly what she felt, seeing Wayne go, and do you know what she said?"

Amelia can barely breathe. "What?"

"She said, *Tiggy, I felt free.*" Tiggy shakes her head wistfully. "I suppose it doesn't matter what people thought of her. Molly certainly didn't care. It's just my pride in her, getting the better of me." She looks down and touches her ice cream gently with her spoon. "Did you know she traveled the world? She took me on my first trip to New York. It was after my second son was born. All expenses paid, on her dime. For a week. We visited all the museums and sights. We went to the top of the Empire State Building. We saw *Once Upon a Mattress* on Broadway, and I got my *Playbill* signed by Carol Burnett about a month before she was nominated for the Tony. It got thrown out somewhere along the line, probably by one of my kids. But that was one of the best weeks in my life."

"Wow."

"And before I moved into the home, I was in Florida, and she came and stayed with me every winter."

"We thought she was alone up at the house all those winters, mourning him," Amelia admits, almost embarrassed.

Amelia feels dizzy, getting these glimpses of Molly's life. For

siobhan vivian

so long, she's been immersed in Molly's past. And that past is what defined what people thought of her.

Tiggy doesn't appear at all surprised. "She didn't care that people pitied her or thought Wayne was some hero." Tiggy groans. "I just wish more people knew that. Molly lived exactly the life she wanted."

Tiggy takes her last spoonful of ice cream and then gets up. Amelia helps her to the stand door, where Tiggy pauses, holding up a finger to tell the aides lingering at the picnic table that she'll be a minute. "You said you forgot to wear the Head Girl pin today. But you do still have it, right?"

"Yes. Right here, actually." Amelia fetches it from the desk drawer. She thinks of Cate when she holds it in her hands.

"Make sure you don't lose track of that. It's a real diamond in there, you know. Her engagement ring."

Amelia reels as Tiggy hobbles over to the picnic table and, with the aides' help, climbs back into the van.

Amelia heads up to the house.

Grady's not there. She goes right inside and heads for Molly's bedroom—not the childhood one, but the one Molly stayed in most recently, down the hall from the kitchen—the one where Grady looked on that first day for the recipes.

She has never gone into this room before.

Inside, there are pictures of Molly and Tiggy on a beach in what must be Florida, taken maybe twenty years ago, from the style of their bathing suits. Another of them at an outdoor café, stucco in Easter egg colors: Miami. Molly's bookshelves are lined with travel books, books about places she's been. Inside the travel books are receipts—for meals, for souvenirs, for hotel rooms.

It seems there were two Mollys: one before Wayne went off to war and one after.

Amelia takes the diary out of her tote bag and flips to the final entry, the announcement in the newspaper for Wayne's memorial service.

The opposite blank page, she now realizes, has a ghostly impression of writing on it from someone pressing through the page before. Amelia sees that several sheets have been carefully torn out.

Using a pencil, she rubs the tip over the grooves and a missing entry appears.

December 29, 1945

Yesterday, sweet Mrs. Duncan broke into sobs when I passed her on my way out of Blauner's. She melted into me when I hugged her, her head resting against my shoulder, her tears dampening my coat. What a tragedy, to have lost the barn. She promised to pray for my family, and especially for me and for Wayne, along with the other lost young men, and for the countless other girls in the same situation, forced to pick up the pieces of our shattered dreams and find something to keep living for.

When she said that last bit, I did well up out of sheer gratefulness that I escaped that fate. What would my life have been if I

siobhan vivian

hadn't figured out what I did? And just in the nick of time, too?

I played the part. I solemnly thanked her, and my mother thanked her too.

I can never tell Mother the truth. Now she thanks God for my ice cream. Without our dairy, my brothers will need to find work elsewhere and it will be left to me to care for Mother and Daddy.

This will be my life through winter, and I am resigned to it. Grieving someone lost to me. In some ways, I can do it honestly. I do miss Wayne. Or the man I hoped he was.

In spring, I can begin to smile again in public, delicately, modestly.

And then, next summer, I will bloom.

Molly didn't stop living when she lost Wayne.
She started.
Ice cream didn't save her.
Molly saved herself.
Everyone thought the stand was a way for Molly to hold on to Wayne, a way to avoid moving on with her life. But it was just the opposite. It wasn't a consolation prize, a thing she settled for.
It gave her exactly what she'd wanted.

Amelia had hoped Grady would save the stand as desperately as she'd hoped Cate would be picked to be Head Girl. Why? Because she didn't think she could do either on her own, couldn't rise to those challenges, despite the fact that she desperately wanted to.

But maybe the only things stopping her were the limits she put on herself.

Amelia goes upstairs and returns the diary to its place under the mattress on Molly's childhood bed. Now she understands why Molly left this room. Not for the reasons Amelia thought, but because the room belonged to the *old* Molly.

Before Amelia leaves the farmhouse, she takes something else.

Grady's business school textbooks from the trash. She's due for some new reading material anyway.

siobhan vivian

CHAPTER FORTY-FIVE

AMELIA CRAMS LIKE IT'S SENIOR YEAR FINALS ALL OVER again, only for classes she didn't know she was enrolled in. The textbooks are more conceptual than practical, but she still does her best, trying to soak up relevant information as fast as she possibly can. The math is a little over her head too. There are, obviously, a million things she'll need to learn.

She'll get there.

She is at the library when it opens, pulling business books off the shelf. Making photocopies of pages, highlighting more paragraphs than not.

Hours pass and she's not even aware.

Whenever Amelia watched Grady study, his posture was hunched; he'd groan like reading was physical labor. But every sentence she absorbs gives Amelia energy, motivation.

She does her best to put together a business plan. What she might need to get set up and running. How much things are worth—from the equipment to the recipes.

So Meade Creamery can't survive in its current form.

That doesn't mean it needs to fail.

Instead of being rigid, holding on so tightly to the way things have always been, Amelia now focuses on the fresh. The possible.

The ice cream will never change. But why couldn't everything else?

There's only one thing standing in her way.

Money.

Over dinner that night, she shares her plans with her parents.

"I have some news. Grady Meade has decided to sell the Meade family farm. But I'm trying to find a way to keep the ice cream stand going."

Her mom and dad share a look.

"I want to buy the business. Molly's recipes, her equipment, and an old food truck that Grady bought at the beginning of the summer. I thought he was nuts, but now I think that could be Meade Creamery's new home. All I would need is a space to produce—"

"I'm sorry," Mom says. "I'm confused. You want to buy the ice cream stand?"

"What about college?" Dad says, baffled. "Are you dropping out of college?"

Amelia laughs. "Of course not! This isn't going to derail anything. I can do it just like Molly did. In the summers. And actually, I might even try to take some business courses at Gibbons." From her bag she pulls out Grady's dog-eared textbooks. "I've been working on a business plan. Mom, I'd love you to take a look at it. It's probably not formatted correctly, but maybe you can help me with that."

Amelia pushes the papers across the table. Her mother glances down briefly, hesitant to really look.

"This is a thing that I love and I'm good at," Amelia says. "I thought you'd be happy for me." In fact, she's stunned that they clearly aren't.

"But there's a whole wide world out there, Amelia. Why stay tied to this place? What if you find a great internship?"

Amelia knows it's true that she'll be giving up something to do this. Some of the freedom of a "typical" college experience, because she'll be dealing with the real issues of running a business. But that doesn't scare her. "This is what I like. This is what I've always liked. And I have the chance to make it mine." She's pleading, and they are giving her nothing. "Come on, Mom. I know you do this for a living. You help people who need money. I need you to help me."

Instead of leaning closer, her mom sits back in her chair. "Sweetie . . . I'm sorry, but this is a little half-baked, don't you think?"

Amelia's dad stands next to her mother. "Do you know how hard it is to run a business?"

At this, Amelia actually smiles. "Believe me, I do. I truly do."

But they turn from her, begin passing plates and side dishes, passing salad dressing and the pepper mill, saying nothing more. Amelia sits back, dumbfounded. Her parents have supported her through everything.

Years, months, even weeks ago, this absolutely would have stopped her. Or at least, given her pause.

But not now. She's *that* sure of herself.

. . .

After dinner, Amelia goes upstairs with Grady's textbooks. There are other ways of getting money. It doesn't have to be through a bank. She draws her fingers down the index, stopping on the word *Fund-raising*.

CHAPTER FORTY-SIX

AT THE FARMHOUSE THE NEXT DAY, AMELIA FINDS THE hallway lined with overstuffed trash bags.

"Grady?"

"Uh, in here."

She follows his voice into the kitchen, where he is wrapping Molly's dishes in newspaper.

"Hi."

He looks nervously at her, like he's been caught doing something he shouldn't. "I'm sorry. But I'm going to have to deal with this stuff eventually." He swallows. "If you want anything of Molly's, let me know."

"Actually . . . that's why I'm here."

"Okay."

"I have a proposition. I want to take over Meade Creamery."

"I'm sorry, Amelia. I'm already getting bids on the land."

"Sell the farmhouse, sell the land. But I want the ice cream machinery, the rights to the recipes, the truck. I'm going to fix it up, relocate production, and relaunch Meade Creamery as a mobile business next summer."

"Seriously?"

She's angry. Hands on hips. "Don't you think I can do it?"

"Of course I do. I'm just sorry I didn't think of it as an option. That you'd want to do this. You'd be giving up a lot."

She knows. And in a way, she already has. She takes a paper out of her tote bag. "I wrote up an offer, but don't feel like you have to accept it. I know this is really just the first step in negotiating. I want to pay you what's fair."

"You don't have to pay me anything. I'll give everything to you for free."

"I don't want it for free."

He looks at the sheet. "Where are you going to get this kind of money?"

"I have a plan for that. But I wanted to talk to you first, to see if you'd even entertain it. I know how personal this is for you, with your mother and all. But my hope is that, deep down, you want this to go on." She takes a deep breath. "I'm sorry I got so upset. I was putting all my hope in having you save the stand for me, but you've got your own stuff going on—school, your dad, your mom. If I want this place to survive, I need to step up and make it happen."

"Wow. I knew you loved this place, but . . . wow."

"It's more than that—I do love it here, but I love the work too. I love the recipes, and the schedules, and the girls. I love the customers, I love—" She could go on and on, but stops when she realizes Grady is staring. "Sorry."

siobhan vivian

"Don't be sorry. Amelia, I completely get it," he says. "I feel like I've watched you fall in love this summer." Amelia blushes, and Grady quickly clarifies, "This business, making ice cream. And now that you've found your passion, you're going after it with everything you've got. It's damn inspiring."

The redness in her cheeks fires back up even hotter than before. "You don't think I'm crazy?"

"Not at all. I think anyone who underestimates you is crazy." He takes a small step closer. "I know you can do this."

"You'll find what you love too, Grady. I know you will." Amelia really is sure of this, as sure as she is of anything. Grady's a hard worker, kind, generous. He will do great things.

He smiles gratefully. "I'm actually excited to go back to Truman. But . . ."

"What?"

"I'm going to miss you is all."

Her heart speeds up. She, of course, will miss Grady, too. So much it hurts her to think about it. "Well, if things work out like I hope they will, and I'm able to buy the business, you know exactly where I'll be next summer. You can always come back to Sand Lake for some ice cream, on the house."

Nervously, Grady reaches out for her hand. "I hope I don't have to wait that long to see you again. I hope . . ." He drops his head back and takes a deep breath, summoning his courage. "I mean, I hope that if you come to Truman to visit Cate, you'll let me know."

Of course if things were good between her and Cate, Amelia would do this, absolutely. But she can't wrap her head around ever visiting Truman without repairing their friendship first. Running into Cate somewhere on campus, not saying hi. The whole idea of it feels unpleasantly surreal. And way more painful, to be honest, than potentially not seeing Grady again.

"Cate and I aren't in the best place right now," Amelia admits. "I really hope we patch things up, but . . . who knows."

He seems to get it. "Is there anything I can do to help?"

"Not with Cate," Amelia says, and Grady nods soberly. Except this can't be it, this can't be how they leave things. "Hey, look. I know you're over the whole business thing, but I would still love to get your opinion on some ideas I'm thinking about for next summer."

She barely finishes her sentence before Grady's lighting up. "Yes! A hundred percent yes. Seriously, Amelia, you can call me any time you want to talk something through. Really. Any. Time."

"Thank you, Grady. I will."

They embrace, clumsily, earnestly, and both Amelia and Grady melt into the hug with tangible relief. This arrangement seems, at least for now, enough of a promise to satisfy their craving for more of each other. This summer isn't going to be the end of whatever is sparking between them, but potentially just the beginning.

CHAPTER FORTY-SEVEN

AMELIA CALLS A MEETING WITH ALL THE STAND GIRLS the next day. Once she pitches her idea of buying Meade Creamery, they give her what her parents apparently could not—full-throttle approval. And over the next two days, each girl finds her own way to pitch in with a talent to help get Amelia's fund-raiser page off the ground.

They take a million pictures of her, selecting one where she stands out in front of the stand, hands clasped behind her back, mimicking the power pose Grady struck for the *Sand Lake Ledger* that first day.

"I like it!" Amelia says.

But one of the newbies shakes her head. "Your shirt doesn't pop. It's too faded. Here." And she pulls off her shirt, a newer polo, and switches with Amelia. They take the picture again, and Amelia sees she was totally right.

And best of all, they are eager to help her spread the word. They want to tell every customer about Amelia's plans, give them the address of her donation page, but there's one problem: the site isn't yet live.

Amelia's been hesitating. She keeps tweaking her essay about why she's seeking money—not because of any lingering doubts, though her parents' hesitation echoes in the back of her mind. Of course the girls would have her back, no question, but what about the adults in town? They all might have trusted Molly Meade. But why should they trust her? A teenage girl?

This also feels like an opportunity for Amelia to change the narrative of Molly Meade, to show that she wasn't a sad old heartbroken woman. Though her business was small, it afforded her an amazing, adventurous life. Why should that stay a secret? She doesn't want to spill the beans, exactly, but she does want to give Molly her due.

And then there's Cate. There's so much Amelia wants to say. This could be for her, too.

This feels more important to Amelia than her college essay. Way more important than writing back to Cecilia Brewster. She can feel the words begin to come together, the way she wants to speak about herself, and not just as one of the stand girls.

After many, many, many drafts, she finally writes something that truly speaks to her feelings about Molly and Meade Creamery. And this is what she posts.

Hello. My name is Amelia Van Hagen. I started working at Meade Creamery four summers ago.

Those summers were some of the most formative of my life. I could probably fill the pages of a million diaries with the fun I've had, the amazing girls I've met, and the bits and pieces of wisdom I've collected. I say without hesitation or reservation that being a Meade Creamery girl is an experience I'll be forever grateful for.

This summer, after Molly Meade's passing, I had the honor of taking over the production of ice cream according to her heirloom recipes. For me, as I am sure for many of you, her life story preceded her. Though I never had the chance to personally get to know Molly Meade, I feel now as if I understand her in a new and deeper way. Through this experience, I've also learned things about myself. How much I love making ice cream. How hard it is to run a business. How difficult it is to take yourself seriously. How easily and quickly everything can fall apart.

But Molly's resilience, her unwillingness to submit to expectations placed upon her at the time, and her unwavering belief in herself and the girls who worked for her have taught me that if you find something you love, you fight for it with everything you've got. No regrets.

The Meade family is not interested in continuing the stand in its current form, but I have submitted a business plan that they are willing to entertain, to purchase their food truck, the equipment, and the recipes, and relaunch Meade Creamery as a mobile business next summer.

I know I am only seventeen (almost eighteen!) but Molly was the same age when she started Meade Creamery. With your support, I would like to continue her legacy while also beginning my own, and make sure that the Meade Creamery girls who come after me continue to have a place to find themselves, too.

Donations come through from people all over Sand Lake. Each one sends a ping to Amelia's phone.

The mayor gives Amelia fifty dollars.

Teachers.

Neighbors.

Tourists.

Former stand girls donate too. There's even a donation from Frankie Ko.

Her parents don't give her a dime.

But the one that really floors Amelia is a hundred dollars that comes in from Cate Kopernick. Her eyes fill with tears and she immediately hops on her bike.

siobhan vivian

CHAPTER FORTY-EIGHT

AMELIA CLIMBS THE STAIRS TO CATE'S FRONT DOOR, trying to keep her hope in check. If she could fix this, if they could somehow come back together, it would be everything.

Cate opens the door before Amelia can knock. "Me first," she announces.

"Okay."

Cate draws in a breath. "I am pissed at you for keeping secrets, I'm pissed at you for hooking up with Grady, and I'm pissed that you fired me." She shifts her weight, letting that hang in the air. Amelia looks down. "But holy shit, Amelia, you *fucking fired me.*"

Amelia smiles at the pride in Cate's voice. "You weren't that good of a boss."

"I know," Cate says, though not in her confident Cate way.

She seems . . . stunned. "I thought I would be. I mean, I think I did some things well. But it was way harder than I thought. And I didn't like how it made me feel, to not be good at something. I haven't had that happen to me before. And it got me thinking about Truman, all the smart people that will be there. What if I'm not who I think I am? What if I can't make friends? What if the classes are hard?"

It's crazy to think Cate is struggling with the same things Amelia's been dealing with all summer—crazy, yet also comforting.

"You know who you are, Cate."

Cate shakes her head. "I had a terrible nightmare last night," she says.

"What?"

"I was away at Truman. Walking around. And I saw you there with Grady. You came to see him but you hadn't told me." Her eyes brim with tears. "And it was because I'd pushed you to make a choice, except it wasn't a choice at all. I didn't support you, like I should have. I know you were only trying to save the stand. I know you weren't trying to hurt me."

"You weren't wrong, Cate. There were times I picked him over you, over the other girls."

"Yeah, but how could I blame you for that?" Cate shakes her head. "I didn't have your back. I didn't make it easy on you. In fact, I made it almost impossible, because it was a conversation I didn't want to have." She looks up. "I don't want you to leave for Gibbons and me to leave for Truman and for us to not be who we are to each other anymore."

"Cate, that's not going to happen! Please don't be jealous of the stand or jealous of Grady, or any of that, because you're the most important person to me."

siobhan vivian

"I shouldn't have said Grady was controlling you. That was insulting. I mean, it kills me to think that Grady was more supportive of you than I was." Cate sniffles, tears streaming down her cheeks. "You always think you're nothing special—but don't you see how many people seek you out? Frankie Ko picked you to work at Meade Creamery. Molly picked you to be Head Girl. Grady picked you to fall for. And I picked you as my best friend."

Now Amelia's crying too. "I love you and I'm so incredibly sorry."

"Can I please have my job back? I know I don't deserve it and I know the stand's only open a couple more weeks, but—"

Amelia rushes forward and hugs Cate tighter than she's hugged anyone before.

It goes without saying that Cate's not coming back next year to Sand Lake. And Amelia will be running the stand in a different way. This really is the end of an era. But a good end. A happy one. The kind best friends like them deserve.

CHAPTER  FORTY-NINE

IT'S KIND OF INCREDIBLE, HOW FAST CHANGE CAN happen when you let it.

In two weeks, Amelia has raised all the money she's asked for. The last few hundred dollars came in slowly, and there was a moment when Cate half-jokingly suggested that Amelia hock the flower pin.

Like she would ever.

Cate's been reading Molly's diary—its existence is still a secret between the two of them—and has come to a new appreciation of Molly Meade. Especially when, late one night, Amelia reveals everything Tiggy told her.

"I had no idea Molly was such a badass. Then again, I had no idea you were such a badass either."

It's been nice, being out in the open with Grady. They've gone on a few dates. And he took her out to a nice dinner when she hit her fund-raising goal. But it's also been strange, watching the farmhouse get emptied out.

Amelia has decided there are two things of Molly's that she does want to ask Grady for: Molly's high school portrait and the original hand-cranked ice cream maker. She plans to hang Molly's picture up somewhere inside the truck, and take the ice cream maker with her to Gibbons. Hopefully it will help her make friends the way it did for Molly. And she might try to come up with a recipe for a new flavor of her own for next summer. But she's keeping the name Meade Creamery for sure.

Losing the stand is still hard. Every time Amelia is inside it, like now, she tries to remember one more little thing about it. As exciting as it is to be embarking on this new adventure, the process of counting down these last days of summer still hurt— saying goodbye to the stand, knowing that no matter how good a job she does with the new incarnation, it won't be the same. It can't.

She heads outside, a bucket on her arm, and walks toward the truck. Grady and Cate are inside working on it. And she can hear them talking about her. Amelia pauses to listen.

"It sucks that her parents haven't come around yet," Cate says.

"Well, her dad did help her clear some space in their garage for the equipment. And her mom helped us transplant some of the honeysuckle bushes. So I guess in their own way, they are."

"Ugh, this stuff is beyond gross." Amelia peeks in and can see that Cate is on her knees in the truck, using a butter knife to scrape the grease off in waxy rolls.

"Still . . . you've got to admit this was one good idea I had."

"Okay, Grady, okay."

Amelia smiles, heartened that Cate and Grady have been getting along as well as she thought they might initially.

Amelia climbs aboard. "Leave it for me, Cate."

"No, no," Cate insists. "This is penance. Though I'll have you know this is more disgusting than the worst the stand bathroom has ever been."

Grady's phone rings and he excuses himself to take the call. His Realtor has been fielding a bunch of offers. He'll have no problem paying his way through Truman on his own.

"So, are you coming to Truman for homecoming?" Cate asks Amelia.

"I'm not sure."

"But you and Grady are a thing, right?"

Amelia smiles. She's fallen in love with Grady Meade, though she hasn't told him yet. She will. Or maybe he'll say it first.

Cate rocks back on her knees. "So this beast runs now?"

"Yep. She's all tuned up." Grady insisted he would pay to get the truck running for her.

"Have you taken it for a drive yet?"

"No."

"Well, come on! Let's go."

Amelia freezes. "Right now? Will you drive?"

"Absolutely not."

"But I don't even like driving the Cadillac. And this thing is way bigger."

"You've got to get used to it eventually. There's no time like the present! Come on. I'm riding shotgun. I'm tired of driving you around."

Amelia slips behind the wheel, starts the engine. "Are you kidding me?"

siobhan vivian

"What?"

"It's stick! I've never driven stick before."

"It's not hard. Just ease into it. Find the point where the gas pedal and the clutch catch."

The truck bucks, shakes, and stalls twice. But on her third try, Amelia manages to get it out on Route 68. And from there, it's basically a straight shot to wherever it is she wants to go.